The Story of Master Caesar

THE SUBMISSION OF ROSIE CRAMER

A Story of True love and Willing Submission

Introduction

I would again like to thank my beautiful wife who is the reason for the series of books I have written. I want to thank her for her assistance with helping with editing, especially all the volumes I have produced.

I have been an artist all my life, not a famous one but have left works of various kinds on this planet's surface. Some have been acrylics and oils on canvas, and others ceramics. I have even produced some items even in cloth. This is my latest venture and hope it will be a lasting one.

The story is a fantasy and designed to entertain and possibly give some insight on being human. Hope you enjoy this story and my others.

Thank You: Calvin L Himel

November 2019

This book is a work of total fiction. Names, characters, places, and incidents are the products of the author's vivid imagination or are used fictitiously. Any resemblance to actual vents, locations, or person living or dead is purely coincidental.

First Printing: January 2020
ISBN:9780578636740

Cover design by: Lemih

The Story of Master Caesar

The Story of Master Caesar

Chapter One

It was one very damp early Tuesday morning during the first month of spring and the beginning of a beautiful day just when the trees were beginning to show the first signs of the end of winter as the buds in the trees first started to appear. The hidden grass was just beginning to shed its brown color and beginning to turn green after being hidden under the heavy blanket of a long lasting wintery snow cover. There were still some small and slowly melting piles of snow from the seemingly extra-long and snowy winter, but the warming weather was soon taking a quickening toll on the last signs of the past few months, and the light rain that had passed through the area overnight was now speeding up the process. The apartment complex was just coming to life as it did every morning especially during the weekdays as most of its residents prepared to leave on their daily trek to their jobs at all the varied locations around the large urban area. Some worked in the surrounding suburban areas while many headed into the nearby large metropolitan city. The apartment complex was really an exceptionally beautiful place to live and had a relaxed atmosphere with its park like setting with all the buildings being only two stories tall with exposed but covered walkways. Even though they were exposed to the elements, it gave residents direct entry into their own personal spaces. The other side directly opposite the entryways provided each apartment with a balcony or patio and had large floor to ceiling windows with sliding glass doors that ran from wall to wall. The trees and landscape gave you the feeling of actually living in the middle of a park, or forest preserve because as you looked out of your window all you would see were the trees, even in the winter months the view was obscured as you looked across the center of the complex to the other side and would barely be able to make out the other buildings making it seem so much more private. The apartments were one, two, and even a few three bedrooms units, with studio apartments separating all of the larger apartments. The studio and one bedroom apartments were very popular with singles and especially with mature single working women of all ages. The rents were slightly higher than most apartments of the same size in the area, but the location was convenient and the premises were well cared for, even though the buildings were well past what would be considered their prime, and it was one of the reasons why the foliage was so mature and covered the views from all the apartments so well, and besides it had ample parking.

It was just another typical Tuesday morning, especially for Ms. Rosie Anne Cramer, twenty nine, almost thirty years old as she woke from a deep sleep after having spent a very relaxing evening alone after drinking several glasses of her favorite wine the evening before. She climbed out of bed, and headed for the bathroom and began taking a relaxing and warm morning wake up shower as she began her now daily ritual of preparing for her job at the nearby local bank branch as an employee. Rosie Anne was a college graduate, smart, single and with a very bright outlook on life, except when it came to her love life. She wasn't at all satisfied with her love life, and her sexual expectations of reaching true satisfaction were low to nonexistent. She began preparing for work as usual, fixing herself a light breakfast of toaster waffles and a cup of instant coffee after boiling a small kettle of water. Rosie was a very shapely young woman, beautiful, with medium size breast, round hips and very cute even though she didn't feel that way about herself, she stood just five foot one at one hundred and twenty five pounds. Her mother was of Italian and Spanish extraction and her dad German, and American. Rosie had a pretty face and had a beautiful slightly olive completion. After eating a light breakfast and drinking her coffee, she began getting dressed, putting on her crotch less panty hose and panties, and her just below the knee length one piece dress with two inch hi heels, combed her long auburn hair and put on her long winter coat since the temperature outside was still on the chilly side from the presence of the melting mountains of snow that chilled the air even though the temperature was gradually rising into the mid-to upper forties and was beginning to gradually warm up during the predicted sunny spring days ahead. She checked all of her windows making sure they were locked, before leaving for her job at the nearby All American Bank branch.

She exited her apartment, locked her door and headed the short distance to the stairway and then down the steps to her auto. Her neighbor Mr. Roger Caesar Thorn watched her after he noticed her passing by his kitchen window. Roger liked Rosie Anne, and they had spoken many times after she had moved in several months earlier, almost a year earlier. Roger felt very attracted to her and sensed there was something very special but unusual about Rosie Anne ever since he had found out her deepest and most hidden secret one evening while spending a quiet and relaxing evening at home.

Roger Caesar Thorn, thirty six years old, six foot two, handsome, with dark brown hair, and a family heritage that would be considered mixed race or creole, had a beautiful light olive complexion. He considered himself and artist and painted in oils and acrylics and was a true voyeur of bondage pornography and on some amateur web sites considered himself a practicing novice of the Japanese rope art of Sabari and a bondage master. He had two women who submitted to him on a very regular basis, just about every weekend. His relationship with both was very exclusive as he was Master Caesar to them, and the alias he used and was known by on some of the amateur bondage and discipline web sites he frequently visited and subscribed to. He mentally would try and only accept the two women as his slaves, but it was much deeper and much more involved than he would ever admit. He had developed a very warm and loving relationship over time with both women, and truly loved them more than he would ever want to admit to. Even his outlook was beginning to change as he matured, and found himself truly in love with both of them. Roger really inside his heart loved both women very much and they truly adored and loved him also, and even though he would not admit to it, he loved them and would do anything and everything for them and had unconsciously proven it many, many times over and over again. It was why they continued seeing him and submitting to his and their own debasing and perverted sexual desires.

Roger hadn't really worked hard for quite a while ever since he had won the state lottery a little over three years earlier. It was on one faithful afternoon after having stopped off on his way home from work, when he filled up his car with some gasoline, and then decided on the spur of the moment to spend a few dollars and play the state lottery. He didn't play regularly like most players, and if he did, it was maybe twice a year which was very often by his standards and just then decided to spend twenty dollars just this once. He purchased some tickets and just decided to use the quick pick after choosing some random numbers in a couple of games on a couple cards and didn't think much about it, after leaving the tickets behind the sun visor in his car for over five weeks before he even decided to check the numbers. The small television he had was on one evening and the news mentioned that a winner hadn't come forward as of yet to claim the big prize, which made him think about the tickets he had purchased several weeks earlier. So that evening after hearing the news and after having finished looking at some porn sites and down loading a couple of videos from one of his favorite bondage sites decided he probably should check his tickets anyway. He didn't ever expect to win, since it seemed most winners were always old and lived in far off suburban areas our out in the sticks. He thought about the tickets down in his car and decided to check them anyway as he slipped on his shorts and went downstairs to his auto and retrieved the tickets before returning upstairs to his computer and checking the numbers on the official state lottery web site and soon found out he had won the big prize the same week he had purchased the tickets. He knew it would only be about half of what the actual amount was because of taxes and really wasn't very excited as he sat down and contemplated a plan of action. He always had an idea and knew what he would do if he ever won. After a couple weeks, after long and serious contemplation he decided it was time to collect his winnings and went to a lawyer's office for consultation after checking around for those people in the legal field who dealt with finance, and created a trust that he would use to claim his winnings. The prime reason was so he could remain anonymous from the ever prying public eye. He soon claimed the winnings in the name of his trust account and had his lawyer collect his winnings. And just as he had assumed, after taxes the amount on his one hundred forty-seven million dollar winning ticket, he would only receive less than half, seventy-one million which he had deposited directly into a new bank account. He had taken the lump sum payout, and after placing it into his bank, sat down with a representative and began a disbursal of the funds. He only placed twenty thousand dollars into his checking account and invested thirty million in treasury bills and twenty million into two separate certificates of deposits of ten million each for two years in order to get the maximum interest rate of five percent. The remainder, he placed into a money market fund where he would have access to it whenever he needed or wanted it. Roger continued working for another eighteen months afterwards and never revealed to anyone about his winning because he knew just how devious people could be and just how stupid they would act if they ever suspected or found out anything.

Roger didn't have any real close friends except for one and it was rare that they got together since his friend started dating a new girlfriend and was thinking of getting married. He didn't have any close relatives except a half-sister and she was almost a thousand miles away and old enough to be his grandmother. He didn't do anything that would bring any undue attention and continued living his quiet life pursuing what he loved doing most, which was painting, cooking and his close weekend relationship with the two women in his life, and they didn't know or even suspect anything about him winning and never had a clue. Soon after winning Roger started investing in some real-estate, mostly very large tracks of vacant land and some of it farm land for tax purposes. Before he resigned he made some really wise and very important investments, he really liked treasury bills, municipal stocks and avoided corporate stocks and the stock market. He bought several extremely large and empty tracks of nearby farm land close to where there was an expanding housing and industrial developments in several close surrounding areas and had formed a corporation and made himself an employee. He did lease backs with the farmers and made more money than the property taxes he paid which went back into his money market fund. He also purchased a truck rental franchise which allowed him to continue to pay into his social security and created even more tax write offs for himself. He continued to stay in his two bed room apartment and no one knew or suspected he was a multi-millionaire. He kept the same old car that he had been driving for several years, he liked it a lot and had sacrificed a lot when he bought it and it continued to run very well as he kept it well maintained. Being very undecided about buying a house even thought it would mean having more privacy, he did like seeing people around sometimes, he also considered buying the complex he lived in but thought it would be just too much trouble and not really worth the money in the long run, since it was almost as old as him.

Barbara Sims was one of the women in his life he had met several years earlier while still on the job as an electronic laboratory technician and way before he had ever won the lottery. She was four years older, but was and felt insecure as Roger later soon found out after he had befriended her one day at work when the only place to sit was at a table for two where he was sitting at and she asked if the other seat was available. Roger welcomed her to have a seat with him even thought he had seen her often when he ate lunch and she was there around the same time but sitting elsewhere. He struck up a conversation with her and found she was a very likable person. They ate together often after that chance meeting and not long after meeting her, just about seven months later Barbara's husband was killed in an industrial accident along with several other people when the plant he worked at exploded due to a malfunction in a production system, it was in the newspapers and on the television news. Roger out of respect for her friendship attended the funeral and gave her his condolences. After that tragedy their friendship slowly began to grow and they became much closer friends since he had no other intentions other than being her friend. She had very few close family members to comfort her and the few she did have lived farther away than his sister did. And several of them had just cut off all contact with her and her husband years earlier before he died, which made her feel even more isolated, insecure, anxious and feeling very alone most of the time. Roger thought she was very pretty, and had a shapely and very attractive figure, and had told her so. She was still feeling very self-conscious and unattractive because she felt she was overweight. She had low self-esteem because of how she felt about her weight which worked to his advantage all by accident. He hadn't planned on taking advantage of her in any way and never did as their friendship soon flourished. He became closely involved in her personal life. She was five foot six, one hundred thirty pounds. She became his first willing submissive. She always wanted to come over to spend some time with him on weekends and one day he relented and soon their relationship eventually became a sexual one, after a very, very, long non sexual friendship. Soon she wanted and began staying overnight, and began willingly submitting herself to serving him in very perverse ways that brought her and him so much pleasure, and eventually she wanted and became his very willing and totally submissive sex slave which she truly enjoyed being because of her own freaky desires which they both took full advantage of as he gave her the complete satisfaction she had been long looking for. She told him that he gave her life real meaning and she would do whatever Master Caesar asked of her, and said she loved him so very much. Roger wasn't a cruel person, just a little perverse and did to her whatever brought her pleasure and he really did love her, as she grew on him though he wouldn't outwardly admit to it. He took her out to dinner and shows often and treated her on holidays and her birthday buying her gifts. She loved him and they had a very meaningful and loving relationship.

Then Barbara brought along with her one day another woman, whom she had known a very long time and was her closest female friends. She had spoken to Roger about her often in some conversations and she really liked her very much. She introduced Victoria Sampson to Roger because they had so very much in common since both had lost their husbands in tragic accidents. But Victoria's husband had been so much more controlling over her, even physically abusive at times, but she missed having that male domination in her life, and enjoyed it for she was a true submissive. He would make her kneel in a corner nude, sometimes with her hands tied behind her back as he berated and spoke to her in a degrading manner before he made her perform oral sex on him and sometimes whipped her with a belt before having sex with her. She was very insecure without having someone telling her what to do and had confided in Barbara her true inner feelings and said she felt so lost and without any direction. She went so far as to ask Barbara to please punish her so she could have some sexual release, this caught Barbara a little off guard and it's when she decided to contact Roger and asked if he wouldn't mind her joining them one weekend after she explained Victoria's dire situation to him. Roger agreed, and found her to be a very attractive and more than a willing participant. She soon met Master Caesar as he took both women out for dinner one Sunday evening as Roger wanted to size her up and see just where her mind was at. He made her feel so much better especially after their initial meeting that weekend. Roger then arranged for her to spend a weekend with him and Barbara. Victoria would start on Friday evening since he wanted to spend some time alone with her first, and soon found a very sexual and willing submissive female. The more he did to her, the more obedient she became. Soon Caesar had two women. He would subject them to his perverted and sexually arousing will and both were so happy because they now had someone who really paid the close attention to them they craved for so much. He took them out often and made them feel good about themselves and gave them a real sense of security and a feeling of being really loved. The kind of love only a man could give a woman. They both did whatever he asked as he commanded them around like slaves, wearing the clothing that he wanted them to wear sometimes when they went out. He tied them up, dominated them and having sex with them however and whenever he pleased. The more he dominated them the more they enjoyed the full attention he gave them.

Ms. Rosie Anne Cramer went to work every day at the All American Bank branch where she worked; she had perfect attendance and had started as a bank teller and quickly worked her way up to bank representative for all bank accounts. She now sat with prospective clients and people with existing accounts who needed to make changes or adjustments and also as a teller when the branch became extra busy. After working there for five years as a teller, she had taken all the courses the bank offered and also the required courses for a management position since she had her bachelor's degree in business and also one in accounting and had positioned herself to be the perfect candidate whenever a promotion would ever present itself. Rosie prayed that would be one day soon, but soon found out that most employees had waited over ten years or more before they ever moved up to where she was now. Rosie had done this in a short four and a half years, and even though she felt it was slow, knew she was making tremendous progress. Even though she was making progress on her job, she felt so un-fulfillment in her personal and especially her sexual life, since not yet even coming close to meeting the man of her dreams, but felt it would happen very soon, she had a strange feeling he was very close. She was a voyeur of some bondage and porn sites and found several and one in particular which she really was attracted to and really liked and had subscribed to. It was an amateur site where members could download and upload videos and photos of themselves and other likeminded people.

After work sometimes Rosie would do a little grocery shopping since she didn't mind cooking for herself and didn't feel she was the worse cook in the world, it was eatable at least. After arriving home, she would change into some comfortable cloths, usually an extra-large t-shirt and nothing else. After washing up she would begin cooking usually a one course meal with a salad on the side in her sparsely furnished large studio apartment. She would sometimes look at some television, and on many occasions she would just open up her laptop computer and surf the web, check on her e-mails and then go to the amateur porn and bondage sights too look at videos. She was intrigued by all the single women who posted videos of themselves, and some were careful not to show their faces but everything else. She became very excited by the ones where some women were masochist and into self-flagellation and pain, as she liked to feel pain herself, sometimes bordering on the extreme as she masturbated and would sometimes use kitchen utensils or a ruler to spank herself as she fingered and played with her vagina and sometimes using vegetables, like large bumpy cucumbers or gourds and squash. She especially liked using the office type binder clips from work especially on her labia and nipples, they were very painful but she enjoyed the sensation as they really heightened her climaxes as she masturbated. She spanked her clitoris with a ruler or cooking spatula sometimes. But what she really wanted and dreamed of having was a man who would first humiliate, dominate and then punish her in very painful ways and then have sex with her as he took full advantage of her. She would talk to herself in a derogatory manner as she punished and brought herself often to a rousing climax many, many times, but knew she really wanted and needed a man to punish her properly.

Rosie as a child had started becoming more aroused sexually in early puberty and then even more in her early teenage years when her very strict and domineering father and even her mother at times used a very large leather strap on her whenever they decided she needed to be punish her. They brought her up in a very strict household and were fundamentalist Baptist that truly believed in corporal punishment as a form of purifying the soul and removing lust as they made her remove all of her clothing before beginning her punishments and if she didn't stay in place or if she moved they would actually tie her hands to the bed post and even for the smallest infractions she would find herself being severely whipped. If she broke their rules or disobeyed, even as she grew older, and even into her very late teenage years until reaching the age of twenty-one she was severely punished. She would be bent over and tied to the bed naked, and several times she was hung up in the garage stripped naked as she was whipped off and on for several long hours. Her dad liked using a heavy leather razor strap and sometimes used one he had with metal studs on her butt and thighs and as she wiggled around between the strikes she began having organisms while her clit rubbed against the bed or chair, or being struck directly with the strap between her legs especially when he hung her in the garage. This became very intense as she was told it was a sin for a woman to derive or enjoy any pleasure from sex, and now she was having multiple orgasms as she was being punished. One time when she was caught playing with herself, her father tied her down in her bed, face up with her head at the foot of the bed and spread eagle and whipped her between her legs, until her vagina became so very swollen she started having continuous climaxes as he whipped her. He never knew how much pleasure he had given her not ever knowing she was having multiple organisms as she just screamed, yelled and cried. Her vagina and clitoris became so very swollen and enlarged and even more sensitive because of the punishments they administered and after that when she touched herself she became more highly aroused. The punishments they handed out caused her to have a very large clitoris and it would rub against the edge of her bed or the edge of a chair when they had her bent over and many times she would be having multiple climaxes as her body shuttered with pleasure while they whipped her. When her father or mother finished and had left the room she would go to the bathroom and bring herself to another rousing climax as she gagged herself to keep from being heard. And that is how it had all started and how she began to seriously enjoy pain while masturbating and climaxing and the relationship of pain and pleasure in her sex life. The problem now was she couldn't climax without a good hard spanking, or the feeling of some serious pain. She wasn't at all a popular girl and was made fun of most of the time which also made her very shy when she attended school and didn't care for any of the boys. When she attended high school her parents were even much more strict on her and she didn't have many if any friends as they would feel intimidated by her parents when and if they came to visit Rosie, and definitely no boys.

Rosie became and turned into a true introvert and learned to be happy being alone even as she attended junior college as long as she stayed at home with her parents as she took extra classes and earning her degrees and formulated a plan to leave home as soon as she possibly could. She didn't consider herself as being at all attractive and wore the drab second hand clothes her parents had chosen and purchased for her, and appeared as a plain Jane. But Rosie was a very pretty girl, with a slight olive but fair complexion, with a slim but shapely figure and had never done anything to bring out her physical beauty, partly because of her parents and they would point out to her women who wore makeup and dressed nice as being harlots. Rosie worked her way through junior college and had a job as a cashier at a local supermarket and soon bought her first car and soon after finished school. She planned to move away from home as she began to dress a little more her age as she still shopped at the second hand store to save her very precious money and dressed a little bit better especially for job interviews as she attended job fairs sponsored by the college she had attended. After she graduated from college she had applied for several jobs at different banks since she was very interested in finance. She was fortunate because one bank had an apprenticeship program and Rosie more than qualified and was readily accepted and was quickly hired. She was elated knowing this would give her the independence she truly wanted and needed in her personal life and after two months of saving her money, she then moved out of her parents' home and into her own present day small studio apartment. She was happy being all by herself as she could walk around with just a t-shirt on and she could masturbate and feel on herself whenever she pleased, which gave her great pleasure. She purchased a card table and chairs and a cheap futon bed and mattress, an inexpensive set of pots and a small set of dishes for two and was now beyond happy and very much relieved to be away from her domineering parents. She didn't go to church any longer and felt she needed a break from the life she had at home with them and was very happy now and felt free.

When Rosie returned home one evening she could smell Rogers's food cooking since he loved to cook. He had even passed her a few samples several times when he grilled outside on his porch and now his kitchen window was open slightly letting out the heat and hearty aromas. She really liked Roger very much, he was very handsome and there was something about him she hadn't figured out yet but it made her feel warm inside and excited her whenever she thought about him, one time after speaking with him, she had to excuse herself to go masturbate as she became so excited talking with him. He seemed unlike any man she ever knew, which there weren't very many since she only had a couple dates while attending college, she had taken her own virginity as a teenager and the two guys she did date just weren't her type and seemed to look down on her. One even told her she wasn't the kind of woman anybody would ever want and called her a dog, and another said she was nothing but poor white trash, this hurt her deeply inside as she went home and cried all that day, that's why she really liked Roger, he was very nice when he spoke to her and wasn't derogatory and didn't speak down to her whenever they talked, and even told her she was very beautiful. Roger really liked talking to her and had invited her over for dinner several times, but she had declined because she felt so self-conscious and embarrassed, but the smell of his food this time just went to the very pit of her very empty and hungry stomach. She was starving and didn't feel like cooking and hadn't gone shopping all week since her rent was soon due and didn't want to be short when it came time to pay, especially since she was still paying a portion of the security deposit with her rent. She wondered if Roger wouldn't mind if she invited herself to dinner. He had told her many times when he had seen her walking past his kitchen window that she was more than welcome to stop by at any time and to come share a meal with him. She seriously pondered the idea around in her head as her stomach growled; she decided to invite herself this time. She went inside her small apartment and washed her hands and decided to see if her invitation from Mr. Thorn still stood. She hung up her coat and put her purse away, then putting on a long heavy sweater and still dressed in her work clothes. She took her keys, locked her door and went next door and knocked. Roger Caesar Thorn soon came to the door and opened it and with a big smile, he asked her to please step inside from the chilly spring air. Rosie said she smelled his food cooking and asked if his invitation to her still stood. He said for someone as beautiful as you my dear Rosie this door will always be open. His words were always so very kind and warmed her heart and also between her thighs. He said wait here just a minute please; he returned with a pair of comfortable and plush women's slippers in a plastic bag which were brand new and had never been opened as he led her into the living room with a large comfortable leather couch and said, please have a seat and please relax, and take you shoes off. She did and said thank you so very much. Roger said he was wondering when she would ever get around to accepting his open invitation. Rosie said it smelled so good and she had to admit she was so very hungry today and hadn't shopped and didn't feel like cooking. He said he very much welcomed having her here to keep him company.

This was the first time Rosie Anne had been inside his apartment as he stepped away and said and had to watch his pan of spaghetti sauce which he cooked from scratch with all fresh ingredients and it was now simmering. He left her sitting on the large comfortable couch. Rosie looked around the apartment, it was exceptionally clean and the furnishings were somewhat sparse and not cheap but very well appointed and manly. She started noticing small items that were lying around in various places, like a set of several wooden objects shaped like butt plugs and highly polished but they were extremely large, and a whip mounted in a frame. Roger returned with a fruit drink made with a red wine and handed Rosie a glass as he returned and began setting the dining room table. He said it was a real pleasure to have her here and was very glad she decided to come because he would rather eat with someone than to be eating all alone most of the time. Rosie complimented Roger on his décor and asked if she could use his bathroom. He said she was welcome, and it was just around the corner just off the entrance hallway. She soon found the bathroom and enjoyed the decor on her way and took a passing glance into his bedroom, the door was wide open and she observed a large wooden cabinet whose doors were open and inside were hanging several different types and styles of whips hanging on the inside of one door and cuffs and collars, were on the shelves and paddles of various lengths hung on the inside of the other door. She slowly proceeded to the bathroom and glanced at the wall decorations. After she used the facilities and washed her hands, she started becoming sexually aroused. She thought about all of what she was seeing and it excited her very much. She tried hard to restrain her now wandering thoughts. She couldn't explain why seeing the whips made her feel this way. She again looked more closely before returning to the living room after walking past his bed room again, taking a good long look before returning as she sat back down again on his large soft leather couch. She sat and thought about asking Roger about what she had just seen and decided to wait and see where the conversation might lead. Roger had seen her out the corner of his eye looking before she returned and felt her looking was more out of curiosity and said nothing since it was her first time here.

After returning to the living room, she sat on his couch seriously thinking about what she had just seen, she began looking more closely at the art on his walls and started to notice all of the nudes and even some that depicted females in restraints and remembered when she passed by the bedroom door noticing restraints attached to the large bed post. She stood and slowly walked around and began to admire some of the unusual articles that adorned the apartment walls. Roger finished cooking and finished setting the table as Rosie looked at and admired a painting of a woman restrained in chains in a jail cell setting and a man standing over her with a whip about to strike her. Roger said to her that he was ready to serve dinner and asked if she was ready to indulge, and she responded that she was famished. He dished them both up, placing angel hair spaghetti on the plates then his meat sauce on top with meatballs and side dishes of freshly made coleslaw, along with garlic bread, and glasses of chilled red wine. He asked her to please have a seat as he pulled the chair out for her. Then returned to place the plates on the table, then he blessed the food and said I hope you enjoy it. Rosie ate it all and said it was so very good, even asking for a little more after finishing the first serving. Roger went and placed a small amount on her plate. She said that it was the best, she had ever eaten. Then mentioned I know your girlfriends love your cooking. Roger picked up on her comments right away and could see where she was coming from as he said girlfriends; he said that he had no girlfriends. Rosie said she had seen a couple women visiting him on weekends. Oh, he said those two, he said they weren't his girlfriends but his very willing sex slaves and they were here for their discipline sessions which were once a week or whenever they felt the need to be punished and loved. He explained they had a very special and loving relationship before he asked her if she knew anything about bondage and discipline. Rosie said that she did somewhat and had looked at some bondage sites but that was about it. Roger wasn't surprised by the conversation and she didn't shy away from it at all now, and assumed what he thought about her was true. He told her he was there master and they were his willing slaves. When you saw them they were here to serve him and were very happy to do so. He

26

said after she finished eating he would show her some of the devices he used on them and asked if she was interested in the subject. Rosie responded that she was very interested and would love to have the guided tour. Roger knew she might be ever since one night while out on his porch he heard a muffled voice and some slapping sounds and had peered over and around the low divider that separated there porches and there was a small space in her curtain that didn't completely cover the corner and observed her kneeling on her mattress and violently spanking herself with the clamps on herself as she came to a arousing climax and just laid on her bed afterwards very satisfied. She had given him her e-mail address when she had asked about a recipe and he said it would be better if he e-mailed it to her since it was already in his computer and it would be so much easier.

Then one day while on one of the amateur bondage sights, he saw a video of a young woman spanking herself, no face was visible in the video just a very large and swollen looking pussy, with a large clitoris and with binder clamps and a small long cucumber deep inside her ass as she had clamps on her labia as she spanked herself with a wooden spatula until she climaxed. He looked at the video and the background seemed oh so very familiar and the sender's user name was also very similar to the one she used for her e-mail address but wasn't sure if it might be her or not, but the shape of the body seemed to resemble her very closely, thought he wasn't completely certain if it was her or not, and then again it could have been almost anyone.

Rosie finished eating while Roger poured her more of the chilled red wine. She was now becoming much more relaxed and very comfortable around Roger now, but was still very excited about seeing the devices he was going to show her and some of his bondage equipment. He took her on a quick tour of his apartment and left the bedroom for last as he showed her the cabinet full of restraint equipment and explained some of the uses for the various devices and there specific purpose for restraining someone. Rosie had never seen some of the items before close up and now became very excited. Roger could tell she was now in her own created and much heightened state as he led her back to the living room. Afterwards as they sat on the couch together and they continued to talk, he pulled out a large picture album containing photos he had taken of the two women she had seen entering his apartment in various stages of undress and restrained in different positions, and included some before and after photos after being subjected to various punishments. Roger noticed her very intense scrutiny as she closely studied the whipping photos in particular. Roger could tell she was very interested and highly excited now and explained there was a special loving relationship between a master and his slave, and masters weren't restricted to having only one slave. As Rosie looked and closely studied the photos, she never looked up once as she was becoming highly aroused and soon asked him how long had he been a master. He answered and said over seven years now. The women in the photos seemed very content and very satisfied with their treatment even when they were restrained after having been harshly whipped.

Rosie asked him, how do you know what a person's limits are? He reached around into the drawer of an end table and pulled out a form that was about four pages long and handed it to Rosie, saying look this over as he handed it to her, when you finish with the photo album. She soon finished looking at the pictures and was pressing her knees tightly together and Roger knew it was a sign that she was very excited now as her skin color had started to become a little flush then she began to perspire slightly to the point of almost having an organism. She looked at the form Roger had handed her, it had a cover sheet that said agreement between dominant and submissive and below the large bold letters it said, MASTER and SLAVE.

Roger said she could take it home with her and read it over since he sensed she was ready to go in more ways than one. Rosie immediately stood and said she very much appreciated him inviting her to dinner and said it was the best meal she had ever eaten. Roger thanked her for coming by and said he enjoyed her company very much also and that she was welcome to come anytime, even if his two women friends were here because they would enjoy being publicly exposed and maybe she might want to participate. She blushed when he said that and again said he truly enjoyed her company very much and it was a real pleasure. She stood and Roger walked her to the door, as he help her put on her sweater and he told her to keep the house shoes as he placed her hi heels in the plastic bag. She hadn't let go of the agreement he had handed her. He was very surprised, when she turned around and kissed him. She quickly stepped out the doorway and departed next door.

After Rosie departed, Roger went to the kitchen and began washing the dishes and putting his food away and cleaned up thinking about Rosie. He knew she would be back soon especially if the video he has seen was really her, and bet she was now jerking herself off. He was right, as soon as Rosie entered her apartment, she couldn't get out of her clothes fast enough before she lay across her futon mattress on the floor with her dildo pressing it hard against herself, pinching and twisting her nipples roughly and soon having one massive continuous climax as she thought about being tied up and whipped by Roger Thorn before collapsing in her bed and just pulling the spread over herself and falling asleep feeling full and also very sexually relieved.

Chapter Two

Three days later as the weather was becoming more and more pleasant with every passing day and not very long after Roger had finished preparing and eating a light breakfast, early on this Friday morning around ten o'clock and planning on going grocery shopping with a list of some needed items. Barbara Sims, forty years old, five foot six inches, and one hundred thirty pounds, with a very pretty and pleasant face and very shapely figure, dressed in a very short skirt and blouse with a faux fur winter coat down to her lovely ankles, wearing stocking and hi-heels knocked on Mr. Thorn's door. Roger opened the door and Mrs. Sims entered, they hugged and kissed and then she immediately went to the living room as Roger followed closely behind and approached her. She turned and faced Roger and said Master, as she removed her coat. Roger hugged and kissed her as she kissed him back passionately, saying she missed him so very much and just felt she needed now to be with him. He said to her that she would have to go with him since he was heading out to the grocery store to pick up some needed items and had several other stops to make also. She said that was ok with her but asked if master would touch her now, please, please she begged of him. He told her to remove her skirt, which she did, wearing crotch less panty hose just as the master had ordered whenever she graced his presence and also told her to put her arms behind her back feeling her between her warm and smooth thighs. She was highly aroused and became more so as he asked her who do you belong to; you master Caesar as he kissed her. He pressed a finger into her very damp and hot vagina, massaging and touching her now very aroused clitoris and shortly had a massive climax and began shaking violently. Roger reached out and held her and continued to finger her as her come was now dripping from her hot wet pussy as he slowly removed his fingers and placed them in her sexy mouth, telling her to suck them clean which she readily did. After removing his fingers, she said thank you master, kissing her voluptuous and waiting lips telling her to dress and wait for him which she did and then sitting in the big living room on the sofa.

Roger took his time dressing and was then ready to leave on his short but adventurous shopping trip. When he went into the living room Barbara stood, he felt her breast through her blouse and bra and knew she was highly aroused now and told her to remove her bra and put her blouse back on. She did as Roger commanded; now he said they could go. Being dressed like this drove her over the edge and with him having her walk in stores dressed like this brought even more excitement to her usual very conservative appearance, but at least she now had her coat on and didn't feel so exposed. It had been more than two weeks since she had graced his presence because she had to attend a weekend retreat for her job where she was one of the supervising managers and it was a requirement because of her high position. She put her coat on and they walked downstairs to his car as he held the door open for her and then they departed for the nearby grocery store. Barbara expressed how much she missed being with him as he drove and they soon arrived at the supermarket and talked as they shopped. He told her how sweet she was and how much he loved her and what he would do to her once they returned home which excited and aroused her as he looked into her pretty face and said all the things that would drive her over the edge and knew if he just touched her anywhere, she would just about have an organism on the spot. He held her hand and kissed it and told her he loved her so very much and that she was his sweet ass bitch, she asked him to please stop because he was getting her too excited. He said that he would stop when he was ready and said he had missed her sweet ass very much. They finally checked out and pushed the grocery cart to the car, loaded the food into the trunk of the car, and soon returned home after making several more brief stops. Roger made her walk in front of him just so he could look at her. After bringing the groceries inside and putting the food away, Roger was ready to have his way with Barbara.

Barbara was so highly aroused now, and was long overdue for some sex. Barbara was told to undress and leave her pantyhose and hi heels on. After she had complied with her master's wishes, Master Caesar cuffed her wrists and placed a collar around her neck, he kissed her and said she was his property and asked her what was she, she replied that she was his bitch, begging him to take her because she was so very excited and missed him so very much. Roger said not yet because he wanted to look at her fully first as he cuffed her hands now behind her back before leading her to the living room where he had several hooks in the ceiling attaching a chain to one bending her over and attached her arms to the long chain. Barbara was bent over, her very round bright ass sticking out, her ample breast hanging down as master Caesar stood behind her and rubbed her butt and then with a surgical glove on one hand applied lubricant to her upturned anus and fingered her as she squirmed with the building up of sexual pleasure and excitement working one finger slowly inside her, then he worked and eased in the second, and shortly afterwards a third as he checked her response before slowly inserting a very large anal plug into her now relaxed anus. Barbara enjoyed ass play eminently, and after inserting the butt plug Roger unhooked the chain and allowed Barbara to stand upright as he kissed her and now being very highly aroused begged him to let her come. He felt her ample and now very swollen with excitement breast and kissed the highly aroused and swollen and elongated nipples as he pulled them with his lips as she squirmed driving her crazy with even more anticipation before he felt between her beautifully shaped thighs kissing her, telling her she could come while playing with her now very moist vagina as she began having a massive climax, he made her continue to stand, even when her legs began to buckle and then he began spanking her butt, telling her to keep standing. He released her arms from behind and made her stand and had her remove her pantyhose and shoes, which she was more than happy to do, before leading her to the bedroom and making her bend over the end of the bed. He slowly removed the butt plug, then making her lie in the bed on her back as he undressed and climbed on top of her spread legs and entered her very wet but tight vagina as she moaned and climaxed again several times, as she tightly held on to Roger. He then climbed off of her, ordering her to kneel, and now taking her from behind, causing her to climax again, before pulling out and entering her beckoning ass, and reaching around playing with her now large and swollen clit, rocking her with another massive climax, and coming inside her anus. Again she was rocked again by another massive climax as she felt his hot sperm in her butt hole, before she collapsed and he then laid down next to her and she told him she loved him as they kissed and held one another, he loved her and always did. He then led her to the bathroom and they bathed one another; he gave her an enema and a douche. He turned the water off and dried her and himself before leading her back to the bedroom and oiling her body from her feet to her head, he did her front and back as he oiled her very shapely body. Soon she became even more aroused again, she reached up and pulled him to her and held him and kissed him with so much passion and just didn't want to let him go.

Roger loved Barbara so very much and was finally able to free himself from her grasp and stood looking down at her. Barbara was so very beautiful to him as she laid there looking up at Roger as he turned and went into his closet to remove a very warm and soft bathrobe and told her to stand as he wrapped the robe around her. Barbara was surprised Roger wasn't going to make her wear a harness or any restraints. She asked him, and he said don't worry my love, enjoy your free time. The day was quickly passing when in the early evening, shortly after he and Barbara had finished eating a full lunch and cleaning up the kitchen; there was a sharp knock at the door. Roger went to the door, looked out, and then opened it; he was a little surprised to find Mrs. Victoria Sampson standing there. She was thirty-nine years old, and five foot seven, one hundred thirty two pounds, with a very nice and very shapely figure, very attractive, lonely and a true submissive. She had with her a small overnight bag as Roger stepped aside; she entered as he closed the door. She stopped suddenly turned around and set her bag down and couldn't wait to hug and kiss Roger. She wanted him so very badly; it had been a week since she had been here last and Roger didn't expect to see her again until tomorrow. The last time she was here Roger had truly did his upmost to be verbally and physically vicious and heartless as he humiliated her, she truly surprised him, she just reveled in the abuse, and the more degrading he was with her the better the sex with her became. He knew he loved her, not because of the sex, but because he just did as a person, and her perverse ways had bothered him at first, but loved her enough to make her happy. It was just the past weekend when Barbara had been away on a retreat for her job and all of Rogers's attention had been directed at Victoria as he subjected her to several different, varied and humiliating and degrading situations which caused her to become extremely sexually excited and becoming even more passionate and submissive. Over the two days, he even took her outside with nothing on but high heels and a coat. He made her walk down several different streets like a whore with a collar and leash on until she was so wet that when he touched her she just exploded having a massive climax and had to help her to stand up and when

36

she had to pee afterwards he made her squat, as he took pictures of her. He severely whipped her as she wore a cruel harness in her anus and vagina for several hours causing her to have repeated climaxes until she was just too weak to stand and then had to crawl around as Roger continued having his perverted way with her. Roger pressed her against the wall and asked her who her stinking bitch ass belonged to, she said you Master Caesar, Roger held her up by her hair with his left hand and told her to unbutton her coat which she did, then her blouse biting her neck and reaching between her legs, he felt her as she moaned and told her she was his dirty little slut whore. She climaxed and screamed for several minutes before he told her to go undress and hang her clothes up. He kissed her before he released her, as she hugged and kissed him back. After releasing her and heading to the bed room, she was surprised to see Barbara standing with her robe on and open, they kissed one another as Victoria began to disrobe as instructed and when she was completely nude Roger entered and made her kneel and pulled himself out and told her to suck him off. She did as he held her head and when he was fully erect he then pulled her up by her long brown hair, bent her over at the end of the bed and roughly entered her vagina, smacking that ass hard several times as he did. Barbara started to leave. Roger told her to stay and watch as he roughly fucked Victoria and soon she was having a massive climax. He then continued to ram her vagina and fingered her anus and told Barbara to get the lubricant. He began applying it to Victoria's anus as he continued to pound her vagina, then he pulled it out and roughly entered her anus. She gasps and began enjoying the pounding he was giving her having her to climax several more times as he fingering her pussy and clitoris. He pulled it out after coming inside her anus, pulled her up, turned her around, pinched her nipples hard as she moaned, and leading her to the bathroom where he showered again, this time with Victoria douching her and also giving her an enema. He dried her off and himself before bringing her back to the bed room and having Barbara help him oil the now very limp and completely satisfied Victoria.

When they had finished he went to the closet, put on his bathrobe and had one for Victoria, told her to stand there as he put the robe on her. Then he made them stand together as he stood in front of them and felt each of them as they became very excited again. He stopped and decided to feed them first and told them to sit in the living room as he prepared something to eat. The food was already cooked and all he had to do was heat it up. When it was ready he would have them sit at the dining room table. They did as they were told and hugged one another as they waited. When it was ready, he placed plates of his spaghetti before them; returning with glasses of red wine, and garlic bread and blessing the food as they all sat down and began eating together. The women enjoyed the food Roger cooked. He was a very good cook and they love it when he feed them. He had them wash the dishes and pots, since there wasn't anything left over.

Having such a delicious meal, the girls where so pleased and then Roger had them to clean up the kitchen.

He then decided to sit on the couch with both women one on each side of him, kissing them both before asking each a very simple question. Would you, or do you think, you would want to live with me full time? Roger went on to explain that he was seriously thinking of moving into a house. And the house would of course be large enough for each of them to have at least a bedroom of their very own. But then they would be subject to being his slaves twenty four seven. He told them to seriously think about it because they would be subject to whatever he wanted to do with them, or whenever he wanted, and they would have to be really comfortable with the living arrangements he was proposing. He said he loved them both very much, also saying that they had to be sure they really loved him, if they decided to live with him. And would have to be something they truly desired, wanted, and stating he could have his way with them whenever he wanted. Said it would probably be more like having two wives, and should be a more relaxed and less rushed atmosphere for them all compared to just spending the weekends together. He told them to seriously think about it. They had a week before he would like and answer. He then ordered them to stand up, and pulled the curtains closed but left a six inch space on the side next to Rosie Anne's apartment. Since knowing she was probably home by now. He had them remove there robes; he left the room and returned with their collars and cuffs and told them to cuff one another. When they finished he said to them to turn and face one another and to wrap their arms around one another as he clamped their wrist together behind each other. Their ample breasts were pressed together as he used a short chain to hook their collars together. Then he attached their ankles together and had them to spread their legs apart. He then attached a long rope from the ceiling hook through the ring on the back of Barbara's collars and between both their legs and down the crack of her ass and then up through Victoria's ass and through her collar and back to the ceiling hook causing them to be pressed together, against one another. Then he blindfolded each, standing back and looked at the two before attaching a spreader bar to their joined ankles. He left and brought back a leather paddle and sat and looked at the two women standing before him. He stood next to them and asked them what they are. They both replied they were his slave bitches. He asked them what they wanted. They replied to serve their master. He asked them if they wanted to be punished. Yes sir, master they both replied. He then took the long leather paddle and rubbed it slowly all over them both, as they started shaking; not knowing what would happen next as Caesar rubbed the paddle between their legs and up there inner thighs. They soon began to perspire, he then let the anticipation build. Victoria started screaming first, please master, whip me, as she began to tremble and shake, and pleaded with him, please master again and then Barbara said please master whip us please, as the excitement was building and getting to be too much for both, as he gently began feeling between their warm and soft legs and found both women vaginas very, very moist.

Caesar soon left and brought back a gag and gagged Victoria and then she cried as she began trembling even more as Caesar said to her as he grabbed and squeezed her butt cheeks and whispered in her ear that she was a real cunt and would be treated like a slut whore. He licked her face as the anticipation really began getting to her, she was the most highly excitable of the two and said he was going to take her outside naked and fuck her like a dog and then walk her around for all his neighbors to see again, only this time she was going to be exposed for all to see. He placed a plastic drop cloth beneath them because he could tell Victoria might soon lose control and urinate. Barbara begged him to please punish them. He took the gag out of Victoria's mouth and she was so relieved and said they wanted to be punished. He asked what type of punishment they desired. Barbara said whip me please, and then Victoria said please master use the whip.

Caesar brought back the flogger and without notice he began whipping them both as they now jerked and cried, and after thirty strokes or more across their backs, butts and thighs, he stopped and picked up the leather paddle, and struck each woman several times hard on their ass cheeks. Then he said what do you say bitches, both said thank you master Caesar. He let them hang a little while longer. He removed the rope that ran between their legs. But left them standing and blindfolded and took a long handled vibrator and held it to their now touching vaginas until both had climaxed several times. He released the spreader bar and unhooked their ankles from one another and removed the blindfolds, once he had done that he unhooked their arms and made them kneel with their arms behind their backs. Then told them to turn around with their heads on the floor and asses up, returning with two small remote controlled vibrators and two long wide soft butt plugs and some lubricant. With a latex glove on one hand; he first played with both women's anus lubricating them until he had several fingers inside of each and almost his full hand as they moaned and enjoyed the butt play before he inserted the extra-large butt plugs inside of them both and after that he removed his glove and inserted the remote controlled vibrators into their very moist vaginas. He told them to kneel and turn around facing him as he attached their wrist to their collars. Then he instructed them to bend over as he placed a thin pillow under their heads and to spread their legs apart. He then activated the vibrators and sat back on the couch and observed the two enjoying the sensations that rocked their lovely bodies. They soon were climaxing continuously, as he sat back and observed their shaking and quivering bodies while they continued climaxing, moaning and crying with pleasure. When he turned them off he told them to sit up and soon they had the look of complete satisfaction and of true submission on their pretty faces. He made them stand and helped them up as he released their arms, turning the vibrators on again on low after attaching their arms behind their backs and with a leash to each one walking them around the fairly large apartment with continuous climaxes racking their bodies and having difficulty walking. He took the whip and made them walk striking them if they stopped. He lead them back to where they started from and looked at each and asked them who they belonged to. They both replied, to you Master Caesar.

Being in a kneeling position he turned the vibrators off and pulled his hard penis out and had them face each other as the two women anxiously took him into their hungry mouths. He toyed with them until he came and they licked up all his come juice even off of each other's face and swallowing all he had to give. He unhooked their arms and led them to the bathroom where he had them remove the vibrators and butt plugs, having them to wash them thoroughly. He then told them to remove the cuffs and the collars which they eagerly did. Then told them to get in the bed, and laid down between the both of them and rubbing and kissing his two highly aroused women having sex with them both as he talked degradingly dirty to them as they both continued having more climaxes. When he finished with them; he led them to the bathroom and they all showered again after he gave them both a golden shower together. Then after drying off and oiling one another, took them back to the living room and fixing them some drinks. They all sat around in their robes talking. And after several drinks they were totally relaxed, and soon headed to the bedroom sleeping long and hard as well as exhausted, together.

Chapter Three

The following morning when Roger woke, and after getting out of bed and going to the bathroom where he did his usual morning routine and showered, shaved and brushed his teeth. Returned to the bedroom and stood looking down at Barbara and Victoria sleeping soundly. He went to his closet and put on a clean pair of shorts and a t-shirt and headed to the kitchen. He began first by preparing to brew a large pot of coffee, before going to the living room and opening the curtains and then the patio door slightly letting in some fresh air, the house smelled of sweat and sex. He returned to the kitchen and began to prepare breakfast for his two sleeping female lovers. He loved being in charge and they loved being dominated as he began preparations for breakfast, taking out the bacon, eggs, and bread along with his frying pan and placed a low fire under it after pouring a very small amount of olive oil in the pan and placing the bacon inside and covering it. He poured himself a cup of coffee, as he opened the kitchen window slightly and allowed the fresh outside air to pass through the entire apartment. He looked at the clock and saw they all had slept even later than his usual wake up time. It figured since they had such an exhausting evening having sex and then fixing them some very potent drinks afterwards which he made strong on purpose. He loved the two women so very much, but tried keeping them at an emotional distance because he really cared about them but didn't want to be tied down like in a marriage but really didn't find it that difficult because there were two of them and he really deep inside of himself loved them both. He enjoyed having unlimited sex with them and that was all he really desired for right now but that was beginning to change, he had a choice and that made it so enjoyable for him. He watched his bacon and drained some of the grease off, cracked and seasoned a few eggs, added some seasoning salt, before covering the dish. He drank his coffee and turned on the radio to the all-news station and listened to the daily weather report, it was going to be a very pleasant day and much warmer than yesterday, closer to sixty-five degrees, but a little windy. As he was sipping his coffee, it's when he heard the bathroom door close and went to the bedroom and found that Victoria had awakened, but Barbara was still in bed and knew she would soon arise, as he returned to the kitchen. It was a Saturday and he would take the two out shopping, something he did every now and then and he enjoyed buying them the clothes he wanted them to wear just for him, and they happily complied with their master's wishes. He made them feel sexy and had them dress for him in a provocative manner to satisfy his lustful taste.

He was sipping his coffee just when Victoria entered the kitchen with her robe open and flew into his arms kissing him, and saying she loved him and would do anything, anytime he wanted. He set his coffee cup down as he held her and rubbed her inside of her open robe and bringing her to a rousing climax. Victoria was highly sexed, a real sexy and very sensitive woman, who he could just touch sometimes depending on her state of mind and she would just about have an orgasm. He could also verbally stimulate her, and if she was suspended nude and blindfolded, she would just go totally crazy with an uncontrollable sexual excitement. He kissed her and told her she was his sexy bitch which excited her even more. He told her to get herself some coffee, and left to check on Barbara and found her just starting to wake up. He sat on the side of the bed and she opened her eyes and reached for his hand and began kissing it and started sucking his fingers pulling him closer and placed his hand between her warm thighs, he couldn't help himself as he felt her moist and very warm vagina and massaged and rubbed her as she began having a massive climax while her whole body jerked and shook as her eyes became very moist. He started to remove his hand and she grabbed it again and sucked his fingers until he slowly pulled them away from her and said time to get up sweetheart. He left the bedroom and headed back to the kitchen and washed his hands. He thought to himself how very hot these two were, they were very pretty women and in their professional life you wouldn't imagine them being so highly sexed and wild. Barbara had told him once long ago she loved him very much and thinking about him sometimes caused her to become so very excited she would have to jerk herself off and when she was here with him her body betrayed her and she would lose all of her self-control.

As he prepared breakfast he noticed Rosie Anne walking past his kitchen window as she left home, getting into her car dressed in a pair of jeans and the heavy winter sweater she wore when she came to dinner and thought she probably heard Victoria scream yesterday evening and probably peeked around the corner as he put the two through their paces. Roger began preparing the eggs and toast just as Barbara walked into the kitchen and poured a cup of coffee and then went into the dining room and sat down as he handed Victoria the silverware and asking her to please set the table. Very soon they were all sitting down eating together, he fed his women well and they loved to eat and he knew that much about them both. He told them he was taking them shopping today for some of the items he would like them to wear for him and whatever else they might need. After breakfast he said they had about an hour and wanted them to start getting themselves ready. Roger had a dress code when they were with him, and it excited them both very much when he took them out. After eating he cleaned up the kitchen, it had been a little more than an hour since he had seen Rosie Anne leave and now she was returning home with some groceries. He watched the sexy young woman make her way up the steps and pass his kitchen window again.

He asked Barbara and Victoria to wear some jeans, cotton panties, and whatever tops they wanted but with no bra, they were to wear earrings and some athletic shoes because they would probably be doing plenty of walking. They responded yes master, as they proceeded to dress and he let them have the bathroom and bedroom leaving them as he went into his office which was located in the second bedroom and checked his computer and up loaded the photos he had taken of them yesterday from his camera. He would decide which ones he would place under his user name on the bondage web site later when he would have some free time and maybe after another session with the two this afternoon. He wondered about

Rosie Anne and when she might come knocking on his door again and figured most likely she would wait until both Barbara and Victoria had left. He detected her well-hidden shyness. He looked up after about half an hour and Victoria was standing in the doorway and said master, and said she was now ready. Victoria was looking cute and the highly sexed woman was always very excited about going shopping with him since the last time he took them she climaxed in the car after he spoke to her in a degrading and very sexual manner. Barbara took a little longer to get real excited some times, but when she did look out. Barbara came and stood next to Victoria and he could see anticipation growing in her pretty face and a very subdued excitement. Roger turned off his computer and went to wash up as he told them to wait for him in the living room. He left to get dressed and soon returned in his jeans, athletic shoes, sweat shirt and his navy p-coat. He said ladies; and they put on their coats and left the apartment and descended down the stairs to his car. He opened the car doors for them both as they stepped inside, and then he walked around to the driver's side, and he glanced up and saw Rosie looking out of her kitchen window before he got in.

Roger asked them as he drove to the Sexy Things store if there was anything they needed or wanted beside what he wanted to get them. Both said they would like some nail polish and some make up items, and he said ok and stopped at one of the local chain drug stores that he knew had a nice variety and a wide selection of what they were looking for. He let them pick out whatever they needed or wanted and he paid for the items as they returned to the car, then heading for the Sexy Things store. After arriving he showed them the items he wanted them to have, such as stocking with attached garters, open crotch pantyhose, sexy stockings with designs, body suits, nighties, and then said to them to select from the dildo section the ones they would like stuck up either their ass or cunt, which made them both blush especially when he used such vulgar and descriptive terms. When he looked he could tell Victoria was getting excited an growing flush in the face as both of them surprised him with some of their selections, but then again he shouldn't be. He had picked out a maids outfit for both and asked if they were finished shopping, they both responded yes sir. They went to the counter to check out and he again paid for everything.

After getting back in the auto he took them to lunch at the Lucky Seafood Restaurant and after entering they were promptly seated in a large comfortable booth. Roger had them sit together so he could look at them both. He looked at these two beautiful, sexy middle aged women who took extremely good care of themselves and marveled at how extremely sexy they were and how much he cared for them. He truly loved them, and thought they loved him or they wouldn't keep coming back to let him do what he did to them, he knew he fulfilled a need they had as they fulfilled his and would wait the week he gave them for an answer to his question yesterday. The waitress appeared and handed them the menus and took their refreshment orders and departed, then returned and took their orders for the main course. Roger sat and looked at them as they talked and only occasionally added to their conversation, but he did mention to them briefly about his neighbor next door, Rosie and her curious interest in bondage and discipline and said he synced there was something special about her and maybe soon they would meet her. Barbara just looked at him and said really. He had his phone out and took their pictures and they didn't even know he had done so.

Their food finally arrived and the three of them sat and ate as Roger watched them enjoying their meal, he enjoyed taking them out since he loved them and they love the attention he gave them. He also showed concern when they said they wanted to talk to him and even discussed their jobs and how they felt many times. It was as if he had two wives at times, and that was one of the reasons he had presented them with the question about living with him, and besides, he felt it was time to move on and settle down since he was feeling more financially secure and was prepared to spend more time with them and thought they might be ready also.

Barbara and he had become very good friends when he was still working way before he won the lotto and even before her husband had died, they would sit and talk at lunch time. They had met by accident as he worked as a technician at the same location and company that had a fairly large female clerical staff since it was there main office and national headquarters. He worked in the research and development department at the same location but they all shared the same lunchroom and cafeteria facilities. One day the lunch room was very full since some personnel were there for classes on a new product line and the only available seats were singles at various random tables. He occupied a small table for two and was sitting alone as she was looking for a seat and asked if anyone was sitting there and he said no, and asked her to please have a seat. They began talking and soon became lunch buddies after that when she would come to have lunch every day around the same time. After that he soon began keeping a place open for her and not long after they were discussing their personal business and expressing their opinions to one another since she felt some attraction to him. Roger sensed over time she was very unhappy and she had expressed it in subtle ways long before her husband had died in an industrial accident since he worked in a chemical production facility doing some type of construction. When he heard about her loss, he attended the funeral with a few of her other co-workers. After several weeks off when she returned back to work they talked again and he could relate to a death of someone very close as she became even more comfortable with their daily conversations and one day she just decided to ask him out. They spent the day together and Roger acted as a real friend. They went to dinner and the movies and several times Barbara asked him if he found her attractive or was he just befriending her out of sympathy. Roger explained he found her exceptionally beautiful and liked her even before the tragic death of her husband and felt a real attraction to her, but she was a married woman and he respected that and would never asked or do anything that would interfere or jeopardize her marriage and said he respected the institution and felt it was something to be coveted. He said it wouldn't be hard not to love her, and had deep feeling and loved her and was very attracted to her. But he explained he had this freaky side that he kept to himself and would be considered perverse or perverted to some people and that was the reason why he had made no sexual advances toward her and really enjoyed and valued her companionship and friendship more than his base desires. She asked him if he would please tell her, he was very reluctant at first but she insisted and he eventually relented and told her.

When he explained his sometimes sexual desire for bondage, discipline and female humiliation he felt truly very embarrassed. Told her he felt embarrassed just telling her and was afraid it would ruin their friendship, until she expressed to him a fantasy she had always harbored and made her very excited when she thought about it, and since they were talking about their deepest secrets told him it was what she thought about when she masturbated herself, and it was of being tied up, whipped and being anally assaulted. She asked Roger if he would fulfill the fantasy for her and after dinner one Saturday he brought her home and subjected her to his will and her fantasy, and they have been together ever since, theirs was an exclusive relationship and they enjoyed the time they have spent together especially in bed together. It was Barbara who introduced Victoria to him, and it was truly very much unplanned and by chance. Victoria was a very close friend according to Barbara was just about her only friend. When Victoria's husband was killed driving home drunk and ran head on into a semi-trailer truck, it took Barbara to console her. Barbara took several days off from work to console her close friend and when Victoria described her life with her domineering and sometimes abusive husband, describing how he treated her by humiliating her and sometimes he would punish her. Said she would not know what to do without him directing her life, and besides she enjoyed having humiliating sex and masturbated often. After a very short while Barbara felt Victoria was just too vulnerable, and decided to introduce her to Roger. This occurred after Victoria had asked Barbara to spank her as she masturbated and wanted Barbara to be abusive and use a dildo on her. Barbara, after speaking with him, about her asked if it would be acceptable to him to bring her along one weekend, he agreed and that is how they met. Victoria was very pretty and she also found Roger very attractive. Victoria was obedient and a true submissive and this made it easy for both Barbara and Roger as he started commanding her around and she obeyed and started feeling better about herself and her life and became relaxed around him. That was how he came to having these two very attractive and sexy women in his life. Of the two, Victoria was probably the most fragile mentally and was much more of a submissive than Barbara. Barbara had grown to just completely let go and told him she had never had multiple climaxes before her involvement with him and truly enjoyed every minute they had spent together. She couldn't go back to having just regular sex again. Victoria worked as the head teller and second assistant manager at a local bank branch and was financially secure and he notice Barbara enjoyed her company very much and wasn't jealous of her and even had told him it allowed her to recover because his attention was now divided and kept her from just being overwhelmed sometimes.

After they had all finished eating Roger paid the bill and took them to a nearby movie theater complex where they had a choice of several movies and treated them to some popcorn, the movie was one of adventure and love and Roger had allowed them to pick the movie they wanted to see. It lasted a couple hours and Barbara and Victoria said they wanted to go home to relax and Roger had decided he was going to be nice to them this evening and see what was on their minds. When they arrive home carrying their bags inside Roger saw Rosie looking out her kitchen window again and she tried hard to remain out of sight as they entered his apartment. He told Barbara and Victoria they were going to relax this evening and to do whatever would make themselves comfortable. After about five minutes both women were fully undressed and headed to the bathroom since they hadn't been since eating and had to relieve themselves and after both had finished, Roger asked them to shower which they were more than happy to do. When they had finished bathing and oiling themselves he asked them to put on the maids outfits and he would take some pictures as he went to close the curtains leaving a fairly large portion open for his curious neighbor to peep through. They complied and he spent the better part of an hour photographing them in various poses. Then he told them to undress and just wear their robes and while they were doing that he went and showered and then they all sat around in their robes. He fixed them some drinks as they

54

looked at some television. Barbara and Victoria were both getting excited as Roger sat and petted both and felt on them and Barbara was sitting next to him and all of a sudden had and explosive climax while Roger rubbed her inner thigh. Victoria was utterly worked up, as she knelt between his legs and took him in her mouth and after he was completely hard stood, turned around and sat on him as he played with her breast. He then reached for her clit causing her to climax multiple times until she stood and sat next to him exhausted kissing him as Barbara now sat on him the same way, soon she climaxed and stood and turned around and got down on her knees and sucked him off as he soon came in her mouth. Roger just leaned back as both women caressed him all over.

Sitting on the couch for about another hour or more before going to the bedroom, and Roger decided to play some games with them and asked them to show him what they had purchased at Sexy Things. Barbara came back with an inflatable anal plug, and Victoria had chosen a double penis that would go into the vagina and ass together, was U shaped and had a handle at the base. Roger said for them to wash them off before using them and he wanted to see them demonstrate the new items for him. They were very excited after washing them off and soon returning. Roger handed them some lubricant as Victoria laid on her back and lubed up the dildo and asked Roger to do her as he began talking to her in a degrading manner and smacked her ass which excited her even more, then teasing her with it and slowly inserted it inside her quivering body, she became even more excited when Roger said she was a whore working it back and forth as he leaned over and licked her clit. She exploded with an uncontrollable climax and laid on the bed moaning as Roger continued working it in an out of her. She just laid there exhausted. Roger stopped, but left it in her feeling her breast while Barbara lay next to her kissing her, before Roger slowly worked it back and forth again before pulling it out completely. Barbara was next as she placed her head down with her ass up in the bed as Roger lubed her rectum then slowly inserted the rubber plug in her upturned anus and when it was completely inside of her, he gradually inflated it. Gently working it back and forth as Barbara moaned. Roger reached between her legs and inserted another dildo into her vagina and began rubbing her clit as she climaxed violently and wiggled her ass and screamed yes, yes, oh yes and then laid down letting the air out. Barbara and Victoria lay in bed now fully satisfied as Roger climbed in between them and held them both. They held on to him kissing him, Barbara stood and went to the bathroom to remove and cleaned the anal plug and returned kissing Roger as he held her and she started to cry and said she loved him so very much. Victoria laid her head on his chest and he rubbed her then pulled her up and told them he wanted another drink and to come with him and took the two women nude into the kitchen and fixed them some drinks which they quickly consumed before he began touched them all over again and then took Barbara, hugged her tight and felt between her legs. She then was very aroused and sensitive to the touch, making her spread them as he told her she was his bitch and needed her pussy spanked and she said yes, please master, as she spread her legs open again as he spanked her and soon she was having another rousing climax. He rubbed her again and she held onto him as her legs started to buckle under her. He led her back to the bedroom and placed her in the bed and climbed on top of her as he entered her. She screamed and climaxed again as Victoria looked on and then he climbed off of Barbara and turned to Victoria and said come her you piece of shit and pulled her by her arm and told her to spread her legs, spanking her pussy hard several times until she had a violent climax also, then laid her next to Barbara and climbed on top of her as he entered her and she screamed and climaxed again. He asked her who she was and she said your bitch master. They all hugged each other and finally went to sleep exhausted.

Chapter Four

The following morning when Roger awoke, found he was again between the two very warm and beautiful women he loved laying in his bed. The room smelled of sex and after getting out of bed he opened the window about three inches, the temperature outside was around fifty five degrees and made sure they both were covered by the sheet, spread an a light blanket before leaving the room. He headed to the bathroom and took a very warm and relaxing shower before returning thirty minutes later. He put on his shorts and another t-shirt and opened up the curtains and the patio door as he did just about every morning, weather permitting. He saw his camera and returned and took several photos of the two sleeping beauties in bed before leaving it in his so called office before heading to the kitchen. Roger started his day by putting on a pot of coffee before he returned to the bedroom just as Victoria woke, she sat up and he helped her up. She hugged and kissed him; he led her to the bathroom and asked her to shower. He returned to the kitchen and poured himself a cup of coffee and opened the kitchen window and started to prepare breakfast again for his two sexy visitors, after putting on some bacon he checked on Victoria, just as she got out the shower and gave her a large clean bath towel, and then checked on Barbara. Barbara was still asleep and he decided to leave her for now. He gave Victoria a robe and a bottle of massage oil and then led her to the living room and told her to oil herself. He held her in his arms and smacked her on her butt a couple times arousing her again as he reached down and felt her, telling her to finish oiling herself. He checked on his slow cooking bacon before checking on Barbara again. She was just awakening. He kissed her and she sat up hugging him as he helped her up and then helping her out of bed before also leading her to the bathroom and asked her to shower also, and bringing her a robe and a clean bath towel. Then he returned to the bedroom, opening the window wider before returning to the kitchen. He had just about finished cooking the bacon with the toast in the oven, and the eggs were waiting in a bowl to hit the hot pan just as Barbara joined Victoria and began oiling her body also. It was one of the things he insisted on them doing to keep their skin oiled. He detested dry skin and would have them at times just use the olive oil from the kitchen, and they appreciated his attention and concern telling them it was the secret to beautiful and long lasting skin.

He asked them to set the table as he began cooking the eggs and soon they were all once again sitting down and eating together. Each of them was famished, especially after such intense sexual adventures the day before. He gave them each some vitamins to take after eating. After eating, Barbara said she was changing the sheets, as she began gathering up all the dirty towels and bedding and placed them all in a large laundry bag, she also began making up the bed as well, she cleaned up the bed room while Victoria washed the dishes and pans. Roger began straightening up the rest of the house and took out his vacuum and cleaned the carpets. He pushed the garbage down in the can and got it ready to take out. He slipped on a jacket and shoes to take and deposit in the dumpster outside. He soon returned and washed his hands and hung up his jacket. Soon the apartment was again tidy as Roger sprayed air freshener and with all the open windows the apartment smelled fresh again. Barbara and Victoria began dressing, both put on a pair of shorts and t-shirts which was what Roger wanted them to wear when they spent time with him and since he had the Sunday paper delivered they all sat and read it together.

Roger then went to his office and uploaded the pictures from his camera to his computer and reviewed them and placed about ten aside in another file that he would upload under his user name, Master Caesar on an amateur bondage site. They were pictures of Barbara and Victoria in various positions but he was careful that their faces weren't shown and were hidden in all these photos. It wasn't the first time he had uploaded photos of them. He would take more pictures today since they did whatever he asked of them and they both knew about the web site. The hardest part for him was, he actually loved them very much and many times would go out of his way to please them. On valentines, sweetest, and mother's day he always planned something special for them, a dinner, show or something to let them know he cared very much. Victoria came into the room and she kneeled down and placed her head in his lap and held him around his waist, he rubbed her back and when she sat up he asked her if there was anything she wanted, said she just wanted to be with him. Said he had gotten her all excited earlier and she couldn't get enough of him and asked if he was going to play with her today. Roger said he was going to hang her and spread her wide open and place clamps on all her sensitive parts and make her scream and climax at the same time. Victoria shook with excitement, and said oh yes, please master; please, I need it very much now. Roger told her to sit in his lap and as she did he pulled her back and slid his hand under her shirt and felt her breast as her sensitive nipples grew harder and then slipped his hand down into her shorts and rubbed between her legs as her breathing grew more rapid and he said to her she was a dirty bitch, his little slut whore, this excited her even more and said he owned her bitch ass, and was going to fuck her until she was as limp as a rag, as he had two fingers in her pussy and told her she had better not come until he said she could, or she would be punished like never before, by feeling her clit she exploded and he held her and continued playing with her as multiple climaxes racked her body and he bite her ear and called her even more derogatory names and pinched her nipples, while holding her tight playing with her driving her crazy and continued rubbing her hot wet vagina. It became extremely wet with her vaginal mucus. When he loosened his grip on her she couldn't even standup as he held her and placed an arm under her, holding her as she began crying. She eventually reached around holding on to his neck. After about ten minutes she was able to stand, he told her while looking into her eyes, and said you didn't do as you were told, and now I have to punish you, she whimpered as he asked her, do you understand me bitch, she replied yes sir, Master Caesar. He ordered her to go the bedroom where he wanted her to remove all of her clothes and place her head down and ass up in the bed and to remain like that until he returned. He closed the office window as he left the room.

Barbara was still reading the paper. He came to the living room and he sat down beside her, they kissed and he said Victoria's been really bad, said she knew and had heard her. Barbara said the bitch really needs it and that was why I introduced her to you. Barbara said Victoria wouldn't know how to cope if you weren't in her life now, and she seriously needs you. Roger said she was waiting for me to punish her now and would deal with her and if you feel the urge you know you can join in. He asked Barbara to take her paper to the dining room table because he was going to hang Victoria up and needed the extra room. Roger went to the bedroom where Victoria was, she was still in the same position he had told her to assume. He told her to stand and began attaching the collar to her neck and kissed her pretty face, then ordering her to hold out her wrist as he placed the cuffs on her arms and ankles. He then led her to the living room where he clamped her arms together in front of her and tied a rope around the clamp. Then attached the spreader bar to her ankles, he took the rope and pulled her arms up above her head attaching it to the ceiling hook. He knelt down between her legs and felt her already sensitive and moist pussy and pulled the labia majora then attached clamps to each one as Victoria winced and moaned and he then attached some small weights to the clamps. He stood before the wincing Victoria and took a large plastic tie and placed it around her not overly large but ample breast, first one then the other squeezing the orbs and making them bulge out, then attaching a clothes hanger with clamps to her nipples then using a short piece of rope to attach it to her collar. He looked her in the face and said, because you came before I said you could, is the reason why, your slut ass is hanging here now. He took a short narrow strap and smacked her ass cheeks, across her stomach and inside of her thighs. She winced from the pain asking her, what you say now slut, she replied thank you Master Caesar. Roger reached for the long handled vibrator and placed it against her vagina and clit as the helpless woman cried with the pain of the clamps and the pleasure of an explosive orgasm as Roger continued to hold it against her clit. She was rocked by several more huge organisms. He paused for a moment to insert a large anal plug inside of her ass, and after doing so, he again began spanking her and then returned to use the vibrator on her until she just hung limp, and exhausted from having so many continuous climaxes. He removed the hanger from her nipples and the plastic ties and as the feelings returned to her breast, he played with and squeezed them as she moaned, then removed the clamps from her labia and unhooked the spreader bar and just let her hang by her wrists like a rag doll. Roger held her around her waist and rubbed her ass as he played with the plug in her rectum, working it in and out as Victoria moaned before he finally removed it. He untied her wrist and made her get down on her hands and knees, attaching a leash to her collar and made her crawl leading her around the apartment all the while smacking her ass with his strap, and when they returned from where he started from, made her stand up, and then he sat on the couch and had her kneel before him with her arms behind her back holding her by her hair and slapping her face lightly several times as she cried. He kissed her and asked her what she was, who she was, and what she wanted to be. She said she was his bitch, that she was a slut, and wanted to be his slave. He pulled himself out and without hesitation Victoria took him in her mouth and when he was fully hard made her stand and turn around and sit on him and as she moved herself up and down he felt her clit as she climaxed again and rode his hard manhood. She moaned and he felt her swollen nipples as he played with her clit as he came in her ass. She got back on her knees as she licked him clean and when she finished laid her head down in his lap as he rubbed her head. She looked up at Roger and smiled and said she loved him very much.

The highly over sexed Victoria was told to bring Roger his camera and when she returned he took pictures of her with her head down, or hidden as Roger poised her in different degrading positions and then in the bathroom with her head in the toilet before he ordered her to shower again. He brought her towel and her bathrobe before sitting down in the living room again, very sexually satisfied. When Victoria had finished bathing Roger led her to the bedroom where he rubbed her body with the oil, she moaned and kissed his hands and began crying as she knelt and hugged him. He pushed her back down and as she lay on her stomach and randomly smacked her ass as he continued to oil her shapely body. When he finished and turned her over, she sat up and hugged him tightly and pleaded with him to not ever let her go, that she would do anything he wanted, whenever, and wherever he wanted and said she couldn't live without him as she cried, big tears rolling down her pretty face. Roger held her face in his hands and kissed her; as she begged him please master. Roger said he would always keep her close. She began to smile and soon calmed down. He told her to put her shorts and shirt back on, and then left to sit in the living room again.

Barbara came and sat on the other side of Victoria, Roger said that Victoria needed to show her thanks to Barbara, her mistress and told her to get on her knees and asked Barbara to take her shorts off and sit back down, they both did as he had commanded and told Barbara to hold her legs up behind her knees so her ass and pussy was totally exposed, then told Victoria to show Barbara her gratification for bringing her here as he and Barbara kissed. Victoria did an excellent job as she licked Barbara's pussy and ass, and soon Barbara was having a huge organism and told Victoria to continue until he told her to stop. When Barbara climaxed again several times and said she had enough, he told Victoria to stop and go wash her face and return. Roger played with Barbara and kissed her as she climaxed again. Victoria returned and Roger had her sit while he was in the middle and said as he placed his arms around both that he loved them. He kissed both and said he was going to cook dinner for them, leaving them sitting on the couch.

Roger went and pulled out some of his precooked frozen food, foods he had cooked before and only needed to thaw and heat up; he fixed a pot of rice to go along with his southern style shrimp dish that he was going to serve. After finishing the rice he just waited for the main dish to thaw as he very slowly heated it up. Victoria came and pulled him to the hallway as she pressed him against the wall, kissing him and holding him securely as he held her; she looked at him and said she didn't want to be without him, he reassured her everything would be fine and not to worry. He held her as she pressed her head against his chess as he rubbed her back; he pulled her head back by her hair and kissed her, and said he needed to check his food. She released him but followed him into the kitchen. He checked his food and stirred the pot and then sat at the dining room table. Victoria followed and sat also, he looked at her and said you don't need to worry about anything, you have a week before I want an answer and not before. He checked and turned the fire out from under the food and found Barbara laying down taking a nap and woke her and said he was going to fix their plates in a few minutes. He asked Victoria to set the table. He took some plates out and prepared to dish up the food. Barbara joined them and sat at the table as he placed the plates of food on the table and poured them all a glass of chilled red wine, and soon they were eating. Barbara said the food was great and she loved it and wanted just a little more and Roger told her to help herself. Victoria took her time eating and when she finished said she loved it and would wash the dishes. When everything was put away and cleaned up. He checked the temperature, it had risen to a remarkable seventy degrees and he told them they were going for a short walk and he put on his athletic shoes. They walked around the complex for a little more than an hour and felt better by the time they returned. Barbara said it was time for her to head home, and she had packed her small bag and changed her clothes putting on some jeans as Victoria began doing the same. He helped them both with their bags walking downstairs with them to their cars and kissed them both good byes. Barbara said she would have an answer for him by Saturday as she got into her auto. Victoria stood by waiting for him as she hugged him tightly and said she would always miss him and he said he would miss her also as she got into her auto also and drove away.

Roger was kind of glad he would have some time by himself and wondered why he even poised the question to them, but knew he didn't want to be alone any longer, and hoped he wouldn't regret this decision if they accepted his offer. As he walked up the stairs he could see Rosie peeking out her kitchen window but pretended he didn't see her as he entered his apartment. Roger checked around and straightened up and started to fix himself a drink and had all the windows open and sprayed air freshener again and decided to sit on the porch and take in the view and looked at the trees that were just starting to bloom as he thought about his very and intense weekend with Barbara and Victoria. While he was sitting and looking at nature at work, Rosie Anne came out onto her porch and spoke to him. He greeted her and commented on the great weather. She asked if she could speak to him, he said sure anytime. She then quickly disappeared inside, and then he heard a knock at his door. He went and answered, and their stood Rosie. He let her inside and invited her to have a drink, she said yes please, he fixed her one and led her back to where he was sitting outside on the porch. Rosie sat down and said she read the contract agreement between a master and slave, and understood it completely and said she could hear my two visitors and said she had peered around the partition and saw what he had done to them, and it turned her on very much and wondered if Roger would show her, or rather if he would do her the same way. Rosie said she was so turned on by what she saw it was unbearable for her and asked Roger to please take her. Roger looked at her and said; are you sure you're ready to submit yourself totally to whatever I decide to do to you, and said she was very serious and it was a total commitment on her part, and not a joke or game. She pulled from her pocket the agreement he had given her and handed it to him. He unrolled and sat back and read it. Reading it very carefully and all her written comments, he read the medical portion and she was free of diseases, she had agreed to everything in the document, and had signed and dated it. He looked at her and said ok Rosie my dear and finished his drink and after a short conversation led her inside, he pulled the patio door almost closing it completely and pulled the curtain the same and went to the kitchen and closed it completely and pulled the curtain close.

He first brought back his small voice recorder before sitting down with her on the couch and asking her several very important questions. The first one he asked her was, that she fully understood the written agreement, she replied yes, had she ever been with a man before and having sex with him. She replied yes, she had but had masturbated all her life and then explained to him how she had come to enjoy pain as her parents punished her and the various ways they had inflicted pain on her, then went on to explain that she broke her own hymen. He asked if she was sure about what she was asking him to do to her. Said she was prepared to serve him as a slave and would do whatever he asked or wanted of her. He said since she had decided this is what she wanted he asked her if she was prepared to proceed. He had her read the last paragraph of the written agreement aloud. The paragraph where she consented to being tortured, abused, raped, humiliated, sodomized, beaten, tied, whipped and then he turned the recorder off and placed it in his office.

He returned to the living room and looked into her beautiful eyes as he kissed her. He told her to stand as he continued sitting on the couch, he looked at her and she was wearing shorts and a loose fitting t-shirt and he told her to kneel and gave her a pillow to place under her knees. He left the living room and then returned with a collar, cuffs and with a paddle and a box of clamps. She had said she wanted to be verbally abused and he asked her what she was. She stuttered, and then said she was a dirty bitch, and he said very well then. Then he asked her what was her purpose in being here, and she replied to serve the master. He told her to stand and remove her shirt; she was very nervous and had never been nude before a man like this before as she removed her shirt, then he said your shorts, she removed them and she had on panties, and he said those also. Rosie stood before him completely nude as Roger looked at her. She was shaven and Roger told her to spread her legs open and feel herself as he sat back and looked at her, she shook and he told her to stop as he stood and placed the collar on her neck and ordered her to hold her arms out placing cuffs on her small wrists, he knelt down, placing the cuffs on her slim sexy ankles, then stood and hooked the leash on her collar. He looked at her and said you are a piece of shit bitch and you need to be punished as he turned her around, cuffing her hands behind her back, before turning her back around and asking her, what are you now, she said your bitch master. He placed the pillow on the floor in front of the couch and told her to kneel with only her head on the couch. She was bent over and exposed as he looked at her ass and rubbed her ass with his hand, he felt between her thighs as she began trembling with unexpected excitement. He smacked her ass several times and then between her legs as he knelt down next to her left side and placed his left hand on her back, then reached around her leg with his right hand and rubbed on her vagina as he began smacking her ass and playing with her clitoris. Rosie quickly came to a rousing climax and he didn't stop as she was rocked with several more climaxes one after the other. He reached around and pulled out a dildo and worked it into her now very wet vagina as she shuttered and began climaxing again, and then he placed some lubricant on her butt hole and taking the same dildo and slowly began working it inside her tight anus as she moaned and finally relaxed as he slide it in and out while she climaxed again. He stopped and pushed it high up into her ass. Pulling her up to a kneeling position by her hair and said you little slut bitch. He held her face to his as he kissed her and she kissed him back with tears in her eyes as he pinched her nipples as she squirmed. He asked her if she was his bitch now, she said yes sir master, he asked her if she was ready to serve him as his bitch slut, she replied yes sir master. He asked her if she wanted him to fuck her, she said yes please, master sir. He stood and dropped his shorts, sitting down on his couch and pulled her face to his hard cock as she readily placed her mouth over it swallowing and sucking like she was hungry. He pulled her back, stood and removed the dildo from her ass and made her stand, grabbing the leash leading her into the bedroom and un hooked her arms from behind her and held her as he smacked her ass, before making her kneel in the bed with her head down as he took a leather strap, and began spanking her hard before climbing behind her and entered her very tight pussy as he smacked her ass with his hand and told her she was his bitch now as he held her and she continued climaxing over and over again as he fucked her vagina before he then entered her tight ass, and as he took her, he smacked her even more and pinched her tits hard as she continued climaxing as he pumped her anus and filling it with semen. He pulled it out and pulled her around by her hair and had her sucking and licking him clean.

Rosie had never in her short life had sex like that or had that many climaxes ever before, she could hardly stand as Roger removed the cuffs and collar and just about carried her to the shower where she knelt in the tub and he urinated on her as he held her head back and told her to open her mouth which she did and gave the very willing young woman a golden shower. He stood her up and turned on the water and he bathed her and himself. She started to regain some of her strength as Roger took her again in the shower, lathering her anus and entered her as he pinched her nipples and clit. She cried and climaxed at the same time before he finished bathing her and then dried her off as she melted in his arms, he then led her back to the bedroom and spread out a towel and then proceeded to oil her thin and shapely body as Rosie laid there weak and said thank you master. He turned her over and oiled her back, and when he finished, turned her back over and she was laying there weak, telling her she was his bitch now. She said take me master, he told her to open her legs as he massaged her vagina and she climaxed again, he said you belong to me now and only me, and asked her if she understood what that meant, she said, yes sir master, and he pulled her into his arms and she hugged him tightly. He said they hadn't finished their drinks and that she would sleep with him tonight, she said, yes sir master. He handed her a robe as he slipped his on and they went into the living room and he took their glasses and refreshed them and dimmed the lights. They sat on the couch and he had her in his arms and she told him that he was her master now and had wanted him for a very long time and was ready to do whatever he wanted. They finished their drinks and he took Rosie to bed with him. As they lay in the bed Rosie said she wanted him again and she climbed on top of him, sliding down and sucked him until he was hard then climbed back up and guided him inside of her as she laid on his chess and soon she climaxed again before rolling off to his side, and falling fast asleep. Roger lay and turned on his side looking at her, this new acquisition and would use her since she wanted to be used before he turned over and went to sleep.

When he woke the following morning and looked over at his newest submissive slave, he wondered how many women had these types of fantasies and if there wasn't something built into the female psychology that made it part of their nature. He pondered the thought of when Inky created mankind, was this built into our species. He went to the bathroom and cleaned himself up and then put on his morning coffee and returned to the bedroom and lay next to Rosie, and as he rubbed her soft body she woke, opened her eyes and smiled at him as she reached out and pulled herself to him, she kissed him and said she wanted to be with him forever. Roger said don't you have to go to work today; she thought for a minute and said she had the day off but would have to work the next coming Saturday for half a day. She said it was part of her regular schedule and everyone rotated to cover Saturdays which was a half day. When he asked where she was employed, she said the bank, and then he understood because Victoria worked at a bank also.

Roger began fixing them some breakfast after handing Rosie a robe and said that was all she was to wear today until he told her what to wear. He fixed their plates and they sat down and ate a full breakfast. Roger told her that today she was going to learn how to serve her master and that she would be subject to some very new experiences. When they finished eating he washed and cleaned up the dishes and the kitchen, and told Rosie she had some free time and asked if she needed to go home for anything. She said that she didn't. Roger went and gathered the items he would use on her and since the weather was pleasant he opened the curtains and the patio door along with the bedroom window. Roger liked having all the windows open and enjoyed the fresh air and since the temperature outside was going to be in the seventies he aired the apartment out again.

Shortly he told Rosie to remove the robe as he placed a collar and a set of cuffs on her limbs. He attached the rope to the ceiling hook and to both her arms, pulling them up above her head, next he attached the spreader bar to her ankles and let her hang there as he looked at her and asked if she was comfortable, she replied that she was. He admired her slim body, with her small breast with large long nipples, tight small round buttocks, and a wide gap between her thin and firm thighs with the large vaginal lips and clit. He could see the anticipation gradually building up as he said, I saw in your answers you like to clamp yourself, to which she replied yes. He told her he was going to apply clamps to her and if she was ready to serve him and enjoy her most base fantasy, said yes she was. Roger took out two large clamps and attached them to her nipples, they were hard from the inner excitement she was feeling, and she moaned loudly as he clamped them to her, knowing they were hurting her. He knelt down between her spread legs and examined her vagina closely with the large fat labia lips and decided on the large office binder clips as he attached one as she winced and moaned, then the other as they bit into her soft tender flesh, he attached the one ounce weights to both and stood and looked into her face as she felt the pain of the clamps and weights. He kissed her as she kissed him back and asked her what do you say bitch. She said thank you as he slapped her and asked her again, she said thank you master Caesar. He decided to use a zipper on her, and string of clothes pins attached with a small rope and started at her calf and up between her thighs, across her stomach to her breast. He attached two sets as she winced and felt the pinching pain. He took a penis shaped dildo and told her to suck it as he held it to her mouth, she did as she was told. When he removed it he placed it between her legs as she responded to its touch and pushed it deep inside of her, she had the look of surprise on her face as Roger suddenly grabbed the end of one of the zippers and pulled hard as the clothes pins pinched her and she screamed, he pulled the other and she jerked and moaned, breathing hard. He let her hang a long while as he contemplated his next move. He removed the dildo and nipple clamps and as the feeling returned he pinched them as she jerked silently with tears running out of her eyes. He bent down and removed the ones on her now swollen pussy lips and played with them looking into her face and she quickly climaxed, breathing in short ragged breathes.

He let her hang their, for several long minutes before returning with a stand with a dildo attached and an anal plug. He had a tube of lubricant and placed some on her ass and slowly worked the large plug inside of her, then placed the stand where it was directly below her vagina with a large soft latex penis with little ridges designed for maximum pleasure and adjusted it where it penetrated her by several inches. It has a spring that gave it a more up and down action and worked like a jack. Rosie felt it entering her and had the look of pleasure on her face but more was yet to come as he adjusted it slightly deeper inside of her. Roger placed a short penis shaped gag in her mouth and fastened it behind her head, and then he widened the spreader bar some, causing her to be lowered more onto the penis jack. He stood and looked at Rosie as she wondered what would happen to her next and then she saw Roger with the whip, she shook with fear and began to perspire as he approached her and she began shaking her head in a very pleading manner. Besides the whip he had a heavy leather strap that reminded her of the one her father used on her and knew it was very painful, he started out with the whip as he spared no parts of her out stretched body, as he struck her breast, butt, thighs, stomach, back, calf's as he moved around her as the dildo penetrated her even more deeply as she moaned and moved up and down and tried to scream as the gag prevented any of her anguished sounds from escaping. Rosie was starting to have another series of organisms as Roger then used the leather strap on her; she winced after every strike as she continued climaxing as the strap stung her abdomen and clit several times. Roger stopped and Rosie was moving up and down on her own as the dildo penetrated her and her own rapid movements caused it to become fully extended inside of her as she had another massive climax before she fell completely limp and down on the dildo as she soon stopped moving and Roger removed the gag. She looked up at him with such a satisfied look as she tried to speak.

Roger moved closer kissing and rubbing her face as she sucked his fingers. She tried to talk but nothing came out but some garble. Roger reached down and felt her nipples pulling and twisting both cruelly as she gritted her teeth, then he reached for her clit as she flinched and cried and in a weak voice, and said thank you master Caesar. Roger let her hang for a very long time after he placed a thin cloth bag over her head and said he wasn't through with her as she moaned. Roger used the bag for effect, and as she hung there went and got himself a cold can of beer, and his camera, sat and slowly drank about half before he removed the bag from her head. He then removed the dildo from between her legs and the spreader bar. He untied her hands from above her head and had to hold her as he placed her limp body on the floor. Rosie was totally exhausted. She was like a limp rag as she lay on the floor with the plug still in her rectum, hands cuffed together and unconcerned with anything. She had received the pain and pleasure she so much desired like never before in her life that she craved so much for at the hands of her new master and now was his willing slave. After half an hour Roger un- cuffed her wrist and told her to get on her hands and knees which she struggled to do. He attached the leash to her collar and led her around the apartment as he smacked her ass with the leather strap as she continued to have orgasms. He had her place her head down with her ass up and legs spread as he whipped her between her legs as she continued climaxing again several more times before laying down holding herself as he rolled her on her back and she rubbed her now very swollen vagina. He asked her what do you say slut, she said thank you master in a weak voice. He made her stand and bend over as he removed the plug from her ass, followed by the cuffs and collar, pulled her up by her hair as he undressed and led her to the bathroom where he bathed her like she was a baby, she was his now and he knew it. Rosie would never be the same and no other man would be able to satisfy her after today and being with Roger.

He finished bathing her and himself and led her to the bedroom where he laid her on a large towel in his bed and used olive oil on her body massaging every part of her, she pulled his hand between her legs as he felt her and she climaxed again. When he finished he covered her with a light blanket and she fell asleep. Roger left her their sleeping and after two hours went and checked on her, her eyes were open as he sat on the bed besides her and rubbed her, she grabbed his hand and started crying and then curled up into a fetal position as she held his hand tightly. Roger lay beside her and rubbed her and said she wanted to be his slave and couldn't be with anyone else now. Said she loved him and she had never felt the pleasure she felt with him and begged him to please accept her. Roger said he accepted her offer but she had to be very obedient and do as he wished. Said she would as he kissed her, and asked her what she wanted, said she wanted to please her master and wanted her master to take her body anytime he wanted. Roger undressed and climbed on top of the willing and now subservient Rosie as he plunged deep inside of her as she screamed fuck me master as she climaxed several more times before he raised her legs up and entered her ass and plunging deeply inside her until he came. He then lay beside her and felt her and spanked her between her legs as she continued to climax until she was fully exhausted. He led her to the bathroom where they cleaned themselves and then returned to the bedroom where he put his shorts on again. He held Rosie in his arms and they kissed and hugged one another.

Roger said they should eat something and he opened the bedroom window again as he led the nude Rosie around and attached the collar to her neck with the leash. He thought about using the harness but felt she had enough for now and would maybe wait until later. He prepared a nice lunch for them both and placed a towel in the chair before letting her sit down to eat. When they finished eating he asked her if she had a coat or sweater coat. Said she had one and Roger said after lunch to get it and a pair of hi-heel shoes. She could wear the robe and slippers as she went to retrieve the items, she said yes sir master. They finished and Rosie put the robe on and her shoes, picking up her keys and went next door and soon returned with the requested items. Roger said for her to put the shoes on. Soon he had her poise as he took pictures with her face hidden and removed the leash. Roger put on some jeans and a t-shirt and his army jacket and grabbed his SLR camera and told Rosie to put the sweater coat on as he led her out of the door, locking his apartment and putting her in his car, driving to a nearby park where they walked around and he took photos of her with the coat open, bent over and after a while they headed back to his car. After getting in he had her unbutton the bottom of the coat as he reached over and had her open her legs and felt her as he verbally degraded her as she had a massive climax, then he drove back home and they returned to his apartment. After opening the door and going inside he pressed her against the wall and ran his hands over her body under the coat and kissed her. She went wild and she climaxed again. He had her remove the coat but left the hi-heels on as he poised her again in very submissive poses and taking many more pictures.

Rosie had never ever been this excited before as he sat on the couch after putting his shorts back on and had her stand in front of him and handed her a penis shaped dildo and told her to play with herself as he sat and watched and if she wanted to come she had to ask permission, and if she came without asking and receiving his blessing she would be severely punished. He told her to insert it inside of her vagina, she did and started begging for permission right away as the pleasure built up in her sensitive and now very swollen pussy, Roger said after watching her she could come and just then she had a massive climax as her knees buckled and she bent over. And then Roger had her sit next to him as he hugged her. It was mid evening and he asked her if she wanted to go home. She said no that she wanted to be here with him a little longer. Roger fixed dinner and told her she could take the collar and shoes off, she did as he told her and to put on the shirt she wore and shorts but not the panties. As the food warmed he handed her a typed sheet of his dress code. She read it and said she would follow his rules. His phone rang and he looked and it was a call from Victoria, he answered and said hello,

Victoria said she just wanted him to know she loved him and was thinking about him. He told her he loved her also and was cooking and had to go and would talk to her later, she said ok master and hung up. He checked on the food and returned to talk to Rosie. He asked her how she felt now that she had been with him and if her fantasies had been fulfilled. She said all of them and more had been filled and didn't know how aroused she could become and wanted to be his bitch and woman and would do whatever he asked. Said she never imagined the fulfillment she felt just sitting here with him and the love, and said now she understood how the other two women she saw felt.

Roger said you will soon meet them and partake in his group submissions, and she would be welcomed by them and would have to service them if he said so. She said whatever Roger asked of her she would do. He told her very well because you belong to me now and most of all because you want to belong to me. She said yes, I give myself to you willingly, heart and soul to you master. Roger fixed their plates and told her to come eat, she devoured her food as her body demanded it to be fed and she asked for more after cleaning her plate and said it was the best food she ever tasted. Roger gave her a second helping and she finished that along with a handful of vitamins. Roger had her wash the dishes and pots since there wasn't any food left over. When she finished he fixed some drinks and they sat on the couch together, he held her and said you are going to enjoy being my neighbor more now as he kissed the side of her face. She held his hand as he looked at the slender fingers and placed one in his mouth and she moaned. She started to put her hand between her legs and he said you have to ask if you want to feel yourself and the only exception was when she bathed. She said yes master and asked if she could feel herself now. He said remove your shorts and sit back down. She did and he said you may feel on yourself as long as he could observe. She felt and fingered herself as he began talking to her in very derogatory terms; the excitement was starting to build up inside of her as her whole body stiffened and then went limp as she exploded with a massive climax. Roger wondered how much more she could take, or was she like Victoria, constantly and perpetually excited. She relaxed and sat limp as she leaned on him and he told her to drink her drink. He fixed her another and she sipped it and leaned on him again and started to cry and said she didn't want to leave. He said sweetheart I am right next door and you can see me every day if you want and that isn't like living a distance away, ok Rosie my dear. When she finished her drink Roger said you need to go home and get some rest so you can go to work, saying all my women have jobs, it's what the master demands. She said ok master as she stood with just the shirt on and he reached between her legs and felt her and pulled her down to sit in his lap as he played with her spreading her legs open as he spanked her pussy and fingered her clit. She climaxed again and hugged him as he felt her. He told her to stand and he stood with her and the shirt fell below her crotch and to get her coat and put it on and get her shoes and he would walk her home, she gathered the few things she brought and they walked to the door, opening it and walked the very short distance to her front door, she unlocked it and he went inside with her as she turned on the light, she turned and hugged him and kissed him with tears in her eyes as he felt her and said he loved her for the first time. She didn't want to let him go, but he told her to get some rest and he would always be next door and she had nothing to worry about as he released her. He turned and departed as she closed and locked her door. He returned home and straightened up washed the sex toys and closed his kitchen window but left the others open and took a shower and fixed himself another drink and stretched out on his couch. He was glad he had taken his vitamins after eating and felt he really needed them.

Roger looked at the clock and it was almost nine pm, he had spent three and a half days subjecting three women to being his sexual slaves, they wanted it and he was more than happy to give it to them. He hadn't expected Rosie to be so accepting and also so soon, but was glad she had come over, and to just think she was right next door. He went to his office and turned on his computer, checked his e-mails and looked for updates to the operating system and then went to his favorite bondage site and under his username uploaded several pictures of Barbara, Victoria and now Rosie. A little more than an hour had passed before he decided to go to bed so he could check out some real estate for his next new adventure. He needed a dungeon just to help simplify things, like for hanging his submissive females in and maybe a work shop so he would be able to construct his own devices. He decided to call it a day and applied some oil to himself and climbed into bed and soon fell asleep at last.

Chapter Five

The following day when Roger woke, started his usual morning routine, brewing a pot of coffee and soon began sipping on his first cup, all of a sudden he heard Rosie's door close. Then her footsteps as she headed toward the stairs for her trip to work, he stayed out of sight as she passed his kitchen window, and once she had passed, looked outside as the sexy young woman descended the stairs, there was something very different about the way she walked this morning, more sure of herself, and it stood out, a new confidence as he watched her reach her auto, she looked more beautiful with her hair up, with the skirt, stockings and sweater she wore. Roger knew what it was, she wasn't uptight any longer and it really showed in her demeanor. And after he had a long talk with her, he understood what she was looking for in her life; it was personal happiness and a sexually secure and satisfying relationship. Roger fixed himself a light breakfast and cleaned himself up, then went to his office and turned on his computer and searched the real estate listings. He put in what parameters he wanted in a home, four bed rooms, with four baths, basement, living room, and dining room, laundry, and garage. He hit enter and waited for his search to complete itself. There wasn't much that popped up in the areas he would want to live that looked suitable so he decided to get creative and started looking at larger buildings, like small warehouses, old bank buildings, barns and even abandoned power sub stations and more commercial type sites. Then just decided to narrow his parameters and looked at the pictures of some possibilities, and soon decided he would try a different approach, which was to just get in his car, and drive around the different areas that he would want to possibly live in and look around for himself. This proved to be very interesting, seeing quite a few large and medium sized plots that were vacant, and also for sale and the good thing was, he had brought along his tablet with him writing down the addresses and locations and phone numbers that were listed on the for sale signs. Roger rode around about half a day before returning back home, and on the way back stopped off for lunch.

It was early evening and after eating decided to head home so he wouldn't be caught in the rush hour traffic. He had seen several locations he liked and all were vacant ploys of land. When he returned home called and inquired about them, knowing he would purchase most of what he had seen in his quest and found several that would have real potential in the very near future, adding them to his long list of vacant land holdings that he used to lower his taxes. Soon, he was going to lower his tax burden even more by turning some of his stock investments into tax free municipal bonds. After contacting several of the agents listed, he made the necessary arrangements to purchase the land, then contacted his attorney and gave him the list of properties he would purchase. He decided that maybe tomorrow he would venture out a little further and see what else was available.

After a long day of decisions, Roger had to decide what was on the menu for dinner, he decided on some chicken and rice with a green salad on the side. It was a little after five when he finished cooking and his kitchen window was slightly open. The next thing he knew there was a knock at his door, and as he peaked through the peep hole and looked, there stood Barbara, he opened the door and welcomed her inside. He said what a surprise as she hugged him, he hugged her back and kissed her, she said for some reason she just wanted to see him and couldn't explain why, she was dressed in her work clothes, she was looking super sexy with her stockings, hi-heels, skirt, blouse and matching long sleeve jacket with her matching purse. Said she loved him so very much and just couldn't get him out of her mind for some reason and knew he had given them a week before he wanted an answer, but she wanted to tell him now she wanted to be with him all the time no matter what. He looked at her, and said he loved very much and wanted her also. Said that she just wanted to see him and tell him now, but had to go because she had a few other things to do before returning home, she kissed him and departed as he watched her go down the steps to her auto. It was ten minutes later when there was another knock at the door, he looked again through the peep hole and there stood Rosie, he opened the door and let her inside, she kissed him and saw the lipstick on the side of his face and she kissed him again and said she loved him, she had just gotten off work and was looking sexy with her stockings and dress and short jacket. She said she missed him and just wanted to see his face before going home. She asked about the lipstick and said Barbara had just stopped by to say she loved him. Rosie said ok, and then asked if she could come back later. Roger said if he wasn't asleep she was welcome and asked her if she wanted to stay for dinner. Said that she wanted to get out of her work clothes first and would return as she headed for the door and said she would be right back in about ten minutes. When she returned shortly she wore just a much worn out long cotton dress and thongs.

Roger had her set the table as he dished the food onto their plates and poured wine into two glasses. They sat and ate and Rosie said that she had the best day at work she ever had, and for some reason her coworkers complimented her and she couldn't understand why since she had on the same dress she had worn before many times. He told her he saw it in her demeanor when she left for work, that she wasn't uptight anymore and had a new aura about herself, and all because of the way she felt inside, and said it showed and was very happy for her. Rosie said it must be because of him and how he had freed her inner self and thanked him for now being in her life. She complimented him on the meal and said his cooking was so much better than hers. Rosie also wanted to be with him and thought about how happy she felt after spending yesterday with him, and wanting to serve him again if he desired her. He told her to eat first. She finished eating and asked if she could help clean up. He said sure and welcomed her help. They finished eating and Rosie cleaned up, washing the dishes and pots as he began putting the few leftovers away.

Afterwards Roger went to his office and turned on his computer and returned to fix a drink and asked Rosie if she cared for one, she said yes sir master and he fixed a couple of rum and cokes. Afterwards he sat in the big chair in the living room while she sat on the couch. She asked him what have you been doing today. And explained that he was looking for a new residence and it wasn't an easy process because he liked the atmosphere here but felt it was time for him to move on. She asked what would happen to their relationship; he answered her by saying that after she met Barbara and Victoria he would then give her the same choice he gave them, and that is would they be prepared to move in and live with him. He told her not to answer yet because she needed to seriously think about it, and one of the most important reasons would be she wouldn't be the only woman in the household and she would have to feel very comfortable being with two other women, and having sex with them if he ordered her to. Rosie said she would do whatever he asked of her. She sipped her drink and he asked her if she had anything to do before she went to bed. She replied no. She was planning to fix something to eat and maybe look at some television. At least, that is what she had been doing, and even masturbating herself. He asked her what she wanted to do now and she replied to be here with him and do whatever he wanted her to do. He got up and sat next to her on the couch and put his arm around her shoulders. He asked her what she had on under her dress and she said nothing at all. When they finished their drinks, he took her to the bedroom and told her to take the dress off; she did as he looked at her and said you haven't bathed yet have you. She replied she hadn't and he told her to lie down in the bed and spread her legs which she did as he then bent over and smelled her vagina, she didn't have any unusual odors as he stood and told her to stand up, she was excited now and told her to put her dress on, she did and asked if something was wrong and he said no. There wasn't and was very satisfied with her. She put her dress on and asked if he would please feel her. He said she would have to wait until he decided to; he was the master and she the slave, and slaves made no demands. He asked if she understood, she said yes sir master.

He went to his office and put his password in his computer and returned to the living room fixing them both another drink. He told Rosie to sit and enjoy, she asked if she could play with herself, he said yes, you may. She pulled her dress up and spread her legs and fingered herself as he sat and watched her, she soon had a major organism and then sat and just looked at him, and said him watching her made it that much more intense. Said she was happy now as she sipped her drink. And was happy being here with him. Roger looked at her and said you are a very pretty young woman and I want you to think very carefully about what I told you, and remember you are the only one who can make you happy, and the choice is yours and only yours to make. If you decide to live with me or rather us, you need to be very sure, and that is why I told you not to decide until after you meet Barbara and Victoria. She finished her drink and he said I think it's time for you to go home. He said come as she stood and followed him and as they entered the hall he turned, pushed her against the wall, raised her dress up and felt between her legs bringing the highly excited Rosie to a rousing climax while she panted. He kissed her and told her to bathe, and get some rest, and that he loved her. She began crying, hugging him and said she loved him very much. He led her to the door, kissed her and she walked out as he watched her until she entered her apartment. Roger went to work at his computer and after a while left it on while it did some updates. Went back to the living room to watch some television, watching the news, and it would be raining near the end of the week and thought that's ok and it wouldn't interfere with his looking again tomorrow, but would start much earlier than he did today. Roger then took a warm shower and went to bed.

The next day when he woke, he took a shower to wake himself up and fixed his morning coffee and had another light breakfast, dressed in his jeans and prepared to leave, when there was a knock on his door, he opened it and Rosie stood there looking as beautiful as ever and said she wanted to kiss him before going to work and said she felt good and wanted to thank him as she kissed him again and said she loved him, turned and went downstairs to her auto, looking rather cute and sexy as ever. Roger was ready to go also and had checked his computer and it had come up with just two new listings that were just posted in the last twelve hours. He printed the new listings out and grabbed the sheets, grabbing his jacket as he closed and locked his door. He went downstairs got into his auto and set out to look at the two new listings, which were several miles away and drove to the farthest one first, and would then work his way back home.

When he arrived at the first house he found it to be a very large home, about ninety years old in a well-established neighborhood, it was three stories tall and had five bedrooms with four baths, living and dining rooms, den, basement and a two car garage, it looked spacious from the outside, the lot was about an acre, it had mature trees closely surrounding the home and it wasn't a bad looking home, but it seemed a little out dated for what he was looking for, and besides it didn't really quite appeal to him and decided to move on to the next. He drove to the next one on his list, it was closer to where he lived now, and it was a much newer home on a much larger lot, more about an acre and a half, it had six bedrooms, five full and two half baths, the property was fenced and had a large gate, the surrounding neighborhood was much more upscale than the last. The home was just off a major thoroughfare, but it was more private and semi secluded. There were more trees around it but not close to the house and according to the information it was less than one year old. He called the listing agent and made an appointment to see it and had informed the agent he was at the location now. The agent informed him he was fortunate and could see the house within the next hour because he was nearby. The price was over a million dollars, really closer to a million and a quarter but according to the listing, the taxes were lower than the last one. Roger wondered why this home was for sale, and would do some more research on the area but for now would just look around the neighborhood. He drove around looking at the other nearby homes to kill some time while waiting on the listing agent. The surrounding homes were all very upscale and not even close together with very large sprawling yards and all had multi car garages and appeared none of the lots were on less than half an acre as he returned. He waited for the agent to arrive to open the large gate to the home before he could drive in. He soon met the agent, Mr. Brown and introduced himself; he asked the agent why the home for sale. Mr. Brown stated the owners had built the home and hadn't been in the home six months, when the unexpected occurred, their company suddenly relocated out of state which forced them to have to sell quickly, and why this was such a new house and listing. Mr. Brown opened the front gate using a remote and they drove up the long expansive drive way to the front entrance. Roger was impressed with the length of the driveway after he stepped out of his auto.

Mr. Brown stated the area was really desirable and upscale and he didn't expect the house to be on the market very long even at the current asking price. They entered through the front entrance that had large solid oak cathedral style double doors ten feet tall with a carved and very unique oriental design, and after entering he was amazed, it had hardwood floors throughout and a large curved double staircase to the upper floors surrounding a large round entrance hall that had an oculus style ceiling. As Roger continued to walk around the spacious home looking and being amazed by the large living room that had a huge fire place with an open plan leading into the dining room area, then the kitchen just flowed into the space. It was large, but with a well-planned lay out, the kitchen had a central island with a sink, and it was one of two. The floors and walls were completely tiled, with professional grade appliances built in with custom cabinets, the other sink was under the large wide sliding kitchen windows with a view and you could look out and see the large patio that flowed off onto an adjoining deck along with landscaping that flowed down a slight hill. And next to the kitchen was the large laundry room with twin washers and dryers with space and hookups for a third set. They proceeded, as you could make a complete circle around the central core of the home where the large oversized elevator was located and back to the front entrance. They walked upstairs and the stairs were wide and all the floors on the second level were hard wood also. Roger first looked at the master bedroom, it was a large flowing space and as large as his entire apartment, with a walk-in closet the size of his office, and a large fully tiled and beautiful bathroom that was spacious with a large walk in shower with a bench, a bath tub, dual sinks, bidet and toilet, it was all done in white tile, floor to ceiling and had wide sliding windows across one wall above head level and also included a large floor to ceiling linen closet. Roger looked at all the bed rooms; and three were almost as large as the master, and were about the same size, and each with their own private bathrooms and the two smallest bedrooms shared one very large bathroom. All the bedrooms were as large and at least two thirds the size of his apartment. It had an attic with a wide walkup staircase for access; and he looked and it. It was completely finished and dry walled showing no signs of any water leaks. When he asked Brown about the roof, he stated it was a metal roof. They walked back to the second level and then took the elevator downstairs to the basement, it had a very high ceiling for a basement, close to eight foot, and the floor was ceramic tile and had a large half bath with a shower room. The heating and air conditioning equipment along with all the house mechanicals were in a large walled off area. The basement was finished, the walls were in place and painted and the entire basement was open and dry. The property sat on an elevated lot that he noticed when he drove up. They walked upstairs using the wide stairs and Roger was very impressed and the home had a fire suppression system, outdoor sprinkler system, security camera system inside and out and that was all centrally located in a built in cabinet near the kitchen. It was located in the core, which was the center of the home. He asked if he could place a retainer or deposit on the home as they went and entered the expansive and oversized four car garage through the kitchen and mud room. The garage had individual doors for each space and all was painted in primer white as was the entire house. Mr. Brown said they needed to go to his office where he could write up a contract, and Roger said of course.

The home was listed for one million two hundred and ninety nine thousand dollars and it would be no problem for Roger. The agent wasn't sure based on Rogers's casual appearance; his dress would make one question if he was on the up and up, and then the car he was driving also. Roger drove to the real estate office and entered and took a seat and waited on Mr. Brown to arrive. There were several agents present as Mr. Brown entered as Roger stepped over to his desk as Mr. Brown began filling out a sales contract and when he asked what his deposit would be. Roger replied what was the asking price, asking Mr. Brown how much of a retainer would he need. Brown said at least ten percent or one hundred thousand dollars would do it. Roger said ok and said he thought he had seen a bank branch down the street and if he could go and get him a cashier's check. Mr. Brown said he would wait for him to return. Roger walked down the block and returned less than an hour later with a check for the full asking price and sat down and handed Mr. Brown the envelope. Mr. Brown almost fell out of the chair after he took the check and looked at it. Roger gave him a check for the one million two hundred ninety nine thousand dollars. Mr. Brown went and conferred with the managing broker and returned saying he would inform the seller of his offer. Roger said to please keep him informed. Mr. Brown said if he would please wait he would call the seller now to see if he accepts your offer. Roger said he could wait.

Ten minutes later Mr. Brown had an answer and said the seller had accepted his offer and Roger pulled out his phone and contacted his attorney and informed him of his latest purchase. Roger left with a copy of the sales contract in his hand and drove straight home. The day had passed fairly quickly and arriving home in the late afternoon could see Rosie was home as her kitchen light was on and saw her car in the parking lot. He didn't feel like cooking and decided he would get some takeout; he got back in his car, driving over to the Quickie Chicken Shack, and purchased a four piece chicken dinner before returning home. He parked and started walking to his apartment, entered and took off his jacket, washed his hands and went to create a folder for the new property he purchased today and began formulating a plan for operating his new home based on if the three women in his life moved in with him. He took out a couple of paper plates that he had kept handy and brought his food to the table. Started to sit down when his phone rang, he looked and it was Victoria, he answered, she was always happy when she spoke to him and said she had stopped by and wondered where he might have been. He said he was taking care of some business and had just arrived home. Victoria said she missed him and would see him after work on Saturday, and he said ok sweetie, and said she loved him and hung up. He began eating and had just taken his first bite when there was a knock at his door and he wiped his hands and went to see who it was. It was Rosie and he let her inside and said he was eating, she kissed him and said she just wanted to spend some time with him as he closed the door and returned to the dining room table. Being a gentleman he offered her some food which she declined and said she had already eaten. She sat down as Roger ate and enjoyed his food and a beer. He asked her when her lease was up and she said in two months and management had sent a new one already but she hadn't signed or returned it. He said yours and mine are just a month apart, and said he had three months. Then he told her don't sign or return it until after this weekend. He then asked if he could look and see what she had in her apartment and explained why based on her possible decision after this weekend. And just really wanted to know how much furniture she had. She said it wasn't a problem and he was very welcomed. He replied after he finished eating, he would look. She asked if he wanted to see it now, and said yes please as he soon finished eating, deposited his plate in the trash can, washed his hands and went next door with her. After he entered, she said he was the first man to ever be inside her apartment and showed him around the very spacious but mostly empty studio apartment. He looked around and all she had was a futon an with a mattress, a small television on a small short table, and a card table with a couple of folding chairs, she had a small set of pots and a pans, most of what she owned was clothes and there really weren't very many of them either, the closet wasn't even a quarter full. The entire apartment including the kitchen and bath was about the size or smaller than the small bedrooms in the new house he was purchasing. He thanked her very much and headed for the door, she asked if she could be with him a little longer, he said yes and took her hand as she took her keys and nothing else. She wore the same dress as yesterday and her thongs and they returned to his apartment. She asked him why he wanted to look and he explained that he was working out a plan for when he moved and told her he wasn't going to renew his lease and had found and purchased a new home.

The two sat on the couch together and he said he was trying to wait until Saturday when all three of them were here to explain and reveal his plans to them all together and said it would be unfair to Barbara and Victoria to tell her anything now. She told him even though he wanted them to wait until Saturday she had already made up her mind, and was prepared to tell him now if he wanted to know. He told her if it made her feel any better, he was willing to listen, she said that she wanted to be with him no matter what, that if he was afraid she would get pregnant he didn't have to worry because as a teenager, shortly after having sex for the first time with a man, had contracted a disease and later had to have an operation and she was sterilized in the process and couldn't have children, her ovaries had been removed. Stressed that it was a very sensitive subject for her, said her parents were highly upset with her, but her mother was a little more consoling than her father, he said that she had ruined her life and was so very upset; he made comments that she was now just a cheap worthless whore. He was so upset, that he took her and tied her up by her hands in their garage, stripped her naked and whipped her with a leather belt and then leaving her to hanging there overnight in the cold, she said it changed her life so much it caused her to study that much harder, because several times he came to her bedroom, tied her to the bed and whipped her between her legs. She finished high school and really applied herself even more so in junior college. Stressing it's what made her the person she was besides the other severe whipping her parents inflicted on her and to enjoy pain with sex, in a sense she was punishing herself. Roger placed and arm around her as she broke down and just cried. She held onto him as he said that he understood her even if no one else did. Said she just wanted to be loved, to be herself and couldn't help what she had become and had come to terms with what she was and needed. She asked Roger to make love to her now; she wanted to be punished and to feel some pain.

He stood and she stood with him, as he led her to his bedroom.

Roger took her to the bedroom, told her to undress and asked her what was she, said she was his bitch and needed to be punished, he held her face with his left hand and slapped her lightly, he told her he was going to spank her ass and told her to kneel in the bed, she complied, he had her to hold her ankles, as he reached for his large leather strap, he made her kiss it all over before he brought it down hard on her upturned ass cheeks ten times, then standing on the other side of her as she whimpered and striking her another ten times as her cheeks began turning bright red. He told her to stand up, she turned around with tears in her eyes, he undressed and pulled himself out, had her kneel and she knew what to do as she placed him in her waiting and ready mouth and soon he came and told her to swallow it all, she took it all in, then told her to stand and spread her legs, he reached down and spanked her pussy hard ten times with the leather strap as she climaxed, he then reached down inserting several fingers in her moist hot pussy as she began shaking with another massive organism. When he stopped; he wrapped his arms around her as she clung to him with tears in her eyes and said I love you master. He told her to get in the bed as he laid next to her and held her and rubbed her very warm buttocks and shortly after he was hard again and spreading her thighs open, and climbed on top of her and had rough sex with her as she moaned and continued to climax. She said fuck me master. She continued and filled her with hot sperm as he came inside of her. She screamed. He rolled over and lay next to her and she slid down and licked him clean as he ran his fingers through her hair before pulling her up and holding her, kissing him as he rubbed her back and butt allover. They just lay together a long time before he took her to the shower and had her kneel, giving her another golden shower. He then turned the water on and they bathed one another.

Afterwards he led her to the bedroom and placed a towel on the bed and rubbed her with oils and some medicated salve that relieved the stinging sensation of her hard spanking. She oiled him after he had finished with her and then she lay next to him in his arms curling up close to him. It had gotten late and he told her she needed to go home so she could go to work the following day, she said yes sir master, she dressed. He put on a robe and walked her to the door and kissed her, she left and he waited until she entered her sparsely furnished apartment and closed the door. Roger returned to his bedroom after securing the windows and went to bed himself falling sound asleep.

Chapter Six

He woke later than he usually did and only realized it after looking at the clock; he had slept very well again and associated it with having sex the day before with Rosie. He went to fix his morning coffee turning on the radio so he could listen to the weather reports and was happy to hear it was going to be another very pleasant day, the weather was steadily improving. His phone soon rang and his lawyer was calling to tell him that he had scheduled several of the vacant land purchases for the same day and the closing on the house for the same week since there were no leans on the property and it being so new plus the amount of earnest money he had placed down fully covered the asking price. He wrote down the dates and locations along with the times and all would be scheduled for the following week on Tuesday and Wednesday, Roger thanked him and hung up. He sat and drank his coffee, ate a donut before he took and wrote down his thoughts about how his new household should and would be run. Whatever Victoria, Barbara and Rosie and he were paying together in rents plus their utilities he would add up. Their new monthly expenses should be much less and sufficient to cover all the taxes, utilities and any other expenses since there wouldn't be any mortgage payments. The rest would go for food and other necessities and everyone should see a big savings. The thing now is how Barbara and Victoria would take to Rosie and didn't foresee any problems as of yet, but it didn't matter what anyone of them thought he was going to move regardless and would gladly welcome the change. Roger decided he would start looking at some furniture today because he only had a couple pieces he was keeping, one was his dining room table and chairs and the large solid wood cabinet in his bedroom with the restraints and devices inside and the rest he would donate to charity. He would prefer that everything matched or closely matched and would have fun shopping for a much larger bed and knew it would be a king size bed this time. This was tops on his list, with some very large throw rugs or even Persian carpets, he thought hell he should just look around and start making some notes. He intended to move as soon as it was feasible so the sooner he started the better. After eating another light breakfast because he was beginning to become somewhat excited as he thought about the move, dressed and checked around the apartment before locking up and heading for some of the quality furniture stores nearby, avoiding the ones selling cheap and low quality furniture. He wanted quality over quantity and soon pulled up to his first store, they handled bed room suites mostly, and it was there specialty and as he looked around, saw several sets he really liked.

He soon found the king-size bed set he really liked, it was a regular king size platform bed, it had drawers underneath the mattress and he really liked it, as he continued looking at the regular sized king beds and made notes of where they were and the cost. The Alaska or California kings were extremely large. After looking, he left and shopped at a couple of other stores taking notes and looking at rugs, carpets, sofa sets, tables, and cabinets and decided to return home after spending most of the day looking around for furniture and before getting some fast food on his way back and decided to eat at a the restaurant. He felt tired and wanted to rest since this looking at and for furniture and shopping was more tiring than he thought it would be, and besides the weekend was coming and knew he would be busy with his three sexy women, and figured he had a day to prepare before there arrival.

After returning home he undressed, washed up, and put on his shorts and a t-shirt, he laid down and soon fell into a deep sleep. It was very late in the evening when he awoke and just laid there thinking how much more convenient doing his laundry was going to be as he checked his cell phone. There were several calls from all three women, Victoria, Rosie and one from Barbara. He went down the list and called Victoria since she was the last one to have called, and she answered right away. She immediately asked where he was, and said at home and had fallen asleep after lying down and had taken a nap. Said she was very worried something had happened to him, he thanked her for her concern, and said he loved her and would see her on the weekend. Said she wanted to come over and spend the night. She didn't wait until he could answer before she said that she was coming anyway, and ended the call. Roger was barely able to say, ok sweetie before she hung up on him. He called Rosie, she asked if everything was alright, he said he had fallen asleep, said she was coming over also, and hung up. He called Barbara, she said Victoria had just called her and told her you were sleeping before she said she was coming over. He didn't have time to answer before she hung up.

It was late Thursday evening and wondered what was going on. He got up, washed his face just in time and shortly after walking out of the bathroom there was a sharp knock at the door, he looked through the peep hole and their stood Victoria. Roger wondered if she wasn't sitting in her car as she walked in and kissed him, he had just closed the door when there was another knock and he opened the door and Rosie walked inside. He introduced her to Victoria and they knew each other and hugged and kissed one another. They worked at the same bank, but different branches. He asked them to have a seat as they sat on the couch and talked. He went and fixed himself a drink, and sat in his big chair and had just gotten comfortable when he heard another knock at the door, went to answer it, and when he opened it there stood Barbara, she kissed him as she walked inside and he followed her to the living room where she heard Victoria and Rosie talking.

He sat down and said what a surprise. He introduced Rosie to Barbara and she came over, and Rosie stood up and they hugged. Barbara said she wouldn't be here if she wasn't one of us, and knew the young woman had issues or was damaged in some way if she submitted herself to Roger. Victoria was dressed in a pair of long shorts and a blouse with a sweater and Barbara in jeans with a t-shirt and sweater. He said may I ask what brings all of you here, now and today, and all of a sudden, stated that they were concerned that something had happened to him. Said he appreciated there concern very much. Barbara said she was very concerned when Victoria said she couldn't contact you and was worried and was sitting outside and had just pulled up when he called her back. He said Rosie here is a new addition to the group and said he had mentioned it to her the last time they were out. He also said I assume each of you have reached a decision of some sorts, and guess I will accept your answers now a day early since you all seem so very anxious to tell me your decision if you are ready. He said let's start first with Barbara. She said yes she would, and then Victoria said yes and last was Rosie as she said oh yes. He said ok then. I have three months left on my lease, and Rosie here has two, and he asked Barbara and Victoria about theirs. Barbara said three, and Victoria said two. He said I assume you wonder where or if I have found a home for us. He explained that he has, and went on to explain that each would have their own very large bedroom and said it was larger than the size of Rosie's studio apartment next door or slightly smaller than this entire apartment. Barbara said she wanted to see how large it was, and he asked Rosie if it would be alright with her, she said it would be a pleasure and they all walked next door to Rosie's studio apartment. Barbara was amazed how clean her apartment was and complimented her, and turned to Roger and said the bedrooms are the size of this apartment; he said yes and much larger almost double in size and each one has its own private bathroom and a walk-in closet the size of his office.

They all returned back to his apartment and Rosie now sat between Barbara and Victoria. He also explained that Rosie had been his neighbor for a year and they had talked off and on and was now his, asking that they both please accept her. Victoria said she had no problems with Rosie, Barbara said the more the merrier. He explained how the house whole would function financially and how he had come to cover the cost of their new home and the guarantees that he would put in place for them in case something ever happened to him. He asked if they agreed to the new terms saying he would have documents drawn up very soon and would put everything in writing. He said Barbara, would be head mistress, and in charge in his absence, and they were to serve her if she asked or commanded them to, after her would be Victoria. He asked if this was acceptable with all of them, they all said yes sir master.

Since they were all in agreement; he proposed having a toast, and fixed some drinks. He returned and served them. Barbara said master may I ask you where is the new home. He told her the neighborhood but not the address and said they would have to wait until next week to see it after he closed. Victoria said she wanted to spend the night, Barbara said she was and he looked at Rosie and said you might as well also. He said you can stay as long as you all go to work tomorrow. Barbara said tomorrow is Friday and she had taken the day off, but Victoria and Rosie had to work and also on Saturday for half a day. He said then you all might as well get comfortable. Victoria went to her car and returned with a small suitcase she kept in her auto besides the purse and a large bag she brought in with her, went to the bedroom and undressed and put on an oversized smock and Barbara followed her and had some of her clothes in his office closet. They both returned and sipped there drinks as Roger now wondering if this was such a good idea and wondered if his penis, fetish and sexually fiendish mind had placed him in a real true to life trick bag. He ordered a couple pizzas as they sat and drank rum and cokes. About an hour later the pizzas were delivered. They all sat at the dining room table eating when Barbara said she was starting to get excited just thinking about moving, said she had been in her little tight ass apartment to long and was tired of traveling over here and would soon be closer to those she loved and thanked Roger for this upcoming move. Victoria said she felt the same way and would be much happier being with them every day and was very happy Rosie was also now part of the group and told her Roger was very good to them and they were all very satisfied with him.

Rosie said she knew he was good and had also been good to her also and knew that she had issues and he understood her and said she loved him and started crying. She really felt loved and accepted. Barbara was sitting next to her and hugged her as she just continued crying and held her and telling her it's alright now baby girl. Rosie composed herself and Roger fixed her another drink, and everyone else. It was starting to get late and he asked what size beds Victoria and Barbara had. They said twin beds, Roger said we will all have to get king size beds; we need to all have the same size beds, so we will have plenty of sheets the same size and if we all decide to sleep together there will be enough room. Roger said he and Barbara would start looking at furniture tomorrow. He told them to imagine all your furniture in your bed room, and then decide what you would want to keep and what you will want to donate or throw away. He said there is no since paying to move stuff and then throwing it away afterwards, and what we pay together in rents and utilities you will be able to save and furnish your rooms. And said the house is paid for so the expenses which we will all share are taxes, utilities and food. He said the dining room table and chairs and the cabinet in the bedroom was all the furniture he was moving and the rest he was donating and suggested they all decide seriously what they wanted to keep and do, we will all have a fresh start for once in our lives.

He told Victoria and Rosie that they needed to bathe themselves so they could go to work tomorrow. Victoria said she was going to shower and Rosie said she wanted to stay but would go home and return as Victoria said she would go next door with Rosie and asked Roger for a towel and a robe. He said you know where they are sweetheart, as she went to get the needed items and then went next door with Rosie. Roger and Barbara sat and talked about the move together on the couch as she held his hand and leaned on him and said she loved him and said Rosie is really happy being here and thought this move was a very positive one. He said he hoped so and said he saw no reason why it shouldn't work well for all of them, and went on to describe the house to her. She asked him if he would tell her how much, he said no he wouldn't because it was personal and he was doing this for all of them. Barbara said when you worked at the company, something had happened to him and she had noticed a very positive change in his attitude over time, but he never said what had happened and then he resigned. She asked if he would tell her and said she could keep a secret. He looked at her and said he had never told anyone ever what had happened and didn't want to change his friendships or relationships and that's why he never discussed what good fortune had come into his life saying it wouldn't help her if she knew, but said it was wonderful and that he felt it was god given and that he loved them. Barbara said she loved him and wouldn't ever ask him again.

It had gotten close to ten and Roger said he would sleep on the sofa and let them have the bed. He turned on the small television and he and Barbara snuggled up and talked more. Soon Victoria and Rosie returned and he suggested they go to bed; he kissed them both and held them each a short while before he told them to leave some room for Barbara. He sat down again with Barbara as she laid on the couch with her head in his lap as he felt her body and becoming excited when he touch her and had told him he had such a marvelous touch which drove her mad as he pulled up her oversized night shirt and felt between her soft warm thighs and rubbed them and she soon had a fantastic organism. Roger suggested that she get some sleep too. She got up and they hugged and kissed before she joined the others in bed. Roger closed up and made himself a bed on the couch and soon had fallen asleep.

Roger was up early the following day before any of his house guest, making a large pot of coffee and started preparing breakfast for Victoria and Rosie soon after he had washed up. He woke Victoria and Rosie after looking at the clock and after they had washed their faces told them to come eat while he served them breakfast. Soon Barbara joined them, and they all ate together. Roger said my family is here with me now, and said a quick prayer. Victoria and Rosie thanked him as Victoria went to dress and Rosie went next door to dress and soon returned looking very sexy and said she really felt more alive and loved, she kissed everyone as she departed for work and Victoria followed kissing them as she left. Barbara helped him clean up and then she and Roger made love, they always enjoyed each other, then went and showered, dressed to look at some furniture. Roger grabbed his list and Barbara was looking sexy in her jeans and short heels. Roger suggested she wear her athletic shoes because of all the walking they would be doing, she changed her shoes, he turned, kissed and hugged her tight and told her how much he really loved her before they departed.

They left in her car since it was newer and Roger drove, saying I know you want to see the house, yes she replied. I knew you would show it to me first. It took little more than half an hour before they arrived entering the neighborhood. She said I know it's a beautiful home just by the neighbors. He pulled up to the closed gate and she said you're joking, he said no, and then called the listing agent, asking if he could see it again, the agent said sure, give him ten minutes, he was nearby and he would stop and show it to him again. About fifteen minutes passed and a car pulled up, the agent got out to shake Rogers hand and said he was coming by to remove the super key and he was in luck. He opened the gate and they drove up the long driveway leading to the home. He introduced Barbara as his wife to make things simpler as the agent removed the super key and unlocked the front door and they all entered. Barbara was surprised, amazed, and in shock at the same time, and that was before they had entered, she hugged Roger as they entered and Barbara walked around the large home just looking in amazement before she went upstairs, Roger followed at a distance, she screamed and they thought something was wrong, but she said I just don't believe it as she went from room to room, then they took the elevator to the basement. She walked around and almost blurted something out, and caught herself and then they walked up the stairs back to the front entrance as Roger thanked the agent. Mr. Brown said the house would be secured until he took possession and confirmed the date his lawyer has given him. They shook as Mr. Brown locked up and took the super key with him and turned the alarm back on.

Barbara just stood in the driveway and looked before getting in the car as Roger opened the door for her as she slowly got in and he closed the door. He said Mrs. Thorn are you satisfied, she screamed and smiled and began crying and said Roger, this is our house, he said, yes my dear. He told her I hope that since you have seen it you will understand what he had said about the beds. They drove down the driveway and he entered the street heading to their destination, she said based on what you had mentioned yesterday, she understands and told him she wasn't going to be dragging her old furniture around with her either. She said she would donate it all and start over and couldn't wait for him to get to the store so she could hug him again. They reached the bedding store, he parked and Barbara had gotten out, came around and was standing outside the driver's door before he could get out, he stepped out, closed the door and she pushed him against the car kissing him as she cried, saying that she loved him for a long time and knew in his heart he was good, freaky but had a very good heart. He held her kissing her as she cried, he waited until she composed herself, and she said thank you. They entered the store and he showed her what he thought were the best bedroom selections and choices, she agreed with him as she looked around and then left after speaking with a salesman, having him to check on how long it would take for delivery after purchase. He drove to another store and they looked at large area rugs and sofa sets and he explained to her he would have a complete sofa set in his bedroom and a desk. It was close to noon and he decided they should go to lunch to the nearby local sea food restaurant. She told him she was glad Victoria and Rosie were going to be with them because she wouldn't want to be in such a large home all by herself. They entered the restaurant and were quickly seated and soon giving the waiter there orders. Barbara couldn't stop talking and said she hadn't been this happy in a very long, long time. Their food arrived and Roger was happy. She soon became very quiet for at least a little while.

After lunch they made a couple more stops looking; before heading back to his apartment. Barbara said she wanted to go home and pick up a few more clothes; and on the way they stopped and went inside her small one bedroom apartment. It was small and now he understood what she had said about the furniture, Barbara wasn't one for trivial items or clutter and she just had a small variety of things, she had a few clothes since she was a supervisor on her job. She took a small carryon suit case and they soon departed and headed back to his place. He drove home and parked next to his auto since most of the residents were still at work. He carried her bag upstairs. Soon they undressed, she needed and wanted him to spank her, he bent her over and gave her a good spanking on her round butt, turned her around pushed her down in the bed, spread her legs open and laid down between them and kissed her vagina and licked it as she screamed, also he spanked her vagina until she climaxed which wasn't long then he climbed on top of her and they made love again, when they finished with one another they almost fell asleep, got up and showered. They then rubbed oils on one another, and then falling asleep in each other's arms.

When they woke it was because the phone woke them, sleeping a little more than an hour, close to two, again he looked at his phone and it was Rosie. He called her back and she answered right away. She was home and wanted to come over he said ok as he wrapped a towel around himself and opened the door, she entered wearing her long dress. He closed the door and returned to the bedroom and told Rosie to undress, she did and had her lay between him and Barbara. Rosie became very excited and hugged them both as they rubbed on her, she started kissing Barbara she hugged Rosie and held her. Roger got out of bed and told Barbara to move to the center of the bed and he told Rosie to get up, she did and had Barbara spread her legs and hold her ankles and told Rosie to kneel with her head down and lick her mistress as he reached for his paddle and grabbed Rosie by her hair pulling her up and asked her what she was, she said she was his bitch. Roger said do what I tell you, while he pushed her head down into Barbara's crotch. He then rubbed the paddle across her butt continuing to push her head down, then he smacked her butt as Rosie licked and sucked Barbara, Roger smacked her hard several times before playing with her now moist vagina, he reached for a dildo and slowly inserted it inside of her. Barbara climaxed; he told her don't stop as he worked the dildo back and forth inside Rosie and soon she climaxed. He pulled it out and pulled her up by her long hair again and made her suck the dildo clean. Barbara released her ankles and reached for Rosie as they laid side by side embracing and kissing one another. Roger had a wrap and put it on just in time as there was a knock at the door, he looked through the peep hole and it was Victoria, he opened the door and let her inside, she had her overnight bag and headed straight for the bedroom after kissing him. And when she walked in said getting started without me, as Roger walked up behind her and reached around and held her breast in his hands and kissed and licked her neck which he knew would drive her crazy and was told her to undress. Soon Victoria was standing nude and told her to get in the bed with Barbara and Rosie. Rosie was now very comfortable as Victoria kissed her. Roger stood at the foot of the bed and looked at his little harem. He asked if they had eaten, all said no. It was around six and he told them to enjoy each other, leaving then to fix something light to eat. He put on a pair of shorts and a t-shirt and headed to the kitchen. Suddenly he changed his mind and decided he would order out and decided on some Chinese food, took out the menu and his phone and called and placed and order, he knew what Victoria and Barbara liked. He and Rosie would just have to choose from the order and he ordered the extra-large sizes and made sure there would be plenty and returned to the bedroom for his wallet, informing them what he had just decided to do instead of cooking. Rosie was licking Victoria vagina as Barbara paddled her butt and then Barbara fingered Rosie as she climaxed again and then Victoria climaxed. Roger kissed Barbara and returned to the kitchen and pulled out some money for their food. He went back and just stood in the doorway and watched as they had Rosie on her back with Victoria licking her and Barbara sitting on her head they really enjoyed each other. He was happy and saw that they were having fun with one another. He left and fixed himself a drink and set places at the dining room table for all of them. It wasn't but a little more than an hour when answering the door to pay for the food.

Roger informed his beautiful ladies as they were holding and caressing one another and it was a pleasant sight to behold as he stood at the foot of the bed and said my beauties, dinner is now served, go wash your hands and put on a little something and then come and eat. They all got up and went to the bathroom having fun as they cleaned themselves up and putting on their lounging clothes before coming to the dining room and sitting down at the table as he dished them up. Roger blessed the food and said he was thankful to have them in his life. They were all eating together once again, it was more like a family now and would soon be an everyday occasion for them all and the more often it occurred the more he was beginning to enjoy it. Roger served hot green tea with their food while they ate, and it wasn't long before everyone was fully satisfied. Victoria helped him cleanup and soon they all sat around in the living room talking. Roger said Rosie and Victoria should start preparing for tomorrow, they agreed and left together to go next door to bathe and returning an hour later. During that time Barbara and Roger talked about how the expenses and checking accounts should be organized, she suggested he be the second person on all their accounts and all of them on his, he agreed and since all had direct deposit it should be much simpler. He said he though everyone would be able to save more money because of the way the expenses would be handled and said it would take about two or three months to see how thing would work out. Barbara suggested they start with the beds and some rugs before trying to do everything at once. He agreed, because he liked to shop and was in no particular hurry. He said based on what he was moving in, which wasn't very much, there should be a savings if everything goes as planned, with two people moving the same day, but would get some estimates anyway. Soon Victoria and Rosie returned looking fresh and clean. He and Barbara kissed them good night, and said sleep well. He and Barbara sat and talked more about the coming move and writing down some of what they were talking about and how they should organize and combine all the households. After Rosie and Victoria had fallen asleep Barbara turned in. Roger again went around and closed some windows and secured the apartment, making a comfortable bed with some blankets and a pillow on the wide couch. He had a queen sized bed, but it would be one of the many items he would donate or give away in the next few weeks.

That Saturday morning after waking up, Roger went and showered and soon began preparing breakfast for his new family of females, it was all the family he really had considering; most of his relatives were distant or dead. He put on and made a large pot of coffee making a few extra cups and prepared breakfast for his girls. Soon they were waking up, first was Rosie then Victoria and then Barbara. He heard laughter coming from the bathroom. He had the bacon on when Rosie entered and kissed him good morning, hugging her warm body, followed by Victoria who did the same and Barbara as they each poured a cup of coffee. He began cooking the eggs and Barbara helped him serve them and soon they were all sitting down eating together. Barbara helped him clean up as Victoria and Rosie prepared for work and Rosie returned and kissed them all followed by Victoria as they departed for work. He said he needed to do some grocery shopping since he had them over more often and they had been eating regular. The garbage can was full and the refrigerator was bare. He looked making out a list and cleaned out the refrigerator of any too old to eat food before removing and tying up the trash bag, placing a new bag in the can. Barbara showered as he tidied up and ran the vacuum through the apartment, and soon finished.

He stripped down and made up the bed as he listened to the radio for the daily weather report and rain was predicted for the very late afternoon closer to midnight.

He dressed and soon Barbara was sitting next to him oiling herself and putting her clothes on. After dressing they departed, taking the garbage out with him and dropped it into the dumpster, they went to the grocery store and soon were finished shopping. He asked her what suggestions she had for this evening, she said to him you have cooked and made sure everyone was feed and happy and thought it was time they did something for him as they returned and put the food away. Said he enjoyed doing it for them and loved them all, and couldn't be happier, she kissed him and he said lets go around the corner to the closest furniture store and look saying that he was just as excited as they were now. She said ok sure, as he drove she texted Victoria planning on taking Roger out to dinner or do something special. Victoria said she would let Rosie know and they would come home first and decide where or what they would do. Meanwhile he and Barbara looked, got some ideas and told her the entire house is painted white and he was going to add some color to his room. After leaving the furniture store they went to a paint store and picked up several different color charts with all the available colors, and told her he was thinking of doing his own painting. The banks closed at noon on Saturdays a by one o'clock Victoria and Rosie returned home and were talking with Barbara as to what they were going to do. They knew Roger wasn't really a restaurant person so they decided to cook and look sexy for their man and since it was supposed to rain it would make it all that much cozier.

They also decided to clean up the apartment. Roger suddenly decided and left to wash the dirty clothes at the laundry mat; he drove to the laundry mat even thought there were machines in the basement. They were always in use even at midnight and the capacity wasn't as large as the ones at the laundry mat and he thought maybe he should have done this during the week when it wasn't as crowded. Because of the large amount of dirty clothes and bedding he had accumulated it was one of the primary reasons he really wanted to move, it was starting to become a hassle, and some people left the laundry room messy after they finished washing and Roger was tired of all the bull shit. Besides with the money he had, and was making with a very ample income he didn't have to continue living like a pauper, and had finally decided to make a change in his life. He had lived with his money spending it very wisely and waited as his internal excitement had passed, and thought he had made many wise investments and they were returning a nice annual profit. He also had managed to be very conservative with his spending and by keeping it a secret, no one knew and the only one who would have any suspicions about how he came to have it might be Barbara, but had withheld any and all information even from her. He never bragged and continued driving the same car, dressed the same way and knew they really loved him, and not because of his money, but for who he was and how he treated them. Yes he was a master, but was into it before he won his fortune, and now was going to make sure it lasted him his life time, but felt now is the time to become a little more comfortable and generous with himself in this lifetime since you can't take it with you when you die, and being happy is what matters most and what it's all about.

He spent almost three hours washing and drying his laundry and folding them up and bagging them before returning home and making several trips upstairs with the clean clothes, linens, robes and towels. When he entered the apartment door the first time he smelled the aroma of food cooking, and Victoria was in the kitchen and the apartment was looking much cleaner and noticed the wood objects were shined as he started back downstairs to the car for the rest of the clean laundry, after the third trip, he thought again that he should have done this during the week instead of waiting for the weekend, when it was more crowded. He looked around and Barbara was dusting and Rosie was washing windows. He went and changed into his lay around the house clothes which were shorts and a t-shirt. He came out of the bedroom and said ladies. What have we here? They said it was time to tidy up their master's home.

He sat down as Barbara said you need to relax some and brought him a cold beer. He sat and watched them as they finished cleaning the apartment. Rosie had just finished cleaning the windows and Barbara tidying up as she then set the table. Soon Victoria was finished cooking. They told him to wash his hands and then come sit down for dinner as Victoria and Barbara fixed their plates. He sat at the table as Victoria served him; there was baked chicken, rice, vegetables and a salad. They all sat down and he blessed the table and they began eating.

He complemented the cook and thanked them for cleaning up, Rosie said they were getting in practice, and he thought that was so very funny and said that it was a wonderful thing. As they ate, it started getting real dark outside. The weather had changed from sunny to a coming rain storm. He finished eating and said that was a wonderful meal and told them they made him so extremely happy. They told him, he was the love of their lives and he was to sit back and relax, they would clean everything up. He said thank you very much and that he loved them. They worked cleaning up as a team and were finished in no time. He then started putting the clean bedding away along with his clothes. They told him he was sleeping with them tonight and weren't taking no for an answer. One by one they went and changed into nighties, returning while he was sitting down and becoming very excited as he looked at their beautiful figures. They led him to the bathroom and undressed him, had him shower, and then dried him off, laid a towel on the bed and massaged him all over. He was so relaxed he dosed off. He didn't dose long before claps of thunder woke him and they were all together in the bed as they hugged and kissed him. It was raining very heavily and the lights went out and Barbara asked if he had any candles. He told her where to look. She returned with a candle holder and set it safely on the table he had in the bedroom.

Rosie and Victoria held each other as the thunder had gotten very loud as he and Barbara hugged. Roger soon fell asleep again as the storm passed and it just continued to rain. While he was sleeping the power came back on and Barbara was awake and blew out the candle and they all were under the covers and soon asleep. When he woke to use the bathroom he found himself in between Victoria and Rosie and eased out of bed and went to pee. He returned and opened the window a little and climbed back in between the two women. Rosie was awakened by his return and she kissed and snuggled up next to him as he wrapped his arm around her, she reached down and felt him and soon she slid down and placed him in her mouth as he ran his hand through her hair, and Victoria woke and saw what Rosie was doing and joined her then Barbara woke and she rolled over and kissed him, he came and they sucked and licked him until he pulled the two by their hair and they laid back next to him. Barbara switched places with Victoria and kissed him as he held the two of them. He was awake now and the rain had stopped. Being up now he wanted a drink and they all went and had one with him. It was two am as they all sat together and talked about their upcoming move. It wasn't long before they headed back into the bedroom and falling asleep again. Roger had fixed them double Gin and tonics and knocked everyone out.

Early Sunday morning everyone was up, Barbara went to the bathroom and was soon followed by Victoria, soon Roger woke, and then Rosie as they hugged and went to the bathroom together. Barbara had put the coffee on as she and Victoria did breakfast, and soon they were all eating. Rosie and Barbara cleaned up as Roger showered with Victoria, then Rosie and Barbara showered together. They had pulled the covers up and all were in the bedroom applying oils to one another. Roger suggested they go window shopping for furniture, and all were in agreement and very excited to be together as Roger hugged and kissed each one of them. Rosie slipped next door to dress and the temperature was in the low seventies and Victoria and Barbara wore loose fitting cotton sun dresses with sandals without bras or panties and Rosie was wearing a dress a little shorter just above the knees without a bra and panties. They all stood as Roger looked at each of them and said he was very pleased. They left in Victoria's auto and he opened the doors for them with Victoria driving as he directed her to the new house. She pulled in front of the gate and he said this is where we will be living very soon. Victoria said wow, and Rosie said that is enormous. He then directed Victoria to the first store on his list. Had his tablet and after entering they walked around looking. He saw a dining room set that he said wasn't too large or small and wrote down the information and Barbara agreed it was a nice size for them. After looking they headed to another store, it was much more upscale and the floor items reflected the quality. Roger spoke to a sales person about several items especially the couch and sofa sets and wrote down what he thought, and soon the girls were ready to go and said they were hungry. Roger said he felt like something light, and suggested some Chinese food. He suggested they head to an oriental restaurant that served sushi on their menu. After being seated he ordered some sushi appetizers and his main course as the girls studied the menus, and soon placed their orders. The sushi came first and he shared it with them, Rosie had never had it before and liked it. Soon the main course arrived and the food was very enjoyable and drinking hot green tea with their food. When they finished Roger paid and read his fortune cookie and laughed as he ate the cookie. Barbara asked, what did it say, as he handed it to her; she laughed also, and then passed it around the table. Soon they all had a laugh. It said (many women made for many loves and much happiness). Everyone decided on seeing a movie and after several hours out everyone was ready to go home to Rogers's apartment. After returning home, everyone made themselves comfortable, as Barbara outlined what she and Roger had decided was necessary when they moved in as far as the finances were concerned. They were all in agreement with the coming arrangements and Roger said he would be the first to move in and get things organized and after they had picked out a room they could decide on a color if they wanted to have their room painted. He suggested they all go home and get some rest and prepare for tomorrow and for the week ahead. Saying he was going to have a very busy week and would work on getting things ready for them. He said he would text them with updates once he had possession. Barbara and Victoria prepared to leave with Rosie as he kissed each one as they left. He watched them all leave as Rosie went next door, and going to sleep early. He returned inside and since it was late decided to turn in and soon fell asleep.

Chapter Seven

Monday morning started out as a normal day for Roger, getting prepared for the rest of the week using today to get a jump on the following days as he put on his coffee and turned on his computer, and waited for it to finish brewing, soon pouring himself a cup and sat down and thought about what colors he might want as he looked through the color charts. He rethought about the wide notion he had about painting the house himself after looking at it the second time when he showed it to Barbara. He thought about what colors he wanted for his room but the entire home needed to be painted and thought it would be much simpler, quicker and less stressful to hire a professional painter since the house was really massive. When he thought about it the entire house was far from small by any normal accounts. He quickly looked through the phone book and chose a painter at random, called and talked as he explained what he wanted done and when and made the necessary arrangements. Roger really felt very lucky that when he started looking he found something suitable so quickly and said a prayer of thanks for all the good fortune that has come into his life, he felt blessed and was very thankful. He then decided he should and would start packing today and get a few small boxes for his books and some of those large plastic storage containers and would still have some for storage after moving, if he needed any. He didn't have much to pack since he was planning on getting a king sized bed and walked around deciding what of the small amount of furniture he would keep. When he finished it would be his books, most of his small decorative items and his computer, his files along with all his documents, the few clothes he had, his dining room set and the cabinet in his bedroom and that wasn't very much. He would set aside what he was taking, anything else that he didn't want he would donate. He thought about what Rosie had and it wouldn't be more than her clothes since she had very little in her apartment.

He pulled up the listing on his new house again and it now showed as being sold. He read over the amenities again, checking if it was the same, found the original print out, and it was, it was that he had just overlooked several items in his quest to quickly find something he liked. Items like the alarm system, climate control, skylights, and balconies and then looked at all the photos, and was satisfied he had made the right decision, and thanked god he didn't have to spend endless days and weeks looking. He pulled out his bank statements and decided to move some funds around after he closed on all the properties this week and some cash from several smaller accounts he keep on hand. He returned to the kitchen and poured another cup of coffee and had a slice of bread with jelly and decided to go to his favorite bulk retail store and buy some large plastic containers and also get some cardboard boxes or banker boxes. He finished and washed out his coffee pot and went and dressed. He dressed and locked his door and started on his mission and decided Rosie would move when he moved, it would be so much simpler that way and would get enough containers for the both of them since she only had her clothes.

He arrived and instead of the usual shopping cart he chose a flatbed truck this time since what he intended to purchase was large and bulky. He found the isle with the items he was looking for. They were the large multi gallon plastic containers that had locking lids; he placed twenty on the cart. They also had the cardboard boxes for his books, pots and pans and the packing tape he would need. He had all he was looking for and checked out and headed back home. When he arrived home he had to make about three trips to bring all the containers and boxes inside and thought when he finished using them Barbara and Victoria could also reuse them. He set them aside and went to his closet and took his winter clothes out first, folded and packed them and soon filled the first container. He soon had emptied his closet of the clothing he figured he wouldn't need until next winter. It didn't take long and left to print up some labels on his computer, printed them out and taped them on the now full containers. When he finished, he had only used three of the containers and made a space for the items he would take with him and soon he was down to the clothes he wore and would kept the few he needed to wear out. He made up some cardboard boxes and taped the bottoms and started packing his books. Only used about six of the small boxes since the books were heavy, when all was completed he felt good because at least he had started. He took a break and fixed a sandwich and drank a beer, looking at the few items he would take. By moving the furniture around and rearranging the room, he had what he was taking on one side and what he was leaving on the other. Spending the better part of the day packing up all of his small decorative items, pictures and some kitchen utensils and was soon finished. He went to the hall closet and packed up all his extra towels and wash cloths in another container and leaving out just a couple of towels and wash cloths out before calling it a day. It was around six when he finally sat down on his couch and turned on the television thinking he would finally have one of those large flat screen televisions for his bedroom.

There was a knock at the door and he went and answered it and there stood Rosie, she had been home and changed and he just then decided he would give her the spare key before she left this evening. She entered and kissed him, following him to the living room and quickly noticing he had started packing, and the stack of empty containers. She sat next to him and hugged him and said I see you have been busy. He said yes and told her she could take a couple containers with her and had decided she should move along with him which made her very happy. She asked him how soon and he said he didn't know yet, but it would be in the next couple of weeks for sure. Said maybe she should just move in with him now and make it simple and easy for the both of them. He said the things you pack up we will bring here and stack up in one place and maybe we can clear your unit first since your lease is up after next month and you really don't have that much. She said that would work for her and he would give her a key before she left. Said that she ached for him and needed him, he said not now because he was very tired. She was very persistent and this really irritated him and she wouldn't stop. Roger stood and took her by the hand to the bedroom and told her to strip, he said you need to be punished since you are acting like a very stupid bitch now. He told her to put her hands behind her head, she did and he took a plentiful amount of lubricant and applied it to her ass and vagina, he reached and pulled out the harness with the large butt plug for her ass and a dildo with tiny fingers for her pussy and inserted them both without showing any compassion or tenderness as she cringed. As they were inserted, she soon began to feel the effects as he attached the belt portion around her waist, and once it was secure in front had her hold her arms out in front of her as he attached cuffs to her wrist and then attached them to the sides of the belt, and finally the collar around her neck with the leash, then added a belt to her arms at the elbows pulling them behind her, making her chest stick out with her large protruding bell shaped nipples really sticking out. She now became more aroused. He pinched them hard and flicked them with his fingers, then inserting the short penis mouth gag to her and fastened it behind her head. He then walked her around the apartment several times as the inserted devices worked there cruel magic on her and then back to the bedroom taking a wide leather paddle out, smacking her small round ass several times as she began having several continuous organisms, he attached clamps to her nipples as she cringed and spanked her even more. Rosie was having a hard time standing but couldn't sit down with the harness on, he held the leash and slapped her lightly on both sides of her face as tears ran down her face and told her she was his bitch, he owned her now and would fuck her however he wanted and whenever and that she was a piece of shit, but she was strapped up now because she was an insolent bitch and needed to learn her lesson and that her purpose was to serve her master and not make any unnecessary demands. He twisted and pulled the clamps on her nipples before removing them. He then led her to the living room and hung the rope from the ceiling and ran it through the loop at the back of her neck collar and down to the back of the belt as he tied it off and just let her stand there. Leaving her there standing, she was forced to stand as spasms rocked her slim body. He sat and watched the agony she was in for over an hour before he removed the rope and the belt holding her arms, also removing the gag, but walked her around the apartment again before he returned her to the bed room. She was still cuffed, he took the leather strap and bent her over and smacked the cheeks of her ass that were exposed and not covered by the leather harness. He stood her up and looked in her tearful eyes and asked her if she still had a lack of understanding concerning her master's wishes. She said no sir master Caesar. He then removed the harness, cuffs and collar from her and pushed her on the bed and climbed on top of her after he dropped his shorts and entered her very moist and loose vagina. She screamed with pleasure as she climaxed over and over again before he came inside of her. Then he pulled her up by her hair slapped her on both sides of her face, then hugged the limp woman as he spanked her ass more. He released her as she collapsed on the bed now fully satisfied. She slowly rose and said thank you Master Caesar, as he pulled her up by her hair again. Leading her to the bathroom, he bathed her and applied soap to her ass, bent her over holding her arms behind her and entered her anus until he came again, he washed her an gave her an enema and made her sit on the toilet before returning her to the shower as he played with her ass sticking all his fingers in her as she moaned. He played with her clit as she had another massive climax. He bathed himself and her and then rinsed her and himself off and when he finished he help her dry off. Then lead her back to the bedroom and applying body oils to her, as she lay limp, but satisfied in bed. He put his shorts and shirt back on and told her to get up and to put her dress back on. When she did he led her to the couch and he fixed them both a stiff drink. After she finished her drink he told her to go home, and led her to the door, but before she left, took her keys and added his spare door key to her ring, he slipped on his thongs and walked the well satisfied Rosie home and went inside and made sure her kitchen window was closed, kissing her good night as she closed and locked her door.

He returned home and closed his windows, turned off the television and went to bed, he needed to rest for the closings tomorrow as he crawled under the covers and went quickly to sleep.

He woke that morning refreshed and very satisfied and prepared for a busy and fruitful day, fixed his coffee, ate a breakfast sandwich and prepared for his busy day. Went to his office retrieved his notes with the location of the closings and brought his check book with him just in case and his thin briefcase, dressed in his jeans and sports jacket and saw the harness before he left and decided to wash it off. It was early as he caught a glimpse of Rosie as she passed his window and looked out as she walked down the stairs; the more he had sex with her the sexier she seemed to appear. He watched her get in her car and drive off before he prepared to depart himself, check around and locked up and walked to his car heading to the first of two locations today.

He arrived, and it was several minutes before he walked inside, the receptionist checked him in as he took a seat and then his attorney walked in. They shook hands and said three of the properties we would close on here and the last two at the next location. He had the cashier's checks drawn from Rogers's corporate account and soon they were closing on the first one, it went quickly since the property was free and clear, and the closing was completed, then on to the next and final one. The attorney said see you in an hour at the next location, Roger said ok and he stopped on the way for a coffee and small breakfast sandwich and headed to the next location. His attorney arrived, and it took less than an hour to close on two more extremely large tracks of land. They shook hands and he told Roger he would see him tomorrow. It was a little pass noon when he left the last location and headed home.

Roger got home and filed his new acquisitions away in his file cabinet; some of these last purchases would soon sell for much more than what he paid, because they were near where there were new developments, construction, and expanding business opening up, and would soon be prime locations, but for now it would also lower his current tax burden. He soon finished with filing his papers away and left to undress and started packing some of his unnecessary office materials, then left to look into the cabinet where he had his bondage equipment and filled a container with its contents until the entire cabinet was empty. He would take his cabinet since it was solid wood and would blend with almost any decor. Being a little tired and having a busy the day, Roger decided to lie down on the couch and take a nap, he was through for the day. When he woke Rosie was kissing him, she said thank you master, he sat up and she knelt down and placed her head on his lap as he rubbed her head, she looked up at him and grabbed his hand and kissed it, he pulled her up and hugged her, feeling her back and then she just started crying and said she loved him so very much. Leading Rosie to the bedroom, undressed her and himself and got in the bed with her as they hugged, he lay on his back and she climbed on top of him and slid down and sucked him until he was hard then climbed back up and placed him inside of her as he held her with one hand and smacked her ass with the other crying and said she would be a good girl as she climaxed repeatedly. She stopped and just laid on top of Roger as he rubbed her head, he held her and knew deep inside was a fragile little girl still. He rolled her to his side and kissed her holding her tight as she calmed down and told him she wanted to move in with him now, and then she said please master I don't want to sleep alone anymore, please, please. He said go, and bring your clothes and the things you will need to go to work tomorrow and then you can stay. All my bitches work, you understand, she said yes sir master, she dressed and left, she packed a small bag and with her dress on a hanger returned hanging it up and left again, and returned with her make up bag, he asked her if she had locked her door and she said yes sir. It was early evening still and he took Rosie and fixed them both a drink and sat with her and she was alright now as he sat and talked with her and told her she didn't need to feel alone anymore, she was loved and he cared for her and loved her and said she needed to get a grip on her inner emotions. Roger said she was welcome to sleep with him and reassured her again she wasn't alone anymore and didn't have to feel that way. He said if I am not here you will be all right and wanted her to understand that. He told her all this time before now you were by yourself. I know you will be all right after we all move in together and with Barbara and Victoria. He asked her if she understood. Said she did but sometimes a feeling would just come over her and she would feel like she needed to be punished and he satisfied that much needed urge in her. He fixed another drink and when they had finished they showered and went to bed, he held her and rubbed her to sleep.

The following day they woke up together and he made coffee and she dressed and was looking beautiful as ever as they ate a light breakfast of toast and jelly before she left for work, he kissed her as she left and he watched her until she got into her car and pulled off. Roger had another cup of coffee. Today was the closing on his new house, or rather the castle compared to this apartment and was calm as he prepared to take a shower before departing, the closing was to be at eleven and it was eight now so he had plenty of time. He located the phone numbers for various utilities such as electric power, gas, and water and internet service. When he had those he showered and knew today would be longer as he would survey the new premises and start cleaning up the house and would make a list of the supplies he would need. After gathering all the needed information he headed to the shower. Roger took his time and finally after drying off sat on the bed and looked in the mirror at himself, he thought about his life and where he was headed now. He oiled himself and dressed and still had more than an hour, he wore his jeans and sports jacket again just as he had done the day before and a pair of athletic shoes. He checked his thin briefcase and then checked that his phone was charged and departed. He drove to the house because he had time and around the surrounding area before heading to the title office where the closing would be held. He was early as he sat in his auto and had the page with from the yellow pages since he decided to hire a painter and had picked one and had talked to him earlier and would call after the closing. It was time to go when his attorney pulled up; they entered together after shaking hands. They were shown to the room with the seller's agent and the closer, it didn't take long and when it was over Roger received all the needed documents and a packet with the warrantees on all the appliances and a bag with several remotes, one for every garage door and one for the gate and the alarm and door codes which he could change along with information on the town garbage collection and water services. They departed as his attorney said he would soon send him a bill; Roger thanked him and headed for his new house.

Roger arrived at the house and as he sat in front of the gate, looking through the plastic bag of remotes, soon found the one for the gate, he activated it and moments later the two large steel gates began opening, once they were fully opened Roger drove up the long driveway to the front entrance and parked before the stone steps leading up to the front door as he sat and found the information for the doors and the alarm system. He read the information and could change the codes at any time and would do that today. He got out of his auto and ascended the steps to the front door; he unlocked the doors and soon entered the pin, after finding the key pad inside, the light turned from red to green. He slowly walked around the large house looking more closely than before as he started noticing the small and minor details about the home he hadn't noticed before. He entered the kitchen and laid his briefcase on the counter, walking over and opening the two refrigerators and the upright freezer, being new and empty noticed the digital temperature readouts and they didn't have any odors but he would wipe everything out and down before using them. He checked the gas stove and it came on, and the sinks, there were two and the water was on and he waited until the water ran hot before he shut it off. He walked over and unlocked the wide door leading out to the deck, and walked out looking around the long and wide stone patio as it led onto an expansive deck as the ground started sloping downhill and walked down a set of wide steps to the very large yard and walked a short distance and turned around, looking back at the house. He noticed the air conditioner and the backup generator; he also looked up at the bedroom windows and some of the skylights in the roof, and the false balcony's in the bedrooms as he walked back inside. He closed the door and locked it and went upstairs and walked around what would be his bedroom, it was almost the size of his entire apartment. He then looked at the ample number of outlets and the several cable outlets and thought someone really planed this out right, he began walking into the large walk-in closet and thought he would never ever fill this up, it was the size of his smallest bedroom that he use for an office, as he headed for the bathroom. Now this was his favorite place, looking around, he liked the white tile walls, floors and especially the windows high up on the outer wall you could open. He left the bedroom and checked another and though how Barbara would love having the large bedroom, he checked the entire floor before going to the basement and then returning back upstairs.

He contacted the power company first, then the Gas Company and water companies. He went with manual in hand and changed the security codes for the door and alarm system and then the thermostat codes. There weren't any cameras inside the home but a system was installed outside, and he found the control console inside a cabinet between the kitchen and dining rooms, the system was active and changed the access code for it also as he wrote down the changes he had made. He had brought his color chart with him and had changed his mind about painting it himself and had spoken to a painter a couple days earlier and gave him a call, when he had spoken to the gentleman he said he would call back and asked if he could have the job completed in a reasonably short period of time, the man said if the home was empty and without any furniture that had to be moved it would be simple and quick. He called and asked if he could meet with him here now and had previously asked when he called if he would keep the day open for him and would pay him for his time. The painter said he would be there within the hour as Roger continued walking around and went to his car for the color wheel. Roger noticed the house has never been painted and there was only a base white primer on all the walls, and knew this wasn't going to be any cheap paint job and would request semi-gloss throughout the entire home. He went and decided on the color for his bedroom and went downstairs. He looked in all the cabinets and drawers and wondered if the previous owner ever moved in, labels and brochures were still in the drawers and he soon found the breaker panel with the backup generator control panel. Soon he heard the loud chimes and opened the front door and it was the painter, Mr. Harvey, he introduced himself and they shook hands. He and Roger got down to business right away as Harvey looked at the walls and said they have never been painted but had a very good primer on them. Roger told him he wanted semi-gloss throughout the entire house and chose an egg shell white for the two story entrance way, hall ways and wanted a bright white for the ceilings in the kitchen and the master bathroom, and Roger also wanted the ceiling painted and the hallways upstairs white also in the egg shell white. He showed him his bed room and wanted a light blue for the entire room including the high vaulted ceiling with the skylights and the closet also and what little wall was showing. Roger said that was a start either tomorrow or the following day he would be able to give him colors for the other three large bed rooms. Mr. Harvey asked while going down stairs, asked about the living and dining rooms and suggested if he stuck with the same color throughout the entire house he could cut cost some. Roger said ok. Mr. Harvey said it would take him at least a week and that he was looking at a cost of nine thousand for all he had described so far and would charge him another thousand for the remaining bedrooms and suggested doing all the bathroom ceilings in the bright white. Mr. Harvey wrote up a contract, it was very specific and by room and Roger wrote him a check for half the cost of the job. Mr. Harvey asked about access, and Roger said what time would he start and he said between seven and eight every morning. Roger said he would be here and asked that they do the kitchen ceiling first and the one in the master bathroom along with the master bedroom. Mr. Harvey said no problem and would start the day after tomorrow which was Friday and said he would be here Saturday but not Sunday, Roger said that was fine with him, they shook and Harvey left and Roger drove to a burger joint and had his dinner. It was near four pm when he sent a text to Barbara, Victoria and Rosie to meet him at the new house after work and sent them the address. After he finished eating he returned to the new house and just looked around again.

Near six pm Barbara was the first to arrive, as she stood on the steps with Roger, Victoria pulled up and after hugging and kissing her, shortly Rosie's car came up the driveway. They waited for her before entering, they all hugged and kissed. Roger opened the door as they entered and said he had placed the utilities in his name and the painter was going to start Friday and described that he had contracted to have the entire house painted, he asked them as he handed each a piece of paper to put their names on it and the color they wanted and don't forget the color number and a piece of tape, and said after they finished looking around to pick a bedroom. Victoria and Rosie were excited since this was their first time being in the house. Barbara chose the second largest bedroom and attached her name to the door, it was a very nice room at the end of the upstairs hallway and the closest one to Rogers bedroom, it had one large window and one with a false balcony with a sliding glass door which gave the room a feeling of being a much larger space, and a skylight, the bathroom tiles were a pale pink and it had a bidet, walk-in shower and a standalone tub, with a wide vanity sink. Roger had asked them, after they chose the room, to choose a color or otherwise the room would be painted an eggshell white semi-gloss like the rest of the entire home. Barbara chose a warm green color for the walls and wrote the color number below her name. Victoria and Rosie came upstairs and looked at the remaining rooms. Victoria chose hers and it had a false balcony, as did all the bedrooms, and her bathroom was all white tile, she picked a warm brown for two walls in her bedroom, the window and the door wall that was opposite one another and beige for the remaining walls and ceiling and wrote down the color numbers below her name also. Rosie ended up with the last bedroom with its own bathroom, her bathroom was a pale pink and she chose a warm pink for the bedroom walls, and added the color number below her name as she attached the paper to the outside on the door. The two remaining bedrooms shared a bath and Roger would have those painted white the same color as the rest of the house.

Roger waited for them downstairs and when they were all together explained he would give them the door codes after the house painting was completed and he could change the codes again anytime, and said Barbara and Victoria could sync their cars to the garage doors and the front gate since they had the newer cars and told them to wait until they moved. Rosie would move with him since she didn't have much and it was from the same location. He also said as soon as a bed was delivered here he would move in and everyone would have king sized beds and asked if they wanted him to make the choice or did they want to make their own, it really didn't matter as long as it was a king size bed. He asked for the colors they wanted and made a separate list and would give it to Mr. Harvey Friday. He said that's it for now stating he would be busy the following weeks getting things prepared and said he had started packing. He asked if they had any questions, no one did and he said if you do just text it to him. He kissed them all and said time to go and since he was the last to leave locked the door and turned the alarm on, they had all left as he pulled out last and closed the gate entering the street and heading home.

Chapter Eight

Roger was going to be very busy the next few following days as his days started much earlier than usual, and packing a few more things every day. That Thursday he had completely packed up his office and all of his documents. He and Rosie moved his and her remaining clothes into the empty closet space he had created when he packed up his winter clothes and she packed the few dishes and pots and pans she had, as they emptied her sparsely furnished apartment in little to no time after she came home from work that day. They moved all her meager furniture to the center of the room; she wasn't taking any of it. He was up very early the following day and headed to the new house so he could let the painters in and returned back home to pack more items, soon finishing with the exception of a couple pots, his coffee pot being one and deciding on using paper plates until they moved. That Saturday Mr. Harvey along with his three sons had completed the kitchen ceiling and his bedroom, the bathroom along with the closet and had set up the needed scaffolding and began painting the large, tall front entrance hall and had just about completed all the other lower level rooms and had just about finished them by the end of the day including the basement. The entire house smelled of fresh paint. He had spoken to both Barbara and Victoria and let them know what progress was being made. The weather was becoming more pleasant every day as they moved closer now toward the middle of spring. All the windows were opened when they finished painting around seven pm. Roger again locked up and went back home. He would order his bedroom set tomorrow since most stores were open and would take Rosie along with him. When he returned home he showered, ate some carry out and was soon in bed with Rosie next to him as she lay close as they both slept. Even though she was sleeping with him they hadn't had sex since he was too tired from packing, shopping and having to get up earlier than ever before.

Sunday morning he fixed a pot of coffee and when Rosie woke he told her they would go out for breakfast instead of trying to cook. Rosie wore a sexy pair of designer jeans and her athletic shoes, blouse and a sweater. Rosie was very happy since moving in and sleeping with him the past couple days and it was showing on her pretty face, she now felt more secure and was very happy. After he dressed they were on there way and had a wonderful breakfast at a nearby restaurant, and now Rosie had a much better appetite and eating more often just by being with him and he made sure she took some vitamins, and she started looking much better, now with a beautiful glow about herself. Then they headed to the bedding store to order their beds, Roger had his list and knew which bed he wanted, it was a platform with the drawers underneath, and wide dual cabinets on both sides of the bed with a headboard cabinet and mirror above, it stood nearly seven feet tall with a dark wood finish, and a king size plush mattress. Rosie looked around and she found something a little simpler, it was very similar, but the end cabinets weren't as tall and you could place lamps on them if you wanted with a headboard, shelf and sliding doors like Rogers. She chose the rose colored wood finish and both sets were solid wood. After placing their orders they went to another store where they had large area and Persians rugs. Roger had all the room measurements, and when he had finished, had purchased three large Persian rugs for his bedroom and had picked out a desk with a matching file cabinet. The rugs were all wool and imported. Delivery of his bedroom set would be this coming Thursday and Rosie's would be the following week, maybe even sooner and the salesman said he would know for sure by Monday or Tuesday at the latest. The rugs and desk would come the same day but from different stores. Barbara and Victoria had both called him Saturday and said they were in the process of separating what they would move from what they wouldn't and knew he was busy also and they would soon see one another and would let him have this weekend to get things together, as he thanked them both.

Roger and Rosie went to dinner at a different restaurant and had a delightful time and enjoyed their food before continuing to look at more furniture. Rosie said she would like to have a dresser and they left and she found one that was wide and also had a mirror, the wood finish closely matched her new bed and she said that was enough shopping for one day and wanted to return home since it was nearly six pm. Said she wanted to get some rest so she would be ready for work tomorrow and was really surprised how tiring shopping was. They returned home and undressed and used the bathroom together, showered and put on their lounging clothes and Roger fixed them a couple of drinks and they watched some television and finally went to bed. Rosie and Roger kissed, and held each other, talked some and then went to sleep.

They both were up very early since Roger had to go to the new house and Rosie to work, they had their coffee, kissed, dressed and departed and went on their separate ways. Roger arrived and five minutes later Mr. Harvey and his sons arrived. Roger opened all the windows as the painters began painting. Mr. Harvey approached Roger with the colors to be painted in the other bed rooms and said they were finishing the atrium today and would start on the different bedrooms today after they removed the scaffolding in the entranceway. He and Roger went to the garage, it had never been painted either, and asked Mr. Harvey how much more to paint it and he looked at the high ceiling and asked what color, Roger said he was open to suggestions, Harvey said he had more of the white paint than anything else and said five hundred and then he would have used all the paint he had ordered, Roger said ok and reached inside his jacket pocket and pulled out his check book and made out a check for the garage plus the remaining balance of the contract he had with Mr. Harvey. Mr. Harvey thanked him and said they would be finished maybe by Wednesday or Thursday for sure and Roger said he could do the garage last; Harvey said ok and returned to work.

Roger made a trip to the fast food restaurant and called a mover and made arrangements for them to give him an estimate and a date and they said they would see him later this afternoon giving them a time to meet for the estimate. Roger said ok, and headed home to meet the mover. He arrived just in time and showed the man what was going to be moved, and he said five hundred dollars. Roger asked how soon and he gave Roger a date of next Monday, Roger said perfect and the mover said eight in the morning and took down the new address and gave Roger an estimated bill. Roger returned to the house so he could lockup and arrived just in time as the painters were cleaning up after finishing the ground floor. Mr. Harvey said they were finished with the first floor and the atrium, the two storied entrance with the stairway and would start on the remaining bedrooms tomorrow, and the garage, with the four of them things were going much faster than expected; since there weren't any obstructions, he thanked Roger for hiring him for the job and said see you tomorrow. The painting crew departed, Roger walked around closing and locking the windows and liked what he saw, it looked so much better being painted, especially in the semi-gloss as he went upstairs and looked around closing the remaining windows. Roger prepared to leave when his phone rang and it was Rosie. Said she was home and asked if he would bring some food home. He said he would stop and get them some fried chicken on his way back, and hung up. He checked to make sure he had closed all the windows as he walked around before leaving and closed the front door and set the alarm. On his way home he again stopped and purchased a couple of chicken dinners and thought about how he would be so happy when he could again cook. He had the chicken dinners and returned to the apartment where a showered and very hungry Rosie was patiently waiting on him, he handed her the bag with the food, she kissed him and went and prepared their plates as he undressed. He would shower after he ate as he put his shorts on and washed his hands. He sat at the dining room table, as Rosie had fixed his plate, and said thank you as they blessed their meal. They ate and Rosie asked, how was it going, and he said very well, and informed her that next they would be moving in and then would call the donation people to come get the items they were leaving behind. He asked her tomorrow after work to purchase two or three sets of king sized bed sheet sets, and said he wasn't washing any clothes again until after they moved.

Rosie was very hungry and he asked her if she had eaten lunch, she had but it didn't amount to much. He asked her why, said she just wasn't hungry then, he asked if she had money, she said yes but didn't feel like eating. Said he just wanted to be sure if you are alright, yes she replied. They finished eating and cleaned up, he commented cleaning up isn't complicated now. He checked the refrigerator and there wasn't much but some condiments, beer and a bottle of wine. He finished his beer and went to the bathroom and showered, came out and put his shorts back on and sat on the couch for an hour looking at television with Rosie telling her good night, she said wait for her, as she turned the television off and asked her to check the windows as he dropped his shorts and climbed in bed and shortly she joined him. He went to sleep right away as Rosie rubbed on him, kissing him as he slept soundly.

Tuesday Roger woke and shortly Rosie, they had a routine now, fix some coffee, wash and dress, kiss and depart as he went to the house and her to work. He arrived and opened up the house, the odor of paint was everywhere, not as strong but still there as he opened all the windows on both levels as the painters arrived, he had opened all the garage doors and one of his sons started painting in the garage and three went upstairs and each man did a room and by the end of the day the bedrooms were completed as one of them helped the other, finishing the garage and staying a little later and completely finished the job. Roger checked the bedrooms and they were just as he had requested and was fully satisfied. Mr. Harvey came and told Roger they were finished and Roger thanked him and handed him a check for four hundred dollars and said, just a little bonus for you and your sons. Roger said if he decided on any color changes he would be in touch. Mr. Harvey thanked him as they had already packed up their equipment in their vans and drove away. He went and closed the windows downstairs and left the upper ones open slightly before locking up and heading home just as Rosie called and said she had ordered some Chinese and was waiting on the delivery man, he thanked her and hung up as he closed and locked the door and put the alarm on. He arrived just as the delivery was made and went and washed his hands and sat down and ate with Rosie again. He enjoyed the food and thanked her for ordering it as he finished eating and kissed her, said she would clean up as he went and undressed and took a long hot shower, when he finished he put on a clean pair of shorts and t-shirt. Tomorrow he would get a break and stay here but Thursday he would have to go for the deliveries, when he came out Rosie said she purchased two set of sheets and they were still in the bag. He said well that was good, he would wash them before using them. He fixed a drink, sat on the couch and was tired, when he finished went and washed his glass, closed the kitchen window and headed for bed. Rosie followed and Roger lay down and as she snuggled up next to him, he had fallen asleep while she rubbed him until she just dosed off herself.

He woke the next morning and made some coffee, Rosie was up and he kissed her, held her tightly as she returned his affection. He dressed because he was going to breakfast and was going to take the dirty clothes and the new sheets to the house and wash them. He kissed Rosie as she left for work and looked at the furniture he was taking, the wood cabinet in the bed room, his book shelf, and dining room table, everything else he would donate, the couch, chair, bed and desk in his office. He would disconnect his computer today since his new desk was coming and set it up and the cable people said 12 to 3 today for his internet service. He thought he might spend the night there and would bring his television also. He would leave Rosie here maybe or he would come back, he hadn't decided yet. He grabbed his laundry basket and detergent, the new sheets and his and Rosie's dirty clothes and left. He stopped and had breakfast and then thought about toilet paper and went to his bulk store and purchased two bundles of toilet paper and paper towels, more detergent, some light bulbs, batteries and a set of flashlights. He headed to his new home, opened the gate and drove up and parked in front, entered and returned to the car as he brought everything inside. He went upstairs and opened the windows and then downstairs also and went and started two loads of wash using both washers, he had to remove the tape from one because it had never been used, and noticed the same for one of the dryers. He made a mental note that he needed a trash can, or cans. He put paper towels and toilet paper in all the bathrooms, including the first floor and basement bathrooms. When he returned the wash had finished and placed them in all the dryers, using both, he thought it was neat having two and there was a space for a third, and thought maybe he should just buy another set with four people in the house, made another mental note. He figured on getting all the expenses out the way. He washed the sheets last, and knew he would be happy here and would bring some pots and pans tomorrow. It wasn't long before he was finished and looked at the cabinets in the kitchen, they were unique, when you opened them they lowered down so the top shelf was more accessible, that was really cool and the center island had a sink and stove top, besides the stove and built in ovens and the second sink under the kitchen window with a dishwasher.

It was time to go, the wash was complete as he folded everything up and left it on top of the dryer. Closed the windows and locked up and then headed home, closing the gate as he left. Maybe now he would get a new vehicle, it was time and he had the money. He stopped and picked up a couple of chicken dinners since Rosie would be home soon and maybe he would stay awake a little longer this evening. He had the chicken dinners and headed home and texted Rosie after he arrived, and before he went inside, placing the chicken on the kitchen counter, then undressed, took a shower and put on his shorts and shortly Rosie was home, looking sexy. He took a picture of her with his phone before she undressed and fixed their plates this time. When she put her house dress on, she sat down and they ate together again. Rosie told him he looked a little more relaxed today. Thanks Roger replied. Then told her the painters were finished and that he had washed their clothes and the new sheets; and the first few pieces of furniture would soon arrive tomorrow.

Rosie said she was more than ready to move, he said soon my dear in less than a week and then he would clear this all out. They finished eating and he cleaned up. Roger decided to disconnect his computer placing the cables and modem in a box along with the keyboard and mouse packing it all and planned to take it with him and a few other items, like the iron and the ironing board, television and his printer and his most important documents. The documents which he had were going to be left in a large locking cabinet that he found in his walk-in closet. His phone rang and he looked, it was the movers and they asked would Friday work for him, they had a cancelation and if he was available they could move him on Friday, said he sure was, and they said at eight, and would see him then. Rosie was in the shower and when she came out he said we will be moving Friday instead of Monday and told her the movers had a cancelation and moved us up, she hugged him and said great. They went to the bed room and he helped her oil her body, rubbing her and the next thing that happened was she was having a climax as he held her. He had her put her dress on as they went to have a drink together. Roger was elated and Rosie was very happy, and he was super happy as they drank. He said he still needed his rest and needed to get an early start in the morning. After they finished and checked the windows they went to bed, it was still early and Rosie said she wanted her master as she slid down and took him in her mouth and then crawled back and sat on him moving her hips up and down until she climaxed several more times before he came inside of her, and she just lay on top of him as he held her and then they rolled over and went to sleep.

Roger was up at five, used the bathroom, and showered as the coffee brewed and dried off, returning to the bedroom, getting dressed and waking Rosie, saying you need to shower and douche and the coffee was ready. He loaded his computer equipment and records, printer, monitor, and several other boxes into his car, returning just as Rosie came out of the shower, and then helping her oil herself and lotion up before she dressed, as he hugged and kissed her. He took a box of pots and pans down and would leave the rest for the movers. It was time for him and Rosie to go; they left together kissing before getting in their cars and departing. Roger arrived to open up the house and began bringing his equipment inside and placed them inside the elevator and the box of kitchen items in the kitchen, his car was now empty and it was almost eight, so he took his computer to his bedroom and set his boxes to the side and walked around and opened some windows since it was a little cooler today than the past few days. A little after eight the bell rang, and it was the bedroom people. Roger showed them where it was going to be set up, showed them the elevator as they began bringing the pieces inside and upstairs. Roger showed them where it was to be placed and shortly it was completely assembled, as they cleaned up the packing material and departed. Roger went and brought a set of sheets up and a new mattress cover and pad, then made up the bed, and thought here we go now. A couple hours later the bell rang again and the furniture store delivery people had his desk and rugs and they brought it up and he showed them where as they unwrapped the rugs and set up the large modern wood desk, then took the packaging with them. Roger went downstairs on the elevator and noticed it was lined with a thin floor to ceiling padding that hung from clips at the very top so the insides wouldn't be damaged from the moving of furniture and was larger than most home elevators; he thought how thoughtful was the design of the entire home was. The only one left before he could leave was the cable guy for his internet service and they had given him a time. They had said 12 to 3 and were there at 1. It didn't take long and the cable guy was soon finished and departed and said if he had any problems after he set his computer up to call. Roger set the monitor on the desk and the modem and hooked everything up and turned it on and he had high speed internet service. He shut it down and would stop by the post office and get several changes of address cards for himself, Rosie, Victoria and Barbara. He locked up and left and stopped by the post office, picked up the cards and left, he stopped at the Chinese restaurant and picked up some takeout food again for him and Rosie, while he waited he texted her and let her know.

After he received the order, he headed home and arrived just before Rosie had gotten off work and went and undressed, showered and put his shorts and shirt on and packed up everything that was left in the kitchen even his coffee pot, he was ready now. He hadn't taken the television yet and turned it on just to have some noise around. Rosie came in and they hugged one another, she said I haven't told you lately that I love you, but I just wanted to let you know I do very much. He said go take your shower sweetie and get comfortable and then we will eat, she kissed him and left to undress and shower. Roger was waiting for her when she came out as she sat down, he dished them up. He said being with you is a pleasure and I hope you know it and you know who you belong to now. She said to you master and I love you and will do whatever you tell me to do. They ate and even held hands and when they finished, they had eaten everything. Roger washed out the plastic containers and dropped them in the box with other kitchen items that he was keeping, as they both took their vitamins. They filled out the change of address cards, he would drop them off the next day and then everything would be in order. He told Rosie she could just terminate her utilities and close the accounts. They sat and watched some television and said take out what you need to wear tomorrow because everything else is going to be moved by the movers. She said yes sir and left and did as she was instructed. They stayed up a little while longer before securing the apartment and going to bed, as they held each other and

Roger rubbed her head. They soon went to sleep and really looked forward to moving tomorrow.

When Friday morning came they were both up very early and excited, they dressed for the last time in his apartment, Roger sent Rosie on her way and told her to have breakfast on her way to work, he kissed and hugged her and told her as he placed an empty container on the floor to drop their last minute stuff into it, she did and kissed him again and left for work. He prepared for the arrival of the movers and checked to see if he had emptied all the closets, kitchen drawers and cabinets. He checked that he had everything even from under the bed. He sure could use a cup of coffee, and to his surprise Rosie returned and phoned him and said come downstairs, he did as she handed him an extra-large cup of black coffee and a breakfast sandwich. He thanked her as she pulled off and headed to work, he returned and stood and ate at the kitchen counter and was thankful she had brought the coffee. He didn't have to wait long before the movers arrived, and knocked on the door. He showed them what was going and what wasn't as they began loading the truck. It was less than an hour and everything he was taking was loaded. He double checked then locked the door and headed for his car and departed.

He arrived first and opened the gate and the large front doors, and soon the truck pulled up, turned around in the drive way and backed up to the front door, he showed them were the heavy items were to go and most of the plastic containers also, using the elevator saved time and they were quickly finished, they made it seem like he didn't have much compared to the space it was in before. In the apartment it looked like a lot, but here it looked like it belonged to and ant. He started putting his clothes away and that didn't take very long at all, he also put Rosie's away inside her closet, what few she had and started stacking the empty containers. And all the empty containers he had purchased were stacked up and were downstairs as he unpacked the kitchen utensils, pots, pans and dishes placing them on the kitchen counter as he broke the cardboard boxes down. When he finished with that he set the empty containers by the front door and also the boxes. He had unpacked even his bondage equipment and placed all the items back in the cabinet that was located in his bed room again. He made a sink full of dish water and wiped out both refrigerators and he happen to have some baking soda and placed a box in each one for freshness, now he would have to get more, and made out a grocery list. The refrigerators were upscale and would probably keep food so much better than the one at the apartment with its old fashion design. Throwing away the old and bringing in the new is my motto. He made a list of what was needed which was pretty much everything.

He had read the information for the door locks and they used the key pad system and had changed the code and didn't need to change any lock tumblers, so that item he scratched off his list and texted Victoria, Barbara and Rosie that he has moved and texted them the key codes and said the gate would be open. He got in his car and headed to the bulk store and had a cart and filled it with a case of all the necessary cans and frozen foods and refreshed his supply of seasonings, and the basics like rice, beans, sugar, coffee and several other items. Roger had about six hundred dollars' worth of stuff when he checked out and then headed to the fresh fruit market for fresh vegetables and fruit. He couldn't take another day of Chinese, fried chicken or Italian beef take outs and needed and wanted to cook. He also wanted to see how well the new stoves cooked, even just fixing something simple. He bought plenty of fruits and vegetables and intended to have a nice healthy salad. He soon finished and headed home and his old car was riding really low with the load he had purchased. He arrived and made several trips bringing in all his purchases. He finished and looked around and sat in one of the dining room chairs, and was happy he had brought his table and chairs. Shortly after a short rest he resumed his activities, placed the vegetables and fruit in the sink and washed them and let them dry on his dish rack and began arraigning and putting the pots and pans away, then the dishes, the utensils, then the canned goods as he organized the shelves. When he finished he was tired from today's activity and the whole weeks. He went upstairs and unpacked and placed several bath mats in his bathroom along with towels and washcloths, and filled the linen closet and refolded as he arraigned the shelves and emptied several more containers. He took Rosie's clothes that were still in containers and hung the rest of her clothes up and the others he folded and placed on the shelves where she could find them. He returned to his room and removed the bedding he brought like his pillows and spreads and blankets, he left a couple out and the rest he folded again and placed in the closet. Now all the plastic containers he had purchased were emptied. Taking them downstairs on the elevator, and stacked them by the front door, with more of the empty boxes.

Roger was tired now and decided to take his first shower in his new house and take a nap as he went to his new bed room, undressed and turned the water on in the shower and realized he needed some soap and went and looked in the linen closet and took out a couple bars and placed them on the sink and took the other to the shower. Feeling funky Roger stood in the walk-in shower with its rain feature and there was even a seat attached to the wall as he sat down and let the warm water run over him, he bathed and soon finished, dried himself off and put on a clean pair of shorts and a t-shirt and laid down after getting a light spread and covering himself and very soon fell fast asleep.

He was sleeping very well in his new bed and it was about three when he laid down and he didn't wake up until Rosie came in and woke him, he turned over and just looked at her and the next thing he knew Victoria came in the room and climbed in bed with him and said you have done quite a lot baby. She rubbed his head as he just lay there and she kissed him and said she really missed him and loved him. He finally sat up and wiped his eyes and asked what time was it, Victoria said after six. He said he was tired from today and the past couple of weeks. She said I can see why, as he told Rosie I tried to put your clothes away, as she said I see you have and thank you very much. He said he was too tired to cook and didn't want any more fried chicken or Chinese to soon. He stood and asked if they had seen their rooms and if they were satisfied with the paint job. Both said it looks so much better and fresh, but very, very empty. He said yes it does, and said it seemed he had a lot until he moved in here, now it looks like Mr. Ant lives here. They all laughed then went and looked at Rosie's room and in her closet, then Victoria's room. She said beautiful before they went downstairs on the elevator to the living room. He had numbered the remotes and took number three and asked Victoria to bring her car keys as he slipped on his thongs and going out front to her car and said lets sync your car to the door and gate, he had both remotes, they did the garage door first, it took a few minutes before they had it done, then drove to the gate. He then double checked that it was done correctly. He said ok now you can go back and park inside, she backed inside and looked at the inside of the garage and said it looks so clean and bright being painted. They went in through the back door after entering the code and he said it automatically locks behind you. They walked to the kitchen and a few minutes later Barbara walked in the front door and to the kitchen where Victoria, Rosie and Roger were standing and she came and hugged them all as he took the second remote from the drawer and asked Barbara to go back outside as he had her get back in her car and did the sync for her auto, for the garage door and then the gate and had accomplished that portion of his getting everyone settled in and got that out of the way. Barbara said how bright after backing inside the garage as she stepped out of her auto and Roger let her enter the code for the back door and they entered. They went to the kitchen where Victoria and Rosie were having a conversation and he handed Rosie the remote numbered four and explained one button was for the gate and the other the garage door. Victoria said she was going to spend the night and needed to get her bag and Barbara said she had to get hers also, as they returned to the garage to retrieve their overnight bags. Roger moved the empty containers to the laundry room along with the empty boxes and when Barbara and Victoria returned told them they could use them to pack their stuff in and the boxes also and would put the tape dispenser with them soon. Rosie said she was going to take a shower, and Victoria said she would join her as Roger told them where the towels were, if they needed more.

Barbara asked have you eaten, and he said not since this morning and he had been too tired to cook and didn't want any more Chinese or fried chicken but a pizza would be nice and since he had bought a couple boxes of frozen he would fix a couple and told her to feel at home and get used to being here and suggested she go shower also. They went upstairs together on the elevator as she pulled her suit case with her and said he had placed toilet paper and paper towels in all the bath rooms and found Vicky and Rosie in his bath together. Barbara said she wanted to use her own bath as Roger went and handed her a towel, bath rag and a rug, and walked with her to her room as she looked around. She looked in her closet and said the painters did a marvelous job and asked him to stay with her as she bathed, she undressed and hugged Roger, kissing him and said she missed and loved him as he rubbed her body and squeezed and kissed her while rubbing her back. She went into the walk-in shower and turned on the water as he sat on the toilet with the top down and she said the water is wonderful finding the controls for the different modes as he watched her in the shower. It has been over a week since he had seen her and he missed her very much. She stepped out and said how refreshing and told him she would be very happy here and especially with him. He told her he missed her very much, she was the most mature of the three and had known her the longest and they always loved one another, she asked him to open her bag and get her robe out, he opened it and brought it back draping it around her. Roger said the next thing on his list was to measure the windows and decide on whether to have blinds, shades or curtains or a combination of both. And said his room even with the bed still seemed so barren but was going shopping for a living room set for his bedroom and a large screen television. He did decide on having curtains but wasn't sure how he would decorate and said he had plenty of time and he was thinking also of purchasing either a new car or probably a pickup. She said, wow you are going to just bust all the way out now, and said it was about time as they returned to his room and found Rosie and Victoria oiling themselves and each other as Barbara joined in and they helped her and did her back as he just watched them and suggested they put on more than just robes because of the lack of window covering.

Roger said he was going to fix a couple pizzas and if they wanted anything else they were on their own. Heading downstairs to the kitchen and taking out his cutting board along with an onion, jalapeño, and a can of mushrooms and black olives and checked the oven for any packing materials and turned on the built-in double wall oven and set the temperature and took a box of pizzas out and removed two, found his pizza pan and began preparing them. He was soon finished as he sprinkled seasoning, olive oil and shredded cheese on them. The oven heated up quickly and was professional grade as were all the appliances as he popped the first pizza in, he looked and it had gotten dark outside as the sun was setting and after setting the oven timer he walked out on the deck, turned and looked back at the house with the lights on and then walked further out to see how the windows looked from outside and how far inside you could see and walked completely around the large home before returning back where he started from and then went back inside, he had to enter the code to get back inside and liked the security feature. He checked the oven and had about five more minutes before he would place the second one in. He took out his large cutting board and pizza wheel so after he took out the first one, he then placed the second one in. The girls hadn't come downstairs yet and he figure they were looking at and planning their rooms, or even playing with each other. He took out a cold beer from the refrigerator and it was really cold, just the way he liked it. He opened the can and began drinking and thought he would go next week and look to finish some of his furniture shopping and clean out his old apartment and Rosie's, and also see about a new vehicle, it was time for a real change. The first pizza finished cooking and he found his oven glove and slid it onto the cutting board and placed the second one on the pan and placed it inside the oven and turned it back on again and set the timer. He sliced the cooked one and took out the paper plates and placed a couple slices on each one, took his beer and sat at the dining room table. The girls finally appeared downstairs wearing very loose fitting and comfortable dresses and he asked what had taken them so long to come downstairs. They said they were looking and talking about decorating and asked if he was going to measure the windows. He said yes, it was one of his priorities and would start tomorrow. They all took a paper plate and helped themselves and each had a beer and then joined him at the table and said how good the pizza was as they ate and returned for more and soon the buzzer went off alerting him that the oven had shut off and the second pizza was ready as he went and removed it and placed it on the board and sliced it and placed his pan in the sink. He took several pieces and they returned and helped themselves and soon they had eaten both pizzas. After cleaning up everyone sat at the table and talked, Roger said he was going tomorrow and finish furniture shopping for his bedroom and order the television and couches and chairs and a table he had seen that he liked, and would measure all the bedroom windows and said he suspected the sliding glass doors at the false balconies were all the same standard size and would get vertical blinds for them, then asked who wanted curtain rods and he would get them if they wanted or he would give them the dimensions and they could pick up the style they wanted. Barbara said he could get hers, but Victoria and Rosie said they would pick theirs out. Roger said he would probably during the coming weeks buy a new car but more than likely a truck, and had seen one he really liked and then he could eliminate carrying the remotes around. He knew he would have curtains and probably a shade of some type for his window along with the vertical blinds for the sliding glass door.

Roger said he would also look at patio furniture and said there were some awesome sets and would probably order a set and get a grill since he had left his at the apartment, it was old and he had seen several he liked, but there was one he really liked, it was charcoal with a gas start. Then said he was going to bed so he would be refreshed for tomorrow. Victoria and Rosie were off and said they would go with him, and Barbara was undecided what she would do and said now she was seriously thinking of packing and moving a lot sooner and would probably use some of her vacation time, and just get the moving out of the way and said the sooner the better. When she said that it made Victoria reconsider and said she only had a couple months left and should do the same, it didn't make any since drawing things out any longer than necessary, but said she had did the new checking account and Roger was number two and had ordered her new checks and would give Roger her files next week. Rosie said she would do it next week also and Barbara asked Roger when he wanted to go finish making the necessary changes. He said Monday since he had moved and there were several accounts he needed to do the change of address on, but had gone to the post office and had taken care of the mailing address. He said he had to arrange to empty the apartments; his and

Rosie's so he still would be busy another week. He stood and said he was going to bed, and asked them what were they going to do, they all said they were coming and he checked that the garage doors were closed and all the downstairs windows closed and locked, only Barbara and Victoria were parked in the garage. He and Rosie's autos were still outside. He closed the gate from the front door as he walked up the stairs and thought about having some art on the now bare walls.

He brushed his teeth, undressed and climbed in bed as Barbara followed. Victoria and Barbara were now on either side of him and told Rosie you had all week with him as she took her place on the end. It wasn't long before he was asleep as Victoria kissed him and Barbara held him and Rosie held Victoria, and soon they all were asleep.

Chapter Nine

Saturday morning when they all awoke, Roger was facing Barbara and they hugged one another, she rose and Roger followed as they went to the bathroom together. After they finished and came out, Rosie climbed out of the bed, followed by Victoria, as he said the bed has now been christened, after leaving the bathroom. Roger and Barbara put on some clothes, and went downstairs and started breakfast and enjoyed cooking in the new kitchen saying to him, this is so much more convenient and easy while enjoying a breakfast together of bacon, eggs, toast and coffee. Roger still had his coffee pot, and Barbara said with the four of us maybe we could use a larger pot. Roger said or maybe just two coffee pots, since he liked his perked. She asked him if he wanted to use paper plates or the regular dishes, and said regular dishes because he was tired of paper plates and they reminded him of takeout's. They prepared to dish the food up just as Victoria and Rosie descended the stairs talking. They placed the plates on the table as everyone sat down together to eat. Victoria said she was going home and was taking some of the empty plastic containers and boxes and had some serious packing to do. She had some tape and just needed to get started, and staying here wasn't going to help her move any sooner. Barbara said she had decided to also go home and begin, and would just move in like Roger and Rosie before her lease ran out. Barbara asked Roger after he purchased the curtain rods to please put hers up because she had curtains and wasn't planning on buying anything except the bed for now and would let him know when it would be delivered after she made the purchase. Victoria suggested that her and Barbara should stop on their way home and make the bed purchases and get them out of the way. Roger said Rosie's bed wasn't coming until next week and maybe they would all be delivered about the same time. Barbara said she was going to the same store where Roger had gone and wanted the same bed, or something similar to his. He said Rosie's is the same with the drawers underneath, just the side cabinets weren't as tall. He finished eating and said now that was a real meal and was glad to be able to cook again. Victoria and Rosie washed the dishes and asked him about the dish washer and he replied that he probably wouldn't be using it much, but would wait and see. After washing the dishes they all went upstairs to dress and get their day started since the moving portion of his grandiose plan was just the beginning. Victoria hugged Roger and said she wanted him but might return later with some clothes and loved him as they hugged and kissed. She waited on Barbara and would follow her to the bedding store as Roger reminded them of where it was located. Roger looked in a tool box for his tape measure, taking it and his step stool and had Rosie follow him writing down the window measurements as he began measuring the windows for the treatments, after ten minutes he returned and all the windows were the same width which would make buying the blinds and curtain rods easy.

Barbara and Victoria both hugged and kissed him and said they were leaving and he might see them later that evening depending on how involved they got in packing and planning. They all went downstairs. Rosie asked him her car or his. He said his as they watched Barbara and Victoria pull out and close the garage doors as they drove down the driveway. After returning upstairs and putting on some clothes they were ready to depart and soon left, closing the gate and headed to the furniture store where he had seen the set he really liked most of all. Arriving there and going inside and soon found an eager salesman and Roger informed him of the set he wanted to purchase. Roger had his list as he looked at the set again, it had medium high backs, wide deep firm cushions making it wide enough to lay down on comfortably and with low armrest; the color was a dark blue with thin gold stripes, and was a soft but durable cloth material. The set consisted of a wide couch, and matching love seat and a large wide matching chair. Roger also chose a low cocktail table of solid wood with a ceramic tile inlay with matching end tables. He found a lamp he really liked and purchased just one. He placed the order and was informed it was in stock and could be delivered on Thursday. He thanked the salesman and checked that off his list of wanted and needed items. Eventually then made their way to the nearby electronics store.

While leaving he asked Rosie if she wanted to order any furniture, she said no and would wait considering how her finances were first and said she had the bed and dresser coming and those were the most important things for right now. Rosie thanked him and said he had done more than enough for her already. Roger looked at her as she looked back and kissed him and said thank you so very much. They continued on their way and Roger also knew which television he wanted. A salesman then approached and he informed him of the one he wanted, it was 110 inches and would like to have it installed and mounted. The store said, they would be more than happy to install it, he was pleased with that and since he was going broadcast, he would also need an antenna and it would all be delivered and installed together as requested, on Thursday. Next they proceeded to a store that handled just outdoor and patio furniture. He found a patio set with eight very comfortable chairs, a large table that came with an extra-large umbrella. They also had the grill he really wanted, they had it in stock and in the box, he would take it with him but would have the set delivered, requesting this coming Thursday, they said that wasn't even a problem. They departed and he treated Rosie to lunch. They went to a gourmet sandwich shop, sat and ate there food there and after finishing their lunch he told her he had two more stops as he headed to another furniture store ordering a set of cabinets he had looked at earlier and wanted for the living room, it would be delivered on Thursday as well. The last stop was the huge hardware store that was part of a national chain and sold everything you would want or need to fix or repair stuff around the home. He went to the window section, which had window treatments and looked at the shades on display for windows, and found several he really liked, gave the sales lady the measurements and placed the order for his bedroom window. He gave her the window sizes for the vertical blinds and she informed him they were of a standard size and would find them on the shelf, and just had to decide on the color and texture and could take them with him. He found what he was looking for and picked out six sets all in an off white or cream color and also found the curtain rods and chose three sets as Rosie picked hers out taking the blinds and rods with them and finally heading home. He told Rosie that was it for today since it was still early in the evening after arriving home. He parked outside but went through the garage unloading the boxes and laying them against the inside wall. He finished unloading and then unlocked the back door and set the blinds and rods inside with Rosie's assistance. Roger closed the garage door and they loaded them on the elevator and took them upstairs. Rosie went and placed her curtain rods and a set of blinds in her room then a set in the remaining bedrooms.

Roger took a short break and told her he was going to install the blinds and curtain rods and went to retrieve his set of battery powered tools. It didn't take long to install the vertical blinds since the windows and blinds were a standard fit and soon he had the curtain rods installed, then taking the vacuum and cleaning up the plaster dust. Rosie asked him what she should cook. He said whatever you want. She decided to make a tuna salad; he said it was fine with him, as she left to change her clothes before going downstairs to prepare the salad. He soon had all the vertical blinds installed and the curtain rods in his room, Rosie's and Barbara's; he cleaned up the plaster dust and was finished. He washed his hands going downstairs to the garage with the empty boxes and started assembling the grill, and a little more than half hour later rolled it through the kitchen to the patio and set it to one side, he would have to get the propane gas canisters and charcoal for it another day, but at least he had gotten started. He returned and went to the washroom by the laundry and washed his hands. Rosie said come eat. She fixed his plate, lettuce with salad on top with crackers and a couple slices of cheese on the side. He had noticed there were ceiling outlets for lights; but none were installed except in his bedroom and had plastic covers over them. He thought that was good because he preferred to choose his own light fixtures. Rosie and he ate and were glad she had fixed the salad because he didn't want anything too heavy. He complimented her on the tasty salad, she said it was probably the best thing she had ever fixed as far as creating a meal and felt she really needed to learn more about cooking. Roger said don't worry you are here with me, and when Victoria and Barbara move in you will learn a lot more and it's never too late to learn. After they finished eating he placed the remaining salad in a sealed container, putting it in the refrigerator as they cleaned up the kitchen. Roger had his notes and went around looking at the ceiling outlets and made notes. At least the entrance was done and it had a large and beautiful light fixture, that looked like a crystal chandelier and it had a beautiful sparkle to it and provided plenty of light and with the white walls the entrance just glowed. He figured he had done enough for the day, but went and measured the windows in the living and dining rooms along with the kitchen, and once he had those measurements, he would decide what to place there. But for the kitchen he was thinking the short vertical blinds or maybe a shade and would see what was available. Roger went to the laundry room and wrote down the washer and dryer model numbers so he would purchase new ones of the same make and model and have a real laundry room. He had placed his ironing board in here and there was enough room to leave it up if he wanted.

He decided to call it quits and Rosie looked as if she needed some personal time. It was just the two of them and said he was going to take a shower and then relax and have a drink, she seemed relieved when he said that and followed him, undressing also and went with him and they showered together. While showering with soap and some shower gel she took him in her small soft hands as he sat in the shower, kneeling and placing him in her warm mouth until he filled her mouth with his sperm, he watched her as she swallowed most of it and after washing her face she stood before him as he felt her, inserting his fingers inside of her vagina as she soon began climaxing, then holding her quivering body as he stood rinsing off and kissing her, then stepping out to dry off. They went to the bedroom and placed a dry towel on the bed and began to oil one another. Soon his phone rang and Victoria called and said she was going to stay home and had gotten involved in packing and would see him very soon, told him she loved him and would keep in touch, also would let him know when her bed would arrive. She hung up. After he and Rosie had put there robes on with a pair of shorts Barbara called, saying that she was coming back and would see him very soon, he said they would be waiting, as she disconnected. He took Rosie by her hand and they walked downstairs and he fixed a couple of gin and tonics with some fruit juice as they sat at the dining room table gazing around thinking how it would all look one day very soon.

He and Rosie were sitting and drinking when they heard Barbara open the back door and enter, said she hoped she wasn't too late as he stood and hugged her and said they were on their first one, she said good struggling with a very large suit case with more clothes that she brought and had a couple of bags in her car asking Roger to get them for her. He said sure and went barefoot to the garage bringing two large trash bags from the open car trunk and went inside as Barbara returned and removed one from the back seat and reentered the house. He said what do we have here, she said just some clothes and said one was her dirties and would wash them here to avoid having to use the one at the apartment in the basement and stated she was out of quarters. He laughed and said, I've always hated that part and then getting there and someone had all the machines in use. He said the blinds and rods are up, she said that's good because she had brought a couple sets of curtains. Said she wouldn't be long, she would take these upstairs and take a shower and return and said don't get wasted before she could return, and they said ok; they would wait for her. Roger left Rosie sitting at the table and went upstairs and found Barbara placing the clothes in her closet and helped her out, she emptied the suit case and they started on the garbage bags, she had some bath mats, towels, wash clothes and curtains. She hugged him and said she would shower and had her soaps and gels and other stuff as she began placing them in her bathroom, she turned on the water and undressed and stood under the water as he turned around and returned downstairs.

About fifteen minutes later Roger returned upstairs and helped Barbara oil herself, she had a towel wrapped around her head and her robe on as they rode the elevator downstairs together and joined Rosie. Roger fixed her a drink and refreshed his and Rosie's as they sat and talked. Barbara said all this week she would pack and on Monday or Tuesday make arrangements to have the movers come and get it at least by the following week, and then would probably take a week or two of vacation time since she had accumulated more than three months' of vacation time available. And said she didn't have very much once she went home and started filling a couple of containers with her household decorations and without the bed decided she would just purchase mostly new furniture and there were only a couple large pieces she might move here but was still undecided whether she would or not. Roger commented it's so much simpler and easy to just let go sometimes. Barbara told him not to buy any curtains yet because she had quite a few still at home, and the ones she was keeping were long enough for all the windows. She asked Rosie what she was going to do. Rosie answered that she would wait until she had paid her last month's rent and the utilities and would know just how much cash she had in her account before purchasing anything else. She did the bed and a dresser and that was the most important thing for her right now, and it was more than she ever had before. They sat and drank and walked around discussing ideas for decorating downstairs. Roger said he was moving the dining room table to the section in the kitchen that seemed to be a space for a small set rather than leaving it where it was, and Barbara said that makes sense and it wouldn't seem so out of place and would fit that space nicely. Barbara told him before she forgot that her bedroom set was coming this Thursday. Roger said looks like Thursday is the big day, commenting his television, and the furniture for his bedroom were all coming that day. He said Victoria's and Rosie's might come together and would call the store to see if they could do it that way and make it simple. He said you know we still need more sheets and bedding, like mattress covers, blankets and pillow cases.

It had gotten late and Roger said he was very tired as they cleaned up and closed up downstairs before heading upstairs and climbing into bed together. Roger was in between the two as he and Barbara kissed and soon Roger was asleep as Rosie snuggled up against him.

The following morning when Barbara and Roger awoke and coming out of the bathroom together and putting on some clean shorts and t-shirts. The two of them went downstairs together and found Victoria in the kitchen fixing breakfast. He said what a surprise, as they all kissed and he asked her what prompted her to come back. Said the packing could get done quickly and stated it was more like cleaning house and had more stuff she was throwing away than keeping, and wondering what had possessed her to keep it all this time. Roger asked what kind of stuff you are talking about. She responded, old clothes along with some old furniture and was starting to see that all she really needed to move were her clothes she wore now, her shoes and cookware and dishes which she was thinking might become clutter here. She asked if Roger would come and see what they might need and the rest would just have to go. Roger said he would because it didn't make sense moving it if it wasn't necessary. He said since we are all here let's move the table. He and Barbara moved it over to the new location in the section of the kitchen where it belonged and Victoria moved the chairs. Then Rosie came downstairs and soon they were sitting down and eating together. He said we will get it all together very soon. Roger suggested since it was Sunday we all go with whomever wanted to be first, Barbara or Victoria and start helping one or both decide what they wanted or should move and start to get things moving. Barbara said she pretty much had already decided and just needed to pack up what she was bringing which wouldn't be very much and suggested maybe we should just go help Vicky and speed up the process. Victoria said she welcomed the help, as Roger said he would bring the remaining containers and boxes. Barbara said that sounds like a plan to me as they cleaned up and Rosie said she would like to help as Victoria hugged her and told her to get dressed. So they decided to go to Victoria's apartment and help her start packing as Roger, Barbara and Rosie got dressed in jeans and t-shirts. Roger loaded some of the empty containers into Victoria's auto along with the boxes and packing tape. Barbara and Victoria drove their cars and Roger and Rosie followed in his.

When they arrived Roger stopped in front of Victoria's apartment, took the containers and boxes out as Rosie started taking them inside and he then parked the car, returning to bring the remaining boxes inside. Soon all of them were inside helping Victoria pack an what she was going to take as Roger went through the kitchen ware and packed what they needed, like her dishes, silverware and soon was finished and had wrapped all the items and labeled the boxes and began stacking them and in a couple of hours had just about packed Victoria completely up. Victoria said hell; I am ready to move now. She decided to keep a hutch and her dresser and the cocktail table and said the rest she would donate. The apartment was a one bedroom and said she had stayed in it because the rent wasn't expensive and she could save more money, saying the banks weren't the most generous employers. She stated she would call the movers tomorrow and see how soon they would come and then donate the rest. Roger had created a nice pile of containers and boxes of what she was moving and the clothes she would donate she placed in large trash bags and would take them to a nearby donation center operated by a veteran's origination. Victoria was thankful for the help and said she would treat everyone to dinner. Roger said now he could eat some Chinese food and knew Victoria liked it also. She said ok, and they all left in her car going just a few blocks away to a very nice restaurant for a sit-down dinner. They entered and soon ordered and talked as Roger looked at Barbara and said your next my dear. Barbara suggested next weekend, and then she could call sometime this week and arrange for a moving date. Victoria said she had to now and hoped they had a day available this coming week. Their food arrived, they were all hungry, and Roger said this is really good since he had ordered a spicy Hunan dish. Everyone enjoyed the food and Victoria said she would take a week off after she had a moving date and told Rosie she was lucky she had moved because she had lived next door to Roger. Rosie replied she didn't have anything to really move.

Soon after they finished eating and Victoria paid the bill as Roger asked Victoria if there was anything she wanted him to take back with him. She responded some of her winter clothes and a few other things; he said ok, as they rode back and went inside and she had placed some in bags but had kept others separated from the ones being donated. He took out about five bags and Victoria said that was it, and he asked her for some hangers and said he would hang them up for her, she had a pile and placed them in a bag and took them to his auto. He returned and hugged and kissed her and said he missed her as he and Rosie along with Barbara departed and headed for their autos. He and Rosie hugged and kissed Barbara, as they headed their separate ways. When they arrived home they went in the front door and brought all the bags to the elevator first; then closed the front door and went upstairs taking the bags to Victoria's closet and Roger said he would come back later and finish but needed to take a shower first and relax. Rosie said she agreed with him on that and needed to relax also, as they headed upstairs together. Rosie said she had a full day and Roger agreed with her and said many more to come before we can enjoy the things we did before with each other, and Rosie asked why not. He asked her what was on her mind, she replied, she wanted him to spank her and that she was overdue for one and really desired it, and wanted to play with herself but knew she needed permission.

He said very good Rosie my dear, you little hot sweet bitch, as he grabbed her and pushed her against the wall. She all but melted in his arms as he kissed her and felt her while she still had her jeans on. Said when he got things together he was taking her outside naked and walking her around like a pet with the collar and leash on as he began feeling between her legs as she climaxed. Said when he talked to her that way it made her so very hot and wet and she couldn't restrain herself from becoming so excited. He told her to go to her room, undress and return, she left and he went to her room to undress then returned, standing nude before him. He opened his cabinet with his equipment and told her to come over here, he placed a collar around her neck and attached the leash, asking her who she was, she replied, she was his bitch. Rosie was even more excited now as her nipples stood up and Roger thought about how he was going to punish her, his willing submissive, and decided the harness was what she needed. He reached for it and she began shaking her head and said please no master not that again, he said why not, you have been very bad and need to learn how to obey. He found the lubricant and began applying it to her and decided on the spreader bars and cuffed her wrist and ankles, then attached the spreader bar to her ankles, then he pulled out a second and attached to her arms and had her kneel on the rug and took a third bar and attaching both of the other bars in the center of each which held her in a kneeling position she couldn't move from. He knelt down next to her and felt her quivering body, caressing and feeling her breast and between her thighs in a sensual way, then reached around and found an anal plug and slowly worked it inside her anus until it was fully inserted. He stood and took out his long leather strap as she looked up at him, he told her to count as he spanked her ass, she counted one, thank you master, two thank you masters, she was at twenty as the strap found its mark between her legs, down her thighs, and across her back, stomach and breast. He knelt down and pulled her head up by her hair and looked at her and asked if she was satisfied now, she said yes sir master Caesar. He said I think not bitch and removed the bar that held the two others apart and the one on her arms and cuffed her wrist to the same one as her ankles; her butt was now thrust up and fully exposed as he inserted a vibrating dildo inside her vagina while she began having several continuous organisms. He left it inserted inside of her. He slowly removed it as he then began after doubling up the leather strap whacked her butt several more times very hard as she began crying. When he finished he left her in that position for half an hour before he decided to released her.

Roger was finished with Rosie and removed the cuffs and made her stand leading her around with the plug still inside her rectum, he held her face in one hand and asked her who she was, and she replied, she was his bitch to do whatever he wanted with, he took her downstairs on the elevator and walked her around the large basement then stopped and made her spread her leg open as he spanked her pussy with the leather strap until she began climaxing several more times, then walked her up the steps all the way back to his bed room where he bent her over on the rug in a kneeling position and removed the anal plug from her ass, then the collar as she continued to kneel inserting himself inside her very hot and moist pussy as she continued climaxing before he pulled out and then inserted himself in her now relaxed an open ass, roughly plunging in and out until he felt himself come deep inside of her, afterwards pulling her up by her hair, turning her around as she kissed and held him thanking her master. He led her to the shower and turning the water on both of them. He bathed her and she held on to him kissing and thanking him for treating her like he did and knew he also loved her. She bathed him and they soon exited the shower and dried off, going to the bedroom as he rubbed her with oils as she moaned, clinging to him, kissing him and thanking him for being in her life and taking her with him. He rubbed her to sleep as they lay under the covers, before he finally went to sleep himself.

Chapter Ten

Monday morning, the first day of a busy week to come for Roger, as he woke sitting up in bed, he started getting out of bed just as Rosie sat up, and jumped out of bed, coming around as he stood and reached out and held her. Roger stroked her head, and said you don't want to be late baby girl, as she looked up into his face and said thank you. He released her as she turned and headed to wash up in her own bathroom. Roger put on his shorts and t-shirt and went downstairs and prepared to fix them some breakfast first, putting his coffee on first, when Rosie came downstairs dressed for work. They sat and ate together. She was smiling, said she was so very happy. Roger said that's a good thing as he drank his coffee and poured a second cup. Soon Rosie finished eating, washed her hands and brushed her teeth in the small washroom, coming out as he finished cleaning up and she kissed him, said she loved him as she headed for the front door on her way to work, he said have a great day baby. She exited the front door and was quickly gone. Roger returned upstairs to his desk and proceeded to file his papers away and started putting them back in order into his new file cabinet. After an hour he had accomplished the first of many more files to come as everyone would eventually give him there files, bills and check books as be began consolidating the new household and was now finished for now. His briefcase was filled with the documents and papers he would need as reference as he changed addresses on the various accounts today at several different banks. He needed to go, there were three separate locations he needed to visit then all of his business would be back in order once again.

He dressed in jeans, running shoes, t-shirt and his sports jacket looking casual but business like and then headed out the front door. His car was outside and would see how long this all would take as he departed. He soon arrived at the first bank, it didn't take very long and afterwards he called Barbara and asked if she would meet him shortly at the second bank for the account changes and she said sure. He arrived and waited in his auto until she arrived. When she pulled up he waited and they walked in together, signed in and waited a short time before a bank representative took care of the needed changes to his account and hers since they both banked there. Finally finishing with all the necessary changes being made and walked out together, they hugged and kissed. Barbara said she had called the movers and set a moving date of a week from this coming Wednesday and just needed for them to come over and do for her what they had done for Victoria, he said no problem, and reminded him her bed was coming Thursday, said he hadn't forgotten, and complimented her on how sexy she looked and said he couldn't wait for things to get back to normal with her in his bed. Said she felt the same way, they kissed again and departed. Roger was ahead of schedule as he headed to the last bank on his list and in no time was finished. He was soon on his way back home, stopping at the dealership where he had looked before at the vehicle he wanted and had checked on the manufactures web site, it was fully loaded and just what he wanted and the right color. He inquired about it and if he purchased it today, it would be five thousand off the list price. It had the features he had read about, after looking at their internet web site, sun roof, navigation, 4x4, with extra-large capacity gas tank and off road suspension, and it just happened to be the color he wanted and told the salesman he would like to purchase it. The salesman wrote up the sales contract and gave him a final price and he used his corporate credit card and made the purchase and then went and removed from his old car a few of the things he kept handy, like a flash light, the remote for the house and some odds and ends that he kept in a plastic bag in the glove box and some maps. They gave him eleven hundred for his trade in and Roger used that for some dealer installed options like mud flaps and rear bed cover. They were happy to make the sale and transferred his veteran's license plates. The salesmen giving him a brief explanation of the vehicle and helped him sync his phone. Soon Roger was off and stopped and filled the gas tank. Roger headed home and after pulling up to the gate read the book on sync, and paired his entrance gate and garage door to the truck and soon had that accomplished, it was the same as he had done in both Barbara's and Victoria's autos. He got out and looked at the truck and was happy to have purchased it and then went inside after parking inside.

Roger went to his desk after washing his hands and filed his papers away and looked at his finances. He totaled up the cost of the house, truck, and furniture and had used one of his corporate accounts, he was an employee of his own company, which consisted of investments, stocks, bonds, municipal bonds, vacant land,

and income properties and provided him with a more than a reasonable annual income which he gave to himself on paper. It really was much more; but he had always been conservative with his spending. He never gave the outward appearance of being a millionaire, and wore jeans most of the time. He spent more on his women than he did on himself, it's what made him happy and saw no reason to change now. He locked his file cabinet and thought about what should he do for the rest of the day since it was just one in the afternoon and decided to go downstairs to look around in the basement and wondered what should he do down here, then remembered the washer and dryer and went back to his bedroom, pulled out his list scratching off the items he had taken care of and noticed that the washer and dryer were still on the list. Today was Monday and he hadn't expected to accomplish all he had done today. So far the truck had been listed something he planned on doing Tuesday, and now he had two free days. He was determined to finish his list and decided to order the washer and dryer, going to the appliance store and it was the same one where the original washer and dryer had come from and had seen their name stamped on the bag containing the instruction manuals. He left home and after arriving informed the salesman of the models. He then looked at refrigerators. He was thinking he would like a bar in the basement and would need a refrigerator, explaining to the salesman why and what he wanted it for and didn't need the bins for vegetables or food. He showed him something similar to the upright freezers and said this would be ideal for the purpose and had a freezer for ice and just shelves inside and said it was designed just for the purpose he wanted it for. Roger made the purchase and set a delivery date and the salesman said he could have it by Thursday, Roger said that's great. Roger completed the transaction for all the items and as he departed, wondering about the bar and who he could get to install or built one and decided to look on the internet when he returned home. Driving home and loving his new truck since it had been a long time like maybe ten years since he had purchased his car remembering where he was at that time in his life.

Roger took himself to lunch and went to a Mexican restaurant this time, and had a burrito and decided to look for some furniture for the living room. Arriving at a major store he had visited earlier, he walked around looking and really didn't like their selection and he had a tendency to like more of the expensive well-made furniture, not because of the price but because of the quality and style. He went back to the store he had ordered his set for the bedroom from, and looked around and found a very nice large area rug for the living room, but was undecided and would wait until Barbara and Victoria moved in, he valued their opinions and since they would be there he felt it was only fair that they should have some sort of input. Realizing he needed to go to the old apartment and see what was there and called the donation people for a pickup. He drove over and parked, calling from the truck and making the arrangements for a Tuesday pick up and they gave him a time of ten am. They thanked him. Roger headed upstairs to the apartment and entered. He looked around a thought about all the good times he had here, having fun with the girls, as they crawled around and of meeting Rosie. He looked through a box of small items and decided he had made a wise choice and looked around next door at Rosie's, but didn't stay long before locking her door and checking the mail boxes before leaving. He headed home since it was early afternoon before the rush hour; soon Roger arrived back home and was admiring the new features on his truck as he opened the gate and the garage door and backing inside. He had some research to do as he entered the house and took out a couple of chicken breasts and would have a chicken salad for dinner.

While the chicken thawed he decided on looking up where or who had bars and he always wanted a billiards table and would search through the internet to find one. It didn't take long to find bars, going through the varied styles and decided it would take time to decide and would put it off for a little later. He saw it would take some time and thought before he would have a bar, he would just continue with getting things settled in the house first, and get Victoria and Barbara settled in. He undressed and decided to lie down for a bit; it had been a busy day and would rest a little. While lying down he then thought about Rosie and decided to start cooking. The chicken was almost thawed. He started preparing it and placed it in the oven and washed his hands and took out a head of lettuce and chopped it up and prepared two large bowls and added cucumbers, radishes, onions and tomatoes and would boil a couple eggs. He covered the salads and placed them in the refrigerator and would add the chicken and eggs later, the eggs were soon done as he cooled them in cold water and waited.

It wasn't long before Rosie pulled up and parked, and entering the front door and was surprised to see him since he had been parking outside. She said you must have parked inside, and he replied yes and told her to go look, she was cute in her hi-heels and short skirt as she headed for the backdoor. She screamed so loud when she saw the truck and came back and hugged him. She said that's beautiful Roger. He told her if she was real good he would take her tomorrow and trade her car in and get her a new one. She said really, you would do that for me, he told her yes and she started crying and hugged him, he told her she was his and has proven that in so many ways, and yes he would do it for her. She held him tight as he hugged her and they kissed. He told her how cute she was looking as he unbuttoned her blouse and felt her breast and she told him she would do anything for him; he said I know you will and told her to go put on something comfortable. She went upstairs and when she returned was wearing the dress she wore around the house as he hugged and kissed her. He said they were going to be eating soon as he shelled the eggs. Rosie had that look on her face and sat on his lap as he felt her and she climaxed saying I love you master.

The oven buzzed, and Rosie had to get up as he went an took the pan out with the chicken and placed it on his cutting board slicing it into chunks, and then took the salads out of the refrigerator and asked Rosie to please set the table, and bring the salad dressings as he began adding the chicken and eggs to the salads. He washed his cutting board and placed it in the dish rack as he let the dish he cooked the chicken in soak in the sink. He brought the salads to the table and sitting down and eating, Rosie said wow this looks great. They each chose a different salad dressing and enjoyed the salad as they ate. While they ate his phone rang and he saw that it was Victoria, he answered. Said that she had contacted the movers and they would move her this Thursday and she was taking that day off and Friday and the following week and would see him then, said she loved him and hung up. Roger said Thursday is the big day it's going to be busy around here and explained to Rosie all that would occur. She said you will be busy around here and at least we won't be alone anymore. Roger ate half his salad and placed the rest in a container for later, as did Rosie, she was very excited and told Roger she was and wanted him to take her upstairs and have his way with her.

He cleaned up and she helped and then they went upstairs and she undressed and stood before Roger, and said master I am here to serve you. Roger sat on the bed and told her to play with herself, she started and he said you dirty bitch do you need a spanking as he stood and opened his cabinet pulling out his strap and rolling it up as she began feeling herself, then he went and took a dildo out and handed it to her and pulled her by her hair and said you little bitch whore you better fuck yourself good and he struck her ass with the strap, she was so very excited now she could hardly stand as he stood back and took several swings at her striking her thighs and ass, then her back as she erupted in another massive climax and had a hard time standing as he held her by her hair, smacking her between her legs as she quivered with a continuous climax. He released her as she sunk down kneeling and bending over as he struck her butt several more times. He told her to lie on her back on the rug, she did spreading her legs wide open, he knelt with his knees on both sides of her head as he rubbed the strap across her wet vagina and whipped her until she climaxed again, and he felt her again causing her to climax until she was completely exhausted. He stood and told her to stand, she had a difficult time as he pulled her up again by her hair and held her as she trembled and holding on to his shirt. She looked up at him and asked him to take her, said she was his bitch. He picked her up and carried her to the bed and laid next to her as he rubbed her head as she pulled him to her kissing him and said please master, please use me. He took his shorts off and spread her legs open and inserted his hard penis in her very wet vagina as he fingered her ass as she climaxed again and he just laid on top of her moving slowly as she cried yes master and had several more organisms as he rolled over placing her on top of him and told her to fuck me bitch as he spanked her ass and he finally climaxed inside of her, and collapsed on top of him holding him tight as he rubbed her back. Rosie began crying as she held on to him tightly. He told her that she was his pretty little bitch and she looked at him and finally felt his face and said please love me forever master. He rolled her to his side as she just curled up in his arms like a baby. He held her until she relaxed, then he led a well exhausted Rosie to the shower where they bathed and soon returned to the bedroom. He oiled her body causing her to climax again and when he finished covered her up, kissed her and he went downstairs to fix himself a drink.

Roger fixed his drink and sat at the table and looked around and thought about all he had accomplished, how he had done it and who was in his life. Just as he finished that thought he looked up and there stood Rosie, standing nude and looking at him as she came and sat in his lap hugging him with tears in her eyes and said she wanted to be with him always. He told her to go put on something; she went upstairs and returned wearing her robe. He fixed her a very potent drink. He returned to the table and placed the drink before her and sat down as she reached and held his hand, kissing it and he asked her, how are you feeling right now. She replied, that she knew he loved her and that was all she needed and wanted and was to serve him, he made her so very happy inside and out. Said she wouldn't know what to do without him now. Told him she knew that was crazy, but he was a savior to her, he satisfied her sexual and mental needs, and couldn't fully explain it but felt blessed to be here with him, she began to cry again. He told her don't cry but to drink up. She sat close to him and he placed a hand on her thigh, she wanted him to feel her, he did and told her she was so very beautiful, cute and sexy. She stood took the robe off and sat in his lap and said she always wanted him to touch her as he did feeling her all over. She loved Roger touching her as he felt her and pinched her nipples as she cringed and smiled at him kissing him again. Rosie had a beautiful shape and it had become more so since being with him in such a short time, she ate much better and more regular, she was happy and told him so and was sexually satisfied. He told her to put her robe on and sit and relax and drink her drink. He had her place a foot in his lap as he rubbed her sexy foot and ankle and calf as she moaned and asked if she could feel herself since he was sending sensations through her, he said you may, as she rubbed herself and he felt her sexy leg and soon she jerked as a climax rippled through her. Roger stopped. They had finished their drinks and he led her upstairs to his bedroom. She climbed into his bed and as she disrobed and laid in the bed he took her feet caressing them as she laid back takin short breaths then he sucked a toe and licked and biting her lightly as he worked up her spread inner thighs, gripping the sheets with unending sensations of pleasure like she had never before experienced working his way up to her vagina, biting her as she screamed and climaxed; as he held her legs apart and licked her clit causing her to raise up and scream as he continued up her body reaching her breast and she was frantic, as he lightly bit her swollen nipples and sucked them and reaching her neck. She was going crazy, he licked her face and fingered her vagina and she just exploded again. She collapsed breathing hard and rapidly as he held her trembling body and began crying again. Roger just pulled the covers over them and held and caressed her until she calmed down. He petted her; she looked at him and smiled. Rosie finally fell into a deep sleep. Roger covered and kissed her, went and checked the house, returned and went to bed and soon fell asleep besides his Rosie.

Chapter Eleven

Very early Tuesday morning Roger woke, went and showered, he returned looking at the clock and woke Rosie; she looked up at him, rubbing the sleep from her pretty eyes, sat up and hugged him. Said she should shower and pulled her up and couldn't help himself, hugging and kissed her on the forehead and looked at her, he couldn't help it but she was looking better every day, he noticed it and she did to and said she had gained five pounds and felt better since Roger had her taking vitamins. Her butt was more firm and round and her breast was starting to get a little larger. She went to her bathroom to shower. He dressed and went to her room and when Rosie came out told her to wear the stocking with the attached garter and then wear her panties over them, she said yes sir master. She asked if there was anything else; he said no, other than eat some breakfast before you leave, yes sir, as he went downstairs to prepare a light breakfast for them both. He had everything ready by the time she came downstairs. Rosie was looking amazingly beautiful and asked her if there was something she had done differently. She said no, only it's a feeling that I've never felt before and can't describe it, but she knew what it was, it was meant for her to be here with him and very soon Victoria and Barbara, missing them both very much. He made her so happy inside just thinking about being here with him gave her great joy and happiness inside. He said have a seat as he prepared her plate. She kissed his hand and said last night was indescribable just thinking about it made her extremely happy. Roger instructed Rosie after eating breakfast to head straight home after work. I will be waiting for you here. Ok Rosie replied. She kissed him and said she would try to get off early if she could, he said ok baby girl see you then, as she departed for work.

He cleaned up the kitchen and knew today was the day he would meet the donation people at his and Rosie's old apartment, and Thursday was Barbara's bed, the furniture for his bedroom, the washer and dryer and refrigerator for downstairs, the television installation, delivery and setup, patio furniture and the rug delivery for the living room. Victoria would also be moving in. An hour after Rosie had left for work she called and said the bed store had called her and asked for a deliver date and told them Thursday, and wondered if that was all right. Sure it is and good thinking baby, said she loved him and ended the call. Soon after Victoria called and said the bed store had called her and asked for a deliver date and wanted to know what day was convenient, he said tell them Thursday, she said she loved him and would call back after they confirmed the delivery date and approximate time. Ten minutes later she called back and confirmed Thursday afternoon. He said very well then. He thought all three bedroom sets on Thursday plus Victoria moving in, was a plan in motion and knew Thursday would just be a hive of activity here. Starting the plan in motion Roger went upstairs to Victoria's closet and began taking the clothes out of the large bags and hanging them up looking at some of the sexy dresses which she has worn in the past when they went out.

He almost forgot as he looked at the time, he had to go to the old apartment and let the donation people in, having more than an hour, as he headed to his bedroom and dressed, and prepared to leave. He would be happy getting this out of the way. He arrived several minutes before the truck arrived and opened the doors to both apartments. The two men soon emptied both apartments and Roger locked up and walked over and checked both mail boxes one last time. Good there wasn't any mail in either one as he now headed over to the apartment complex office and informed the agent that he had moved and also Ms. Cramer. Roger asked for an early termination release or could he schedule a formal inspection. The agent asked if he could inspect the apartments now. Roger said he sure could, as they walked together back to the units and the agent had inspection sheets for both apartments. The agent found both units clean and in very good condition and released Roger and Ms. Cramer from their leases. Roger then handed over both sets of keys. Rosie for a month and two months for him as Roger signed for the both of them, and the agent handed him the release form for both the apartments. Roger also gave him the new address where to send their security deposits checks to. Shook the agents hand and said thank you very much as he departed. As he left he thought, finally that was all taken care of and would inform Rosie when she came home as they went for her new car as he got in his truck and now drove home.

After getting in the truck, thought they would need more bed sheets and soon was parking in front of a large department store. He entered and headed straight to the linen department and picked up three kings side mattress covers and six sets of sheets in various colors. He thought this should be a good start for them and knew over time everyone would eventually purchase additional sets. When he finally returned home decided to eat the rest of his unfinished salad from the day before. He sat down after opening a bottle of chilled red wine and started to have lunch and to his surprise, Rosie walked in and kissed him. She had taken the rest of the day off early as she washed her hands and took out the remainder of her salad also. They sat and had lunch together. He informed her she didn't need to pay the next month's rent and had acted on her behalf as far as her lease was concerned and they would also send the security deposit checks here, and had her release form. After eating and cleaning up he asked her if she was ready, she said yes sir with an air of excitement in her voice. He asked her to go get the title to her car, as she then scurried off upstairs to retrieve it, she soon returned with an envelope and handed it to him, he checked the contents, it was her title and they prepared to leave.

He returned to the same automobile dealer where he had purchased his truck. They rode together in Rosie's old car; it was much older than his old car and the exterior wasn't in the best of shape but it ran fairly well. He would handle this as a corporate write off on his taxes and would do the same for both Barbara and Victoria, paying off the remainder of their auto loans. He believed in treating them all the same in a fair and equitable fashion, since they were all very committed to him, and didn't want one thinking they were more or less special than the other. He and Rosie walked inside and the salesman he had yesterday approached and asked if he had a problem. Roger said oh no, he was here to purchase a car for his lovely secretary. Roger asked Rosie to look around and pick the one she might like. The salesman showed her several models with a variety of options. Rosie soon approached Roger asking if she could get anything she wanted, he said yes. After a short time looking around and sitting in several different models, Rosie showed them both the one she really wanted; it had all the options, was a burgundy color and was on the lot outside. The salesman said they would very soon have it ready and he asked about the trade in. Roger said its parked right outside and asked them to transfer her license plates, the salesman said that was not even a problem and then asked about financing. Roger handed him his corporate card, again. The day before Roger had checked his balance and kept a sharp eye on his personal finances knowing this was just a drop in the bucket, it he didn't spend it he would have to pay tax on it. Rosie was now very excited as Roger told the salesman to put Ms. Cramer's name on the title, he said no problem. While the salesman filled out the paper work, Roger whispered to Rosie to go to the washroom and take her panties off and return and be sure she didn't touch herself, she blushed and did as Roger asked, returning shortly.

The salesman was soon finished with the paper work before Rosie returned. He went to check on how much longer the preparations would take to the car and returned saying it wouldn't be too much longer as Rosie returned and signed the sales receipts and the other needed paper work as Roger just sat looking at her. She looked like she had gone to heaven and returned. It wasn't long before they pulled the car around in front and the salesman asked Rosie to come with him as Roger followed. The salesman opened the door for her while stepping inside her new auto, he help show her how to sync her phone and explained where the different controls were. Roger asked where's the garage door remote, she answered it's in her purse. She familiarized herself with the controls and the salesman thanked Roger again shaking his hand as he got inside. Rosie then pulled off. He asked her to check the gas tank and told her to stop and fill up. Roger did the honors and got back inside as Rosie now headed home. She thanked Roger for the car as they approached the gate, Roger asked her for the remote, and paired the gate to her car and once that was done had her pull in front of the last garage door and paired that one also, then explained she didn't need the remote any longer and would kept the remote in the kitchen drawer along with all the others. They stepped out after she backed inside the garage and she was so very excited and hugged Roger and thanked him again and started crying and said no one had ever done what he had done for her as he held her close. They went inside and she hugged him again and he told her it was time for some pictures and they went upstairs and he poised her sitting at his desk and when he was finally finished she was only wearing her stocking and high heel shoes. He then held her and asked who she belonged to, she replied that she was his bitch, as he felt her now very wet with excitement vagina causing her to climax repeatedly. She held him tightly kissing and thanking him before he released her and told her to go put on some clothes. She came back bare foot in her dress and hugging him again. Roger told her she made him very happy as well, before heading downstairs to cook. It was a nice day outside as he opened the kitchen windows and prepared some fish and a side dish of vegetables with a salad as she assisted him and they talked. His small television was on the end of the counter by the window as they watched the early evening news and began cooking, setting the table and holding one another.

Rosie said thank you again as she looked at him and tried to hold back her tears, and then she just began crying profusely, as Roger came and held her again as she clung to him. He held her, caressing her as she slowly calmed down and pressed against him having another climax. Roger held and kissed her and asked her to pour them a couple glasses of wine. Roger picked up his phone and called Barbara and asked her to bring her payment book for her auto loan, she said ok, and would see him soon. He then called Victoria and asked her to do the same thing. Victoria replied she would just bring the box with all her records and information since she didn't trust the movers with it and didn't need them now anyway. He had fixed enough for all of them, and asked Rosie to set two more places. They talked and commented on the news and within the hour Barbara walked in the front door and not long after was soon followed by Victoria with her banker's box, setting it down near the stairs. Roger asked Barbara and Victoria to wash their hands and have a seat, after they returned he explained that he was going to pay off their auto loans. Barbara had just purchased her auto six months ago and Victoria a little more than nine months earlier. He explained he had purchased a new truck for himself and a new car for Rosie; and decided they all needed a fresh start. This would be a write off for him and would allow him to see how their expenses here would be, and it would save them all money and allow them to furnish their rooms the way they wanted, including the entire house over time. Barbara said she wanted to see the new rides as her and Victoria excitedly headed to the garage and when they returned Barbara hugged him and said it's about time and Victoria said thank you master. The food was done as he and Rosie prepared everyone's plates and set the food on the table. They said grace together as he poured wine for all and they began eating, Victoria asked for seconds and he said help yourself and told them they didn't have to ask because they all lived here. He and Rosie cleaned up the kitchen and washed the dishes.

Soon after dinner Barbara hugged him and said she wanted him now and to please take her upstairs. He and Barbara went upstairs and undressed, climbing in bed as he felt and kissed her, licking her vagina before he spanked her. She moaned and said I love you so much master as she climaxed before he climbed on top of her; they had sex and soon climaxed together. She was now very satisfied as they went to his bathroom and showered together having more sex and telling him it had been too long being away from him and was glad she was moving in next week. She said Victoria is about to go crazy since she hasn't had any sex since the old apartment and when she moves in will be all over you. Roger said he could see it in her eyes now and would be ready for her. She thanked him for paying off her loan. She loved him so much as tears formed in her eyes as they held each other. He told her they made him so very happy with them in his life, it was the least he could do and just liked making them happy also and besides he needed to spend it or have to pay tax on just having it. She kissed him and didn't want to let him go and said she needed to get back home for now so she could go to work and said she felt so much better now. They dressed and headed downstairs where Victoria and Rosie were hugging one another and crying, and when he appeared they came and hugged and kissed him. He said ladies please, as they said you are too good to be true, and we love you very much.

Barbara said she had to go and thanked him for dinner and took Victoria by the hand and said to her you need to get ready for Thursday and know you have to work tomorrow. He kissed them both as they departed and looked at the clock. He thought about tomorrow and would take care of the auto loans early and prepare for Thursday and try getting a little rest. The rest of the evening he and Rosie drank wine and finally closed up the kitchen. She went and showered in her bathroom and returned as they climbed in bed and kissing before going to sleep. The wine and excitement of the day took its toll as Rosie soon began sleeping very soundly.

The following morning after he and Rosie woke up, they cleaned up, dressed and had breakfast together. He asked what she was wearing underneath her dress, and she replied what the master required of her, which was the crotch less pantyhose. He said good girl as he hugged her and she departed for work with the biggest smile on her face ever. He took his time since it was still early and finally dressed after cleaning up the kitchen and deciding what he would prepare for dinner. His phone rang and it was Barbara, he answered and she said that she loved him and just wanted him to know and how happy she felt and wished him a very happy and wonderful day. Said he loved her and wished her the same as they disconnected. He sat at his desk as he retrieved Barbara's paper work and payment book and slid it in a folder, then looked at Victoria's and did the same and placed them both in his briefcase and soon headed out. He got in his new truck and was happy as he pulled out and watched the garage door close and headed to the bank where Victoria worked and had financed her auto loan. After arriving he signed in and waited for a bank representative to appear, amazingly it was Victoria, she said please wait a moment as she felt someone else should handle this and knew he was here for her loan. A few minutes later a man appeared assuming it was an employee and asked Roger to follow him and to sit down asking him what can he do for him today? Roger replied I'm here to pay off a friend's auto loan and made sure they had the correct address. It was confirmed that they did as he used his business card again, and shortly the transaction was completed. Roger stood up and shook his hand and thanked him. As Roger was about to leave Victoria walked up dressed very professionally and looking very sexy and thanked him. He then bent over and kissed her cheek, whispering to her what he had in store for her tomorrow night. While she blushed, turned and departed to her desk watching him leaving. She stood and watched him leave before returning to her desk, then went to the washroom after thinking about what Roger said that had excited her so much as she went to go relieve herself and calm down.

He then drove to the second location which was the credit union where he used to work and where he had also met Barbara. The credit union was open as Roger approached the counter and explained why he was there, and was asked to have a seat at a nearby desk. Roger remembered the man who came to assist him. He also remembered Roger as they shook hands. Mr. Tomas took the information and Roger handed him his corporate card and paid off Barbara's auto loan and did a change of address for the title and soon that business was finally completed as Mr. Tom inquired as to how he was doing. Roger responded he was doing very well as he stood to leave; he thanked Mr. Tomas and departed. Roger got inside his vehicle and was happy that he had accomplished all he had set out to do and that his girls would be free and clear on their finances once they had moved in. He took himself to lunch again and decided he wanted an Italian beef sandwich and French fries and stopped at a nearby restaurant and placed his order along with a small pasta salad. While he sat an ate thought about dinner and what he should cook, thinking he should fix something that they could have for tomorrow since he wouldn't have time with all that would be going on. He finished his lunch and decided to do some grocery shopping and would buy some frozen Italian beef and bread which would make nice snacks during the busy day tomorrow.

Roger stopped at the nearest grocery store to the house and none were in walking distance. The neighborhood was all large homes on large lots and you definitely needed a car. Shopping was a favorite of Rogers because he loved to cook and eat. He shopped and purchased some fresh condiments since he had trashed everything from his old refrigerator. Finally he finished shopping and checked out, noticed he had spent close to a hundred dollars, and found it convenient placing items in the back of the truck and had asked for some boxes before he left the store. He drove home and backed inside setting everything inside the back door first. He washed his hands and put the food away and then took his briefcase upstairs taking the documents out and left them on his desk and would total everything up after he changed clothes. He changed and sat at his desk and began totaling everything up and filing the documents away for when tax time rolled around and left Barbara's and Victoria's documents out for them to look at if they wanted to see them before he would file them away in his new filing cabinet. He decided he would fix some spaghetti sauce, and then tomorrow all they would have to do is heat the sauce and boil some pasta.

He headed downstairs to accomplish his next mission, removing enough ground meat from the freezer and taking it out to thaw. He then went through the house opening some windows an arriving back in the kitchen as he turned on the television. He listened more than looking at the noon day news that was almost over and soon turned it off and turning on the radio instead. He began taking out his ingredients, and removing his large Dutch oven from the cabinet. Dinner was on Rogers mind and was getting hungry and decided to cook some of his tasty spaghetti sauce which everyone loves and then tomorrow all they would have to do is heat the sauce and boil some pasta. After preparing all the ingredients to go into his sauce he started cooking, putting on a large pot of water for the pasta. Then he sat and had a glass of wine, and was happy that this week had been very productive as he cleared up old business, for instance, donating his and Rosie's old furniture, buying his new truck, and her new car, paying off Barbara and Victoria's auto loans and getting ready for a new adventure of actually living with the women in his life all under one roof. He knew this might be a mentally trying experience, but should prove to be beneficial for all of them and much more convenient and financially a step in the right direction for them and him also. He stood and decided to start cooking now and watched as his vegetables sautéed in the pot and covered them and sipping on more wine, and returned to open the cans of tomatoes and mushrooms mixing and seasoned them in a large bowl before he would add them as he turned the fire down to simmer. One thing Roger noticed was how much better this stove cooked than the one at the old apartment, and he thought you do get what you pay for, and you shouldn't ever be cheap with yourself, something his mother used to tell him. Roger watched his food, and as the vegetables simmered he added the tomatoes and began placing the thin angel hair pasta in the boiling water, then taking out his collider and had it ready as he stirred the pasta, it wasn't long before it had finished cooking and he placed the collider in the sink and poured the pasta out, drained and rinsed it and then let it sit in the pot on the stove covering it. He stirred his sauce as it simmered and was soon turning the fire out. He looked at the clock and it would be a little more than an hour before Rosie arrived home. Going upstairs he sat at his desk and looked for landscaping companies and had seen a few working in the neighborhood and had written down their phone numbers.

The grass outside was getting very long and hadn't been cut in two or maybe three weeks and the bushes needed trimming and were showing new buds as the signs of spring were abound, one thing for sure with a lawn this large he would be crazy if he thought he could manage it by himself, just like painting the house. The other thing he knew for sure was he really moved up scale when he moved here and now would need to use more maintenance services, besides; he wasn't a renter any longer. He called one maintenance service and asked them to come today and give him an estimate and they said not until Friday. So then he called another one, and asked the same thing. The last company he called said they would come today in about an hour and were nearby in the neighborhood. Soon his doorbell was ringing and a man appeared at the front door; his truck and trailer were in the driveway loaded with equipment and his crew. He and Roger walked around and surveyed the property and the man, and older gentleman with a pleasant smile, a

Mr. Rodrigues, said he would charge him three hundred a month and that would include any and all landscaping and would include trimming the trees also. He said they would come once a week on, as he pulled out a slightly worn note book from his shirt pocket and looked and asked if Wednesday was ok. Roger felt it was a very fair price since it included everything and being on over an acre knew it was no small task and more than he could ever handle by himself. He shook Mr. Rodrigues hand and said it was a deal. Mr. Rodrigues said he had contracts in his truck and Roger said fine and asked if he would give him a moment as Roger went inside and soon returning with his check book. Roger signed a contract for one years' service and paid him up front for six months. Mr. Rodrigues said to call him Juan and said he would begin today, and also informed Roger that they plow the snow during the winter months. Roger thanked him as Juan returned to his truck and five other men got out and took out there equipment from the large trailer attached to the rear of the truck and three rode out of the back on mowers and began cutting the grass and cleaning up the property. Roger called the first company and cancelled the appointment, and thanked them. They asked why he had cancelled and Roger said he found someone else and hung up.

Juan's crew quickly went all around the house cutting grass and pruning bushes and trimmed most of the trees cutting back the low hanging limbs and pruning others and cleaned up the entire property as Roger looked out from inside. They handled the job in no time with the large ride around mowers as the three whizzed around with one guy trimming the trees as he walked around and a third trimming bushes then having a leaf blower blowing the small clippings and trimmings away. There were two more men with blowers and they finished and cleaned up and prepared to leave as Roger came outside and thanked them for the fine job. He and Juan walked around and Roger said he was very satisfied with the way things looked; it made the house stand out so much more and didn't look neglected any longer. It was looking like someone lives here, as he walked around and thought about next year, thinking what he might add to the landscaping or would just leave it the way it was since it was designed to be low maintenance and in the winter there was plenty of room to push the plowed snow off to the side. He sat on the front steps and admired the foliage and thought about where he had moved from and the park like setting and now felt like he moved to the center of the park. He was becoming more and more satisfied with his new home and his decision to move as every day passed and didn't know how long he had sat there before Rosie drove up the driveway and waved as she drove pass heading to park inside the garage. He watched the garage door close and a few minutes later she came out the front door and sat beside him, kissed him and said she noticed the change as soon as she pulled off the street and drove down the driveway and commented on how much better it now looked. He said yes and stated he had a gardener now and they would come every Wednesday.

They stood and went inside the house as he hugged her tight and said how sweet she smelled, she smiled and told him she wanted to change and could smell the food and said she was very hungry. Rosie went upstairs to change. Roger went to the kitchen and took out the plates and silverware to set the table. Rosie came downstairs relaxed and as lovely as ever and he asked her to fix her own plate if she wanted and she did just that. He had purchased some readymade coleslaw and placed some in two small dishes for them. They sat down eating together and drinking red wine telling him about her day at work and how her coworkers asked her where did she buy her new car. Said they wondered how she could drive such an expensive auto on her salary. She told them she had saved up for it and that she deserved it. Roger said that was a very good answer my dear and that people are always trying to get into other people business. Rosie said the food was delicious, as Roger said he prepared it for tomorrow because with all the planned activity he wouldn't be able to do much cooking and had bought some Italian beef for sandwiches also for tomorrow. She understood and got a little more and returned. He said that's where the five pounds came from. And said from you're cooking. She complimented him on the dinner and would help clean up. Roger finished eating and sat back and drank his wine and looked at her, she smiled back at him and blushed. He told her she was a lot of fun as he stood and rinsed his plate off before placing it in the sink while she began washing the dishes. Soon they had cleaned up and he said the sauce would have to cool a little while longer before he could put it away. He stated one day we will be able to walk around the corner there and sit down on our new couch, but tomorrow we will be able to at least sit outside on our new patio furniture.

She said oh great my bed will be here. He said yours, Victoria's and Barbara's and wondered how many trucks they would send or if they figured that one out yet. She laughed and told him you will soon find out. He said lets walk around outside to look around the grounds since he hadn't done so since moving in. She said she needed some shoes and ran upstairs and returned with her running shoes in her hand slipping them on as they walked out the front door. They circled the house as he looked at the exterior more closely and then they walked further away where the trees stood and there was a fence bordering one whole side of the property and then in a corner another fence and beyond that a large expansive and grassy area. Roger knew that was part of the church grounds next door, and could hardly see the house from here because of the trees that hadn't fully bloomed yet as they walked the perimeter of the property following the fence line then to another corner where the tall decorative fence began which eventually led to the front gates. Walked pass and continued to follow the fence until it ended in another corner and they came to a tall wood plank fence that evidently belonged to their neighbors and followed it until it ended and then another style of wooden fence began, it ran about halfway until it came to a tall cyclone fence that connected with the fence on the church side. Every time they had looked back toward the house they could only see a portion of it, maybe a wall or the roof and only really could see it clearly when they had crossed the driveway from the front gate. They walked back toward the house and the grounds where all the grass and trees bordering the perimeter were and the house was really hidden out of sight to be in such a large open area. Roger was glad the trees weren't very close to the house as they walked back sitting on the front steps as Rosie sat next to him, she reached and held his hand and kissed it.

After a short while they decided to go inside and Roger checked his pot and it had cooled down enough to put the food away taking out two large plastic containers. He filled both containers and what was left in the pot was slightly more than another full container and placed that in a smaller pot for tomorrow as the containers went to the freezer and the pot the refrigerator. Rosie washed the large Dutch oven as Roger poured another glass of wine. Rosie set the large pot on the rack and joined him. Roger soon closed the windows downstairs and said it was time for them both to shower and he was going to bed early so he could be on top of things tomorrow. She agreed as they went upstairs and showered together, both bathed one another as she made love to him as the water ran over them and was happy when Roger came in her mouth, she swallowed all his come as he felt her and she climaxed several times. After they finished, oiled one another as he felt her and she climaxed again before climbing into bed, hugging him until he turned over and went to sleep.

Chapter Twelve

Thursday, the big moving and delivery day had finally arrived, and Roger, woke refreshed, and was more fresh and calm than usual, probably because he had beautiful sex with Rosie, who helped him to become more relaxed now and besides he had accomplished quite a bit since first proposing the question of merging and combining households to Barbara and Victoria. He went and did his usual morning wakeup thing since getting up earlier than normal. He didn't wake Rosie, he just let her sleep. He went downstairs and opened the kitchen windows a little since it was a little nippy outside as he put on his morning coffee, turned on the television, and listened for the weather report knowing that delivery men and movers always got an early start. He headed to the front door and opened the panel with the gate control opening them, he could see them from here and it looked almost far away but wasn't as he returned to have his first cup of coffee. He started to prepare breakfast and decided to have some cheese toast this morning with onions and peppers in his eggs. He placed his bacon in a pan with a little oil over a low fire and covered it, then began preparing the eggs, turned the oven on, took a flat pan out, and began laying out several slices of bread for him and Rosie. Placed it in the oven and took out the cheese and laid some slices to the side as he ate a couple, then took out an onion and bell pepper. He decided, looking at the clock to wake sleeping beauty. While going upstairs she was just waking up. They hugged then she got up to go to the bathroom. Roger went back downstairs and drank more coffee. He opened the oven door and turned his bread over and then checked his slow cooking bacon and turned it over and prepared an aluminum pan lining it with paper towels placing the bacon in the pan when done. Soon he added the cheese on the bread in the oven and began dicing his onions and bell peppers preparing to scramble his eggs. Breakfast was ready when Rosie walked downstairs saying it sure smells good and I'm starving. She was dressed very nice and ready for work. Roger really admired the woman she had become and was very proud of her. In the meantime he fixed their plates as they both sat down to eat. Rosie finished eating and said it was early and had another cup of coffee. She again thanked Roger whom she adored for a wonderful and delicious breakfast. Rosie told Roger that she was sorry because she wouldn't be with him when her bed arrived but will be happy to get it and Roger said he would to, as she looked a little disappointed by his comment. He noticed her look and said you won't be alone any longer.

They were sitting and talking when the doorbell rang and Roger answered it. He opened the door and it was the bedding store delivery people and he recognized the man from when his bed was delivered. The deliveryman said he had two bedroom sets and needed to know where to place them, Roger said they all go upstairs and asked what were the names on the orders, he said Rosie Cramer and Barbara Sims, Roger took him up on the elevator again and the man said he remembered being here because of the elevator which was such a huge help. Roger said the Sims set goes here and Cramer over here. Roger asked if he was bringing all the pieces up first before setting them up and he answered yes. Roger said to get him if he had any questions about placing the furniture, and asked if he would give him a minute. Roger brought Rosie upstairs and told her to show the man where she wanted her bed to go. He thanked her as she turned to Roger and said she better leave now while she could, she kissed him and said see you later, as she departed for work. Roger then showed him where Barbara wanted her set placed. He thanked Roger. Roger had more coffee and cleaned up the kitchen and opened the windows as the outside temperature rose to more comfortable levels. After forty minutes the bed delivery men had brought both sets upstairs and Roger asked if they would pull their truck closer to the side of the driveway because there were more deliveries coming, they said sure and pulled up turning around and down the driveway.

It was good Rosie left when she did which was a little early for her by almost half an hour because soon another truck arrived and Roger was glad he had such a large area for them to turn around in, and it was the patio set, he directed them to the quickest way around back, it didn't take them long before the set was sitting on the raised patio deck, Roger inspected the set, signed the receipt and they departed just in time as Victoria pulled up and opened her garage door and backed inside. She was followed by a truck a few minutes later. She left the garage door open came and kissed him as her truck backed up to the front doors. They opened the back door and extended a ramp to the top step and Victoria showed them where her things were going and the elevator they could use. The bedroom setup took about half an hour for each set. The delivery men were taking out the packaging materials as Victoria's movers were finished moving her belongings inside. Roger checked the new bed installations making sure they didn't block any receptacles when they were finished setting them up and signed for them both. They took the paper and plastic wrapping with them as they departed, then Victoria's movers were soon finished and quickly departed. After that another truck came and the men brought the large area rug for the living room rolled it out and soon departed after Roger signed. Soon after they had departed, the furniture truck arrived with his couch set and Roger showed them where it was going and soon they had it all set up in his bedroom, he showed them where the largest couch would go including the end table, love seat and chair. They finished rather quickly and took the packing materials then departed. Ten minutes later Victoria's bed arrived, a different crew this time and Roger showed them the elevator and introduced them to Victoria as she showed them where to set it up, fortunately the elevator had pads to protect the inside and Roger had never taken them down and was glad he didn't, but knew this was the easiest way to move furniture with the house having six huge bedrooms to move into and fortunately it was oversized and the door height was taller than he had seen in other home elevators, they were eight foot tall, and the load capacity was 4500lbs. Roger returned downstairs just as the electronics store delivery men came along with a separate instillation crew and Roger showed them what wall he wanted the television on an fortunately Rogers bedroom doors were eight foot double doors, the ceilings were very high on both levels, no lower than eight and the average was about ten. After they arrived the washer and dryer came along with the fridge for the basement and Roger let them in thru the garage since it was the shortest route to the laundry room and basement. This was almost the last of the all-day deliveries, as Roger looked at the clock and within another couple of hours Rosie would be returning home. The washer and dryer were installed and the refrigerator was installed and plugged in, Roger signed again, thanked them as they departed. The technicians located the wall studs and had installed the wall mount for the television, Roger thought 4K, the technology continues to advance and found it fascinating since he had worked as an electronic technician. He had purchased the best and most advanced, and so this should be very enjoyable since it would be Wi-Fi ready. They worked on the portion of the wall mount that attached directly to the television and hung the huge screen on the wall mount and it came with extra-long cables which he requested when he purchased it. The salesman showed him some shelves and he showed them where he wanted them placed; and next hooked up the antenna, positioned it where Roger would receive the most stations, then hooked a long cable near the window programed it again and it received the same amount of stations. The tech compared it to a list before they mounted it behind the television out of sight and preformed another tuning test with and without an amplifier and it had the max amount of stations for this area, 56, that was great. The best he had ever received at the apartment complex was 50, and was satisfied with the reception and the clarity of the picture. They checked with Roger to see if he was satisfied as he signed and all of them packed up and departed. They finished just about the same time the bedroom people had finished setting up Victoria's bed. The last delivery came, his cabinets for his bedroom and the living room furniture, he showed them where and they loaded them up on the elevator and into his room and set the other in the large living room. All the movers and delivery people had come and gone, he finally was able to close the front doors and the garage doors.

Everything that was to be delivered had arrived as Roger went to his bedroom and made some minor adjustments to the new furniture, arranging it some before he sat down and looked around. This made a big difference now that he was able to sit down comfortably as he turned the wall on, that's what he called it, The Wall because even though the ceiling was ten feet, it looked like the wall had come alive after looking at small screens until now. He sat for several minutes just looking but was beginning to get hungry since he missed lunch and turned the TV off and went downstairs taking out the pot of spaghetti sauce from the fridge, turning on a very low fire on the stove and taking out a larger pot and began to boil some water for some pasta, and he still had some coleslaw left. This won't take long as he went and sat out on the new patio furniture set, it was very comfortable and he enjoyed how comfortable it was. He went back inside and checked on his water, it was boiling, he added his salt and a little cooking oil and a package of pasta and slowly stirred it and watch it closely, he detested over cooked pasta, he checked it and waited until it was just right and tender, pulled a strand out and ate it, waited another minute as he stirred it and checked it again, and poured it into the collider, rinsed it and let it drain over the pot on the stove. He stirred his sauce as it was almost ready as he took out some French bread, slicing it and arranged it in an aluminum pan and warming it in the oven as he made some homemade garlic bread, melted some butter and adding garlic salt, when he finished, coating the bread and placing it back in the oven they would have some garlic bread, then turned the sauce off. It wasn't long before he went upstairs and found Victoria, she was busy in her room as time had just passed her by and that's when she realized she was hungry, suddenly Rosie walked in from work. He told Rosie to wash her hands and said dinner is served. He fixed there plates and poured some wine with bread and coleslaw on the table. They all said their blessings and began eating. Roger was a very good cook and could season food really well. Roger wasn't talking much because a headache was bothering him and he knew why. Their food was so delicious and Rogers's headache had subsided once he started eating. While eating Barbara entered through the front door and washed her hands joining them. Roger wasn't surprised that she was here because he knew she wanted to see her new bed. They ate and there was plenty for all of them. When they all had finished he rinsed there dishes off and left them in the dish water until later, as they all ascended the stairs. Barbara got in her bed as Rosie headed to hers. Barbara said now all we need are some sheets and on my way home I will pick up several sets. Roger then remembered he had the two Rosie had purchased along with extra mattress covers. Barbara kissed him and said she would see them Saturday. Roger walked her to her car as they kissed. He said he would buy more sheets tomorrow and she didn't have to stop, she said ok and told her they would be over early and would bring the containers Victoria had and help her finish with her packing. And since he had the truck he could bring her delicate things, documents and papers, and her pillows and stay here until the movers came. She said that sounds like a plan, he said not unless you have a better one, she shook her head no as she got in her car and turned around and headed home.

Roger went inside after saying goodbyes to Barbara and started cleaning the kitchen, washing the dishes and pots, and cleaned up the table. Took his vitamins and drank half a bottle of water and went outside and sat down on a patio chair, looking around and saying now he had a starting point, he had a grill and some chairs and that was a beginning. It wasn't long before Victoria came outside and hugged him and said I'm here, and what was that you said to me the other day at work, told him it had made her so excited she had to go calm herself down and said you are a dirty old man as she sat in his lap playing with his hair. He opened her blouse and rubbed her firm round breast in his face as he tried to grab a nipple with his mouth and she let him, then she sat in the chair next to Roger and asked if they had any beer, he said yes as she stood to go inside and asked her to bring him one also, she came back with two very cold beers and they sat and she looked around saying it is really beautiful out here. He told her about Rosie and him walking around the fence line yesterday and then him having hired a lawn service and how you hardly could see the house. She said this is like being in a park and more so than your old apartment, he responded that he agreed with her. Said he was tired from all the activity today and would go inside soon and then asked her if she was squared away. She said almost and had put most of her clothes away and arraigned her room and would see as time went on what else she wanted or needed. He said the same for him, since the couch came today along with the television. Victoria opened her blouse and said that feels so good and looked at him looking at her and smiled as she jiggled them at him. He knew he was tired and she did to, and after they finished drinking they went inside as he commented he hadn't seen Rosie. He closed up the downstairs as she went around with him as they checked the house before heading upstairs and soon found Rosie asleep on his couch. They left her and he grabbed his robe and towel and went with her to her bedroom and they put the mattress cover on her bed and he went back and returned with the only other set of sheets he had washed so far and then made her bed up and Victoria threw a spread and a blanket on the bed and they left to shower together.

It was his first time in the her bedroom other than looking at it and hanging her clothes up; they undressed and showered together, they both were very tired and just bathed and dried off one another then oiling themselves, climbed into her bed, kissing and hugging and a short while later both had fallen asleep.

Friday when Roger woke, he looked over at Victoria and climbed out of bed. He went to his bathroom and Rosie was still sleeping, only she had gotten in his bed sometime after he and Victoria had gone to bed. He went and washed up. Got dressed and went downstairs to fix his coffee. He pulled out some coffee cake waiting on the coffee to brew. When it was ready he poured a cup, cut a piece of cake, sat down and drank his coffee and ate the cake. A few minutes after eating his cake and pouring another cup of coffee Rosie came downstairs in her robe, she hugged him and poured herself some coffee also, saw the cake and cut a piece for herself and sat down. He asked her how she slept; she said very well, saying the couch is very comfortable. Yes we know when we saw you were asleep which we figured was a clue. Victoria came downstairs in her robe and kissed them both and poured herself a cup of coffee and sat down with them. Rosie looked at the time and said she had to get ready and ran upstairs. Vicky asked him what was on the agenda for today, he said sheets; he had to get enough sheets and said it was time to wash the ones on his bed. He then poured another cup and brought the remaining coffee cake to the table and Victoria ate some this time. Victoria said she would spend the day with him, and he replied that sounds so wonderful. He cleaned up and rinsed the pot out as Rosie came downstairs and said she would stop for breakfast on her way to work kissing and hugging them both and departed.

After Rosie left, Victoria and Roger returned upstairs and went to their bedrooms to dress and when Roger finished he stripped the bed of all the linen and would place it in the washer on his way out. Roger looked around and thought there still was a lot to do as he checked the weather and headed downstairs with the dirty linen placing it in the washer and added the detergent and set it to wash in cold water and waited for Victoria, then remembered about the sheets in his truck and went and brought them inside along with the mattress covers and placed the new sheets in the other two washing machines. Victoria came down shortly and they headed out in his truck left to have breakfast and arrived at a restaurant enjoying a great meal. They talked about decorating the house. After they had finished, he drove to the bulk retail store which sold sheets as he checked the thread counts and they were 400 and better but he felt there sheets were overpriced. They went to another department store and they had a better quality and the count was above a thousand and was forty dollars a set and purchasing eight sets in various colors. They went to the bed store and they had 1500 thread count for forty dollars a set and he purchased ten more sets. He asked her if she had anywhere she wanted to go and she said no, just wanted to finish unpacking and getting her room together. After arriving back home Roger dropped all the sheets in the laundry room and began washing them after placing the sets he had washed in the dryer. He placed three sets in each machine and started them up; they were extra-large capacity washing machines which was great as he left to put his shorts on since Victoria had already gone upstairs. He needed to collect her empty containers and bring them downstairs for tomorrow to help Barbara pack. He went to Victoria's bedroom and stacked all the empty containers gathering all the lids and brought them to the elevator and returned for the empty boxes, broke them down as Victoria said leave one please, he did taking the boxes and going downstairs to the laundry room and opened the door and propped it open and opened the truck bed and placed all the containers and boxes inside and closed the tail gate.

Beginning to get hungry he returned inside he began to prepare lunch, they would have the Italian beef, he took it out and ran warm water over one of the containers since he had bought several and loved having the upright freezer right here with its large capacity. He took out a pot and a couple jalapeno peppers and a bell pepper, cleaned and sliced them and with his small fry pan adding oil and soon added the peppers to a pan with a low flame and did the same for the beef and covered both as he removed the bread and took out several of the small buns and placed them in an aluminum pan and placed them in the over at a low setting. He returned upstairs to Victoria's bedroom and found her finishing up, he said he was going to change and would return shortly and had started fixing lunch. He changed and went downstairs and turned the fire up a little higher under the frozen beef and covered it. He went to the laundry and placed the sheets in the dryers. He took the remaining sets and placed them in the washers and returned to the kitchen, stirring the beef and taking the bread out and turning the oven off. He stirred the peppers and covered them again.

It wasn't long before lunch was ready, turned the stove off, the beef and peppers were done and took out the mustard and went and found Victoria. Brought her downstairs where he fixed the sandwiches placing the peppers and mustard on them. He looked and took out the remaining coleslaw and placed it on the plates with the sandwiches and took everything to the table where Victoria was patiently waiting. She enjoyed the sandwich and slaw since he said this was a light lunch. Roger went and brought back two glasses and a bottle of red wine that was from yesterday, and they drank the remainder.

He cleaned up after they ate and went upstairs with her and said she was going to finish up as he went to his bedroom and started arraigning the furniture in the room. He arraigned the cables under his desk and moved the cabinets where he wanted and had everything neatly arraigned to his liking, with the widest couch facing the television and turned on his computer, the television and went into the setting and connected the television to the WI FI, once he had that accomplished he could project the computer to the television and it was connected to the internet. He turned to a broadcast station before he turned it off. He went downstairs and finished washing the sheets placing the remaining ones in the washer and taking the dried ones out. Victoria found him and helped him fold the sheets that were in the dryer. He then took the ones that were washing and placed them in the dryer. Roger started upstairs putting a mattress cover on her bed and the freshly washed new sheets on Barbara's bed and proceeded to do the same for Rosie. After finishing Victoria brought it to Rogers's attention that she had been really a bad girl and giving Roger hints on what she wanted from him. Soon he surprised her and they headed to her bedroom and he told her to undress. Victoria was so horny when he held her, spanked her a couple times and made her bend over as he spanked her again and feeling her warmth, she just exploded with a loud moan. He pushed her down on the bed and rolled her over as she reached up and pulled him on top of her kissing him madly as she opened her legs then he entered her taking a nipple in his mouth as she climaxed several times until he pulled out, raised her legs up and entering her anus as he came inside her, then laid next to her as she held him and they kissed madly.

They both were exhausted from the day's activities, even though they continued to feel on each other. It was early evening and they just lay in each other's arms. Victoria said she really missed him. He said we should shower and they decided to use her bathroom, he had showered in Barbara's and now it was Victoria's turn. They entered and her bath was similar but different as they entered the walk-in shower together and turned the water on and had to wait until it heated up. Victoria bathed him and he bathed her; as they felt one another and she climaxed again as he felt her all over with the soap. Soon they were finished, drying each other off and returning to spread the towels out on the bed. Victoria being a feminine woman loved her scented oils and got a bottle from her dresser and they began oiling each other. After finishing and being a little exhausted they both climbed into bed falling asleep in each other's arms.

When they woke it was Rosie coming home as she entered she started looking for them after seeing their cars in the garage and finding the house so quiet, walking around until she found them, saw that they were sleeping together and decided to wake them up. He and Victoria had slept at least three to four hours. We both needed and wanted sex and it was so good. After Rosie woke them she left to change into something much more comfortable. Roger then gathered their dirty clothes and he put on some clean clothes to go downstairs to finish washing. Victoria came downstairs and helped him fold the sheets again as he finished with placing the others from the washer into the dryer and placed their clothes in one of the washers and started it up. Roger and Victoria left the laundry room and went and sat together in the kitchen holding hands as Roger said we are sleeping together tonight as Victoria smiled at him. Rosie came downstairs and sat down with them and said what's for dinner, Roger and Victoria looked at her and said do you have any suggestions. Said that she could fix her world renowned tuna salad, Roger suggested she use the canned chicken instead. Ok replied Rosie, as she went to boil some eggs taking out her veggies, and started the preparations for the salad. Rosie looked at the two of them and could tell they were still tired and knew this week had been very trying especially for Roger and appreciated all he had did for her, and would gladly fix them dinner even if it was simple. Roger stood and took out a bowl and took three cans of chicken out and opened them after he whipped of the tops and dumped them in a bowl. Rosie kissed him and said she loved him and continued with her preparations. Roger opened up a bottle of wine and grabbed a couple of glasses, just as he did Barbara entered from the garage, she said she had some stuff with her as she brought in several large trash bags filled with her pillows and some bedding. She hugged everyone and asked Roger and Victoria if they would help bring in the rest from her car, Roger and Vicky went and found several garbage bags filled with clothes and more bedding and brought them inside onto the elevator. They returned to the kitchen and poured some wine and watched Rosie prepare her salad.

Barbara came downstairs and asked where were the bags and he said in the elevator upstairs, she said you two look very tired as Roger and Victoria held hands, he said they were and had put her mattress cover on and made up her bed and purchased more new sheets, washed and folded most and said the weeks activities were catching up with him. Rosie said that's why they are sitting down watching me. Barbara said she would be back as she walked upstairs and Roger knew she was getting the bags out of the elevator and went to help her, and bringing the bags to her room as she unpacked them and placing the items in her closet. She thanked him and said she was happy as she hugged him, kissing him and rubbing him back. Said she was ready for tomorrow and it wouldn't take long since all of them were coming and said then things would smooth out more. She slipped out of her clothes as she stood nude before him and slipped on a dress and he told her if you have any dirties just bring them downstairs as he turned to return downstairs taking the elevator. She knew he was tired because he didn't act excited, she knew him and knew he had accomplished quite a bit this week. But also knew he was determined to finish what he started and wouldn't pressure him, she loved him and knew Roger was good and true.

Roger returned as Rosie finished the salad dishing up their plates for them as Barbara came downstairs and helped her serve. Roger blessed the table and gave thanks that they were all here together, and began to eat and complimenting Rosie on the salad pouring wine for all. He said if he seemed a little out of it was because the past week was catching up, but had one last mission to complete this week and that was to help Barbara pack up tomorrow and then they could relax and get things much more organized and was glad they were all here with him, and said we have each other, as he then proposed a toast to them all. They finished eating and Barbara told him she would handle cleaning up as Rosie helped her, they put the left over salad in a container and knew how tidy Roger was and would maintain his standards. Roger stood and wanted to hug them all and said he love each and every one of them, they were his world and nothing else mattered to him but them, he kissed and hugged each and went and sat outside and asked Victoria to come with him as Barbara said she was going to take a shower and Rosie likewise. He sat outside with Victoria sipping their wine and talked until Barbara and Rosie joined them as he sat just looking at the sky as the sun went down, before he said he was going to bed and wanted Victoria with him tonight. They all went inside and he locked up the house suggesting they all get some needed rest, and then slept in Victoria's bed with Victoria. Before he went to bed told Barbara tomorrow he was going to sleep with her. Barbara and Rosie slept in Rosie's new bed. It wasn't long before Roger and Victoria were sound asleep as they held each other; they slept soundly until they woke the next morning, as Barbara and Rosie enjoyed feeling and pleasuring one another soon they slipped off into a deep sleep with Barbara holding Rosie.

Chapter Thirteen

The very next morning Roger woke up feeling refreshed and more alive than ever, the nap he had taken with Victoria and a good night's rest did him wonders. He felt so much better and the thought of finishing the last major portion of this huge move and change in his life and the way he would be living, gave him renewed energy. He turned over and looked at Victoria as she awoke and kissed her, rubbing her head before he got out of bed and heading to his bedroom and bathroom, he began washing up and decided to take a nice warm shower all alone. Victoria soon climbed out of bed and went and refreshed herself with a shower also and putting on clean shorts and t-shirt. She headed downstairs and found Roger preparing to brew his morning coffee. Hugged him again and said she loved him so very much, and would help prepare breakfast; she found the pans that she needed to use. Vicky had prepared breakfast for them before and knew just how much to fix, it wasn't long before the smell of bacon and coffee was in the air as Roger opened the kitchen windows, he loved fresh air in the house as he thought about he still had quite a few things he needed to take care of next week. Window treatments do so much for a room making it warm and cozy Roger thought and was surprised that the previous owners hadn't put any window treatments up, blinds or curtains of any type.

Barbara and Rosie soon came downstairs in their usual attire. Victoria was preparing to serve breakfast as Rosie assisted her. Barbara set the table and shortly they were all sitting down eating. Roger said this was the last big mission until the movers actually moved Barbara's furniture and her containers Wednesday so today should go pretty quick and then we can cool out some and begin to relax a little. Barbara and Rosie cleaned up as Roger and Victoria emptied the dryers and folded the last of the sheets and placed all the dirty clothes in one washing machine. Barbara and Rosie were heading upstairs to change into their jeans as he and Victoria rode upstairs together to do the same. It wasn't long before Barbara and Rosie pulled out of the garage, followed by Roger and Victoria in his truck as they headed to Barbara's apartment for the final phase of packing. When they arrived Roger backed into a parking space as he and Victoria along with Rosie and Barbara made one trip each with the empty containers to her unit. They were all inside the small apartment and Barbara had separated what she was taking as they wrapped and filled the containers. Roger stacked them to one side and after a couple of hours they were completely finished. Roger took a couple containers and several bags filled with clothes and shoes to his truck along with the unused empty containers and boxes as Barbara checked all the drawers. She was leaving the bed, the kitchen table and chairs, but had decided on taking her dresser, a chest and her television. Roger returned and brought her flat screen television and DVD player downstairs and placed them inside the rear of his crew cab portion of the truck. Barbara didn't have very much, it was about as much as Victoria had when she moved and would be glad when Wednesday comes. Barbara walked around and Roger knew what she was thinking, after being there so long, she told them that was it and they could go home now. Barbara had moved almost all of her clothes and all of her documents and papers as they loaded up and headed back home.

It wasn't long before they all arrived back at home. Roger backed inside the garage and opened the back door and placed all of Barbara's stuff inside the elevator and emptied his truck and placing the empty containers in a corner of the laundry room. He left the empty boxes in the garage against the wall. Soon Barbara backed up inside and he helped her take what she had brought with her to the elevator and when he was finished rode upstairs and placed her television in her room on the floor, Rosie, Victoria and her emptied the elevator and brought everything to her room. Roger said he had a run to make and would be back shortly. Victoria asked to go with him and he said come on and was headed to buy some propane gas canisters and some charcoal for his grill. While shopping he picked up some wet mops for the floods and some dusters and more bathroom cleaning supplies purchasing enough for everyone. They headed back home, and he and Victoria stacked the supplies in the laundry room temporally. They took what they needed to their bathrooms. Roger was a clean man and dirt was not his thing, he took the wet mop and started cleaning the floor in his room and when he finished Victoria came and took it and did her room. Roger then sat on his new couch and it was very comfortable, the firm seating was a pleasure to sit on and he had an excellent view of the television. Soon Victoria came and sat with him and asked if he was going to use his grill today, he said he had almost forgotten and headed downstairs and took some chicken out then went outside and installed a gas canister on the grill, set the bag of charcoal next to it and returned inside.

As she was coming downstairs Victoria asked Roger. What are you going to do next? He told her he was waiting for the chicken to thaw and then I can season it. Ok she replied well that will take a while in the meantime I have something for you to do and would you please come upstairs with me. He went upstairs with her to her bedroom and she pushed him down in the bed and climbed on top of him and said she wanted him now as she kissed him and pulled his jeans down, then she stood dropped her jeans and swung herself around so her crotch was in his face as she placed her mouth on him, he breathed in her scent and played with her as she move up and down on him, he licked her and soon she climaxed as he held her legs so she couldn't move as he titillated her even more pulling her into his face even more. He soon relented and she turned around and sat on him and laid her chest on top of his as she moved her hips climaxing over and over again as he held her until she just lay on top exhausted. He rolled over to her side and rubbed his hand through her hair, said she needed that, then he rolled her over on her back and was on top as he penetrated her and slowly worked back and forth inside of her as she moaned and climaxed several more times. Roger didn't come because he was still in recovery mode but would satisfy Victoria, and knew she was hot for him after moving. He thought Barbara would be next and had just let Victoria have her way with him because he had gotten her highly excited and she couldn't satisfy herself completely during the past week because of moving. They laid together for a long while as he felt on her and played with her until she was fully satisfied, she finally said thank you master as he kissed her and told her how sweet she was, and then said to her, I think the chicken should be ready by now, they left and washed up in her bathroom and got dressed and went back downstairs together.

The chicken had thawed so then, he began cleaning and seasoning it, placing eight large pieces in a bowl and placed it in the refrigerator. Victoria asked what you think we should have with it. He said a salad and some boiled vegetables would be good. He asked Victoria to take some potatoes and carrots out of the refrigerator and a pot from under the counter. Victoria cleaned the potatoes and carrots and he went outside and placed some charcoal in his new grill and added some lighter fluid and remembered it was gas ignition, turned the gas on and hit the lighter button; it started to smoke and was soon lit. He turned the gas off as the flames started burning the charcoals until the fire died down. Victoria had cleaned the potatoes and peeled, diced, and rinsed them and put them in the pot on the stove then added some seasoning. Roger watched as the flame died down and the charcoals started to glow as he returned to the kitchen for the chicken and a pair of tongs. He took the chicken outside to the grill and set it on the sideboard of the grill and began placing the chicken on it and covered it up. Returned inside and took out a can of cold beer then grabbed Victoria and kissed her. She took out a can of beer also, and they went outside together and sitting in the new patio chairs. He told her she was sexy and was so happy her sexy ass was here now with him, she asked him to stop because he excited her so much when he spoke to her that way. He stood and checked his meat and turned it over and said he would be right back. He went inside and brought out an empty aluminum pan to place the chicken in when it finished cooking. He sat down and held her hand and felt her breast through her t-shirt getting her excited again. He then mentioned they hadn't seen Barbara or Rosie for quite a while and wondered what they were up to, and said he was going to see and would be right back. He entered the house and went upstairs and found them sitting in Barbara's room on her bed talking. He entered and said ladies, he had started cooking and was wondering what had happened to them. Barbara said they had put away all she had brought and would be downstairs shortly as they continued to sit and talk. He returned downstairs. Roger had to check on his meat and Victoria said she turned it over again and it was almost done. Victoria went inside checking on the vegetables, and turned the fire down, returned and commented about the stoves, saying they cooked so much faster and much better than any she had used in the past, as he checked the chicken again and sliced one and it was very tender and not over cooked, as he placed them in the pan and then took them inside and covered them, and returned and smothered the fire after he had brushed the grill off. He and Victoria sat a few more minutes outside before returning to the kitchen and preparing the salad together and were soon finished.

Barbara and Rosie came downstairs finally and joined them, setting the table and taking the plates out and placing the condiments on the table.

They all sat down after he and Victoria dished everyone up and Roger poured everyone a glass of his favorite red wine. He said it was a pleasure to have them all here with him finally, and was very pleased they were all together now in one home as they toasted and enjoyed the meal together. After they finished eating Rosie and Barbara washed the dishes and cleaned up, putting everything away. Afterwards they all went outside and sat in the new patio chairs. Rosie commented that she was ready to buy some more furniture for her room and would like to go tomorrow and had seen something that she really liked when she was with Roger. It was an area rug and couple of chairs and would love to order them. Roger said all she had to do was go. Then said she would like Barbara to go with her, and Barbara said she would love to. Roger told them about the cleaning supplies in the laundry room that he and Victoria had purchased and said it was time to clean there bathrooms and he would spend tomorrow cleaning his room and maybe decorating. And next week would look for and probably order some window treatments for the living room and dining room windows and probably purchase some more patio furniture and maybe a fire pit if he found one he liked. They all sat around talking for over an hour as the sun went down before going back inside. Roger closed the windows downstairs and checked that the garage doors were all closed and turned the alarm system on before going upstairs and preparing to shower again since he smelled like smoke from cooking on the grill.

Barbara said she was sleeping with him tonight and she was going to get her towel and robe and join him in the shower. Victoria and Rosie said they would shower together and then go to bed. Everyone was very tired from all the activities of the day. Barbara came and she dropped her dirty clothes on top of Rogers as they embraced each other and went and bathed in the shower and they enjoyed feeling on one another. After taking their shower together and drying off he placed a towel on the bed as they oiled each other bodies and put their robes on and then sat on the couch as he sat down and Barbara stretched out with her head in his lap. He turned on the television and she said you can't miss seeing that can you. Making a joke, Roger said I just turned the wall on and asked her how she liked it; Barbara responded it made sense since the walls are so large. He said downstairs will be something he wanted everyone's input on so we can start using it, and said he started when he purchased the rug and the cabinet but valued their opinion and since they also lived here felt they should have some choices. He rubbed her body as they continued talking and said she missed him touching and rubbing her. Victoria and Rosie came in and sat together on the small couch in their robes and were mesmerized by the large picture as he told Barbara he could project from his computer to the television and then they could see videos of themselves. He continued feeling on Barbara as she was getting very excited and soon she shook while an organism racked her body. He continued touching her as she reached out and held his hand and kissed it trying to calm down. Victoria and Rosie asked if they could have each other. Roger said yes and told them they didn't have to ask him any longer since they all lived here together now. They kissed him and Barbara heading off to Rosie's bedroom. And Roger turned the television off as he and Barbara soon decided to go to bed and pulled the covers back and climbed in as they held and caressed one another and pleasuring each other while Barbara had multiple organisms and he climaxed then they just held each other as he turned out the lights and they went to sleep.

Chapter Fourteen

It was Sunday when he awoke, and after he came out the bathroom, climbed back in bed with Barbara. He began rubbing her soft body; she soon woke, kissed him and also went to the bathroom. When she returned they engaged in more loving and sensual sex and soon both were very satisfied as they continued hugging before bathing together. They continued kissing before drying off and oiling one another. Roger put on some clean shorts and t-shirt as Barbara grabbed her robe and headed to her room doing the same and changing into something much more comfortable. Suddenly Barbara decided to gather up all the dirty clothes even stripping down his bed, bundling everything up and headed downstairs on the elevator. Roger had gone downstairs and began making the morning coffee as Barbara came down with the dirty clothes and headed to the laundry room and started several different loads. Shortly Victoria and Rosie appeared downstairs and began to prepare breakfast. After everything was ready they sat down eating together again. Roger informed them he knew they all had laptops and needed the WI-FI name and password and it was on his desk and for them to enter it into their computers and cell phones. He also asked for their checkbooks, the last two months of bills and their bank statements so he could work on the new household budget and close any of their open utility accounts. He asked Victoria to call for a pickup of the items she was donating that were left at her old apartment and he would also need the keys. Rosie asked Barbara again if she would go shopping with her today to look for some rugs, chairs or a couch and maybe a television. Roger asked them to decide what they wanted to have for dinner and who should cook, or should they cook as a group. Barbara said lets cook as a group and for dinner maybe something light, like some seafood. He said he preferred them cooking together also because it's much faster and was more fun. They finished eating and everyone helped clean up before Barbara and Rosie went upstairs to prepare to go furniture shopping and maybe he and Victoria would go to look at some window treatments for the living and dining rooms. He was still waiting on his bedroom shade to arrive, which he hoped would be delivered soon.

Barbara and Rosie had dressed for their shopping adventure while Roger decided he would have some fun with Victoria first. He was sitting at his desk when they said they were on their way out and kissed him before they left. As they departed Victoria sat on the couch and stood, walking over to her and said you know you have been a very bad girl, she replied yes sir master, as he told her to undress. She did as instructed, he opened his cabinet and took out a collar and placed it around her neck, she was always highly excited as he spoke to her in a demeaning manner, and told her she was his little tramp bitch and he was going to fuck her tight little ass after he spanked her. He placed his hands between her legs and rubbed her firm soft thighs as he moved his hand to her vagina and asked her what she was. She responded she was his bitch and was here to serve him. He told her to kneel as he removed his shorts and she automatically took him in her hungry mouth and when he was fully hard told her to bend over as he knelt down behind and entered her doggie style in her now very moist vagina as he smacked her ass cheeks as she quickly climaxed, as he continued to pump her. He reached around and fingered her clit until she was racked with multiple climaxes, he then pulled out and turned her around by the collar and had her suck him off until he climaxed in her mouth ordering her to swallow it all, then pulled her up and wiped her face with his hand as semen dribbled from the corners of her sweet lips. He held her with one arm around her and was pressed against him as he spanked her butt and she whimpered and held on to him, looking up and telling him how much she loved him.

He stood and pulled her up with him as he stood and kissed her passionately and felt between her smooth thighs again causing her to climax several more times as her held her and making more derogatory comments as she began shaking uncontrollably and continued climaxing as her body was totally racked with multiple orgasms. He led her to the bed where he laid her down, she held on to his shirt and he continued caressing her. Soon she had calmed down and he put his shorts back on and brought her clothing over to her and sat her up as she said thank you master, he then removed the collar. He told her to clean herself up and then they would go to look for some window treatments and she could decide if she wanted a curtain rod for her bedroom; she departed as he decided to wear some jeans after he cleaned himself up and changed. Soon Victoria reappeared, her hair was combed and she had changed into a longer pair of loose fitting shorts and a blouse, said she was extremely happy to be with him even more now as she came and kissed him again and he hugged her. Victoria was so in love with him; her thoughts of him would make her so sexually excited she would have to masturbate to make the feeling of him subside enough to carry on with her day sometimes. Now being here with him and living in the same house help her have better control of her emotions. Just going to the store with him helped calm her feelings so much now and sometimes when he touched her she felt like someone who gets and electrical shock from a static electrical charge. Now she was so very happy just being with him.

They went downstairs to the garage and decided to go in her car. Roger asked her to drive, she asked where to, and he directed her to where, and then they were off. They soon arrived and headed to the window treatment department of a major hardware chain, the same one he had purchased his bedroom shade from and the vertical blinds he had put up last week. He knew what he wanted and asked Victoria what she thought. She said that they were exceptional shades and would be perfect for the living room and dining room area and complimented him on his selection. He placed the order for the three large living room windows and the two in the dining room and had the measurements with him, since they were custom made. The store clerk informed him the ones for the kitchen were of standard size and could find them on one of the nearby shelves as she led them to the shelf, they looked around and soon found the ones for the kitchen after checking the measurements, he purchased two sets. He asked Vicky if she wanted a curtain rod as they looked at the different styles, she picked on out and he placed it in the shopping cart. He paid and they left the store and would make one other stop and went to the bedding department of a major department type store and picked out four different kings size blanket sets with matching pillow cases. They looked around some before leaving, Roger paid and they headed home. After bringing everything inside Roger began preparing to install the kitchen blinds and went and took out his tool box and his drill and within an hour they were up. Victoria cleaned up the dust soon after he finished with the installation. After putting up the vertical blinds in the kitchen and doing the curtain rod in her bedroom, he and Victoria fixed some sandwiches and sat down and had lunch with some red wine, when they finished they both went upstairs and changed clothes and then sat together and watched some television.

Victoria said now that they were all together asked him how was he going to run his new household, how were the finances going to be handled, he explained to her since they were all starting out with new accounts and the balances were transferred from the old accounts, and everyone was in the process of terminating all their past utilities, and with the payoffs of their auto loans and the termination of paying rent, they had no expenses other than their charge cards for right now. All they would need now would be a portion of what each of them was spending before. Told her that after her lease ended, or if you can get out of it sooner, you will see a big savings, especially in your bank account and asked if she had spoken to her landlord yet. Victoria said she had left a message on the rental agency's answering service but they hadn't returned her call yet, and that she needed to have the donation people come and then maybe she could avoid the last month's rent payment. He asked her to leave the information for him and to contact the donation people. Said she had and they said Tuesday at eleven, he went to his desk and made a note of that and asked for the key. She left and returned with a box and gave him her check book and all her documents as he went through them putting everything in order. He wrote her name on the front of the box and placed it on top of the ones he had for both Rosie and Barbara.

Roger had created a new file for the house and it would soon be the only working file with the exception of all their checking accounts. He told her it was going to work out very well; after everyone's old business has been cleared up and closed. He then returned to the couch and sat next to her again. She kissed him as he placed his arm around her shoulders. She said shouldn't we put the blankets on the beds, he said maybe later while they watched television. It was early evening when Rosie and Barbara returned from shopping. The girls had so much fun and were elated on finding sales on different household things. Barbara purchased several king size spreads. Rosie purchased a rug which would be delivered Wednesday. Barbara couldn't resist and saw one also, purchased it and would be delivered the same day. They both were so surprised and happy. They kept looking around and came upon some beautiful bath mats on sale. They ended up buying more because of the sale; then they decided that it was time to head home. Arriving home they showed Victoria and Roger what they had purchased before deciding to go change into something more comfortable. Barbara returned wearing a loose fitting dress with nothing on underneath and Rosie had changed into just a very long t-shirt. Now all of these women loved Roger and he knew it. Barbara then sat next to Roger and he gently felt between her warm soft thighs. She willingly opened them and allowed him to feel her. He asked what's for dinner. No one answered. Roger replied, saying I guess it's up to me then. He thought about having baked fish, mashed potatoes and a delicious tossed salad. He stood and headed downstairs and began taking out what he needed. Roger started, dumping the fish in the sink and with the four of them that was the entire bag, six large potatoes and a head of lettuce. He opened the bags containing the individual pieces of fish and placed them in a pan and began to season them, then peeled the potatoes, diced them and placed them in a pot of water and let them soak and pulled out two large baking dishes, oiled them and then placed the fish inside, as he turned the oven on setting the temperature. Then drained the potatoes, refilled the pot with water added salt and placed them on the stove turning a fire on underneath. He placed the fish in the oven, as everything now was in motion. He cleaned his cutting board and then chopped the lettuce and took four salad bowls from the cabinet just as Victoria came downstairs and began helping him. She set the table and took the salad dressing out as he opened a bottle of red wine and poured himself a glass. He took out a stick of butter and a package of cream cheese and as the oven let him know it was at temperature set the timer. Victoria poured herself a glass and he kissed her and felt her through her shirt. Barbara and Rosie came downstairs and noticed the blinds and commented that they looked very nice. He checked the potatoes; they had boiled and drained the water from them before adding the butter and cream cheese and mashed and stirred them then covered them and waited on the fish. He had placed the lettuce in the bowels, as Victoria placed them on the table and the oven dinged and he removed the dishes and started placing the fish on the plates, and then he scooped up the mashed potatoes as Victoria placed the plates on the table. They all sat down as he passed the wine around and everyone poured themselves a glass.

He blessed the table, they all were eating, and to his surprise when he asked what's for dinner. No one had any suggestions. Roger thought this is strange, very strange. Since they all ate like they were starving, as they each went back for more potatoes and shared the last couple pieces of fish. When they finished, everything was completely gone. Barbara said Rosie cleaned up and washed the dishes as Victoria helped clear the table as he sat and watched them. He thought who or rather maybe he should punish all of them tonight. They were acting like they wanted it, and thought he had to maintain control. As he watched each one, thought about what he would or should do, they needed to be spanked and played with and that was the reason they were eager to move here with him, and he would fulfill their wishes completely, tonight. Then was pissed as he thought about they had no suggestions when he asked what they were going to eat, he knew women loved food, and especially these three and was surprised at their non-response. He waited until they had finished cleaning up and told them to come sit down as he looked at each of them, then he had them line there chairs up next to one another, and had Barbara first then Victoria, and Rosie last. They all knew then that he had something in store for them as he looked at their anxious faces. He asked them who he was, they all responded he was their master, and next asked them what were they here for, and they said to serve him. He told them to pull their shirts up and spread their legs wide open, they all did. He told them to feel themselves until they climaxed. It didn't take them very long since they were now very excited after he told them to line their chairs up and knew he had something in store for them and was going to have his way no matter what and they each wanted it badly. Barbara was the first to climax, and then Rosie and Victoria climaxed together. He told them to finger themselves and after about a minute told them to suck their fingers. After they had did that he told them to put the chairs back and to go upstairs, undress and stand at the foot of his bed with their hands behind their heads, legs spread, and before they did that if they had to use the bathroom to do so now. They all stood and departed to follow their master's orders.

He washed his glass and was the last one upstairs; as he entered his bedroom he found them all just the way he had instructed. He opened his cabinet then he told them to turn around and bend over with their hands on their knees, told them all he wanted to see was ass, they turned around and that was all he saw, was ass. He found three anal plugs almost the same size, he put on a pair of surgical gloves and took out a tube of lubricant before going down the line and lubricating each anus and then began inserting an anal plug in each as they moaned. After inserting them, he told them to stand up and turn around with their hands behind their heads. He removed three dildos of similar size and stood before each woman and placed one inside each of their mouths. Then came back to the first and lubricated it and inserted inside Barbara, being the first she moaned and took out a piece of rope and doubled it wrapping it around her waist and looping it thru the rope in the front and between her legs and looping it once around the dildo holding it in place between her legs and through her ass crack and tying it securely in back, next he did Victoria the exact same way and making her extremely excited by calling her his little slut whore as the excitement built up in her quickly as moisture ran down her thighs. He made sure their clits were between the two ropes, when he did Rosie, she had become so excited, calling her a slut and telling her what he was going to do, she climaxed as he tied the rope behind her back. He smacked her ass several times hard for climaxing without permission. He placed collars on each of their necks and cuffs on their wrists while hooking their cuffed arms behind them. He attached a leash to each one, and led them to the elevator as he brought with him several different straps and whips of various types. They descended to the large empty basement where he led them around. They tried very hard not to climax and told them they had to ask permission first, if they wanted to climax, and as he did Barbara begged him with tears in her eyes and climaxed before he could give his permission, for this she received ten lashes with the light whip all over her body as she continued to beg and holding her up by the collar as she climaxed for several minutes. Rosie and Victoria begged and made the same fatal mistake, and received the same punishment as multiple climaxes racked their sexy bodies, he held them up by their nipples as they screamed and continued to climax over and over again. He untied Barbara's hands and had her to get down and start crawling and then did the same to Victoria and Rosie using the heavy leather strap on them as they crawled around on the cool tile floor.

Then he made them stand as he looked into their tearful faces and continued to jerk from the ropes biting into their tender flesh and clits sending spasms through them. He kissed Barbara and she said thank you master, he untied the rope and told her to jerk herself off as he watched, she worked the dildo back and forth inside of her until she had the most intense orgasm ever as he held her up in a standing position by the leash then telling her to place the dildo in her mouth and suck it clean like it was real and play with herself as he degraded her while she climaxed again as he let her sink to her knees in total ecstasy. Next was Victoria's turn, he had her do the same thing as he degraded her even more as she started climaxing and hers was even more earth shattering and lasted longer. He held her up by the leash and her hair as she sucked the dildo and Barbara was forced to kneel and made to watch. It was now Rosie's turn and she climaxed when he just touched her and degrade her as he untied the rope. She was racked by continuous climaxes and she shook uncontrollably and sucked the dildo and playing with herself as her knees started to buckle. He eventually caught her and eased her down to the floor.

He made them all kneel holding their ankles as the anal plugs were still inserted and while they were bent over, he whipped them again and again as they cried and moaned and flinched using the flogger whip and making sure he struck them between their legs several times. He told them to stand and they did, they were fully satisfied now, it showed as he kissed each one and they said thank you master. He told each to turn around and bend over as he removed the anal plugs and handed it to them, when he finished he ordered each to their individual bathrooms to wash themselves and the plugs and dildo. He told them when you finish he wanted to see each one and they were to oil themselves as he watched and to bring a clean shirt with them but not to put it on. He asked, do you understand, they all replied yes sir master. They all went upstairs together. He replaced the whips and straps back into his cabinet. He showered and oiled himself putting on some clean shorts and a t-shirt also. The first to return was Barbara, she hung the collar and cuffs up and placed the cleaned plug and dildo in the cabinet and he had several large towels spread out on his bed and Barbara sat down and started to oil herself. He came over and oiled her back. She then grabbed and kissed, and hugged him as she cried and said she loved him so much and told him that was so intense; as she laid on her back as he oiled her thighs, legs and feet and had just finished oiling her when Victoria came in and placed her equipment away and cried and held him and said thank you master, then he and Barbara helped her apply oil and then Rosie entered and they did the same for her after replacing her restraints away with the plug and dildo. She sat on the bed and hugged him tightly and thanked him as they all oiled her and then he told them to put their shirts on. Telling them to go downstairs where he fixed them all martinis and they enjoyed them, he knew they would sleep very well after several and so would he. The martinis he made were mixed with tonic and were very potent and since they were all sexually satisfied, it would really relax them and they soon would be ready for bed. When they had finished, having at least three drinks apiece he escorted them upstairs. Victoria and Rosie went to her bedroom and Barbara slept with him as he held her in is arms and she soon dosed off very happy and satisfied.

The following morning Roger woke up after having a very restful night's sleep and headed downstairs and opened the kitchen windows, and made his usual pot of coffee. He looked at the clock and thought he needed to wake Rosie and Victoria so they wouldn't be late for work. He returned upstairs and found Rosie in her bathroom and Victoria was just getting up and heading to her room. Barbara sat up and he went over and hugged her. She rose and headed to her bedroom. Barbara was off this week he remembered and would be with him. He went back downstairs and took out some donuts, and when he turned around Victoria was entering the kitchen and poured a cup of coffee. Roger said you're going to be late, she told him she had taken the week off so she could get her room squared away, take care of the donations

252

and possibly end her lease. She began preparing breakfast; Victoria was real big on having breakfast and was always the one who helped him prepare it most of the time. Soon Rosie came down almost dressed for work followed by Barbara. Roger knew Barbara was off this week but had completely forgotten all about Victoria. It didn't take long with Barbara's help for Victoria to finish preparing breakfast and soon they were all sitting down eating and everyone was satisfied. Rosie returned to her room to finish dressing for work. Barbara and Victoria cleaned everything up and soon returned to their rooms. Roger said he was washing his bathroom down since he had used it and knew it was long overdue for a cleaning and would wash the walls since he hadn't cleaned it since moving in. It had gotten quite a bit of use. He brought the bucket and mop upstairs from the basement and more of the cleaning supplies including some of the items he purchased on one of his shopping trips and a bottle of pine cleaner and bleach, some rubber gloves, old towels, and rags and headed to the bathroom. Roger opened the bathroom windows and began with the walls and when he finished started with the sinks, shower, and bath tub which he had yet to use, the bidet, and toilet and did the floor last, the bathroom took him a good hour to do and the smell of pine cleaner permeated the bathroom and then his bedroom. He dumped the bucket of water in the toilet and rolled it into the hallway. He placed the cleaning supplies in the vanity for the next time. Looking around he saw that he needed to strip his bed down, and began changing his sheets and pillow cases; then he opened the sliding glass door and windows; as the pleasant smell of fresh air passed through his room. So refreshing he thought. Soon Rosie said goodbye and kissed each one of them as she headed to work.

Victoria walked in and asked if he was finished with the bucket and he said yes. She took it to her room and began making a bucket of hot soapy water. She then began to clean her bathroom also. Barbara came and she had stripped her bed and Rosie's and was headed downstairs to start a wash load as she took Rogers as well. She returned shortly and helped Victoria by her wiping down the walls. Cleaning all of the bathrooms was not planned but they needed to be cleaned and made the process much faster. Barbara asked what about the last one, the smallest one. Ok they replied and it took no time doing it and the downstairs bathroom and the one in the basement as well. When they finished, felt they had accomplished a major mission. Roger said this wasn't planned, but I'm glad we did it.

They began preparing lunch, some sandwiches, and talked about the next few days, Tuesday which was tomorrow they would clean out Victoria's apartment and Wednesday Barbara's movers would come and then arrange to donate her old stuff away, and she and Rosie's rugs were also to be delivered. Barbara suggested they apply some wax to the floors and Roger said he needed to go to the hardware store and pick a few things up. Barbara and Victoria said they would like to go so they all left and prepared to change clothes. Roger wore some jeans and a sweat shirt and Vicky and Barb wore the similar outfits since it was in the upper sixties outside. They closed all the windows throughout the house and prepared to leave and left in his truck. He headed to the hardware and Barbara asked about the living room windows and he said it would take about two weeks and the shades would be delivered sometime later next week; and the one for his bedroom window should arrive very soon. They arrived and taking a shopping cart, soon found a floor wax that was easy to apply; since the entire house had hard wood floors. They followed Roger and went to the lighting department looking at fixtures, he didn't care for the ceiling fixture in his bedroom and was looking for something more compatible with his décor, he found one he liked and Barbara and Victoria also had a ceiling outlet for a light, but no fixture and he told them if they found one he would install it. They looked around and Barbara found one and Roger felt it was her style, it was beautiful and soon Victoria chose one also. Then he looked around for the hooks and soon found the shelf and the boxes with the size he wanted in the hardware section. It was the hooks he would install in the ceiling where he could hang them from if he decided to punish them that way, he had hooks in the ceiling at the apartment, they enjoyed being hung up as he toyed with them. They also looked at some outdoor furniture and Barbara said she liked the rattan and especially the lounge chairs, but said she would wait a little longer until they went on sale. Soon all of them headed for the check out and then back home. Arriving home he backed inside the garage and started to unload the truck. Barbara said she wanted to wax her floor before the movers came. Her and Victoria decided to go upstairs together and asked him to roll the rugs up in her room and Rosie's and they would do all the bedrooms and hallway and suggested to Roger a nice long runner or several shorter ones for the hallway would look great with the addition some colorful pictures eventually.

Roger rolled the rugs up and after doing that he started installing the new light fixtures, everyone had a mission. Barbara and Victoria read the directions and used the wet mops to apply the wax and with the two of them they completed the waxing much sooner. Roger soon finished installing the light fixtures in their bed rooms. He took the one he removed from his room and placed it in Rosie's. He thought about the trash pickup and contacted the town and found out pickup was done by a private contractor and he called to make arrange for a pickup and found out it was on Thursday only, and they would deliver receptacles and he had two but probably could use two more and made the request, they said he was now on their list, and gave them the routing number the village had given him. Well, that was taken care of filling both waste containers since moving in. These were things he didn't have to be bothered with in the apartment but was still glad he had moved. Barbara and Victoria had completed the upstairs and decided to do downstairs as they rolled the living room rug up and before he knew it they were finished. He went and rolled the rugs out upstairs after the floors had dried and they looked so much better. He decided on a shrimp and rice dish for dinner and with four people it was easier for him to cook since he had a tendency to fix too much. He was getting a picture of how to shop and being aware of buying too much. He watched what they used the most of and would soon have it down to and art. He took the shrimp out and instead on one bag, would now be using two and his large pots more often than before and arranged the pots in the cabinets much better now since it has been a couple of weeks and the addition of Victoria and Barbara's cookware helped a lot.

The house smelled clean, of pine cleaner and bleach and now the lemon sent of wax. The entrance looked exceptional and Barbara said they should look at more large area rugs and made a list out of where as she and Victoria measured the spaces, and said after Victoria's donation pickup they would look and shop and asked Roger if he would go with them, and he said yes, of course he would love to. They said they were through for the day and liked the light fixtures and now along with her lamps Victoria stated her lighting was now complete giving more light. They asked if he needed any help and he replied yes, the vegetables and took them out and the cutting board, and the rest of the ingredients; as they all chipped in and help Roger. Soon all the prep work was completed and he took out and poured them each a glass of wine and he took them in his arms and hugged them, and told them he loved them very much. Vicky had cut the vegetables and diced them and Barbara had cleaned the shrimp and he had taken and prepared his tomato mixture, and now he was ready as he put on some rice and prepared the big pot for the main course. They all talked and discussed how well things were starting to work out. He asked them to write down what he needed from the grocery as he looked in various cabinets and dictated to them the needed items and soon had a list; it wasn't long but needed larger quantities of certain items more than others.

He had started cooking and soon the rice was finished, and the shrimp dish was simmering as he waited to add the shrimp last. It wasn't long before he was finished and had turned off the stove as they sat and talked. All of them had decided to go change into something more comfortable since it had warmed up some and they were still wearing the jeans they had cleaned the house in. They had finished with a major house cleaning project which they hadn't really planned on doing. Roger looked at the clock; it would be less than an hour before Rosie would return home. He decided to install the hooks he had purchased and took his tool kit out, the hooks, step ladder and his stud finder and went to the basement and soon found the ceiling joist and installed the first of six hooks three feet apart and was soon finished, putting his tools away and changed his clothes and felt he had at least the basics installed. He joined Victoria and Barbara sitting downstairs in the kitchen and they would wait on Rosie to return home from work to sit down and all eat together. Barbara started setting the table. Roger went to the basement and brought back a chilled bottle of wine, and began taking out the dinner plates, then a lettuce and washed it and after it drained, chopped some for several small salads and wrapped the unused head and returned it to the refrigerator. Shortly, after Rosie entered, she was told to wash up so they could eat. Roger and Victoria dished and served and soon they were eating. They asked Rosie how was her day? Good she replied, and felt much better now being home with them. After eating Barbara and Victoria said they would clean up and put the food away as Roger helped them. Rosie stayed downstairs until the kitchen was cleaned up and then Victoria and Barbara sat on the patio-deck. Roger went upstairs with Rosie. Roger showed her that her bathroom had been cleaned and all the floors waxed as she undressed and told her he was going to have her show and give special thanks to Barbara and Victoria later for cleaning her bedroom and bathroom. She put her t-shirt on and came and hugged him as he felt her allover asking her who she belonged to, and she said she belonged to him and then they joined Barbara and Victoria on the deck. They sat and talked for a while and Barbara talked about decorating after her furniture and other things were moved in and Victoria talked about adding some large very colorful pictures since the walls were all white.

Roger went inside and fixed them some drinks and returned with a tray and four glasses, and said ladies something special for you as he passed them around. They sipped their drinks saying these are really good, and Roger left and returned with a pitcher for refills. They sat and sipped until the pitcher was empty and then went inside as Roger washed up the glasses and pitcher, closing the windows and turned on the alarm. Having Victoria and Barbara sit on the couch in his bedroom and telling Rosie it was time to thank both women by preforming oral sex on both. Roger said Rosie wants to give you two a special thank you as Barbara pulled her shirt up exposing her thighs as Rosie knelt between them and licked and sucked her until she climaxed, then she had to do Victoria and she soon climaxed also.

Afterwards, Victoria and Barbara went and showered. Roger had Rosie between his legs as she sucked him off, then he stood and bent her over the end of the bed taking out a belt and smacked her ass several times before he entered her as she climaxed several times. He pulled her up and pushed her down to her knees and entered her mouth again and climaxed as she swallowed, saying thank you master, as he again pulled her up and took her to his bathroom having more sex with her playing with her as she continued climaxing. They finished bathing and dried off having her to oil him and then he did her. She held his hand and placed it between her legs as he applied oil to her and she climaxed again. Barbara and Victoria returned after oiling each other. Roger said Victoria was sleeping with him and told Barbara to sleep with Rosie in her room. Barbara and Rosie kissed him and Victoria and then departed. Roger took Victoria by the hand and kissed her as she hugged him passionately and they climbed into bed as he turned out the lights. As he lay in bed with her feeling her body as she gladly welcomed his touch and roving hands and told him how much she loved him and would do whatever he wanted of her. He told her of the things he would do to her that made her highly excited. And knew she had a very vivid imagination then she soon erupted with a massive climax as she held on to him and then he rubbed her to sleep as she curled up close to him, and soon Roger was asleep also.

Barbara and Rosie climbed into bed together, the king sized bed gave them plenty of room as Barbara pulled

Rosie to her and they kissed as Barbara felt between Rosie's thighs and the highly sexed young woman was soon overcome with lust for her older companion as she quickly climaxed and Barbara caressed Rosie and she slid down between Barbara legs and licked her again as Rosie felt on herself. They were thankful Roger had now allowed them to have one another without asking permission and soon Barbara erupted with a massive climax as Rosie fingered her vagina and licking her clit, and Barbara held Rosie's head to her until she couldn't stand it any longer as Rosie slowly climbed back up and licked Barbara's nipples and Barbara held her tightly. They kissed and soon fell asleep with Rosie in Barbara arms and both were very happy and now very content.

Chapter Fifteen

Roger woke; the mornings were becoming a lot more routine and more relaxed now as he went to the bathroom and returned, looking at the beautiful and sensuous woman sleeping in his bed. Victoria soon began to wake up and feel for him, then opened her eyes and saw him standing there looking down at her, she rose and climbed out of bed reaching out and hugged him; and then headed toward the bathroom. When she returned he took her in his arms and got back in bed where he caressed her smooth, soft body and she automatically responded, holding him close as he whispered, in her ear that he loved her so very much, she buried her head in his chess as he ran his fingers through her hair. Victoria loved him so much when she thought of him sometimes at work she would have to go to the washroom and relieve herself. He kissed her once again and said you know we have to clear your apartment today sweetheart, she said yes I know and I guess we need to get started; they soon climbed out of bed but only after Roger hugged her and told her she made him very happy, she kissed him on his lips as he held her tight. He released her as she headed to her bedroom after putting on her long t-shirt as Roger headed downstairs to fix the morning coffee.

It wasn't long before Barbara, Victoria and Rosie soon appeared downstairs. They all had slipped on shorts and t-shirts as Barbara started to prepare breakfast. All of a sudden all three girls hugged and kissed him and one another. Roger thought he had turned his weekend exploits into a full time occasion with the four of them all living together now and there were only three things left to do. Victoria's donation and cleaning out her apartment, then tomorrow when Barbara's movers would and move the last of her belongings here and then the very last thing left to be done would be cleaning out her old apartment and having her donations picked up. Then we would all start to begin seeing the savings and the adventure of decorating the new house together. Rosie assisted Barbara with breakfast, and everyone was feeling great. It was a family gathering and everything has been well planned. During breakfast all of the girls started commenting on their new life and looking forward to love and happiness. Barbara commented on how well she had slept last night, and every night since being here. Victoria said she has been sleeping so much better also since moving in and said she didn't have any more restless nights like before when living alone and said she felt safe with them here. Rosie also said since being with them she slept so much better and evidently it shows because of all the compliments she has been receiving at work. Roger expressed the concern he had for Barbara and Victoria saying he was relieved how they have pulled things together knowing they felt safer than ever being very happy and more than satisfied that things were working out and making life more pleasant for them all. After breakfast Roger and Rosie cleaned up and then she left to prepare for work. He went upstairs to his bedroom and sat at his desk, and decided to turn on the television to look at the morning news. It was disappointing as usual and after a short while looking at it soon ended up turning it off. He found it much more relaxing listening to the radio since it was more soothing to his brain.

While listening to the radio Roger stood and proceeded to sit on the couch. Barbara came in and sat next to him, kissed him and mentioned what a wonderful time she had with Rosie yesterday. Thanking him as usual. No problem Roger replied, anything to make my girls happy and obedient. Barbara chuckled. Barbara also mentioned how everyone loves where they are now, saying in some ways we were all lost and then you came into our lives and changed everything for the better. From the bottom of our hearts we thank you so very much master and always will serve you. Roger smiled saying I enjoyed this little chat with you it means a lot to me and not every woman could share a man together. Just then Rosie came in kissed them both and said she's leaving for work and to have a wonderful day. They replied you too sweetheart. Victoria entered, then said to Roger shouldn't we be getting ready. Yes Roger replied, we should and get some of the trash out of the way before they come for your stuff. Barbara said I called the donation people for a pickup and they had an opening for Thursday and gave me a pickup time. That's great Roger replied then everything will be out of the way by this coming weekend. I also got in touch with the landlord and he agreed to meet me there on Thursday to terminate my lease and save me the last two months of rent.

They drove and he made a quick stop, picking up some coffee on the way. It wasn't long after arriving when the donation people pulled up and were sitting in there truck drinking there coffee before they came and rang the doorbell. The apartment was empty in fifteen minutes and Victoria had left some garbage bags and a broom, along with a dust pan and she cleaned up and soon the apartment was empty and swept up, she left the curtains and rods and to her surprise the leasing agent appeared. He stated that Mrs. Sampson had contacted him earlier and left a voice message for him regarding today and he was prepared to inspect the apartment and terminate her lease a month early, they welcomed him inside and he was satisfied saying he was very sorry to see her go. Victoria signed and gave him her new address for her security deposit refund and he handed her a copy of the release form. She saved a month's rent and thanked the agent and handed him her keys and they all departed and was debating whether to go have lunch or go home. Barbara said she wanted to see if she could find a large round rug for the entrance foyer and had the measurements with her, so they headed to the store where they had seen so many different styles and shapes of rugs and carpets before and after arriving looked around. It didn't take long before she found one, and asked Roger and Victoria what they thought. It was beautiful; it had plenty of color and had a design similar to a compass face. Barbara made the purchase and it would be delivered in a couple of days. They continued to look around and decided to return home to relax and enjoy each other's company. As they entered the driveway as the mail man was just leaving; and Roger stopped and got out and spoke to him and confirmed all the names that resided here, the mailman thanked him and asked him to please leave the gate open so he wouldn't have to return their mail to the office, it had happened only once so far. Roger said it wouldn't be a problem again and thanked him. He parked inside the garage, as they entered he found a pile of mail inside the front door and Roger sorted it and pulled out all the bills, and handed Victoria and Barbara all the catalogs that had arrived, and taking the mail he had upstairs placing it on his desk and knew the shredder would soon be getting a work out.

Roger started undressing and went and took a quick shower since he felt dirty after cleaning up Victoria's apartment. Before he finished bathing both Barbara and Victoria entered and undressed and came in with him and they had a good time in the water, Roger was feeling very relaxed and taking the shower really helped and bathing together was always a special bonus for him. They soon finished and then dried off and went to apply some body lotions as they sat on his bed. Knowing cleanliness was next to godliness, Roger lay down just to chill and maybe take a nap; the girls decided on lying down with Roger and giving him a hands on massage telling him they loved him for all he had done for them and before that they loved him anyway. Roger loved this and they knew it. He was slowly falling asleep. Barbara and Victoria turned him over and as soon as they did he was fast asleep. They lay besides him and just pulled the covers up over them and they all just took a well-deserved nap as he lay between two of the three women in his life. And very soon they were all sound asleep. Several hours had passed when everyone woke up and the girls started kissing, hugging and feeling on Roger again. He surly didn't resist as they had their way teasing him.

Vicky asked what should they have for dinner, he said Rosie, and they laughed and said no, food. He said it didn't matter to him and had to decide if they wanted baked, fried or grilled. Barbara said she didn't feel like eating anything heavy and suggested making some salads. Roger suggested a grilled chicken salad since they had tomatoes, cucumbers, peppers and radishes and eggs and he would grill the chicken. Victoria said that sounds like a winner as they went to their respective bedrooms to put on some clean clothes and Victoria came in and went into his bathroom and picked up all the dirty clothes and took them downstairs with her and started a load of wash. Barbara took the chicken out of the freezer and placed the individually wrapped pieces in the sink and ran warm water on them. Barbara and Victoria cleaned and chopped the lettuce and other vegetables and put some eggs on to boil while Roger went outside and lite the grill adding a few more charcoals. Roger went back inside after lighting the grill, grabbed a bottle of red wine and placed three glasses on the center island and poured wine in each one. And he held up his glass, gave a toast to us, he said as they clicked glasses and repeated to us and sipped. It wasn't long before Roger sprinkled some seasoning on the chicken and washed his hands taking the bowl and a pair of tongs outside and placed the chicken on the hot grill and covered it and returned for his wine glass and went back outside and sat down as Barbara and Victoria soon followed and joined him. The eggs had boiled and were cooling in cold water. Roger turned the chicken over and returned to the table as Victoria said; this is great and asked Roger if he had thought about an outdoor pool. Said he had, thought about it but didn't want to get too far ahead of himself and wanted to decorate more of the house first. Roger kept a close eye on the chicken as he turned it over then went inside for a pan and a knife and placed the pan on the side board, and sliced into a piece, then gave it a few more minutes and sat down and felt on Victoria's thigh and tickled her as she said stop please. He stood and checked the chicken and cut into another piece, then removed them placing them in the pan, brushed the grill down and smothered the fire closing the vents on the grill, taking the chicken inside and setting it on the stove and covering them.

He returned with the bottle of wine and refreshed their glasses as they sat and sipped and Barbara looked at her phone to see the time, and said Rosie should be here soon just as she walked out on the patio-deck. There stood Rosie looking stunning in her work clothes and appeared to look better with every passing day. Barbara commented on her appearance. Roger said to Rosie she could shower first if she wanted, said she would and kissed him and them as she went back inside. Little more than half an hour later Rosie appeared and had brought with her a wine glass and poured herself a glass full as she sat down and said what a relief and told Barbara how much she enjoyed being with her last night. Barbara told her it was very pleasurable and since they were all here they would be together again. After about half an hour Victoria said she wanted to eat and they all returned to the kitchen as Roger chopped the chicken and Barbara placed the bowls where he could add the chicken as Victoria peeled and rinsed the eggs, Roger passed the bowls to her while she sliced and added the eggs. Rosie took out the dressings and set the table and Barbara put there glasses on the table and they all sat down and began eating. The salad was very good and Roger thought about the last time he had a chicken salad and couldn't eat it all and knew it probably would happen again. All of them took their time eating, and enjoyed it very much as they savored the flavors, and sipped the wine. Roger actually finished his salad this time since they hadn't eaten since breakfast. These weren't as large as before and he didn't feel stuffed which was a good thing.

Rosie said she would clean up since they had dinner waiting for her as Victoria put the dressings away as Roger noticed when they ate together they consumed one bottle of wine and would make a mental note of that when he went shopping. It wasn't long before the kitchen was cleaned up and all of them went back outside to talk and enjoy the pleasant weather before turning in for the day. After a long while as the sun went down they went inside and closed up the lower level since everyone had bathed. Roger kissed Barbara and Victoria good night as he took Rosie with him. Barbara said she needed an early start as she went with Victoria to her bedroom.

Roger climbed into bed after undressing and so did Rosie, she hadn't slept with him since Victoria and Barbara moved in and was all over him and asked him to spank her. She bent over in the bed without being told. She welcomed a spanking from Roger and asked that he use a belt on her. Roger got out of bed, went to the cabinet and removed his wide leather strap and walked over and pulled her up by her hair, looked into her face and kissed her, she said please master spank me, he asked her why. He knew she felt guilty about something, said she had jerked herself off earlier today and that was against his rules. He knew she wanted to be punished and may be lying about playing with herself as he told her to stand, and removed some office binder clips and had her spread her legs as he applied them to her now more plump pussy lips, only this time he added two smaller ones along with the larger ones, then he applied long plastic ties to her now slightly larger breast pulling them tight causing them to bulged out, then he applied the binder clips to her nipples. Rosie really enjoyed the clamps and was used to the feeling since she used to apply them to herself, but now she seemed to cringe since it had been a while. He asked her what she was, she replied she was his bitch, he said that's right and told her to turn around and to place her hands behind her head; she did as she was told. Roger decided to use a narrow leather strap this time with two one inch wide thin ends as he brought it down on her butt and thighs and as he whipped her it wrapped around to her breast and vagina and upper thighs. He told her to turn around and she did as he looked in her tear filled eyes, her breast were now swollen as he twisted the clips on her nipples before removing them and then touching them as he removed the plastic ties and as the feeling returned he pinched them, she cringed but enjoyed feeling the pain, he told her to turn around and bend over and spread her legs with her hands on her knees as he pulled the clips on her vaginal lips, removing them before taking the wide leather paddle and spanking her hard on each cheek five times, then having her stand and turn around to face him again. He looked at her and asked if she was sorry she had broken her masters' rule, she said yes sir master. He knew and she knew that she wanted his attention and this was her way of getting it.

Roger would be sure she was fully satisfied when he finished as he looked at the small narrow marks on her body and knew she needed more. He placed his hand between her legs and felt the moisture from her highly excited state, he told her to bend over on the floor with her legs spread wide, head down, arms besides her head; she complied, as he took the wide leather strap from the cabinet, his favorite. Standing before her and told her to hold his ankles. She did as he whipped her between her legs and down her thighs as he made her count, one, thank you master, until she climaxed at fourteen and continued till she reached twenty. She climaxed several more times, then made her stand and not touch herself, she did as he felt her again, climaxing and she reached and kissed his other hand climaxing with a loud cry saying thank you master. She climaxed again as he held her between her legs and closed the cabinet and ordered her to kneel. She then took him in her eager mouth, and after a few minutes he ordered her to the bed and to lie on her back as he climbed on top of her as she eagerly awaited his penis penetrating her very hot pussy. She continued climaxing as he came inside of her and she held him and climaxed again. He laid on top of her as she looked at him with a loving expression of complete satisfaction. He moved over and laid next to her as she took his hand and placed it between her legs and he felt his and her love juices as he rubbed the come over her clit. She continued to climax again squeezing her thighs tightly together pressing her head against his chest. He hugged her and said she loved him and shortly after he climbed out of bed taking her with him to the shower where they bathed and made her douche; as he held her and stroked her head. They soon finished and dried themselves off and quickly oiled each other. Said she was happy now as they returned to the bedroom and climbed in bed and she curled up next to him kissing him and placing his hand again between her legs and said it was his and she finally went to sleep fully satisfied. He eventually turned on his side and turned off the last light and falling asleep.

Chapter Sixteen

The next morning after waking up and coming out of the bathroom, he returned to bed, it was too early to get up and he couldn't go back to sleep and turned over looking at Rosie. He decided to take some photos of her, as she laid there sleeping and posed her without waking her up. He finished his little exploit and returned to bed. She began to wake up as he stroked her head. Then she smiled snuggling up against him, holding him while going back to sleep as he continued rubbing her beautiful body. Looking at the clock with just a couple more hours before he knew that she had to get up for work. He eased out of bed and slipped on his shorts and t-shirt and walked around the house as he looked at Victoria and Barbara soundly sleeping in Victoria's bedroom. The sun was just about to rise as he looked at the clock and it was five thirty so he went downstairs and put on a pot of coffee. Knowing everyone would wake up between six and seven, taking some donuts out and sat down and drank his coffee. Well, today Barbara would completely move in and the moving in part of his grandiose plan would then be complete. As he sat and thought about Rosie, he felt it was fate that had brought her to him, just as Barbara had entered his life and then Victoria. His thinking was you should be happy, and that he was, very happy and would leave it at that. And they were happy also and knew you had to make your own happiness in this life time, and to stay happy was the real challenge and felt he wasn't doing too badly for himself. He heard the elevator and looked at the clock and it was six fifteen as Barbara entered the kitchen; she came over as he stood and hugged her. She looked at him, kissed him and said thank you for making me so, so very happy as tears came to her eyes and she looked at him and kissed him again. She took out a cup from the cabinet and poured herself a cup of coffee, sat down and held his hand, and said she loved him and felt blessed to have him in her life. He started to say something, but decided not to, and just accepts what had just happened.

Said she and Victoria had talked a long time before going to sleep and they felt blessed to have him and now each other, being here together. Told him as they held each other they were so very thankful to have him in their lives. Soon Victoria came downstairs and kissed him and poured herself a cup and said she loved him, as Barbara said we are very happy to be here with you Roger. Victoria said they needed to eat a little something before getting started. Roger said he would be right back. He went upstairs to check on Rosie. After entering the bedroom Rosie had just turned over and started waking up; then Roger came in, sitting on the side of the bed and started touching her, and looking at her closely, noticing that the marks on her where now barely visible. She then sat up and placed her arms around him and began crying as he held her. She said please never let me go, as he rubbed her back and said to her it was time to get up sweetie, she kissed him as he helped her up and handed her the t-shirt she wore last night. She went to her bedroom and he returned downstairs as Victoria and Barbara had breakfast well under way. Rosie came downstairs and set the table as Barbara filled four glasses with orange juice. Victoria dished up the breakfast of eggs, ham, toast and jelly. They all pulled up a chair and Barbara said grace, while eating in silence Roger said, hope you all have a blessed day. Barbara, Victoria and Roger cleaned up as they told Rosie to get ready for work. They were finished in no time since it was getting to be a regular routine with them. They all left to prepare for Barbara's moving in.

Roger was dressed and looking at his desk, and decided to take care of the bills later. Rosie looking sexier than ever as she came in and he asked her to wait a moment as he snapped several more pictures of her; she hugged him tight and kissed him and told him she would always be his. He kissed her back and told her to be safe. Before departing she turned, departing only after she had hugged and kissed Barbara and Victoria. Barbara and Victoria were dressed and Barbara said she was leaving now and wanted to be sure she had everything ready, she kissed them and departed. Roger and Victoria checked the house and then departed soon after. They arrived about half an hour after Barbara and found her cleaning up and soon the movers arrived. Barbara showed them what to take and it took less than an hour after loading up the truck and where on their way. Roger and Victoria waited for Barbara and they all drove home passing the moving truck and arriving just in time as it pulled in and backed up to the front entrance. Barbara left her car outside as Roger parked inside the garage. She showed them where her things were going by loading them on the elevator and in less than an hour they were completely finished. Roger then changed clothes and sat at his desk and started opening the mail and the bills for everyone's accounts; and after an hour, he had a stack of bills ready for the mail man and bundled them up and took them downstairs, before he came. He returned as he began filing the paper work away and checked off the closed accounts for everyone and there were only a couple that he hadn't received yet. Checking on Barbara to see what she was up to, saw that she was busy arranging her room and helped her move a couple pieces of furniture. She then stated it now looks more like a room with someone living in it. It wasn't long before the mail man came and took the bundle Roger had left as well as dropping off today's mail delivery. Victoria came in and she had been folding clothes and had quite a bit too wash. She stated that she would cook and was deciding what to fix for dinner. Eventually she needed to make out a grocery list which she and Roger had discussed earlier.

They went to the kitchen and discussed dinner and looked and decided on mixed vegies, and a meat loaf with a salad. Victoria said she would make the meat loaf but would have to wait for the ground meat to thaw as she took it out of the freezer and placed it in the sink in some warm water. Roger said we can wait as he picked up todays mail deliver and returned upstairs, he sorted it out and went through it separating the junk from the remaining bills that had arrived and proceeded to open them and placed them in a stack. He looked through the rest of the mail and shredded it as he went along. He had the last three bills that he was looking for and wrote out the checks and scratched them off the list and filed them away. He again checked on Barbara. He found her straightening and putting things away as she looked up and saw him enter and commented that the room was as big as her entire apartment. She hugged him and said thank you and kissed him and they embraced. Said she was so excited and asked him to touch her as she unfastened her jeans and he reached down and slid his hand inside her jeans and felt her, holding her with one arm and kissing her, using his other hand to finger her and gently moved it around inside of her, soon she climaxed and bit his neck. He held her tight as she jerked having climaxed multiple times then Roger massaged her knowing where her most sensitive spot was since as he had done numerous times before. Roger removed his hand and held her up with both arms placing his knee between her thighs as she slowly calmed down and thanked him again kissing him until he just held her tightly. Said she was all right for now, informing her that Victoria and he were going to fix dinner; he released her and returned to his room for the outgoing mail and went downstairs and placed it in the mailbox outside the front door and then returned to the kitchen.

Victoria was preparing the ingredients to go in her meatloaf. Roger found the grocery list and did an inventory of their food stocks and Victoria said to him that since being together this short period of time she found herself eating much better, but less often, and felt good and had noticed a change in her overall appearance. Said eating fresh everyday had it benefits over eating in restaurants and fast foods. Roger agreed with her as he took out a pot for the vegetables that he would prepare, and said to her just look at Rosie, she looked almost anorectic when he first saw her, now she has filled out more. Victoria told him that she has gained five pounds and felt she was looking and feeling so much healthier. Victoria asked him if he was trying to fatten them up, and he responded no, but you are what you eat. He also said being together and eating well is much healthier for all of them and being loved is also good for everyone. He walked past her and smacked her on the ass and said see it's plumper and firm now, she responded that yes it is and had noticed it herself. He told her she was looking better and walked back pass her again and kissed her and said, she had more ass for him to feel on and could spank her better and this excited her as she begged him to please stop. Roger called her his sweet little tight ass bitch and she begged him to please stop, as he filled his pot with water. She told him she would have to jerk herself off if he kept it up, and he replied no problem as he walked behind her and told her he liked feeling her sweet ass. She turned around to faced him and said please master, he did sliding his hand into her jeans as she unbuttoned them, pulling the zipper down and sliding his hand in her panties and feeling her shaven vagina, feeling the dampness as he squeezed her placing pressure on her swollen clit, then she held him for dear life as she was rocked with a massive climax as he was pressing her against the counter top. She cried, thank you master, oh god thank you, as he removed his hand and stuck his finger in his mouth, she kissed and hugged him as he asked if she was all right now, and she replied, yes sir and just don't talk to me anymore until I finish please. He laughed, kissed her and began preparing the vegetables as he washed them. Very soon Victoria had the oven on and had mixed the meat and ingredients together and placed it in a baking dish, before placing it in the oven, and had the water boiling with the potatoes and carrots. Then he took out the lettuce and she removed bowls from the cabinet, he chopped the lettuce and said you know a salad for all of us uses a whole head of lettuce then she washed some tomatoes. She commented that the grocery list is not that long but the amounts are larger, and we should see a savings on groceries soon, he agreed. They prepared the salads and washed up their utensils. He told her he would have to double his wine purchases because you only could get four glasses out of one bottle, then took one out with a couple of glasses and poured them each a glass.

He handed her the glass and told her he loved her and she had some sweet pussy and would molest her later and eat her as she blushed and said please stop. Roger laughed since he liked her reactions when he talked dirty to her since being highly excitable and very sexy. Barbara soon joined them and asked if there was anything she could do, Vicky said she could set the table and Barbara proceeded to do just that. Roger said well tomorrow we will finish up with the moving portion and that part will be completed. He told them he had the last three final bills from all their utilities to pay and they had just come today and would have them in the mail by tomorrow. Barbara poured herself a glass of wine and they all sat down. Barbara and Victoria still had their jeans on and Roger suggested they go put on something more comfortable so he could fondle them. Victoria blushed and Barbara said yes sir. They went upstairs and changed clothes and returned both wearing loose fitting thin dresses. Roger said that's better ladies as he stood to check on his veggies turning the fire down to low. Barbara said her room feels so much better with her furniture in it and can see how really small her apartment was. Now she has everything she owns in one room. Victoria said that realization came over her also when her furnishings were moved in. Roger looked at the clock and said it was nearly time for Rosie to come home and fifteen or so minutes later she walked in and greeted and kissed them all and went upstairs to change and soon returned saying that she was so happy to be home and missed them all so very much.

Soon the oven chimed and Victoria took the oven gloves and placed the meatloaf on the cooling rack, as Roger turn the fire off from under his pot, and they went and drank more wine as the food cooled down some. Roger and Victoria went and prepared the plates as Rosie placed them on the table and Barbara took the salads out of the refrigerator. They all sat down to eat. Roger commented about Victoria's earlier remarks about eating healthier and less often and Rosie's weight gain. Barbara said she felt better also since being here together and wondered if being happier and having a more secure feeling about your surroundings had anything to do with it and with Roger having them taking vitamins. Rosie said her complexion has cleared up and with Roger insisting everyone applying oils and lotions to their bodies she has seen a marked improvement in her overall appearance and skin tone. Victoria said she just felt so much better, and soon they had finished eating. Barbara cleared the table and Rosie washed the dishes and Victoria put the uneaten leftovers of meatloaf in a container Roger handed her. The veggies were all gone so cleaning up was a breeze. When everything was cleaned up Roger said they were going for a walk, and would walk around the property and said they needed some shoes. Roger went upstairs and brought his shoes and Rosie's downstairs. Barbara brought Victoria's shoes down with hers. They went out the back door to the patio and put their shoes on and Roger led them down the wide patio as it transcended into a deck. The yard slopped downwards and down the wide stairs onto the expansive grounds. They walked the grounds together for the first time and experienced the natural surroundings as he showed them how much space surrounded the house. After they had made it around the first time he told them they were going around again because he didn't want any of them getting fat on him, and when they returned they were happy to be back. Barbara commented that you can't see the house from the grounds and Victoria said that was good in case she wanted to stand in the window nude.

While they sat outside Roger went inside and brought back four bottles of water for them. Roger said to them they were looking good to him and said he was going to take a shower and get some rest and headed inside and they all followed as he closed up the downstairs before going upstairs. He went to his room and found the clothes Victoria had washed and folded and placing them in his large closet. His bed wasn't made up but he had straighten it up earlier as he undressed and put his shorts and shirt on a chair and headed to the shower, and turned the water on and entered and showered alone for once or at least that's what he thought before Victoria entered, came in and disrobed getting in the shower with him and said he had gotten her all excited earlier and it hadn't went away and needed him to cool her down. He laughed as he played with her as she climaxed several more times before they exited and dried off. Roger spread a towel out on his bed as they oiled each other and when they finished he told her to go sleep with Rosie and play with her. Victoria said she wanted to be with him and he got in bed and said ok but he was going to sleep. She climbed in with him and massaged him as he quickly went to sleep, and soon Barbara came in and got in bed with him also, he didn't wake up as she rubbed him also. Rosie entered and then Victoria got out of bed and took Rosie to her room and left Barbara with Roger. Victoria and Rosie caressed each other and soon fell asleep. Roger was tired, more tired now that three women were with him not just on weekends, but every day and all day. He slept very well now every night, that's what he was thinking, but the girls had other ideas.

Chapter Seventeen

It was early Wednesday morning when Barbara woke and Roger continued sleeping, she headed to the bathroom and looked at the lighted clock, it was four thirty. Both of them went to bed early before ten, she got back in bed and laid down looking at him as he slept, he turned over and faced her, slowly waking up, yawned and opened his eyes, looked at her and reached for her as she touched his face. She said sweetie as they touched, snuggling up and he soon went back to sleep. She held him, and shortly he again woke up, climbed out of bed and went to the bathroom and shortly returned refreshed. Roger looked at the clock, it was now a few minutes after five; he returned to bed and reached out to caress her and they hugged and kissed. He told her it was a pleasant surprise seeing her here with him and said he couldn't go back to sleep and she said the same. They talked and debated whether they should get up as they hugged and kissed saying that he loved her and was glad she was here with him now and every day. She felt the same. They both wondered why it took them so long to be together. Said she knew why and it was her reluctance to make any sort of commitment. He said it wasn't just you, he had felt the same but over time became more concerned about her safety especially becoming more emotionally attached and in love with her and said he was glad that part was over. They then decided to have some coffee and got up and he put on his shorts and a shirt, she put on her robe and both of them headed downstairs as the sky grew light now from the rising sun. He made the coffee and she took out the donuts as then they went outside on the patio and took in the morning air, looking at the dew that clung to the trees as they hugged and kissed again before returning to the kitchen, pouring their coffee and sitting down as they just lovingly looked at one another. He said, well today we wrap up all the moving and finally can start operating as one household. She reminded him about the rug delivery, the rug for the front entrance. He said Victoria can handle the delivery and said he would go with her. They sat drinking their coffee almost an hour before Victoria came downstairs. Said she looked for them in their bedroom and that she and Rosie were up also since everyone had gone to bed so early.

Rosie was next to come downstairs and entered the kitchen and said good morning family as she kissed Barbara and Roger, and went and poured a cup of coffee. Everyone appeared much rested while Barbara stood and began to prepare breakfast, as Victoria and Rosie assisted her. Roger sat and watched. Barbara said she was going to change clothes and was soon followed by both Vicky and Rosie. They all quickly returned as he made another pot of coffee and soon breakfast was served. Roger said he had never had breakfast this often in his life except in the army. Rosie told them she hadn't eaten this regular since she was a child and hoped she didn't get fat but said it was hard to resist good food. Victoria told Rosie she needed some meat on her bones and was looking so much better than when she first met her and was now filling out. They soon finished and Rosie cleaned up and Roger gave her a hand.

Everyone went to their bedrooms to dress for the day. Roger decided when they were out he was going to the sexy store and buy them some stockings and was going to take them out one day soon maybe this weekend. He sat at his desk and finished with the last of the closed utility bill accounts and wrote the checks from their various accounts, filed the statements away and made sure he had the account numbers on the checks before he sealed them and placed a stamp on the envelopes. He was finished and headed downstairs and placed them in the mail box outside and opened the gate and decided he would no longer close the gate because of possible emergencies. It was Wednesday and Juan and his crew would be here along with the rug delivery. When Victoria came down he informed her of the rug delivery and about the lawn care people coming and then asked her to decide what they might want for dinner and take it out early if it needed defrosting saying he had the grocery list and would pick up a few things while he was out with Barbara. Rosie came downstairs and kissed them and headed to work. Victoria asked for the list and added a few more items to it. Barbara came downstairs and said we are a little early and he said we should go anyway. They departed and he rode with Barbara as she drove to her old apartment. They arrived, parked and entered, she looked at what she was donating as they cleaned up and after an hour the truck arrived and two men came and verified the address and name and fifteen minutes later everything was gone. It wasn't long before her landlord appeared as Roger took the last of the trash out. When he returned the landlord had given Barbara her lease release papers and a copy of the inspection sheet and also gave him her new address and handed him her keys to the apartment, he wished her well as she departed along with Roger.

They left and Roger asked her to please stop at The Sexy Store before getting the groceries. Barbara knew where it was as they pulled up in front and went inside together. Roger knew what he wanted, and purchased three pair of one size fit all stocking with the attached garters, three fishnet body suits and three crotch less pantyhose along with two more restraint harnesses with the attached butt plugs and short penis shaped dildos and was finished. Barbara purchased a very larger dildo. They paid and departed, then headed to the grocery store and Roger spent most of his time in the produce department and only purchased a few other items that Victoria had added to the list. He checked the list before they checked out and they headed home. It wasn't long before they arrived home and brought the groceries inside. Victoria said the rug came, as they went to look. Barbara had made an excellent choice, it filled the space perfectly and Roger ascended the stairway and looked down, saying it was spectacular. He went downstairs to wash the vegetables and the fruits and washed the several melons off. Roger was taught at an early age that you should always wash your fruits and vegetables. Noticing Barbara and her body language Roger knew that she wanted some attention, so he went upstairs with Barbara and sure enough, she wanted him to play with her.

Knowing Barbara well Roger knew what that meant as they undressed in her room and he asked about the dildo and she took it out, removed the packaging, and went to wash it off, and told him she needed to take an enema first. Roger knew what that meant, she like him playing with her ass and went to his bedroom leaving all his clothes and brought back a pair of latex gloves. The last time they went to the Sexy store she bought the inflatable dildo, but this one was slightly larger, longer and solid, when she returned from the bathroom Roger knew he would have to play with her anus. Roger was overwhelmed as she spread a huge towel out on her bed and brought a jar of anti-bacterial lubricant and he knew just what she wanted. She hugged him and they kissed. Roger replied it has been a while as he talked to her dirty and spanked her as she bent over as he put a surgical glove on and using some of the lubricant began playing with her anus and used his fingers on her, massaging her anus and slowly playing with her pussy with the other hand. She became more and more excited. He took the large dildo and placed lubricant on it and placed it at her anal opening, he moved it slowly around her anal opening pushing it inside her willing ass before he then suggested she sit on it as he stood and pulled over the solid wooden chair she kept and used for her anal play. He set the dildo in the chair holding it as she slowly began sitting on it, he played with her clit and continued talking dirty to her as she now slowly went up and down on it. He played with and licked her vagina and sucked on her protruding clit causing her to climax as he continued holding the dildo and it began sliding easily up inside her anus. She then stood and bent over in the bed as Roger worked it in and out of her; then he inserted a vibrating dildo in her vagina causing her to have another massive orgasm as Roger continued working it in and out of her anus and becoming more aroused and pulled it out then slowly inserting his hand, working it inside her anus as she told him to fuck her sluttish ass. Barbara said that felt wonderful as he fist fucked her anus. Roger enjoyed playing with her when she felt like this and she climaxed again soon. Afterwards he slowly removed his hand and being highly aroused, Barbara turned around and took him in her mouth where he soon climaxed. Then they went to the shower where they continued with the large dildo and some soap as Barbara knelt down and he gave her a golden shower, then they bathed and washed off the sex toys and continued feeling each other saying to him that she was long overdue for that. He loved playing with Barbara and she loved him for his discretion and being adventurous with her fantasies. They bathed a long while before they came out and made sure everything was cleaned up. She willfully placed another clean towel on the bed as they oiled each other. Roger continuously played with Barbara as she acted like a dog in heat. He focused on her anus which he knew she was a freak for. He then sucked and licked her clit causing her to climax several more times. They were all over each other, soon Roger got up after fulfilling her fantasies to wash his hands. They hugged and kissed some more and Barbara said to him she never got enough of him on weekends and now since they're living together she's so very happy now and know that he will always be here for her. She dressed in a loose fitting clean cotton dress and gathered the towels and there dirty clothes and took them downstairs. He also left to do the same and headed downstairs hearing the sound of lawn mowers and looked outside and saw Juan and his crew were busy cutting and sprucing things up outside.

Barbara came out of the laundry room and Victoria said they would be having baked fish, broccoli, and rice with a salad. He asked what part she wanted help with; she said the rice and the salad. Barbara said to Victoria you like to cook don't you, and she replied yes it was very enjoyable and calming for her. Roger felt on Victoria's butt and said it has a nice shape to it now, and she said to him he should know. He asked her if she was still excited from yesterday and she said yes and still wasn't completely satisfied yet. He said it sounds like you need a spanking across you slutty little ass and maybe while your tied up. He knew this excited her as she rubbed herself against the counter and asked him to please stop or he would have to do something sooner and not later. He grabbed Victoria and turned her around and said you need it now and took his hand since she was wearing shorts, slid his hand inside them and felt her as she became more aroused and he talked to her dirty as she became very wet and he fingered her as she wrapped her arms around his neck and he inserted two fingers inside her as he whispered in her ear and licked it and she erupted with a massive organism. He then held her up as she was racked with several more climaxes and her breathing became short and ragged. She said, please master, as he continued before abruptly stopping and just held her. He asked her if his little slut had enough for now, and she said yes sir master, as he released her. Victoria had to go sit down and get herself together while Barbara stood and watched the encounter.

Vicky finally stood as he washed his hands and began preparing the rice for dinner. Vicky came and kissed him and proceeded to begin cooking and Barbara said she would do the salad. Soon the dinner was underway, the fish was in the oven, the broccoli was steaming, and the rice was done along with a green salad. Roger opened a bottle of chilled red wine and the three of them sat and sipped the wine and waited on the food and for Rosie to come home. The lawn care people had finished and departed as Roger looked outside and everything looked good. He told them about his decision to leave the gate open, and the reason why and they all agreed with him. Soon Rosie arrived and they told her she had time to change and wash up. She went upstairs and soon after the oven dinged, and Victoria removed the hot dish from the oven and set it on the stove top. Barbara set the table as Roger refilled their glasses and Victoria dished up their plates and Rosie soon came downstairs and they all sat down and began eating. The food was delicious. They sat and ate and Roger said after dinner he wanted Rosie and Victoria to shower because he wanted to see them all and had some special clothes he wanted them to wear for him and would take pictures; Barbara knew because she had seen what he had purchased.

After finishing a wonderful and delicious meal everyone seemed to be well, content and full. The girls helped clean up and when they finished left to go upstairs following their masters order. Victoria and Rosie left to shower. Roger therefore, handed Barbara the fishnet body suit telling her to wear some black hi- heels and he would take pictures. While they dressed Roger spread out large towels and their old bedding he had saved covering the cushions and backs completely and covering the sofas and chairs along with the cocktail table. Victoria and Rosie had showered together and oiled one another as Roger came and handed them the packages telling them what shoes to wear. He returned to his room where Barbara was already seated, she had fixed her hair and had some earrings on. She looked marvelous and he started taking pictures of her and posing for him, then Rosie and Victoria walked in and Roger told them both what he wanted them to wear. For Rosie he wanted her hair in an upsweep and Victoria he wanted her to wear some earrings. The girls were posing one after the other and individually, then as a group. Upstairs, and downstairs with explicit photos for his collection and then told them to undress and return with nothing on.

He went downstairs and secured the house, fixed some drinks bringing them up on a cart as they were all seated, passed the drinks around and said you all look very lovely. It was still early and he informed them he had decided to play a DVD he had compiled; since he was into computers and had combined several short and long videos together and made several two hour disc, which he had compiled in his spare time. Before he started he went to his cabinet and removed several dildos and clamps along with some lubricant and placed all the items on the table which he had covered with a soft blanket. He explained that they were about to see some bondage and discipline movies and told them they were free to feel themselves and one another and could have sex with one another and it was ok to do whatever they wanted, and for them to enjoy watching and would be filming them for his own pleasure, he passed out the drinks and put the DVD in the player and started the movie with them looking at the large screen television knowing they wouldn't miss seeing anything. It wasn't long before Rosie had her hand between her legs and soon Victoria followed as she now had her legs up and reached for a dildo and some lubricant and massaged herself and soon climaxed several times. It was good Roger had placed towels on all the cushions earlier knowing he was going to treat them to a show. Barbara came and sat by him placing his hand between her legs as he felt her and when a scene of a woman inserting a large dildo in her ass appeared on screen she climaxed and held Rogers hand tightly between her thighs. She finally released his hand and picked up a dildo and began massaging her anus with it as she played with her vagina and continued climaxing. Rosie was sweating as she climaxed several times and continued feeling herself as she lay down looking at the large screen and not taking her eyes away from the action. The DVD Roger had put in had several stories. The three women couldn't stop looking. One story had a woman tied and hanging, being whipped and then a baseball bat inserted in her rectum and a dildo in her vagina, another scene a woman had clamps with weights attached, and another a woman was demeaned, spit on and urinated on before preforming oral sex. Roger had made the DVD and included what he knew turned each one of them on as they enjoyed themselves. Rosie reached for the clamps as another story played and a woman had clamps on her sensitive parts and Rosie clamped herself, her vagina and nipples, pulling and twisting until she screamed and climaxed. It was a pleasant evening and the outdoor temperature was above seventy as he had opened his window and the sliding glass door. They sipped the drinks as they enjoyed the video, there were scenes of two women with one dildo between them and a real good variety of bondage and discipline, and some sadism and masochism, one of a woman being led around on a leash, and in a cage and lots of other cruel stuff. The DVD lasted two hours, and he placed another in and these were even more demeaning than the last, as they continued masturbating, then Victoria came and played with Barbara and ended up fisting her anus with her small hands as Barbara climaxed and knelt on the short solid cocktail table as they faced the screen not taking their eyes off the action and then Rosie joined in and they were having an orgy and he was filming them with his stationary cameras, and had one he used for close ups. When the second DVD ended they were exhausted and sat and laid and rubbed on each other as Victoria left to wash her hands since she had them up Barbara anus and then returned as they sat and hugged and kissed each other. He turned the television off and made them all go to his shower and wash. He followed and told them to continue and they happily did, applying soap and shower wash to one another and Victoria fisted Rosie in her ass again with her small hands, then Barbara fisted Victoria and he gave them the enema bag and they just had a good time before they were all finished. They spent almost an hour in the shower and made sure they were clean as they came out. Telling them they would have to clean his bathroom tomorrow and making them oil themselves even thought they were totally exhausted. The girls were lying on several large towels on his bed as they oiled themselves. Roger took more pictures of them. They were now fully satisfied and totally exhausted. He told them to go sleep and he would see them tomorrow. They kissed and thanked him and he patted their ass as they left.

He picked up the dildos and returned the clamps to the cabinet and washed the dildos in bleach and warm soapy water, dried them and returned all the items to the cabinet. He straightened out his room with only a few of the towels he had to place in the dirty clothes pile he created by his bedroom door. He folded the bedding that was used and returned it to the closet. Roger uploaded the video from the cameras he had taken from a couple of stationary positions and the angels were very good and it captured all the action. Roger left to check on the girls and to his surprise they were all sleeping in their own beds alone, totally exhausted. He kissed and covered each one of them, saying finally. While the girls were all sleeping Roger started cleaning up. Placed the glasses and ice bucket on the lower shelf of the cart and the dirty towels and bedding on top and went and took everything downstairs to be washed. Roger started a load of wash using all the machines then to the kitchen where he washed the glasses and pitcher and left them to dry on the dish rack.

Roger was more than satisfied when he returned to his bedroom, it was almost ten pm, the girls were all very sound asleep and he would also get some needed rest now. He thought about how they had just let themselves go, how they felt at ease with one another and how their inhibitions had totally left them. He was happy they felt free with him watching them. He undressed closed his sliding glass door and window and climbed into bed, and pulled the covers over himself and quickly fell asleep.

Chapter Eighteen

Friday morning came and Roger woke around six, he got up and went to the bathroom, came back and climbed right back into bed. As he laid there it wasn't long before Victoria came into his room with her robe on, took it off and crawled into bed with him cuddling up next to him and kissed him and told him she loved him so much and thanked him for yesterday, and how exciting it was as she snuggled up close as he held and caressed her. She laid their kissing and caressing him back. As he lay there with her not to long after, Barbara entered completely nude and climbed in on the other side of him snuggling up next to him and feeling his face as she kissed him. Said she would always be his, and then Victoria reached down and gently held his penis and began massaging him, it soon began to stiffen as Barbara slid down and took him in her mouth, then Victoria slid down also with her and they both licked and sucked him as he felt their warm mouths and tongues on him. He pulled both women up by their hair and held them close as Victoria managed to climb on top of him and slid down and guided him inside of her and moved slowly on top of him; as Barbara licked his ear, Victoria soon climaxed as her body stiffened, then relaxed before she rolled off to his side; Barbara then got on top and she slid down on him also as Victoria kissed him and he played with Barbara's breast causing her to soon climax also and then just laid on him until she rolled over to his other side. Roger was still hard and now climbed on top of Victoria and whispered in her ear how she was such a slut and needed a good fucking and began pumping her hard as she moaned and said fuck your nasty bitch master as he fingered her anus and she climaxed again. He continued as she was racked with another massive climax. He sat up and raised her legs up and entered her now tight ass as she screamed and he slowly slid inside of her and pumped her and soon climaxed filling her anus with semen. He pulled out and lay back down between them both as they licked and kissed him. They all briefly closed their eyes before getting up together and going to the bathroom and taking a nice warm shower and washing one another. When they came out of the bathroom Rosie came in and hugged him as he was putting on his robe and sat on the side of the bed. Rosie thanked him also for last night, and said she was his and would do whatever he wanted. Barbara had left and returned with her robe on as her and Victoria stood holding hands. He stood and said ladies lets have some nourishment. Rosie said she had taken the day off because she wanted to be here with them and they all went downstairs to have breakfast.

As usual Roger put on the coffee and the three of them fixed breakfast together, and soon were sitting down eating and nourishing their sexually ravished bodies. Roger brought back the coffee pot and refreshed there cups. Came back and sat down after everyone had finished eating. Barbara had something to share with the family saying that last night was the most enjoyable and exciting time she had ever experienced with them or anyone as far as she was concerned and wanted Roger to take her and have his way with her again. Saying that she just felt freaky and let her hair down got loose. Rosie said she wanted to be punished, and Victoria spoke up and said she wanted more but couldn't explain why she felt the way she did. But Roger knew why, he had unlocked their deep inner feeling and they were able to show their true selves. They began cleaning up and were soon finished, and they surrounded Roger and asked him to take them and do whatever he wanted to them and said they needed him to punish them. Barbara said some of the videos he showed excited her and even now as she thought about them made her feel very excited. He said to give him some time to think and reminded them they were supposed to clean his bathroom and suggested they do that first. They went upstairs and he was in his bedroom and soon began smelling pine cleaner and bleach.

Roger had to sit and think about what he was going to do to them and soon decided he would have them wear the body suits and cuff and hang them and degrade them since they wanted to feel used. He had shown them some video scenario's they probably would never have thought about otherwise. He decided he would have them sit down and talk to him more about what they saw that turned them on after they finished cleaning the bathroom and after putting the cleaning supplies away. They had finished when he asked them to come have a seat and told them he needed to talk to them some more. They sat down and he started with Barbara, he asked her how she felt right now. She told him she really felt truly free inside and uninhibited, but wanted to explore more of how she felt. He asked if what she had seen had anything to do with how she felt. She replied yes it had and it excited her so very much and said now she wanted to be played with again. He asked her what she wanted done to her. She replied the anal play with the bondage and humiliation was such a big turn on. He asked Victoria what she wanted. She replied to be tied up and humiliated verbally and the spitting and slapping with the urination and sex made her so extremely excited and couldn't explain why it was such a turn-on saying she was hot now as she thought and spoke about it, as she pressed her knees tightly together, and added the anal play was new to her but she really enjoyed it very much and was surprised how good it felt. Rosie was next and said the clamps and whippings along with the penetrations and being verbally humiliated, but said she enjoyed feeling the pain on her genitals most of all. Roger said he just wanted to know what and how they felt. He asked them if they were prepared to play all day. They all responded yes. He said ladies I respect you and love you all very, very much, and I know you trust me and it's the reason you are here, and told them he would help them fulfill their sexual needs and desires. He told them they had an hour to do whatever they needed and to return wearing nothing but the body suits from yesterday and they had to address him in the proper way when they returned, they all said yes sir master, as they left his bedroom.

He went downstairs and took out the roll around cart and an empty box and brought it upstairs to his room and placed the ropes and whips, clamps and paddles in the box along with his video camera and SLR. He put on a jockey strap and his leather motorcycle chaps and his leather vest and a pair of socks and his black cowboy boots. When the girls appeared he asked them to put on their black hi-heels. He took a second camera and tripod placing it in the box. When they returned he placed the collars on their necks, cuffs on their wrists and ankles as he kissed each one. They all headed to the elevator and went downstairs to the basement. He took photos of each one individually and had them poise and expose themselves, he was excited just looking at them as he made them line up and began verbally degrading them as he took out several lengths of rope. He suspended each woman from their wrist cuffs with rope to the hooks he had placed in the ceiling. After they were all secured he came and first kissed Barbara, he told her she was his slut as he felt her between her legs and she became even more excited than she already was an began so perspire. He next moved to Victoria, he kissed and tonged her, then told her she was a tramp ass bitch and just another dirty cunt, but she belonged to him as he felt between her legs, and she climaxed, he said she would receive extra punishment because she climaxed without his permission as she shook with even more excitement. He now moved to Rosie, kissed her and told her she was a trash ass bitch also and felt her as she shook, trying not to climax and couldn't help herself and jerked as she was overcome with excitement an climaxed anyway. He took pictures as they stood with their hands above their heads looking very sexy and helpless. He set up his cameras on a couple of tri pods and set them to video record his session with them. He approached Rosie again and tore the net around her nipples as he applied extra-large clothes pins to her aroused and now swollen nipples, standing before her and holding her face with one hand as he told her she was a piece of shit and slapped her lightly several times and spat in her face as she cried and said yes sir master. He told her she deserved to feel even more pain and brought back the spreader bar, bent her down and attached it to the ankle cuffs spreading her sexy legs open for easy access to her now wet and dripping pussy, then placed the large office binder clips to her now plump vaginal lips and pulled the hood back from over her large clitoris and attached an extra-large clothes pin over it as she screamed out loud, he checked that it had plenty of skin so it wouldn't come off then hung on some weights from the binder clips; he stood up and looked into her face as he placed a finger inside her vagina, then two fingers as she became extremely wet, then withdrew them and stuck them in her mouth as she began sucking them as tears ran down her cheeks and called her a tramp ass whore.

Moving close to Victoria, Roger told her that she was a slut whore and took a tube of lubricant out, put on a latex glove, and began to liberally apply it to her anus and very slowly started working several fingers around until he had three inside of her and she really seemed to enjoy it. He then kissed her and she kissed him back before he began inserting a long and wide anal plug inside of her now very relaxed anus then returned to look her in her face as he wiped his gloved hand on a towel and found a soft latex penis shaped dildo and inserted it inside her dripping wet vagina before he doubled and tied a rope around her waist and between her legs, tying it snuggly at the small of her back as he returned and took a small very worn piece of nylon scrubbing pad and soaked it with lubricant and then pulled the rope back and placed it where her clit was beginning to protrude as she cringed and then smacked her on her ass as she climaxed violently. Barbara was next as he stood before her, he slapped her, spit in her face and told her she was a piece of shit bitch; he pulled her by her very long and swollen nipples, then ripped the rear of her fishnet using his gloved hand applying a liberal amount of lubricant to her anus as well and began playing with her until he could easily insert several fingers inside of her, then he inserted the large inflatable dildo inside of her anus and slowly pumped it up. He stood before her and rubbed her vagina and bent down and licked it as she jerked and he began sucking her clit, soon she erupted with a rousing organism. He stood back and looked at them all and began taking pictures.

Roger suddenly took out his long leather flogger with several long narrow ends. He looked at them; they all were on the edge of losing all self-control and he knew it, he had been with them all long enough to know there limits. Rosie was about to climax again. She shook and Victoria was shaking also. He started to whip them but checked on the clamps that bit into Rosie's vaginal lips. They were stretched and decided to add a couple smaller weights. He then decided to blindfold each woman before whipping them again so they wouldn't be able to anticipate any of his moves. He began to whip all three across their bodies, as the whip landed on their thighs, stomach, butt, breast, backs and calf's as they all moaned, whimpered and cried as organism after organism rocked their bodies, shaking uncontrollably. He stopped and took more pictures of them climaxing.

Victoria climaxed and urinated. He whispered in her ears that being a tramp whore she would have to lick it up as she urinated again even more. He approached Rosie, removed the blindfold, bent down and removed the weights from the binder clips before he removed them as she cringed as he felt the now swollen vagina lips; she screamed and had a most violent organism ever then she urinated also. He then pulled and ripped the fishnet and lubed her anus and soon had three fingers inside of her and then worked another large long and wide plug inside of her anus. He stood and came and held her head up and looked as tears ran down her beautiful young face as she tried to kiss him. He then moved back in front of Victoria, removed the blindfold and asked her what was she, said his worthless bitch, she shook as he spat into her face and grabbed the dildo inside of her and worked it into her slightly, and then back in as she climaxed again and he licked her face and told her she was his bitch and she said, yes sir master, and he just let her hang as she began climaxing again while her knees buckled under her. He now stood before Barbara and ripped the net around her nipples as he took and pulled them, pinching them since they were very swollen from the excitement she felt inside as he felt and spanked her vagina and told her she was his bitch, she also climaxed. He then removed the blindfold and kissed her.

Roger released Rosie from the spreader bar and untied her from the ceiling and had her kneel, and then did the same for Victoria and finally Barbara. They were all kneeling when he told them to stand. Although the hi-heels made them look exceptionally sexy, they still had the anal plugs inside their asses as he went and cuffed their hands behind their backs. He attached the leashes to the collars and then led them around the large basement while they walked around looking sexier, leading them back to where they had started. He took Victoria and removed the rope from around her waist and knelt down and removed the pad and anxiously looked at her very swollen and over sensitive clit and slowly removed the dildo and licked and sucked her clit as she shook, screamed and climaxed repeatedly again. Roger stood there and held her knowing she might collapse as she looked at him and said in a weak voice she loved him. He kissed her and spanked her butt, she kissed him back. He released her hands from behind her while she held on to him and shook again with another climax. Roger told her to get down on her knees and lick up her piss, and she did as master ordered, he then moved to Barbara and released her arms, telling her to get down on her hands and knees also, and then he released Rosie, and told her to do the same. Being amused by it all Roger knelt behind Rosie and worked the butt plug back and forth several times before pulling it out slowly. Next he went to Barbara, letting the air out of the anal plug while working it around arousing her thoughts and feeling before pulling it out of her slowly, and then did the same to Victoria, pleasuring them to the upmost and fulfilling their fantasy. He told Victoria that's enough and lined them up, told them to put their heads down, ass up and arms out in front, with legs spread. He took his long strap and went down the line as he whipped each between their spread legs three times before telling them to play with themselves, they did and all three climaxed and Victoria just lay down on the floor as she climaxed continuously. Roger rolled her over and looked at her as she slowly came around and calmed down.

He made them all kneel and had them lick his boots and they seemed to really enjoy being subjected to his will. He told them to stand, then told them to undress and when they were completely nude he told them to take each other as they felt and licked and used the dildos on one another climaxing until they just laid on the floor in each other's arms and in the urine. He told them to clean up the floor and the dildos and when they finished to shower, oil themselves and wear some loose fitting dresses and nothing else, and said he wasn't finished with them and said remember this is all day. They said, yes sir master, as he picked up the restraint equipment and pushed the cart to the elevator and returned after he fixed a bucket of soapy water for them to use, making them busy themselves cleaning the dildos and anal plugs in the basement washroom, picking up their clothes and shoes and mopping up Rosie and Victoria's urine and their sweat. All of them had finished and went and showered together in Barbara's bathroom. Roger went and undressed and showered again and put on a clean pair of shorts and a t-shirt, it being his favorite attire.

The Master Caesar was sitting in the large plush chair in his bedroom about an hour or so later when they all entered and he told them to line up, they did and he stood and walked over to Barbara, looked her in the eyes and asked her who was she, said she was his bitch slave and was here to serve him. He kissed her and told her to sit on the left couch, she did so sitting down. He then stood in front of Victoria, looked her in the eyes and asked her who was she, said she was his nasty bitch and was here to serve him. He told her to sit on the right. Then he approached Rosie, looking her in the eyes, asked her who she was, she replied that she was his dirty slave bitch. He told her to sit next to Victoria, she did. Roger sat in his chair and asked them how they felt now. They all said they felt very happy, good and very satisfied. He said I think you all have had enough for today, and if not, for right now at least as he stood and hugged each one. He suggested they go have something to eat and they said yes sir, master. They all went downstairs together and he said soup. He took out a pot and four cans of mushroom soup and three cans of mushrooms and prepared the soup and very soon they were eating.

When they finished eating he said they were free to do what they wanted, he was finished with them and told them he hoped they were fully satisfied, then he asked if they were satisfied, and they all replied that they were, and told them to get some rest if needed and he would see them whenever, it was early evening around four and he said he would clean up and wash the dishes. He soon finished cleaning up and when he finished went around and made sure downstairs was secure before going upstairs to his bedroom and lying in bed. Several minutes later Victoria came and lay next to him and held him as he rubbed her head, she dosed off and went to sleep. He looked up and Barbara was next as she came and lay down also and kissed him, she turned over and then Rosie came in and crawled into bed besides Barbara.

Said she wanted to be with him also, and soon she fell asleep also. He dosed off as they all lay in his bed fast asleep.

Already in their dresses when he woke up; sleeping for a couple of hours it was almost seven when he looked over at the clock. He had to pee. He then eased out of bed and went to the bathroom. They were sleeping soundly when he returned, grabbed a pillow from the closet and lay on the long couch with a light blanket over him as he dimmed the lights. A couple hours later he woke up again and it was almost nine pm and sat up, they were all sleeping soundly as Barbara woke, she went to the bathroom and came over and said she wanted him. They went to her bedroom and they undressed and she made love to him. Holding him and cried and said how happy she was as she sat on top of him placing him inside of her as she kissed him and climaxed. Roger said he hadn't built up enough strength to come again. She understood and just held him tight as they fell asleep again. It was near midnight when they woke again and Roger said he wanted a drink of water and he and Barbara walked downstairs and went to the kitchen and took out a couple of bottles. Barbara said what he did to them made her feel so alive inside and being here with him was a dream come true, and was glad it had really come true. They walked back upstairs and he looked in on Rosie and Victoria and they were holding each other and sat up when they saw him and Barbara. They each said they wanted him. He said he couldn't right now. Rosie asked him if he would just lay with them and Victoria said please master. He climbed in bed with them thinking these girls are truly in love with me and seems to me they cannot get enough. Oh well Roger thought, so they all hugged and rubbed him and Barbara laid next to Rosie and they all went to sleep again.

Chapter Nineteen

It was Saturday morning when Roger woke up; he found himself surrounded by three hot and very beautiful women who thought the world of him. He knew he would never sleep alone again in his life. That was not going to happen not ever again. The girls were up and all over him rubbing and kissing him as he struggled to go to the bathroom to pee. After using the bathroom Roger returned to bed and laid down between them. He said ladies, I suggest we go and eat and then decide what's on the agenda for today. They agreed and began getting out of bed and went to their bedrooms to freshen up and dress. Roger decided that the girls should go shopping and would give them a list of what he wanted them to purchase that would be for his eyes only. The girls were elated to be going shopping and Roger was thinking this would give him a chance to relax and next week they all would be back at work.

Roger went downstairs and the girls were all there and had started preparing breakfast and put on a pot of coffee. They told him they had everything under control as Rosie brought him a cup of coffee and a donut. It wasn't long before he was surrounded as they all sat eating and looking at him and smiling, Roger wondered what was up, had they or were they conspiring or planning something. He commented that he had a list of things he wanted them to purchase for themselves and hoped they went shopping for themselves today. Barbara asked, what were the items that he wanted them to purchase. He said that he wanted them to get some black tube dresses and a pair of open toe black hi-heels.

Victoria said that sounds sexy and she knew where he had seen them and also who carried the shoes. When they finished eating they cleaned up and were finished in no time. Victoria said she would do anything he asked of her and told Barbara and Rosie we should do whatever Roger ask of us. Rosie and Barbara agreed and told him they would purchase the items today. He said thank you ladies; as he stood and left the table and they all returned upstairs to dress and go shopping. Roger sat at his desk and turned on his computer and then stood and brought his cameras over and soon was downloading his pictures to one of his hard drives and going through the photos he had taken the past couple days and placing them in different files.

A little more than a half hour had passed when Barbara, dressed and looking very sexy in jeans and a blouse with a light sweater and running shoes came in his room and said they would be leaving soon and asked if there was anything else he wanted or needed. He said no, but if you see something for the house and for downstairs feel free because he trusted their judgements. He walked over to her as Victoria looking equally as pretty joined her and then Rosie appeared and they all looked stunning. They kissed him and said they were off and would see him soon. He said take your time, and then he said wait a moment as he went to his closet and opened his cash box and returned and handed each a hundred dollar bill and said you girls take yourselves to lunch. They kissed him and departed as he watched them all leave. He returned to his desk and viewed the videos and edited certain portions going through the photos and pulled out a select few for uploading to his favorite bondage and discipline web site. When he finished he looked at the clock it was nine and opened all the windows upstairs and then downstairs, in the living and dining rooms where the windows were up high and returned upstairs and made up his bed and then laid back down. He soon dosed off, sleeping very well, when he woke it was almost one, as he washed his face and now felt so much better. Playing with the girls was very exhausting and would have to work out a schedule in his head for dealing with them. He went downstairs and fixed himself a sandwich, took his vitamins again and chuckled; he had taken some at breakfast and needed to build up his stamina.

He thought about when they returned what he would do to or with them and knew they expected him to have something planned for them. He thought about how they would look with the stockings and tube dresses with the hi-heels on. It was a beautiful mental picture he had in his mind of them dressed. Then he thought about the two additional harnesses he had purchased, and would see what state of mind they were in when they returned. He opened a can of beer and went back upstairs going thru everyone's bank statements and had a good idea where they would all be in a few months money wise and he would keep a list of all the household expenses and the utilities and figured water would probably be at or near the top of the list. He put everything away and was finished and went and sat in his large comfortable chair and looked at some television, watching the evening news and it was close to six pm when he heard them returning. He heard laughter and their sweet voices as they appeared standing in his bedroom doorway. He stood and walked over to them as they hugged him and said thank you very much, saying that they had a wonderful time together. Each and every one of them had several large bags and soon went to their bedrooms.

Rosie was the first to return wearing the black tube dress with the tags still attached and the open toe hi-heels and asked for his approval, she was followed by Victoria, and then Barbara. It was just as he imagined, perfect, and they returned to their rooms before Barbara returned and sat on the couch closest to him. Barbara said they had a wonderful time together and thanked him again and asked why those particular dresses. They look good on you girls and with the stockings it looked extra sexy, to him. He asked her why she asked. Because she felt they are what sluts wear. He said you are my sluts. He stood and went to his closet and took out the stockings he had purchased and returned, handed her a pair and told her to go put them on with the hi- heels, the dress and nothing else. She stood and left to do as she was told. When Victoria and Rosie appeared he handed them a pair and told them to do the same thing. He readied his camera. Barbara returned and she looked extremely good to him as he stood there and asked her what she was. She said she was his bitch, he said that's better and if I want you to look like a slut you will, do you understand, she said yes sir master. He kissed her and put his hand between her legs and she was as hot as a firecracker and climaxed in less than a minute. He said see, you are my slut bitch, as she blushed and the excitement in her began rising.

She said master please take her, he said you will have to wait and asked if she could feel herself, and he said no, and told her to have seat.

Victoria appeared and then Rosie. He asked them how they felt about the clothes. He said Barbara felt they are what sluts wear, and that's why you are all wearing them now. Victoria said yes she agreed with Barbara, and Rosie said she agreed also. Roger said what if I took you all outside wearing them just the way you are now. He said I bet you two are highly excited aren't you, as he reached under Victoria's dress and felt her, she was even wetter than Barbara, then he fingered her and she climaxed right away. He felt Rosie and got the same result. He said see you are all sluts. He told Victoria to sit down, as he opened the cabinet and told Rosie to pull the dress up and place her hands behind her head. He reached in the cabinet, pulled out the lubricant and an anal plug and lubed it and inserted it inside Rosie's anus. He turned her around and took one of the new harnesses out, lubed the penis portion and inserted into Rosie vagina and fastened it around her waist and pulled the strap up between her legs and fastened it. Pulled her dress back down and told her to have a seat, if she could. He called Victoria over, told her to raise her dress and put her hands behind her head, as he applied lubricant to her also and used the old harness on her as he lubed the anal plug and then the vaginal one, fastening it to her. He finished and pulled her dress down. Barbara stood knowing she was next; he looked at her, and told her you are my slut bitch as she put her hands behind her head and he raised her dress up. Roger found the large anal plug and inserted it inside her anus; he took the other new harness and lubed the penis portion and inserted it inside her wet vagina and fastened it up, and pulled her dress down. He looked at them and made them standup as he began attaching the collars to their necks, then the leashes. Looked at Barbara and said you think you are a slut now, she said yes sir master. He told her if I want you to look like a slut, for me you will; now I am going to walk you bitches around. None of them protested as Roger grabbed the leashes and his camera and took them downstairs on the elevator and out the front door, that's what shocked them. It was unbelievable as he stood back and took pictures while the dildos and anal plugs took their toll on them and led them down the driveway almost to the front gate before he turned them around and then back to the house. Roger had never seen sexier walks in all his life. He walked them around back to the patio, and when he stopped they were all holding one another and had climaxed several times and were still going strong. He asked them what they were, they said almost in unison, his bitches. He told them what he liked about their dresses as he approached Barbara, is that he pulled it down in front and her perky and aroused breast were exposed and you can pull them up also as he raised the bottom above her butt. He looked at her and said that's real slutty, then caressed her butt. Roger kissed her and she tonged him back deep throat style, he said you still want more as he held her ample breast in his hands and played with them, licking her nipples. She moaned and then he spanked her rectum several times as she shook with a violent organism, holding onto him as he continued spanking her, she continued climaxing again and shook violently. Roger waited until she calmed down some. Victoria and Rosie watched. He undid the harness from Barbara while standing outside with her being totally exposed; he handed it to her as he rubbed her butt and kissed her passionately.

He told her he loved her very much and she could go take the plug out of her anus and return with her loose dress on so he could play with her some more, she kissed him as she went into the house. Victoria was next and knew she was probably ready to climax again as he pulled her by the leash and said come here you nasty bitch, Victoria climaxed as soon as he pulled her over to him, pulled her dress up and said you are a real slutty bitch, as she climaxed again, pulling it down exposing her very swollen and sensitive breast as he squeezed her long nipples and she shook again. He smacked her butt several times as she was overcome with intense shaking, sweating and having multiple orgasms racking her shapely body as she climaxed over and over again. He said you are my very special bitch as he unfastened the harness and allowed it to drop and it was dripping wet, as he held her head back by her hair and tonged her as she responded right away, he handed her the harness and said you know what to do don't you, she said yes sir master as he made her suck the dildo that had been in her vagina. He told her to wash it good and he then let her depart. At last it was Rosie's turn now. Rosie was somewhat of a nymph and hungry for anything Roger had to dish out, and he knew this. He then pulled Rosie over by the leash, and said you dirty little cunt, told her to pull her dress down, and then the bottom up. Roger looked at Rosie and she was game for whatever he had in mind. He then spanked her hard and much longer than the others and just watched her as she was racked with several massive organisms shaking uncontrollably for a several long minutes. Roger pinched her nipples hard and twisted them as if squeezing a rag. She climaxed while her knees buckled and crying out loud. He held her up as she began crying, and removed the harness and made her suck the dildo, watching as she swallowed it completely down her throat, before he removed it. Master Caesar gave her an order to wash the toys and remove the plug that was still in her anus as he allowed her to go inside.

Roger hoped they had, had enough and fixed him a stiff drink, and went around and secured the downstairs windows and then went upstairs and went to his bedroom and took a much needed warm shower. Barbara must have been waiting for him as she entered wearing her robe and hung it up and came in with him and begged him to take her as she knelt down and he had to urinate and did so on her as she raised her face and opened her mouth and it was a long one as she rubbed it all over her body, then took him in her mouth and as he became aroused, he pulled her up and had her face the wall applying soap to her anus and entered her as he reached around and played with her vagina. She climaxed several times, then he squatted down and lathered her anus and worked his hand slowly inside her and the other hand went inside her vagina as she moaned and said yes and had a huge orgasm, they bathed and he shampooed her hair and she washed him. When they stepped out the shower he dried her off and she helped him as they went to his bed where they oiled one another, then laid and hugged. She cried profusely as tears ran down her beautiful face and said she was so turned on by what he did to them she had lost all self-control and when she came upstairs and used the bathroom she just had to have him. He held her feeling on her. She asked him not to stop. He continued feeling her, as she made the statement, saying that she was obsessed with his touching her and couldn't live without him now and asked him what he had done to her. He said I freed your inner self and told her she would come to terms with how she felt. He told her it was there inside of you all the time, now you don't have to hide or have any inhibitions and asked her don't you feel so much better. She said yes, much better, free and safe that she can be herself. Told her she should be very happy, said she was already and was so much in love with him. He told her he needed a drink, he put on his robe and she went and put hers on and returned and they went downstairs together and he fixed her one.

Victoria and Rosie came downstairs wearing their robes, as he and Barbara were sitting at the kitchen table drinking. Rosie came to him and knelt down in front of him and placed her head in his lap as he rubbed her head. She looked up and said she loved him. He knew she wanted something, and the last time she placed her head in his lap she wanted a hard spanking. Said she wanted him to spank her hard as she handed him the rolled up leather strap from the pocket of her robe. He told her to remove her robe as he pulled a chair out and had her fold her robe and place it in the chair then place just her head on it and told her to hold the back of the chair, and spread her legs wide open. He gently felt her thighs, back and butt, then he doubled the leather strap up, and brought it down across her butt hard several times, then stood where his strikes would go down her thighs and between her legs until she climaxed several times and continued whipping her as she whimpered. He stopped and rubbed her redden butt and thighs and felt between her legs and played with her vagina as she climaxed again as he continued rubbing her, then pulled her up by her hair hugging her, as she said thank you master.

Barbara looked at her and knew how she felt, he was their master, he satisfied their urges and they loved him for it. Victoria stood and watched as Roger whipped Rosie and had gotten turned on again as Roger looked at her. She wanted to feel herself, she asked him for permission, he said you may but take you robe off and to stand in front of him. He told her to spread her legs and put her hands behind her head, she did as he rolled the belt up and shortened it and he stood and rubbed it gently over her nipples as she became highly aroused. Victoria had a beautiful body, he suddenly began spanking her vagina as her clit stood out. He stopped and told her to feel herself now and she did and climaxed as he told her don't stop, and continued as she had another massive climax. She calmed down some and she and Rosie were still unclothed. He told Rosie to go to the laundry room and bring a blanket from the dryer, she left and returned. He took it from her and spread it on the floor and told her to lie on her back, and then told Victoria to get down on her knees while Rosie spread her legs open and lick and suck each other as he and Barbara held hands and sipped their drinks. He struck Victoria across her back and butt with the belt a couple times, and then told them to change positions with Rosie on top as he struck her also as they soon began climaxing together. He told them to lie head to head and have each other so he could whip them both. They now were having repeated organisms. He told them to kneel before him and play with themselves as he stood, walking behind them and whipped them with the strap and said look at the sluts as they climaxed several more times making all kinds of degrading comments and then made them knee face to face and hold each other as he whipped their butts as they slowly turned red. He stopped and sat down as they shook and cried and held each other, he told them to kiss and if they wanted each other to go ahead and do so. They did as he sat and watched. Barbara said she was turned on as she knelt down before him and took him in her mouth and he was hard and then Rosie came and sucked him along with Victoria. Next thing that happened, he was laying on the blanket as Victoria sat on him as Rosie licked his ass and Barbara had her vagina in his face as she climaxed and he fingered her, Victoria climaxed and then sucked him then Rosie sat and rode him as Barbara and her kissed, Rosie climaxed and then Barbara laid next to him as Rosie licked her vagina as her and Roger kissed. Barbara got up and they all licked and sucked him together. He climaxed and sat up and said oh my sweet bitches.

He stood and put his robe on and made himself a fresh drink and returned and sat down as Rosie and Victoria lay on the blanket kissing Barbara as she rubbed them both. He watched them and then told them to kneel before him, which they did. He asked them if they were satisfied now or needed more. They looked a little confused; he told them to clean themselves and return, and not to put any clothes on until he told them to. They went to the small washroom by the laundry and returned, he told them to spread their robes over the chairs. He fixed Rosie and Victoria drinks and refreshed Barbara's. He sat and looked at them, he made the drinks potent, and they began drinking heavily and asked if they enjoyed themselves. Rosie said she was happy as she rubbed herself, and Victoria told him she had never felt so uninhibited before in her life, and was so very happy. He knew how Barbara felt, but said she was so happy now, as she leaned over and kissed him. He asked if they were sexually satisfied now, after the exploits of today. They said yes, as he told them to sip their drinks. He asked if they wanted to see more videos because some he considered as too cruel he hadn't shown them. They all said they understood his love for them and his reasoning but wanted to see them anyway. He said ok, before we turn in he would let them look after they finished their drinks. Roger thought about the ones he would show them now, he considered them extreme and couldn't see himself subjecting any of them to such punishment because he loved them, but wanted to see their reaction.

They had finished their drinks and he cleaned and washed the glasses and told them to put their robes on. They were more relaxed now and it wouldn't be long before they would be ready to get a good night's rest after all they had been through today. He had them get the extra-large towels he had purchased for them one day while shopping and he also had one, he asked them to put them on the couch where they were going to sit and said they were free to touch and feel themselves and each other as they took their robes off and made themselves very comfortable. He brought up his computer and turned the television on and as they connected, he started showing them the videos and closely watched their reactions. They all watched intently and after half an hour Rosie had her hand between her legs as she watched a woman cruelly whipped until the whelps on her butt started to bleed and she became bloody. Another video showed a woman who had clamps on her private parts as her vagina was stretched open, and hot wax poured on her. Rosie and Victoria climaxed together as they watched a woman hanging, being whipped and an electrical prod applied to her vagina as she shook violently. That one caused Barbara to have and orgasm also, as he showed them videos for over an hour, as all three had climaxed several more times. He turned it off and they said they wanted to see more and he showed them a few more for about another hour, as they continued to feel on themselves and have multiple organisms. He was surprised at their extreme interest and reactions, and it surprised him how often they had climaxed. He had never known women who had as many organisms as these three, and wondered if it was the food, the vitamins or how he treated them or how they felt about being here. He eventually turned it off as he observed them and felt they needed some rest telling them that the show was over and to go to bed. He said he felt they had enough for one day and for them to leave as he kissed them good night and made sure they went to their own beds again for the second time and tucked each one in as they all soon fell asleep. He went through the house and secured the windows as it began to rain outside and he checked the climate control and climbed into his bed and turned out the lights. He laid down thinking about them, he either had the three freakiest women in the world or he didn't have any meaningful understanding of women at all, he smiled and thought, but he was extremely happy with them in his life, and their fantasies and hang-ups as he dosed off into a deep and very restful sleep.

Chapter Twenty

   Sunday morning when Roger woke, he went to the bathroom and returned, looking at the clock, it was five thirty five; he decided to check on his girls and found them all in their beds still sleeping soundly as he returned to his bed to lie back down and was thinking about the day to come. In the past when he was younger and dating different women, he would find them, feed them and forget them, being eager for sex. And at the apartment not long ago he would feed them and play with them before sending them home, and he fell in love with them over time and now would love and take care of them. Roger thought about what might occur now that they were all here together, at their new home and his. One thing for sure was it seemed all there inhibitions were now gone or leaving, and was very happy for them. He thought about what he would do today, he had two options, one was to take them out to dinner, or two fix something here and just enjoy their presence. Roger thought about last evening and didn't know what might be on their minds. They had shown him that they were far freakier than he had ever expected and was caught very much caught off guard on how they truly felt and what they would do or wanted done to them. But he had certain limits as to what he would physically do to anyone of them. But they seemed to want more and the problem was with him, he loved them very much and really deplored the thought of hurting them or anyone. The question now for him was if he was prepared to fulfill their deepest most perverted desires. He decided to just play it by ear today and see what they would do or what they might ask him to do for or to them it was something to seriously think about as laid there pondering his thoughts.

He turned over and dosed off again and soon was awakened by someone crawling in bed with him. He didn't turn over as this warm body snuggled up next to him, feeling a very warm naked body against him, as a leg was placed over him and someone taking his hand as he lay on his side and moved it between their very warm thighs. Roger could feel a very moist vagina. A soft voice he recognized as being Victoria's, whispered and said all she wanted in the world was him, as she took his hand and rubbed it against her very moist vagina and soon climaxed. He felt her wetness on his hand. She climaxed several more times before he turned around to face her, and squeezing her butt and placing one of his legs between hers and held her tight, he caressed her butt rubbing and squeezing it, spanked her as she jerked and cried and began climaxing again uncontrollably, he held her tight and she couldn't move as he kissed her. She slowly calmed down. Roger again held her as she kissed his neck. Victoria was crying and her pretty face was wet with tears. She loved him so much. He asked her what should he do with her, she looked him in his eyes and said she didn't know. He asked her if she was in control now, said she thought so. He said he needed to know for sure. Said she wasn't sure. Oh my god Roger replied.

He said to her maybe you want me to tie you up and take control, and asked her if that's what she wanted. Said she wasn't sure, except she loved him very, very much. Roger asked her, how you are feeling right now.

She said seeing that woman tied up, hanging, and whipped and being placed in a cage. Do you have a need to be placed in one? I don't know she replied. He asked her what you want to happen to you right now. Said she wanted to be his bitch and serve him. He held her tight with one of his legs still between hers and spanked her butt very hard and told her she was his slut bitch as she had several more climaxes as he held her tight. He held her until she calmed down again, then reached into his headboard and took out some lubricant and applied it to her vagina, and soon felt how swollen she was. He reached for an antiseptic cream and applied it to her, holding her hand. Her swollen vagina was the main reason she was having trouble controlling her passions which wasn't like her. She said it was feeling much better now as he kissed and held her. Getting really excited and turned on, he climbed on top of her and shoving his hard penis inside of her as hard as he could and having her going completely out of her mind while he constantly talked dirty to her as organism after organism racked her body so intense that Roger had to hold her as he filled her cunt with his hot semen. She completely lost it then as he pulled out of her and then shot a load of hot semen into her face as she gladly licked it with a look of complete satisfaction, and then taking her hand and rubbing it all over her face. They both got up and went to the bathroom where they showered together. He lathered her up with a shower jell and a soft soap then pressed her against the wall while his penis was being aroused again. He then bent her over holding her arms behind her and fingered her anus, Victoria had never been taken like this before;

he continued to fuck her like a whore then he entered her ass as she was racked with several more climaxes. When he finished she then sunk to the floor of the shower completely used as he reach down and pulled her up to finish bathing, he dried her off and then himself, wrapping her in a large towel and led her to the bed; he massaged her with oils. Roger rubbed antiseptic cream and salve on her swollen vagina and now worn out pussy having her lay down in his bed for a moment, then covered her up and soon she was sound asleep being completely used and exhausted. She definitely had a work out. Roger left Vicky and changed into usual attire before going downstairs to brew some coffee which he surly needed.

After his coffee had brewed he had a good idea now where this day was headed. He poured a cup and smelled the aroma of the coffee that was tantalizing and tasted so good with a donut. It wasn't long before he was joined by Barbara wearing only her robe. She kissed him and asked him to stand as she opened her robe and rubbed against him, taking his hand and placing it between her warm thighs, she was soaking wet and soon climaxed. She held him around his neck and began kissing him wildly. She then poured herself a cup of coffee, sat down and took a sip. Roger thought about what would happen next when Rosie woke up. Barbara said she was surprised Victoria wasn't fixing breakfast. Roger informed her about what had happened this morning and said she was sleeping now. Barbara asked him if he wanted breakfast, no he replied, saying he was going to rest today if he could. Barbara said that sounds good and would try to do the same and would go lay with Victoria and see that she was all right. Rosie came downstairs and kissed them both and poured a cup of coffee and joined them at the table. Barbara finished her coffee and said she was going back upstairs. He sat with Rosie looking at her as he picked up on her vibe, it was her eyes that betrayed her inner feelings and Roger thought to himself, OMG.

Rosie then asked him to take her to the basement and said she wanted him to tie her up and whip her. He asked her why, and Rosie said she felt like she needed it. He said when, now, please master please. Roger was definitely not surprised knowing what type of women he had. Oh well he thought to himself. After finishing their coffee, they went upstairs together to his bedroom where he opened the cabinet as she stood close by; he placed the cuffs on her arms and ankles the collar around her neck and took out a spreader bar, and a leather whip and strap with several lengths of rope and also placed some clamps in a small canvas bag. He attached the leash to her collar and led her to the elevator as they then descended to the basement. She removed her robe and placed it on the floor as he attached the rope to the ceiling hook and had her stand underneath as she kissed him passionately and told him she was a nasty dirty slut and needed to be punished. He knelt down and attached the spreader bar to the cuffs on her ankles and adjusted it with her legs spread wide apart, he stood and cuffed her arms behind her and attached the rope and pulled it up causing her to be bent over with her arms above and behind her. He took the leash off the collar and ran a rope from it to the loop in the center of the spreader bar and fastened it to hold her neck in place in a secure and bent over position. Leaving her there to get his camera and returned taking pictures of her from all angles. He laid the camera on her robe as he walked over and felt her body all over and reaching in the small bag attached large cloths pin type clamps to her now large and swollen nipples before bending down attaching some to her vaginal lips. He asked her what she was, she said his worthless slut. He reached for the leather strap and struck out striking her butt several times standing on both sides of her, striking her inner thighs, lower leg, back and stomach. Then he used the whip on her as she whimpered and cried out. He asked her what do you say slut, she said thank you master in a halting voice. He removed the clamps from her vagina and used the strap on her placing several hard strokes between her legs as her knees bent causing pain as well as excitement. He continued then stopped and left her hanging, picking up the camera and taking more pictures. He left her and went upstairs to the kitchen for a bottle of water.

While he was in the kitchen Barbara returned still wearing her robe and asked where was Rosie? He explained to her about her request and said she was hanging in the basement. Barbara said she wanted to see Rosie. Roger said if she did it would be because she would be hanging with her. She insisted, and took her upstairs and attached a collar to her neck and cuffs to her arms and legs as the excitement began building up in her. Roger could see her nipples starting to get hard. He grabbed the other spreader bar and more rope, attached the leash and took her downstairs to the basement. Told her to remove her robe as she folded and placed it on the floor next to Rosie's and then he led her and positioned her below a ceiling hook and attached the rope to the hook with her arms behind her back, looking over at Rosie, she began to perspire. He attached the spreader bar to her ankles and adjusted it as her legs were spread wide apart also and he pulled the rope as she was forced to bend over also. He removed the leash and attached the rope to her collar and then to the bar, taking the slack out of the rope. He stood back and admired his handy work, taking more pictures of them both. He decided to place clamps on Barbara's fat vaginal lips, she cringed as he did and placed some on her nipples, she whimpered. He felt her body, feeling the soft skin of her legs and inner thighs and stomach touching her all over as she became even more excited just from his touch. He picked up the leather strap and began whipping her as she flinched but couldn't move and she cried with a loud cry. He stopped after a while and removed the clamps and then used the whip on her, then the strap again striking her between the legs and went back to use it on Rosie again. Rosie had several more organisms while he used the strap on her and went back using it on Barbara as an organism racked her body. He picked up his camera and took plenty of photos and close ups of the two women. After a while he released their necks and untied their hands and allowed them to stand as he fastened their arms in front and reattached the rope pulling their arms up again, this time above their heads. He stood in front of both and took the whip and whipped their breast and stomachs and between their legs. He stopped and felt each between their legs inserting several fingers inside of their wet vaginas as they climaxed uncontrollably, and then just let them hang there for a long while after taking many pictures.

Roger left them hanging and went upstairs and checked on Victoria, she was just waking up, she saw him and sat up as he sat on the edge of the bed and said thank you. She got out of bed and went to the bathroom and soon came out and put her robe on and asked about Rosie and Barbara. Roger said they are just hanging around in the basement because they asked to be punished. He took her to his room and placed a collar on her and cuffs on her wrist and legs and attached a leash and brought a large dildo along and led her to the elevator and took her downstairs to the basement where she saw Rosie and Barbara hanging with their legs spread apart with whip marks and small whelps all over their bodies and he told her to remove her robe. Roger cuffed her arms in front of her and made her kneel and bend over as he then took the strap and whipped her back and butt hard as she began to cry before making her crawl over as he handed her the dildo and told her to kneel before Rosie and give her pleasure, as he watched Victoria insert the dildo inside of Rosie and licking her clit as she climaxed again several times. Then pulling Vicky by the leash in front of Barbara and told her to do her also, it wasn't long before Barbara's knees bent as she climaxed. He made Victoria stand as he placed a rope on a hook and pulled her arms above her head. He removed the spreader bar from Barbara and attached it to Victoria and taking the whip, whipping her all over her body as she whimpered and soon began crying profusely as tears ran down her face. He then stood before her and inserted the dildo in her mouth, having her suck it before he inserted it in her vagina with her climaxing repeatedly until she just hung with her knees bent before she slowly stood back up. He left them hanging, went upstairs and looked to see what time it was. It was a little after ten, and had spent the early morning punishing them as he returned to the basement and removed the spreader bars from Rosie and Victoria. He held Rosie's head up looking at her and asked her if she wanted more, she said yes master, please punish me, he slapped her and kissed her as he gazed at the small red marks that covered her body. He held her head pulling her hair and said to her he would give her only a few more, she said thank you master as he stood back with the leather strap and struck her butt several more times, as she swung by her wrist when her knees buckled, he stopped and looked at the large whelps on her ass cheeks. He asked her if she was satisfied now, she said yes sir master as tears ran down her pretty face, and he kissed her and untied her from the rope in the ceiling as he laid her down gently on the basement floor where she knelt, saying thank you master.

He stood before Barbara and she was completely covered in sweat; he looked at her and asked if she needed more, she said yes master, please whip me again master. He looked at her body and asked her if she was sure, she said whip me please master. He took the strap and doubled it up, making it twice as painful and held her around the waist and spanked her hard across her buttocks and upper thighs and then he felt her between her legs as she climaxed and jerked on the rope. He untied her as she sunk to the floor and laid on her side. He approached Victoria, looked at her and asked her if she needed more and to his surprise she said yes please master. He stood back and used the long wide leather strap on her, it wrapped around her as he counted to ten and then stood before the whimpering Vicky and kissed her as she hungrily kissed him back and said thank you master and then released her from the rope. He left the ropes hanging from the ceiling as he took more pictures of them on the floor with their hands still cuffed. He unhooked the cuffs freeing their hands, and told them to stand. They slowly did as they were told to put their robes on and to return the cuffs and collars to the cabinet and wait for him upstairs. He took his camera, bars, whip, straps and dildo with him. They all took the elevator upstairs on orders from the master and replaced the cuffs and collars in the cabinet, he carried the dildo he used on them.

He said to them as they stood before him that he hoped they were fully satisfied, and instructed them that they were to take a warm bath and to soak in the tubs and let the warm water relax them, and he would be around to check on them and to stay in the water until I give you girls the ok to get out. He asked them if they understood, they all said yes sir master. Go and I will see you three very soon. Roger thought to himself he would have never imagined what had just transpired this morning even if he would have tried to think about doing what he did. They should have had enough by now to last them the rest of the week and would see as the coming week transpired.

Roger was beginning to get hungry since breakfast was very light consisting of just coffee and donuts. He also knew with a hectic and pleasurable day the girls had to be hungry as well. Roger decided on ordering either Italian or Chinese, and remembered he still had his menus for the Italian and Chinese restaurants that delivered and had very good food. He decided on Italian, taking out his phone and they were in his contact list, he looked at the menu for the Italian restaurant and looked at the time, it was noon and placed the large order, he ordered beef sandwiches and French fries, pasta salad and two extra-large pizzas. He gave them the new address and they said it would be a little more than an hour, and gave him the cost; he said ok and would just give the driver a bill when he came. He thought he would wait a few minutes before he would check on his women. He wanted them to relax and soak their swollen and sensitive vaginas after subjecting themselves to their own very vivid imaginations and extreme fantasies. They would all be going back to work tomorrow and didn't want them to appear too whelped up and he would personally rub each one with oils and especially Victoria with the antiseptic, then he thought they all probably would need some also. Roger checked first on Barbara and found her soaking in her tub, he knelt down as she rose up slightly to kiss him and he bent over and washed her back and told her when he returned she then could get out. He found Victoria in her tub and knelt down and washed her back as well as she cried and said she loved him as she takes his hand and places it between her legs and has an orgasm and he tells her to stay until he returns, and she says yes sir master, as he heads to Rosie's bathroom and she is soaking using some bubble bath as he kneels down and she grabs his hand and kisses it, he scrubs her back, he tells her also to stay until he returns. Roger lets them soak quite a long while before he goes back to Barbara's bathroom and helps her out of the tub and to the shower to rinse off and wash her hair then wrapping her in a large clean towel and tells her to lie down while he gets Victoria and Rosie. He goes and helps Victoria and has her wash her hair and rinse off in the shower also, wraps her tightly in a towel as he heads to Rosie's bathroom and helps her out and to the shower to wash her hair and rinse off. He leads Rosie to Barbara's bedroom and returns for Victoria. He goes to his bedroom for the antiseptic salve and has them all open their legs wide as he applies very liberal amounts to each woman's vagina before he tells them to oil themselves as the doorbell rings and he departs downstairs.

Roger grabbed his money from the counter as he heads to the front door. It's the restaurant delivery man. Roger opens the door and the man hands Roger a couple of large shopping bag and two large pizzas. Roger hands the man a one hundred dollar bill and tells him to keep the change. He thanks Roger and departs. The food has arrived and Roger takes the food to the kitchen and returns upstairs to see what the girls were doing, where he finds them oiling themselves. Having them showered and squeaky clean and their hair washed, Roger orders them to put on some perfume with some comfortable clothes. Rosie and Victoria wrapped in towels head to their bedrooms to do as Roger ask as he returns downstairs and begins to set the food out on the kitchen island counter and takes out some picnic plates placing them on the counter top along with the paper towel holder. To his surprise they all come downstairs dressed in the tube dresses and nothing else. Roger opens a bottle of chilled red wine as they gathered around and fixed their plates as everyone heads to the kitchen table sitting down together as Roger blessed the food. It was around two when they sat down and ate. Everyone was very hungry since they had skipped breakfast and were pretty famished after a very intense morning. Roger complimented them on their beautiful appearance and especially how good they looked and smelled. Barbara tells him they did it for him because they know he loves and cares about them. When they finished eating, every one of them thanked Roger for the food. Roger reminded them about when they all lived in separate apartments telling them to go home after feeding them. He said now times have changed and we are all here together. Now let's go outside and enjoy the nice weather and each other's company.

Enjoying the fresh air, after eating and sipping on the wine everyone helped clean up. All that's left was about half a pizza and left it on the counter as they took their glasses outside and Roger opened another bottle of a very good red wine he had chilled as they sat outside and it isn't long before Victoria pulls her dress up and down exposing herself, Roger just sits and looks and doesn't say anything as he wants them to feel comfortable and at home. He looks at Victoria and smiles and tells her you are at home my dears and if you took the dress off it would be fine with him. Victoria stands and takes it completely off and sits back down as he enjoys the view. Barbara and Rosie both stand and remove their dresses also and sit down and the conversation continues uninterrupted. Barbara said soon they would look at some furnishing for the rest of the house and take their time so Roger can get a handle on the house hold expenses and their accounts can recover somewhat. Roger said he thinks in about a months' time they will all be doing very well financially. He expressed his deep appreciation in them being here with him and hoped they were all satisfied with their fantasies and sexual desires and living arrangements. As the sun began going down they went indoors and Roger secured the lower level and suggested they prepare for tomorrow and said he would miss them but knew they would be home every night. He said they should get some rest and go to work happy now that they were all settled, secure and their minds were free. They all kissed him going to their bedrooms to prepare for tomorrow. He looked at the clock and it was close to nine and decided to look at the news, he watched and it was some good and some sad stories as usual and then the weather and sports. He watched and then sat at his desk, turned his computer on and finished downloading the photos that were taken earlier in the day. He checked and it had several updates in progress and leaving it on while taking a nice warm shower alone, finished and sat on his towel as he applied some oil to his body and feeling so refreshed. He checked his computer and it needed a restart and he did a restart with shut down, turned the television off, and turned off his bathroom light and started to climb into bed when he looked up and noticed Barbara standing in his bedroom doorway. She approached him and bent down and kissed his face and asked to sleep with him as he pulled the covers back and she got in with him and he turned the lights off. He turned over and kissed her and said he was going to sleep. He turned back over and pulled the covers over both of them as she placed an arm around him then he dosed off after a very exhausting day.

Chapter Twenty One

The following day, Monday would turn out to be Rogers first normal day in a couple of weeks, or rather the first day alone since moving all three of his women into the same house with him. It would also be their first day back at work since moving especially for Barbara and Victoria as he really looked forward now to some time alone and planned to enjoy the day and look at some more patio furniture, something more relaxing to sit on similar to loungers. After he woke up Barbara had rolled over, as he headed to the bathroom and when he returned noticed the time, it was five thirty sharp and put on a clean pair of shorts and t-shirt. As he dressed, Barbara slowly turned over and soon opened her eyes; she said good morning love as he sat at the edge of the bed. She then leaned over and he touched her face, bent over and kissed her. She climbed out of bed hugging her as she put on her robe and went to her bedroom. Roger headed downstairs and made his morning coffee as usual and made the now new normal of twelve cups, enough for everyone. He decided on having breakfast this morning taking some bacon out and decided to cook it in the oven. The coffee was ready and so was Roger as he poured himself a cup, taking out the donuts, with only two left. He drank some coffee and ate a donut preparing to fix some cheese toast. After preparing the cheese toast decided on cooking eggs with diced onions. He evidently had an appetite. While sipping his coffee Victoria came downstairs looking very happy and wearing a house coat. She kissed him smiling and saying good morning, pouring a cup of coffee and began saying. I see you trying to start without me. Roger told her you are oh so welcome to take over as he went to the oven and with an oven glove on and a pair of tongs turned the bread over, then the bacon. He was sipping his second cup and decided to open the kitchen blinds. He turned around and diced an onion and told her she could do the eggs as she began cracking and placing them in a bowl and soon mixed the diced onion in with them. Roger asked her how well she rested, she replied very well thank you, and thanked him for the antiseptic and said she just finished using some more of it this morning. He told her clothing rubbing on it would keep it swollen longer and should keep it open if she could. Said she knew all about that and was planning on doing so.

Soon they were joined by Barbara and Rosie. Rosie had on a smock and Barbara had on her robe as the each went and poured themselves a cup of coffee and Rosie kissed Roger before she sat down to drink her coffee. Roger opened the oven and checked on the bacon and it was almost done as he placed the cheese on the bread. He took an aluminum pan and lined it with paper towels as Victoria began cooking the eggs and not long after he took the oven glove and removed the bacon and set the pan on a rack as he placed the bacon in the pan with the paper towels to drain. Barbara and Rosie set the table and took out the plates as Victoria finished with the eggs and Roger took out the bread turning the oven off and soon they were all sitting down to breakfast. When everyone was finished Barbara and Rosie cleaned up as Roger had the last cup of coffee before he went and washed the pot.

When everyone departed the kitchen, Roger went out on the patio deck and looked around. He thought how pleasant the weather was now but rain was in the forecast and they were expecting a week of rain starting later on today. He was thankful the weather had been pleasant when everyone was moving. He returned inside and headed to his room as the girls dressed for work. He put on a pair of jeans and socks along with a t-shirt and went down stairs after he had found the measurements for the living room and dining rooms. So far he had just purchased a rug for the living room and would look today and see if he could find something he liked. He wished Barbara and Victoria could go with him, but it wasn't necessary but would like to be using the living room and dining room more, he looked at the walls and decided maybe he would start with a television and some cabinets, or even some pictures. As he walked around Barbara came downstairs headed to work wearing a smart fitting business suit and she looked very stunning, she came and kissed him, her makeup was light and the lipstick she wore made her more beautiful than ever and her long hair was in a roll giving her a very pleasant appearance. He walked her to the garage door and wished her a great day. She smiled at him and said ok. On her way to her car Roger noticed she looked so much better and happier than all the previous times he had seen her. He watched as she pulled out of the garage while the door closed. It wasn't long before Rosie and Victoria came down stairs, dressed and also looking very stunning and very happy. Victoria looked exceptional beautiful and happy. She wore her business suit with a skirt that fell well below her knees and the black stocking he recognized as being the crotch less ones he had passed out to them all. They both kissed him and noticed Rosie was wearing a close fitting dress just above the knees with a short jacket. They both were looking very happy and beautiful as they departed and he watched them enter into their autos and pullout as the doors closed behind them.

With a sigh of relief Roger now could start his day and went upstairs checking that no windows were open since it was supposed to rain today as he gathered his wallet and other items that he carried with him and his check book as he grabbed his keys and a sports jacket. He was heading to his attorneys office to pay for his services for the past couple of weeks and have him make out a new will. He went to the garage and got in his truck, pulling out and watched the garage door close as he headed to his attorneys office and had a pleasant drive on the way before he arrived. He didn't have to wait long. Roger soon entered his office and handed him a check for all the closings and the list of new changes to his will. His attorney said it would be another week before the will would be ready for him to sign and would give him a call. Roger stood and shook his hand and departed, his day was now free and all of his time was his as he headed to one of his favorite furniture stores and browsed around looking. He soon came to a set he liked and was informed by a saleslady it was a new arrival. Roger looked at a brochure she showed him, it came in leather or a cloth fabric and the complete set was comprised of five pieces, two couches, and two chairs each in different sizes and had a chase lounge as part of the set. The cushions were firm and the backs were high enough to be comfortable. She showed him both the leather and fabric sets and the choice of colors. Roger liked the cloth and noticed the material was really wearable but thought maybe he should go with leather since he had a cloth set in his bedroom. He decided on the complete set in medium brown leather and what he liked about the set was it didn't recline. He placed the order and it would cost him close to three thousand dollars, and it was well made. The saleslady was happy that he purchased the set as he inquired about a low cabinet that was much wider than most, he ordered one in the light brown color. He liked it because of the intricate wood cut design on the front doors. When he had left the store noticed that he had spent close to five thousand dollars, but was satisfied with his purchase and they would call him with a delivery date within a couple days. It was around noon when he stopped at the grocery store to fill a short list of items and he caught some sales on a few other items, filling his cart and some were frozen and would have to go home now for sure and knew all he had was time. He checked out and was glad every time he carried a load home because of the ease of loading groceries and unloading them from the back of the truck was truly convenient.

He headed home and noticed several long boxes at the front door and remembered the shades for the living and dining rooms were to be delivered and his bed room window also as he backed into the garage. Well the rest of his day was cut out for him and especially if he decided on cooking. He unloaded the groceries and after he had brought them all inside, put them away. He went to the front door and brought in the shades that had been delivered and looked and brought in the mail. He took the shades to the dining room and would purchase himself a collapsible and extendable ladder tomorrow. He found the one for his bedroom and could put it up today, but first decided to take some chicken out of the freezer and let it thaw. He took the shade and mail to his bedroom and he soon had the shade installed and cleaned up and after vacuuming up the dust he vacuumed the rugs before putting it and his tools away then went through the mail. As he went through the mail, found an invitation to attend the neighborhood association meeting tomorrow evening at the church next door, at seven pm. He set it aside and went through the rest of the mail and found two bank statements setting them aside, and the rest went to the shredder. He did the bank statements and they were Victoria's and Rosie's, as he went through their ledgers and marked off all the cleared checks and there accounts were in very good shape now and they only had a couple of outstanding checks for the closed utilities. He finished his paper work and looked at the clock and it was a little after one as he thought about dinner. He changed clothes and checked the outside temperature, it was pleasant for spring close to seventy as he opened his bedroom window before going downstairs turning the climate control off and opened more windows before deciding what he would have with the chicken, and decided on some beans and rice and figured he would start cooking now before they returned home. Roger enjoyed cooking and had quite a library and had at least fifteen cook books which he had decided to keep here in the kitchen after he moved in and they were on the counter under the cabinets where he could use them if needed.

He started the beans and soon they were boiling and turned them out and let them sit as he returned to his bedroom and made up his bed. He then laid down and relaxed and dosed off. Within an hour or more he woke up and headed downstairs to finish cooking, seasoned his beans took a piece of ham out sliced and diced it and added it to the beans and turned the fire back on under them and waited for them to boil again, having the radio on and the weather report was severe storms with high winds were heading this way and to expect very heavy rain fall. He went outside and let the umbrella down and secured it with the straps that were attached to the outside and pushed the chairs under the table and returned inside. He fixed a salad and left it in a large bowl that had a plastic cover. The time was ticking and it was close to four o'clock and would wait to cook the chicken, but he seasoned it and oiled a baking dish and it was all ready to pop into the oven turning his beans down added some more water and let them simmer as he fixed a pot of rice. The rice was soon done and looked into the living room imagining how it would look with the furniture before returning to the kitchen. Then turned the oven on and placed the chicken inside and waited till the oven reached the predetermined temperature. He then set the timer and stirred his beans and tasted them and let them cook. Roger went to the living room and took the shades out of the boxes and checked where the cords would be and laid them under the windows where he would install each of them maybe tomorrow, and did the same for the dining room. He started thinking about when he had closed on the house and found out he was actually buying two lots that totaled more than an acer where this house sat here, and was room for another one or even two but the last owner had combined both lots and sold them all together as one. It was the reason for the gate. He thought if he ever sold he could always split it back up but this was the reason it was over a million dollars and thought he would have an appraisal done, because he always felt it was underpriced when he purchased it and his quick response really caught the seller off guard before they may have increased the asking price.

The oven chimed and he set the timer and noticed it had gotten much darker outside and was starting to rain, he went upstairs and made sure all the windows were closed and turned the climate control back on before returning to the kitchen as he set the table and busied himself. He had the salad bowls out and the plates as he checked the beans and turned the fire down even lower. It was a few minutes after five as the rain really began coming down as he listened to the radio and there were reports of flooding where the rain had passed several hours earlier. Roger checked on his chicken and the oven dinged and shut off as he removed it and covered it up, the food was still hot when Barbara came in the back door from the garage and said it is pouring down. She kissed him on her way upstairs and said she wanted to get comfortable first before dinner. It wouldn't be long before Victoria and Rosie would be here and then they all could sit down and eat as Roger turned the low fire off from under the beans and set the chicken in the now cooling oven to keep it warm. About a half an hour later when Victoria and then shortly Rosie entered, Barbara came downstairs wearing a house coat. Victoria and Rosie kissed him and said they would change and be right back. Barbara washed her hands and helped him fix their plates. She dished up the salad and placed the salad dressing on the table. Victoria and Rosie came downstairs several minutes later as Roger poured some wine in their glasses while Barbara set them on the table along with the salads. Soon they all were sitting down eating and talked about their day at work. Everyone complimented Roger on the food and Rosie even had seconds, getting more salad. When they had finished eating Roger put the left overs in containers, which was just the beans as they had eaten everything else and the girls began cleaning up the kitchen. It continued to rain and it came down harder than before. Roger looked out the living room window and watched as the water ran down the driveway toward the street. The girls went to their bedrooms to shower and relax and he went to his room and watched the news. It was as dark as night outside as he sat and watched television and soon turned it off and went to his library taking out a book to read. Roger read for a couple hours and only Barbara came in and sat with him a short while and he told her about the furniture and the shades arriving, and said he would install them tomorrow. Close to ten Rosie and Victoria came in and said good night to him as he asked them where they were and they said on their laptops shopping and Rosie said she did a questioner for her job, as they kissed him and departed. Barbara asked if he would sleep with her and he said after he had taken his shower he would join her as she departed. He placed a marker in his book and took a long warm shower and then oiled himself and turned off his bedroom lights but left one lamp on as he went to Barbara's bedroom and got in bed with her. They hugged and kissed and very shortly both were sleep.

The rest of the week was much the same as Monday. Roger shopped and found some of the patio furniture that he was looking for and it was a rattan style made of a durable plastic material making it water proof and would be delivered the following day, and the furniture store called and said they would deliver the living room set the following Wednesday. He had purchased a foldup extendable and collapsible ladder that Tuesday and by Wednesday had installed the shades in the living and dining room and making a trip to the electronics store and purchased a television for the living room as large as the one in his bedroom and it would be installed the same week as the living room furniture was to be delivered. How great is that Roger thought? He slept with Victoria on Tuesday and Rosie on Wednesday and alone Thursday, he had normal sexual relations with them during the week and indulged them only if they had a need which most of the time they did if he didn't just go to sleep. By Friday Barbara and Victoria were both sleeping with him. That Saturday Rosie had to do her half day at the bank and afterwards he took them all to the movies and then out to dinner afterwards. A routine was

347

starting to develop and they all were very satisfied with it. Sundays they played some bondage games, not as intense as when the girls were off, but enough to where they were happy and fully satisfied.

The following week the furniture for the living room was delivered and Roger was able to sit and enjoy watching television in the living room and everyone was very satisfied with his furniture selection. After the first month had passed everyone's old expenses were fully paid off and their checking accounts started to grow and everyone including Roger had received their security deposit checks from their old landlords. He now had an idea of the monthly expenses for the house as he took the property tax and divided it by four, then by twelve to determine how much each would contribute monthly, and did the same with the water, gas, electric and trash fee. When he finish with that and then added food, they each were looking at between four and five hundred dollars a month. That was by far much less than the amount compared to what they individually had paid in the past for utilities, rent and car notes. He also had them to buy food on their own and gave them the grocery list most of the time which helped the household budget a lot and then he would just buy cleaning supplies and paper products at the bulk store and soon they had a more than a sufficient supply on hand.

Roger did attend the neighborhood association meeting at the church next door and met quite a few of his closest neighbors. Roger went alone the first time, he went just to check out the neighbors and most of the attendees were couples. Roger was invited to join and play golf which he had never done and was told the local club in the neighborhood provided instructions since he was invited to join which he did, and since he had quite a bit of time on his hands, they also had a driving range which he enjoyed as he worked on sharpening up his newly acquired golf skills. After joining the club it proved to be very financially beneficial to his real estate operations and very rewarding to his bank account also. He actually thought of teaming up with several people who wanted to build a strip mall and while he was part of the small group of only four people who were sitting having drinks one day having a discussion and two were very serious about developing a particular piece of property describing the access and discussed how much it would cost to build and the potential profit from it, but had a problem finding out who owned it. The third person asked where it was located; they gave the location, and said they had problems finding out who actually owned it and all they knew was it was part of a holding company. Roger asked what side of the intersection and knew the area very well that they were talking about as they described it. Saying it was a gold mine if they could get their hands on it. Roger asked how much they would be willing to pay for it, and said two million now, but with the development around it the value would soon be going up. They wanted eighty acers of the location and would build a large strip mall and a couple of condos if they could purchase it. They didn't know Roger owned it and he said three million for the first forty acers, and two million for the second forty away from the intersection. They looked at Roger and said you talk like you own it. Roger said he did, as their jaws dropped. Roger just asked if they were serious. They said they were very serious and were thinking of forming a partnership to purchase and build the strip mall. Roger stated that his research had shown that retail was in a downward spiral right now and there was an overabundance of retail space right now and especially in that particular area and felt now wasn't the time to invest in another mall and pointed out that there was another mall less than a mile away and it had several vacancies and the occupancy rate was just slightly over sixty percent and stated he had purchased a large building on fifty acers nearby that was now shuttered.

Roger pointed out that there were too many empty industrial buildings around also and very near. A couple had just been built and completed in the past year and were still vacant. He said he almost purchased one but changed his mind and was glad he did because the occupied ones were going to be empty soon. He did state that his price was firm; if they were ever serious. They were so shocked that he owned it as he paid for the next round of drinks before deciding to head home. Roger went home to revue his holdings and his ongoing profits from his various operations and was satisfied he had made the right choices. Rogers's business holdings did very well and he was satisfied with his annual earnings.

Now the weekdays at home were much the same, quiet. Almost routine sometimes as Roger would leave the meats out after he seasoned them and would let the girls cook and sometimes he would cook dinner and it would be ready when they came home. They always ate together every day and had formed a real family type bond together. He slept with one of them almost every night and it proved to be beneficial for each. The house slowly accumulated more furniture throughout as they each made purchases on their own and began spending more time downstairs together. He eventually had a professional wet bar built and had the pool table he always wanted. They spent time on the weekends outside or in the basement playing games and even more bondage games together, as he even brought in a large animal cage to place them in sometimes when playing with them, which really excited Rosie and Victoria.

Soon Victoria was made bank manager at the branch she worked at and to her surprise Rosie was promoted to assistant manager but would have to transfer in order to accept the promotion and it turned out to be at the same branch as Victoria, and both promotions came with pay raises. They took turns driving to work which saved them both money. Not to long after that, Barbara was promoted to director from supervising manager on her job as the former director of the department retired. Barbara's raise was truly very significant and beneficial for all of them. Roger bought another small luxury apartment complex and created a new company and added it to his portfolio of real estate holdings.

When winter came Juan provided snow plowing and they always had an easy time coming and going from their home. Well they were all very happy together and loved and played together. Roger was the happiest of all since they were all under one roof and he would never be alone or sleep alone ever again.

FINIS

www.ingramcontent.com/pod-product-compliance
Lightning Source LLC
Chambersburg PA
CBHW070050120726
47909CB00002B/343

* 9 7 8 0 5 7 8 6 3 6 7 4 0 *